"*I have amnesia.*"

She said the words out loud, feeling like a character in a bad movie. Only no one had bothered to give her the script.

"I'm sure it must be unsettling," the doctor said. "Memory loss is unique to each case. Recovering it could take a few days, or…it could take time."

Or she might never recover. That possibility was so frightening, she thrust it from her before it sucked away what remained of her sanity.

"Justine—" the doctor began.

Justine. That damn name again. It set her teeth on edge. "Don't call me that!"

The doctor shifted his approach. "I do have some good news for you," he said. "There are no broken bones, no major trauma and your pregnancy is intact."

"Pregnancy?" she gasped, her throat squeezing closed.

D0451662

Previous titles by REBECCA YORK

43 Light Street books:

Life Line
Shattered Vows
Whispers in the Night
Only Skin Deep
Trial by Fire
Hopscotch
Cradle and All
What Child Is This?
Midnight Kiss
Tangled Vows
Till Death Us Do Part
Prince of Time

Peregrine Connection books:

Talons of the Falcon
Flight of the Raven
In Search of the Dove

**Don't miss these upcoming
43 Light Street books:**

For Your Eyes Only
Father & Child

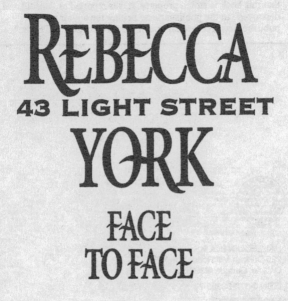

REBECCA

43 LIGHT STREET

YORK

FACE TO FACE

Harlequin Books

TORONTO • NEW YORK • LONDON
AMSTERDAM • PARIS • SYDNEY • HAMBURG
STOCKHOLM • ATHENS • TOKYO • MILAN
MADRID • WARSAW • BUDAPEST • AUCKLAND

HARLEQUIN BOOKS
225 Duncan Mill Road, Don Mills,
Ontario, Canada M3B 3K9

ISBN 0-373-83323-7

FACE TO FACE

To our moms,
Beverly and Fannie,
for nurturing us and our love of books.

Chapter One

Justine Hollingsworth could afford to play with the hired help. It was one of the perks of wealth.

Mike Lancer stood on the corner of Light and Lombard Streets, watching her retreating figure and wondering if it was remotely possible that she hadn't heard him call her name. She was less than fifty feet away.

Her pace didn't slacken as she made for the shelter of the parking garage. Maybe she hadn't heard him over the noise of the midday traffic that was mucking along through the fifth straight day of hard spring rain.

Dodging a double-parked delivery truck, he made it to the opposite curb in time to get splashed by a passing taxi. With a curse, he brushed water from the legs of his jeans.

"Justine Hollingsworth? Were you looking for me?"

The slender redhead didn't turn, and he felt a stab of anger.

He'd seen her leave his office building. Had she come an hour early for their one o'clock appointment, found the door locked and decided to pay him back by ignoring him? So much for the mysterious job she hadn't quite offered him—and the sizzle of sensuality that had crackled in the air of his office last Wednesday as she'd sat across from him. He felt like a film noir character—the detective who's taken in by the sexy client and then ends up floating in the harbor with a bullet in his back.

As he watched her duck under the garage's overhang, he wondered if the gray light was playing tricks with his vision. Maybe it wasn't her. Her rain hat hid her wavy red hair, and he'd caught only a glimpse of her face. Then she turned the corner, and he got a good look at her elegant profile with its high cheekbones and dainty chin. It was the face that had regularly graced the *Baltimore Sun's* People and Places section since she'd married Kendall Hollingsworth and his million-dollar construction company eight years ago. Usually she dressed as if she'd just stepped out of a *Vogue* layout. Today she was playing it low-key, with hardly any makeup and a raincoat that shouted Value City rather than Nordstrom's.

Shoulders hunched, fist pressed against her mouth, she looked as if she was trying to hold back tears. Mike fought an unwelcome wave of concern. Had something devastating happened to her? Earlier in the week, he'd decided she could take care of herself, with or without his help. Now she looked fragile—a flower mowed down by a thunderstorm. The sight of her stricken face made it hard to remember that the attraction he felt for her was dangerous and that he'd be a fool to involve himself with the problems of a woman like Justine Hollingsworth—unless she paid him very well for his time and effort.

Mike's brows drew together in a scowl. He almost spun around and headed back to his office. He didn't need her money. Or the hot jolt of sexual voltage that had flared between them. Yet he quickened his pace to catch up as she entered the garage.

Before he'd taken twenty paces into the darkened interior, a man with unkempt hair and a dirty fatigue jacket materialized from behind a concrete pillar. In his late fifties with weather-beaten skin, the man could have been homeless, using the building for a shelter. However, instead of slinking into the shadows, he fell into pace behind Justine. Ten to one the guy was after her purse.

"Whoa, buddy. Don't even think about it," Mike growled, tensing his muscles and lengthening his stride. The man glanced fearfully over his shoulder. For a few seconds, they sized each other up in the murky light. Then the would-be mugger bolted, apparently deciding to cut his losses.

The delay had given Justine enough time to disappear from view. Listening intently, Mike glanced up and down the row of cars. Moments later, an engine started. Then a teal blue Taurus drove slowly toward him, with Justine at the wheel.

No way could she miss seeing him. He stood on the oil-splotched concrete, trying to look casual. Resisting the impulse to swipe back the dark hair plastered to his forehead, he felt his arms stiffen at his sides. Her eyes locked with his for a split second, and he thought he saw her react before she turned the car toward the parking attendant's booth. After paying the fee, she made a right turn onto Light Street.

Another engine roared. Mike barely had time to jump out of the way as a gray Pontiac Firebird with two men in the front seat barreled toward the exit. After a rolling stop at the gate, they, too, turned right. Mike wanted to think they'd simply happened along at the same time as Justine. His old cop's instincts told him otherwise.

As he climbed into his battered Mustang, he cursed the sixth sense that urged him to follow Justine into the downpour. Maybe he simply wanted to find out why she needed to yank his chain. Bending forward over the wheel, he squinted through the windshield. The rain was coming down harder, the wipers barely keeping up with the deluge. He almost lost the Taurus in the noontime traffic near Camden Yards before Justine turned north again and headed up Charles Street. She was driving as if she didn't know where she was going—or didn't care.

THE WOMAN in the blue Taurus brushed the back of her hand across her eyes and fumbled in her open purse for a tissue. On the street, she'd kept herself from breaking down.

In the privacy of her car, she couldn't prevent the tears welling in her eyes from spilling down her cheeks.

Lord, what a wreck she'd made of her life—and all because she'd been naive enough to trust the wrong man. Now he was trying to punish her for *his* mistake. Her hands clenched painfully on the steering wheel. Until two months ago, she'd been reasonably happy with the niche she'd carved for herself. She'd worked hard to get where she was, but everything was tumbling down like a house built on shifting sand. She couldn't even imagine the future. Like the past, it was shrouded in mist.

Unbidden, the faces of her parents stole into her mind. As she thought about them and what they'd meant to her, what they'd taught her, she worried her lower lip between her teeth. Lucky they weren't here to see what an unholy mess she'd made of her life.

Trying to quell her painful thoughts, she lifted her gaze from the bumper of the car ahead and peered through the rain at her surroundings. With a start, she realized she had no idea where she was, except that she was on a highway hemmed in by high stone walls. She'd been driving for thirty minutes, and she didn't have a clue where she'd been or where she was heading.

It was symbolic, she decided. She didn't know where she was going to end up—on this ride—or in her life.

Several trucks passed her, shaking her car and splattering the windshield with dirty water. Slowing to a crawl, she wondered why she'd gotten herself onto a highway in this kind of weather. An exit sign loomed out of the swirling mist ahead. Falls Road. She turned off, breathing a sigh of relief as the traffic thinned.

MIKE KEPT the Taurus in sight, noting with a kind of grim satisfaction that he'd been right. The men in the gray Pontiac were also taking the same tortuous route through the city.

Coincidence? He'd given up on that concept years ago, growing up on the streets of East Baltimore. He glanced at the bigger car's license plate. It was smudged with mud. Not improbable in the rotten weather, but damn convenient. He could barely read an 8 and an *H*. Inching closer, he tried to make out more.

SHE WAS ABOUT to turn on the radio, hoping music would help change her mood, when she caught an unexpected flash of movement from the corner of her eye. Glancing to her left, she gasped. A large gray car had crept up alongside her on the narrow road. It was in her lane, edging over, crowding her toward the shoulder.

Was she going too slowly for the driver? Hoping the fool would pass, she eased up on the accelerator. The other car dropped back, as well, pushing her farther toward the right. Her chest tightened and her hands gripped the wheel tighter. Sparing another quick glance to her left, she saw a man staring at her from the passenger seat of the other vehicle. The expression on his face made her blood run cold. In the split second when their eyes met, she knew he was enjoying her terror.

Her right tires sank into the shoulder, making her car list dangerously to the right, and suddenly she needed all her skill to keep the car on the road. Everything was happening so fast she barely had time to react. The car started to slide. She stabbed at the brakes and knew she'd made a mistake. Lord, what were you supposed to do in a skid?

Frantically, she tried to turn into the direction the wheels were taking her, but the power steering didn't respond properly. The road took a sharp turn, and she felt herself hurtling toward disaster.

MIKE HAD DRIFTED BACK a couple of car lengths, watching with narrowed eyes as the Pontiac followed Justine onto Falls Road. When the car crossed a bridge, he caught a glimpse of the creek that meandered along the thoroughfare. Usually the water was all but invisible; now it was swollen to an ominous torrent.

A passing van going too fast for the road conditions drenched his windshield with a curtain of muddy water, reminding him that the winding road was treacherous in bad weather. Momentarily blinded, he hunched forward and tapped the brakes. When the obscuring sheet drained away, he realized he'd lost his quarry around a bend.

Taking a chance, he speeded up as he rounded the curve. The Pontiac was pulling rapidly away, and Justine was on the shoulder. Good God, had the other car shoved her off the blacktop? He couldn't be sure; he hadn't seen. But, regardless, Justine was in trouble. For an endless moment, the Taurus clung to the gravel. Then it hit a ramp, hydroplaned and jumped the guardrail, heading toward the rushing creek.

He glanced from the car to the water. It was flowing at least five feet above normal level. And Justine's car was making straight for it.

HEART RACING, she jerked the wheel the other way. But nothing she tried had any effect on the car. It barreled toward the creek; then for several heart-stopping seconds, it was airborne. Time seemed to slow to a series of freeze-frames. She was trapped in an endless ride of terror as the vehicle nosed over a small rise and plunged down a steep incline.

Nothing lay in the car's path to slow its momentum. A scream rang in her ears as dark water rushed up to meet her. Then a sudden impact slammed her forward against the steering wheel, and the world went black.

MIKE WAS ON THE LINE with 911 when Justine's car went over the embankment. He barely had time to choke out the location of the nearest cross street before the Taurus plunged into the foaming current.

"The car's in the water!" he shouted to the dispatcher as he screeched to a halt, perilously close to the roadway, and threw open his door. The voice on the other end of the line

was still asking for details, but he barked out only one more
sentence. "I'm going in after her."

Rain sluiced over his head and shoulders as he vaulted the
guardrail and slid down the muddy bank, following the path
of the car's destruction through honeysuckle vines and tall
grass.

The vehicle was a hulking, indistinct shape in the mist.
When he drew closer, he saw that it rested at an angle, nose
down in lapping waves.

Mike waded into the shallows of the rain-swollen creek,
judging the strength of the main current. He quickly decided it was strong enough to sweep him away if he wasn't
careful. His eyes riveted on the evil-looking water swirling
above the level of the car windows. Then he looked at the
car. Inside he could see a mop of red curls slumped against
the steering wheel, and the water level was rising quickly
inside the vehicle. Damn. She must have gone in at the
wrong angle for the air bag to deploy.

Tossing his leather jacket onto the bank, he waded farther into the icy cold. The current seized him, and he
grabbed a tree limb to keep from being carried down-
stream. He grimaced as the numbing cold rose to his thighs,
his hips, his waist. Letting go of the limb, he reached for the
car's door handle, thankful it was within his grasp. As he
transferred his hold, he found that the door was locked.

He pounded on the window, calling her name, but she
didn't move, didn't respond. Back braced against the side
of the car, he reached down and scrabbled along the creek
bed with his fingers, loose gravel biting into his flesh, until
he found what he was looking for—a good-size rock.
Yanking it free of the muck, he smashed it against the window. The safety glass held. He angled his body away to get
more leverage, horror gripping him as he saw Justine's face
submerge. She didn't even struggle.

Bringing his arm down in a mighty arc, he slammed the
rock against the glass again. The window imploded, show-
ering the interior of the car with tiny pellets.

Reaching through the ruined window, he tipped her head back and held it above the water. Her eyes were closed, her face pale as marble except for the streak of red slashing across her forehead. When he tried to pull her from the car, he realized the seat belt was still locked in place.

With a curse, he dived inside, pushing between her slack body and the steering wheel. Working by touch, he found the metal buckle and released the latch. Then he retraced his path, pulling the unconscious woman with him through the window and into the flooded stream.

She was a dead weight in his arms, threatening to drag them both under. Tightening his grip, he held her above the water as he contemplated the treacherous ten-foot stretch of surging creek between him and the shore. With a technique he'd learned at the police academy, he shifted her to a shoulder carry. Still, negotiating the torrent was a lot harder than his solo journey to the car. His muscles ached from fighting the current. His body was numb from the cold, and his jeans felt like metal weights on his legs as he pulled Justine through the rushing water to the bank.

His jacket was lying where he'd dropped it on the shore. Spreading it out, he laid her down, put his ear beside her nose and felt her chest. She wasn't breathing, but her heart was still beating. Her lips and cheeks were bluish gray.

He tilted her head back to open her airways and checked to make sure that her mouth was unobstructed. Then he began mouth-to-mouth resuscitation, concentrating on forcing air past her icy lips while he slowly counted off the seconds.

He tried to think of her as an anonymous victim. But fear twisted his stomach into a tight knot. When she'd sat across from him in the office with her skirt hitched up to display her well-shaped legs, he'd wanted to touch her. God, what a way to get his wish. Trying to keep his mind blank, he continued methodically blowing into her lungs and compressing her chest.

Somewhere in the distance, he heard the wail of sirens. Then Justine coughed, and all his attention narrowed to her pale face. The blue tinge was gone.

"Thank God," he whispered, gently turning her to her side.

She sputtered and coughed up river water.

"That's it," he encouraged as she began to breathe on her own."That's it."

Above him on the road, tires screeched to a halt. Two men with a stretcher slid down the bank. One of them brushed past him and knelt over Justine. The other draped a blanket around his shoulders, and he realized as he climbed unsteadily to his feet that he was soaked to the skin, covered with mud and freezing cold. Shivering, he pulled the blanket tighter.

"Can you make it back to the ambulance on your own?" asked the paramedic who'd given him the blanket.

. He stared at the flashing light. "Don't worry about me."

"You could go into hypothermia, buddy. And you need a typhoid shot. You'd better let us take you to Mount Olive and check you out. You can ride in the second ambulance."

Resigned, he glanced back at Justine. Her eyes were open and tracking him. He wasn't sure what he expected to see in their blue depths. Certainly it wasn't what he found, a mixture of gratitude and longing that shattered him. In that moment, he wondered how badly he'd misjudged her.

JACK ORDWAY, Jackal to his friends, swore loudly as he craned his neck out the window of the gray Pontiac.

Lennie Ezrine, the car's driver, clenched his teeth to keep from delivering the bitter rejoinder quivering on the edge of his tongue.

Up on Falls Road, traffic had slowed to a crawl, though not because of the rain, which had finally stopped. Drivers were gawking at the ambulances pulled onto the shoulder and the car half submerged in the roiling water of the Jones Falls.

At the next intersection, Lenny turned onto a residential street and pulled into a driveway. After backing rapidly out again, he made another slow pass at the accident scene. This time, he could see two men carrying a woman on a stretcher toward an open ambulance door.

"You stupid shit," Jackal muttered.

Lennie had taken enough abuse. "You were the one who told me to edge her over. You thought it was funny when she looked like she was gonna freak!"

"Yeah, well, it sure as hell ain't my fault she went into the creek."

"Or mine neither. How was I supposed to know her damn car would go over the guardrail?"

Jackal didn't answer as they followed the ambulances down Falls Road.

"Heading for Mount Olive," Jackal guessed. "That's the closest hospital."

"Yeah."

"We better make sure."

Lennie nodded tightly. They were both in trouble, unless they could cut their losses. "She buys the farm, and we never get what we need.

"The stuff's probably at her house. All we gotta do is get the maid and the handyman out of the way so we can toss the place. And if we don't find what we want, we bug the phones so we can follow along on the conversations."

Jackal's eyes widened. "You really think we can get away with that?"

"Why not?"

Jackal chewed on that for a while. "Okay. I guess you're right. Any way we can do it—just so we get results."

Chapter Two

The phone rang, and Maggie Dempsey, housekeeper in the Hollingsworth mansion for more than a dozen years, rushed to the receiver. "Hello?"

"This is Mount Olive Hospital," a man said on the other end of the line.

It was the second call from the hospital. The first had sent her into a tailspin. Hoping against hope, she'd tried to contact her employer to inform him of the accident. But the Alaskan outfitters had relayed what she'd expected to hear: Mr. Hollingsworth was hunting at a remote mountain lake, and he'd left strict instructions not to be disturbed. Did she want to authorize a special flight into the camp?

Maggie had learned the consequences of disobeying instructions, and she'd respectfully declined. But what if Mr. Hollingsworth came home and demanded to know why she hadn't told him that his wife was in the hospital?

Sweating, Maggie had compromised and phoned Estelle Bensinger, the snooty executive assistant who ran Mr. Hollingsworth's office. Estelle thought they were on the same side, but Maggie didn't trust Mr. Hollingsworth's secretary any more than she trusted his wife. But at least she'd shifted responsibility to someone else.

"Why are you calling? Is Mrs. Hollingsworth all right?" Maggie asked the man from Mount Olive.

"She's feeling better."

"Thank the saints," Maggie breathed, hoping she sounded sincere.

"She wants you to bring her a nightgown and toilet articles."

"She does?" Maggie's brow wrinkled. "But I already brought down some things—a nightie and some clothes she can wear home from the hospital."

There was a slight hesitation on the other end of the line.

"Must be a mix-up. We don't have them."

Fretfully, Maggie glanced toward the window. It had been dark for several hours, and her night vision was so bad that she never drove after sundown. Yet there was no question of denying the request. She'd have to get a ride.

"I'll be there as soon as I can," she allowed.

"This time, make sure you come to the nurses' station."

After hanging up, Maggie went in search of Frank, the handyman who took care of the garden, repairs and heavy cleaning on the Hollingsworth estate.

He wouldn't like coming back on duty after his supper, but that was just too bad. They both had it good here, with high pay, medical insurance and a snug roof over heads. They could even eat steak every night for dinner if they wanted, and nobody would be the wiser. In fact, Maggie had thought many times that she was a darn sight better off than when she'd been married to Patty Dempsey, ex-fighter and ex-con. She'd been lucky to get this job, and she was going to hang on till retirement. Whatever it took.

SHE AWOKE from a drugging sleep that seemed centuries long. Yet some self-protective impulse kept her lying very still, wishing that the comforting blackness would swallow her again.

Her brain felt as if someone inside her skull was banging on a kettledrum. Every time she tried to move, her body ached, but it wasn't physical pain that kept her quiescent. It was the fear of some unknown yet terrible threat lurking at the edge of her consciousness, ready to spring if she gave the slightest sign that she had returned to the world.

She knew, however, that she couldn't simply lie here forever. Wherever *here* was. Holding her breath, she cautiously opened her eyes. The first thing she discovered was that the man in the sopping wet T-shirt was gone. He'd been holding her, his strong arms a shield from the terrible cold. She remembered his lips on hers. And his dark eyes, so close, so full of worry. She'd wanted to reach for him, but she'd been too weak to lift her arm. She didn't even know his name, yet with him gone, she felt a stinging sense of loss.

She heard her own ragged sigh in the silent room. Where was she, anyway? She could see plain walls, plain curtains and metal furniture. The serviceable theme was repeated with the crisp white sheets on her hospital bed.

She let that sink in. She was in a hospital.

Yet she didn't know the reason, and her heart started to pound. Raising a hand, she ran her fingertips lightly over her face. Her forehead and cheeks were abraded.

Gingerly, she moved each arm and leg. They were stiff, but nothing seemed broken. And she wasn't attached to any kind of machine. She was breathing on her own.

Breathing. Why should that be a problem? As quickly as the question formed, the answer danced away from her.

In sudden panic, she tried to locate a call button near the bed, but the mechanism eluded her. Feeling trapped, she pushed herself up, then gasped at the sharp pain that stabbed through her head. The room began to spin, and she gripped the sides of the bed, willing the dizziness to subside. When the vertigo finally eased, she drew in a deep breath, staring at a framed reproduction of the Mona Lisa on the other side of the room. The subject of the famous portrait smiled back benignly, increasing the feeling of unreality hanging in the air. She realized she knew the name of the woman in the picture—but she didn't know her own.

In growing terror, she scrambled for the combination of sounds that would deliver her identity. Her name. She had to know her name! But her mind drew a blank. Frantically, she looked around the room, and to her left saw an open bathroom door. Swinging her legs over the side of the bed, she slid to the tile floor and managed an upright position. It was a small victory. Concentrating on each tiny step, she shuffled to the washbasin and leaned against the cold porcelain for support. After switching on the light, she stood, barely breathing, summoning the courage to study her image.

In the end, there was no other choice. The woman staring back at her uncertainly was wearing a silky white gown with tiny lace trim. She was in her late twenties or early thirties with a wild wreath of red hair, blue eyes and skin that probably looked healthy when it wasn't marred by abrasions and a large bruise that spread across her forehead.

Objectively, nothing about the collection of feminine features was threatening. Yet as she peered into her own haunted eyes, she felt as if a chasm had opened beneath her and she was dropping toward the center of the earth.

A cold sweat broke out on her brow. "Who are you? What's your name?" she demanded in a quavery voice.

No answer came, either from the image in the mirror or from the depths of her soul.

A strangled sound welled in her throat. How could you forget your own identity?

Her temples pounded as she tried to remember—anything. But her personal memory started with the moment she'd awakened in the hospital room. No, with the man in the wet T-shirt. He came before the hospital. But she didn't even know the date, the day of the week, the year.

The vacuum gnawed at her; it grew inside her mind, threatened to sweep away all traces of sanity.

"Please. Somebody help me," she sobbed.

No one answered. Her legs were trembling so hard she would have toppled over if her fingers hadn't clamped the cold washbasin in front of her. Hours, or perhaps only minutes, later she turned on the tap and splashed cold water onto her face. It stung her damaged flesh, but it made her feel more alert.

Looking around the little room, she spotted a bar of soap still in its wrapper. Perusing the label brought back a meas-

"Away."

She probably looked stricken because the nurse responded with a reassuring little pat on her shoulder. "He'll be back soon."

She let that comfort her. He hadn't left her to fend for herself. He'd be back.

Kindly, the nurse led her to the room where she'd awakened. As she stepped through the doorway, every instinct urged her to run headlong for the exit, to escape from this nightmare. Yet she knew she wouldn't get far on her wobbly legs. And her legs were the least of her problems. Where would she go?

Her head swam with confusion. The name—Justine Hollingsworth—sounded wrong. But the man felt . . . right.

Feeling numb, she sank to the edge of the bed, her jaw clenched with the effort to keep from whimpering. When the nurse shifted her legs and tucked the covers around her icy body, she didn't protest.

Eyes squeezed closed, she heard the sound of rubber soles receding. Then she was alone again. But she couldn't cope with being alone. Fear seeped into every pore, like floodwater soaking into a low-lying field. She had no defenses. And she knew the rising tide would swamp her.

Blindly she reached out for a mooring. Then *he* was beside her in the dark, a comforting presence come to rescue her from madness.

Do you need me?

Oh, yes. Yes, please.

Perhaps it was only a fantasy. Perhaps if she opened her eyes, she would see that he wasn't there. But as she lay shivering and alone in the dark, her need made him real.

Are you cold?

Yes. So cold.

Let me warm you. He was beside her on the bed, holding her the way he had before, his voice deep and reassuring, his body solid and warm. *I'm here,* he whispered. *I'm here.* He said it over and over, easing the dreadful tension, lulling her into a strange kind of peace. And finally she drifted into sleep.

THE MOMENT MAGGIE stepped from the garage to the service porch, she knew something was wrong.

"Someone's been in here," she hissed.

"You're crazy," Frank snorted as he followed her across the sun room.

Trying to prepare herself for the worst, Maggie sprinted into the kitchen and stopped short. Every cabinet and drawer was opened, much of their contents strewn across the floor as if a tornado had swept through the room.

For several seconds, she stood staring at the mess with Frank right behind her. Then Frank lumbered around a pile of scattered spaghetti and reached for the phone. Maggie moved almost as quickly to slap her hand down on his—hard.

"What are you doing?" she demanded.

"What do you think, woman? Calling the police."

"We can't."

"Why not? Mr. Hollingsworth will be furious about this."

"Frank, think. We've both worked here for years. We know how much he hates the law messing in his business."

"That's true." Frank nodded slowly. "He solves his own problems. But what are *we* gonna do?" he asked, looking in dismay from her tense face to the ravaged room.

"Clean up."

"But—"

"You want to call the police, you take responsibility."

Frank looked unhappy.

"You find out where they broke in, and fix it up," she said. "I'll start cleaning. And until Mr. Hollingsworth gets home, one of us stays here."

"Yeah. Okay," he agreed.

With a sigh, Maggie started on a tour of the house. The kitchen was in the worst shape. The only damage to the living room was the pile of sofa and chair cushions in the middle of the rug. And the office had hardly been touched, thank the saints. The worst surprise was in Mrs. Hollingsworth's bedroom and her walk-in closet. Maggie stared in horror at the clothing, cosmetics and contents of drawers and shelves scattered everywhere. Mother Mary, how could she ever put everything back in the right place?

As she surveyed the damage, another thought struck her. Snatching up a phone book lying in a heap of papers on the rug, she called Mount Olive Hospital. When a woman's voice answered, she asked, "How can I find out if a patient received the things I brought over to her?"

"You could check with the nurses' station."

Ten minutes later, Maggie had the information, but it didn't make her feel any better. There had been no problem with the first bag she'd brought. Sitting down heavily on the bed, she squeezed her hands into fists. The call had been a trick to get her out of the house. If she'd had her wits about her, she would have phoned the hospital before rushing down there again. Now she'd have to pay the price for her stupidity.

"JUSTINE?"

She ignored the thickly accented male voice coming from a few feet above her head.

"Mrs. Hollingsworth, I know you're awake."

The man's tone was kind but insistent. "You can't hide forever. Please open your eyes."

There really was no alternative. She obeyed and found herself staring into a round, brown face. Behind horn-rimmed glasses, the eyes were dark and liquid. Sympathetic. Or perhaps that was what she wanted to think.

"I'm Dr. Habib. We met earlier. Do you remember?"

"No."

Over his shoulder, morning sunlight streamed into the room. It did nothing to dissolve the choking knot in her chest. Under the covers, her hands clenched at her sides.

"I'm not Mrs. Hollingsworth." She made an effort to keep her voice steady. "Why are you calling me that?"

"I see your memory has not returned," the doctor said, his voice matter-of-fact. He was short and round, his body poured into an expensive-looking suit. "I know that must be upsetting."

She gave a little ironic laugh.

"Do you remember what happened?"

She shook her head.

"You were in an accident. Your car went off Falls Road and into the water. The Jones Falls is at flood stage." He paused, giving her time to assimilate the information.

She felt her features freeze into a mask of shock.

"Let me make you more comfortable." The offer came from a moon-faced nurse standing behind the doctor. According to her name tag, she was Mrs. Janet Swinton.

Lord, she'd have the staff memorized before she knew her own name.

Mrs. Swinton came forward and touched a button, raising the head of the bed. "Better?" she asked.

"Yes."

Dr. Habib continued. "You were rescued by a passing motorist and brought to Mount Olive Hospital."

A motorist? The man with the T-shirt and the muscles. Last night, she'd imagined him cradling her trembling body in his arms, shielding her from the abyss.

"Who is he?" she managed to ask.

"Someone named Mike Lancer."

"Mike Lancer," she repeated. It was a strong name, strong like the man. But he was a stranger. And apparently *not* her husband. In the dark, she'd conjured his comforting presence, but she couldn't rely on him now. She had to rely on herself.

She fought to stay calm, to collect data, search for clues that would explain the bizarre misunderstanding about her name. "I was driving Justine Hollingsworth's car?"

"Uh...no." For the first time, the physician looked a bit uncomfortable. "Apparently you had a rental."

"Then I had Justine Hollingsworth's purse. Her identification?"

He spread his hands apologetically. "I'm sorry. The river was moving very fast. Everything inside the car was swept away."

She gave him a sharp look. "Then why are you so convinced of my identity?"

"Mr. Lancer recognized you."

She searched his eyes for signs of duplicity. Listening to his outlandish story, it was hard not to come back to the conspiracy theory she'd dismissed the previous night. Only this time, she wondered if the man she remembered as her savior was part of the plot. She fought the tightness in her throat. "Let me get this right," she enunciated carefully. "I was driving a rental car. I had no identification. But someone I know just happened along?"

The physician favored her with a little smile. "You're a well-known member of Baltimore society."

"I look like Justine Hollingsworth?" she clarified.

"Yes. Except that you've cut your hair. In recent months, you and your husband have attended a number of charity events. The Mount Olive Ball, for example. And the fundraiser for the aquarium. Your picture has been in the paper."

"And that special feature on the Channel Eleven evening news that they shot at your lovely St. Michaels vacation home," Nurse Swinton added brightly. "Your husband made a very substantial donation to the hospital fund. Which is why we're taking such good care of you."

Habib gave her a quelling look. "As you're well aware, we take excellent care of *all* our patients, Mrs. Swinton."

Color rose in the woman's cheeks. "Yes. Of course. I only meant..."

The exchange barely registered with the patient sitting in the hospital bed. She was trying to imagine herself at a glittering media event or owning a vacation home. The picture simply didn't fit her image of herself. She sucked in a little breath. What image? She didn't have an image.

"Unfortunately," the doctor continued, "Mr. Hollingsworth is on a hunting trip in Alaska and can't be reached until he returns to Anchorage. But we contacted your housekeeper, Mrs. Dempsey. She brought several night-gowns for you to wear and some other personal items.''

Silence filled the hospital room while the patient tried to come to grips with a truth that was becoming harder to deny.

"I have amnesia," she finally blurted out, feeling like the main character in a bad suspense movie. Only no one had bothered to give her the script.

"Amnesia. Yes, that appears to be true," Dr. Habib agreed as if he'd been reluctant to put a name to her afflic-tion and was grateful she'd relieved him of the onerous task. "I'm sure it must be unsettling—not remembering your past."

She gulped. "Yes. Why did this happen to me?"

"We're not sure. You apparently hit your head against the steering wheel."

She nodded tightly. Now that the doctor had apparently decided to speak frankly, he went on for several minutes with technical information about brain tissue and neuro-logical trauma. Most of it eluded her, but a pertinent phrase penetrated her numbness.

"In addition to the inability to remember your personal history, you might have other problems, as well."

"What other problems?"

"Well, you might have trouble remembering informa-tion that's told to you."

"How long will I be this way?"

"We can't be sure. Each case runs its individual course. You could regain your memory in a few days. Or..."

"Or what?"

"It could take time."

She shuddered, reading between the lines. She might never recover. That's what he meant. The possibility was so frightening that she thrust it from her before it could suck away what remained of her sanity.

"But we're here to give you all the help you need, Jus-tine," Dr. Habib concluded on an upbeat note.

Justine. That damn name again. It set her teeth on edge. She sat very still, afraid that if she moved, she might shatter.

"Don't call me Justine."

Habib gave her a paternalistic smile. "It's your name."

She looked down at her hand, watching the fingers pleat the rough fabric of the hospital sheet. "What if it upsets me?"

"I'm sorry."

Her eyes darted around the room and settled on the reproduction of the Mona Lisa she'd seen on the wall the night before. "If you have to call me something, call me..." She might have said Mona. Somehow that didn't seem much better than Justine. But Lisa sounded...more familiar. "Call me...Lisa," she almost shouted.

Habib looked startled. "What?"

"Humor me. Call me Lisa," she said with more force than she'd mustered since the beginning of the strange interview.

The physician started to say something, then he shrugged. "If that makes you feel more comfortable. But really, it's best if you try to work toward the familiar."

"Lisa," she insisted.

"All right. We can...uh...do that for the time being." He shifted his weight from one foot to the other. "I have some good news that should cheer you."

"What?" she asked cautiously.

"Our staff physician did a thorough examination when you arrived in the emergency room. You have no broken bones or major physical trauma."

She nodded.

"And your pregnancy is intact."

"Pregnancy?" she gasped, her throat squeezing closed.

Chapter Three

"Are you telling me I'm going to have a baby?"

"Yes," the doctor said. "You're about two and a half months along."

Tiny shivers raced over her skin. She stared at Dr. Habib, unable to absorb this new shock that was somehow greater than all the rest.

"No. I can't be." The denial rushed out of her as if saying it quickly would make it true.

"In your present state, the news could be a little disturbing," the doctor allowed in a soothing voice that chipped at her uncertain mental health. The bland look on his face was the last straw.

"Stop it!" she screamed. "Stop being so damn calm and reasonable. My whole world has fallen apart! I—I—" She stopped simply because she wasn't sure what to say.

Dr. Habib took a step back. "I see you're upset..." He hesitated. "Mrs.... ah... Lisa, why don't I give you some time to adjust, and we'll talk later."

She nodded tensely, wanting nothing more than to see him vanish. No, she wanted this whole nightmare to vanish.

"You just take it easy, and we'll be in with breakfast in a few minutes," Nurse Swinton added soothingly.

Dr. Habib and the nurse stepped into the hall, no doubt to hold a whispered conversation about the deranged behavior of the patient.

With a little moan, she slumped against the raised head-board. Eyes closed, she clutched the bedding, doing her best to hold tight to reality. Yet reality had no meaning. Pregnant. She couldn't be.

Trying to read the signs of her body, she cupped her hands under her breasts, testing their weight. They were full and rounded, but she had no basis for comparison. She hiked up her gown, peered down at her middle, and with shaky fingers, she stroked her hand across the ivory skin. Did her abdomen curve outward the barest amount?

Again she touched her breasts, gliding her thumbs gingerly across the pale nipples. They were prominent and tender, almost the way they felt before she got her period. She clutched at the tiny bit of self-knowledge that had popped into her mind. Yet she didn't know whether it was real memory of her own body or merely something she'd read in a magazine.

Her heart was slamming against the inside of her chest. All at once, she knew that she couldn't stay in this place, couldn't wait for the next startling revelation from Dr. Habib. What would he tell her next? That her husband was running for president of the United States and she'd better not screw up his chances for election or maybe this was like that movie where a devil-worshiping cult helped the Prince of Darkness impregnate an innocent woman. What was it called? Something about a baby... *Rosemary's Baby*. Yes, that was it.

The crazy idea sparked a hysterical laugh. Then the worst thought of all shot through her mind. Habib and Nurse Swinton had destroyed her memory with drugs, and they were holding her here against her will. They wouldn't let her go until—she felt a surge of panic and struggled to suck in a breath—she docilely went along with the fable that she was Justine Hollingsworth.

The last vestige of rationality fled. Terror gripped her and wouldn't let go. She had to escape, had to find someplace safe. Someplace where she could get back her memory, where she could start to string one coherent thought after another. Figure out what was going on.

In that moment of terror, she wanted Mike Lancer, the man who had looked as if he cared about her, to stride through the door and whisk her away. But he wasn't coming. She couldn't count on him any more than she could count on the doctors and nurses here.

With a furtive glance toward the hall, she slipped out of bed, tiptoed across the room and quietly shut the door. Then she opened the closet. Inside were clothes she didn't recognize—a classically styled aqua silk shirtwaist and a matching tailored blazer. There was no purse. No identification. Quickly she searched the jacket pockets and found two folded twenty-dollar bills that might have been tucked away for an emergency. They'd have to do.

Imbued with a sense of purpose, she pulled the nightgown over her head and reached for the undergarments folded on a narrow shelf in the closet. The panties and bra were thin and silky. They didn't look or feel like the sort of things she'd pick. But then, neither did the dress, really.

The panties rode low on her hips. The bra was a little tight, but her pregnancy could account for that. She was adjusting the waistline of the dress when a flash of movement made her turn.

Nurse Swinton had opened the door and was standing there uncertainly, a tray of food in her hands, a startled expression splitting her moon face. "Mrs. Hollingsworth, what are you doing?"

Lisa froze.

The nurse spoke firmly. "Please get back into bed. I'm going to call Dr. Habib."

She had no intention of obeying. With a violent shake of her head, she went down on her hands and knees and retrieved the aqua pumps sitting side-by-side at the bottom of the closet.

Clearly giving up on further protests, the nurse silently backed out of the room.

Lisa knew they would cut her off at the pass if she didn't escape in the next minute. Clutching the shoes, she made for the hall. But it was already too late. Nurse Swinton had jettisoned the tray and was heading back toward her room. Dr. Habib was right behind, his hand pressed close to his side. But she saw what he was trying to hide—a hypodermic needle.

She screamed as her tormentors bore down on her. Flinging the shoes at them, she ran. She made it as far as the next room before strong hands grabbed her shoulders and wrestled her against the wall.

"No. Let me go," she cried out.

An orderly pushing a gurney stopped in midstride. Patients came out of their rooms to stare at the spectacle.

"Help. Please, somebody help me."

But none of the onlookers sprang to her defense.

She tried to fight, striking out wildly with her fists, hitting Swinton's shoulder, knocking off Habib's glasses.

"Mrs. Hollingsworth," the nurse gasped, "you'll hurt yourself."

Relentlessly, they moved her down the hall and back into her room. Then a jab stung her upper arm, and she knew she'd lost the battle and probably the war, as well. She tried to hold on to consciousness, but it slipped though her fingers like water through a sieve.

ESTELLE BENSINGER'S long fingers drummed against the receiver as she impatiently waited for the supervisor to answer the call. Normally she was bedrock-steady, but the events of the last twelve hours had crumbled her composure.

Finally, a woman's voice came on the line. "This is Mrs. Swinton, nursing supervisor. Can I help you?"

Her angular features sharpened. "I'm Estelle Bensinger. I want a status report on Mrs. Justine Hollingsworth."

"Are you a relative?"

"No, but I *am* Mr. Hollingsworth's executive assistant." Estelle put as much authority into her voice as she could muster. As Kendall Hollingsworth's office manager, she screened his calls, answered his correspondence, scheduled his meetings, researched his associates and competitors and performed other duties, as required. Like her boss, the head of the K.H. Group, she was accustomed to people jumping to her commands. This morning, she only hoped she didn't sound too eager.

Rocking back and forth in her custom ergonomic chair, Estelle listened to the nurse.

"Mrs. Hollingsworth has suffered a mild concussion and minor abrasions. She is listed in stable condition."

"Are there any serious problems?"

"We're not allowed to release those details," Nurse Swinton clipped out.

Estelle tried several more interrogation techniques but kept coming up against a brick wall. Then the nurse abruptly said she had to attend to a patient and hung up.

Estelle rubbed the tension lines in her forehead as she tried to regain her usual composure.

She'd been on the wrong side of thirty with no hope of marriage when she'd won the plum job as Kendall Hollingsworth's executive assistant.

God, what a man he'd been back then. High-energy. Strong. Self-confident. The distinguished dark hair with a touch of gray and his conservative good looks hadn't hurt, either. They'd simply added to his aura of power and wealth.

She squeezed her eyes closed, trying not to think about subtle differences that only a wife or mistress or longtime private secretary would notice. It was more soothing to remember the good times, when everything was clicking along. She'd been his unflappable, reliable assistant for almost ten years. They'd been a great team despite his marriage to Justine. As far as she was concerned, Justine was trouble from the top of her salon-styled red curls, to the toes of her five-hundred-dollar Italian shoes. For at least a year—maybe longer than that—the marriage had been on the rocks. Anybody could see she and Kendall were all wrong for each other, that their breakup was only a matter of time. So why hadn't Justine left town the way she was supposed to?

"Oh, God, what do I do now?" Estelle muttered. For starters, she needed more information. Like what, exactly, had put Justine in the hospital. An accident or...something else? If the answer was something else, would Justine be foolish enough to tell her doctor the whole truth?

MIKE LANCER BRUSHED several wayward yew needles from his dark hair and sighed. Since five that morning, he'd been stationed in the bushes of a small park in Catonsville, waiting for Mr. Clyde Patruski to take out his trash.

Mike was stiff and bored, and he had to take a leak. But he wasn't about to leave his hiding place until Patruski showed.

It wasn't until seven twenty-two that the barrel-shaped Patruski emerged, carrying a green thirty-gallon trash can. With a smile of satisfaction, Mike began to snap pictures of his quarry muscling the can down seven steps and then twenty feet to the curb. As a dividend, he got several shots of the jerk picking up a tricycle from his front walk and slamming it onto a neighbor's lawn. So much for the story that Patruski had wrenched his back so badly on a work assignment that he was incapable of doing more than shuffle from the sofa to the bathroom. When Able Exterminators showed the man the pictures, he'd be smart to drop his medical claim against the company—if he didn't want to face a charge of insurance fraud.

As Mike slid behind the wheel of his car, he breathed out a long sigh. After reading Patruski's case file, he'd have bet money that the guy was faking the extent of his injury. But up to now, Patruski had been careful not to do anything in public that would give him away. He'd even had a neighbor kid unload grocery bags from his car. A week of shadowing him had netted nothing suspicious. Mike had to admit, it had been one of his better ideas to watch how Patruski got his trash to the curb.

Whistling the theme song from *The High and the Mighty*, Mike headed toward the beltway and then to I-95. But, the jaunty notes of the song tapered off and finally stopped as he neared the Russell Street exit. Truth be known, he hated this kind of two-bit assignment. He'd take a good murder investigation any day, except that there weren't enough of those to pay the rent. A private eye had to fill in with what he could get.

At 43 Light Street, he stopped in the newly opened lobby café for a large cup of coffee, then took the elevator to the office he'd been sharing with Jo O'Malley since last November. Formerly the sign on the door had said O'Malley and O'Malley; now it read O'Malley and Lancer. He'd begun taking over some of Jo's business after she'd been shot by a couple of thugs trying to steal some of her husband's custom-designed electronics equipment. He and Jo liked each other and worked well together, and when she'd gotten pregnant, she'd asked Mike to come in as a partner. Since she'd gone part-time, he'd been carrying the major caseload.

Sipping his coffee, he leaned back in his desk chair and started listening to his messages. Three years earlier, he hadn't been sure he could make it as a private detective, not after resigning from the Baltimore police force under pressure. As far as the powers that be were concerned, he was a bad cop who'd taken the easy way out—which was hardly a great recommendation for getting jobs in the metro area. But he was good at his work, and the clients kept coming. And he had the satisfaction of helping people who had nowhere else to turn.

After noting a phone number from a child-custody case, he jabbed at the button on the answering machine and waited for the next message. It was from someone who identified himself as Dr. Habib at Mount Olive Hospital and who spoke with an East Indian accent.

"Mr. Lancer, I was told you were the man who rescued Mrs. Justine Hollingsworth from the Jones Falls. Mrs. Hollingsworth appears to be suffering from amnesia and is having some difficulty coping with her lack of personal memory. Your account of the rescue would be helpful.'' He ended with his phone number.

Mike sat forward. Since the accident two days ago, he'd been trying—and failing—to put Justine Hollingsworth out of his mind. He pictured her again, first as she'd looked outside the parking garage, then on the bank of the rain-swollen creek, her face white as death, her red hair streaming, her body limp as a broken doll. Her eyes had focused on him with an unnerving intensity that had made him want to scoop her back into his arms and damn the consequences. Almost but not quite, that look had held the power to wipe away everything else he remembered about her.

The doctor said she had amnesia. That certainly put an interesting twist on things. Could this very convenient illness possibly be real? He was listening to the tape again, trying to read between the lines, when a noise in the waiting room made him twist around.

Jo was standing near his door, looking disheveled but cheerful. A royal blue diaper bag was slung over one shoulder, and a molded-plastic infant seat, complete with a two-month-old sleeping occupant, dangled from her other hand.

Mike grinned at the peacefully sleeping baby. "Getting Scott started in detective business early, huh?"

"I hope he's going to be an electronics genius like his father. It pays a heck of a lot better."

"Tell me about it."

As he watched her carefully set the baby carrier on the rug in her own office and crack the door, a stab of envy took him by surprise. She had it all—a husband who loved her, a child, a job that she could shift into low gear while she concentrated on domestic life. Did she know how lucky she was? Mike struggled to contain feelings that rarely got the better of him. If things had worked out differently, he might have had a wife—even a family—by now. Below the desk, the hand resting on his knee clenched.

On her way back to his office, Jo scooped up the pile of mail he'd stepped over in the front hall. Sitting down, she set a couple of envelopes on the edge of his desk. "So what was that intriguing phone message I overheard? Are you working for the famous Justine Hollingsworth?"

"She interviewed me for a job, but she didn't get around to telling me what it was."

"Hmm. Did you really rescue her? How come I didn't read about it in the paper?"

"Maybe the hospital kept it confidential. We're talking about a socially prominent woman who wouldn't want that kind of publicity." Keeping his voice carefully neutral, Mike briefly related the details of the accident and his suspicions about the guys who'd been following her.

"It's possible they deliberately ran her off the road," he concluded. "Or they could have been trying to scare her and screwed up. Or maybe they were only trying to pass illegally."

"But you don't think it was a coincidence," Jo clarified.

"At this point, I have no way of knowing. I'd like Justine's take on it. But if she really has amnesia, maybe she doesn't remember the accident—or why she wanted to hire me in the first place."

"Why do you think she's faking?"

He sighed. "It could be a ploy, an expedient way to duck out of a bad situation. What if she has a secret she doesn't want her husband to find out? Amnesia gives her some breathing space."

Jo continued to sort through the mail. "I suppose you didn't talk to the police about seeing the other car following her?"

He ticked off three very good reasons on the fingers of his right hand. "The license number of the other car was smeared with mud. I can't prove I saw anything sinister. And they're going to wonder why I'm dragging the name of a well-known citizen into the mire. So going to the police will only set me up for a hostile interrogation. I think my best bet is to forget Mrs. Hollingsworth ever contacted me," he muttered, tipping back his chair again and trying to appear relaxed. But he suspected from Jo's expression that she could read the tension in him.

"It's not that easy," she said.

He sat up straighter. "Oh yeah?"

Jo passed a piece of mail across the desk to him. It contained a brief note explaining that Justine Hollingsworth wished to retain his services—and a check for five thousand dollars.

Chapter Four

Benita Fenton took the stairs to the second floor like an ancient train chugging up a mountain track. Every step was an effort. At the top, she held on to the railing and gasped for air. It had been four months since her quadruple bypass. She was only seventy, but she felt more like a hundred. Ed had turned his study into a temporary bedroom until she got better—if she ever did. The operation might give her a few more months, a few years at the most. Regardless, she was going to have to suffer through whatever time she had left.

Today was May twelfth—Andrea's thirtieth birthday—and Benita was determined to visit her daughter's room. She moved slowly down the hall of her Philadelphia row house. The floor squeaked, the carpet needed replacing and the roof leaked in a few spots when it rained really hard. But they didn't have the money for repairs.

When Benita reached the last room on the left, she pulled a key from her pocket and unlocked the door. The musty smell made her cough, but she stepped inside, anyway. Her eyes watered as she looked around the sanctuary that had remained virtually unchanged from what it had been when Andrea was a teenager, except back then, clothes and shoes had been slung carelessly around the room. Lord, they'd had some real knock-down drag-out fights. Andrea had been determined to show her independence. Benita recalled that she had been just as determined to make her daughter toe the line. Then Andrea had taken off for good—and left an empty place in Benita's heart.

Benita's gaze swept over the room, letting the familiar furnishings comfort her. The canopy bed; the flowered, handmade quilt; the Billy Joel poster on the wall; and the tray of eyeshadows, lipsticks and nail polish on the dresser. A fine layer of dust lay over everything like a blanket. Several industrious spiders had taken up residence in the corner where three Barbie dolls sat. The room hadn't been touched for over six months, since she'd started having chest pains. Now she had a compulsive urge to clean, to make the mirror above the vanity sparkle in the morning sun, and to wash, starch and iron the faded pink-checked curtains that hung limply at the window. But her days of compulsive housekeeping were over.

Benita pulled out the photo album from below the nightstand and sank onto the bed. As she turned the pages, she tried to recapture the joy she'd felt when they'd first brought little Andrea home. They'd waited so long for a baby.

Pictures of Andrea in the bath . . . in a pink snowsuit that clashed with her carrot-colored hair. . . in her first frilly dress for Christmas Eve—she'd looked like an angel come to earth. Benita's heart clenched at the memories. She'd tried her best to bring up the perfect child. It was a parent's responsibility to keep her offspring out of trouble and make sure she was a credit to herself and the community. She'd heard Pastor Downing say that dozens of times. So why had she been punished all these years for doing her duty?

Her fingers traced the edges of Andrea's confirmation picture. The girl had been so obedient when she was little, but from the time she'd turned fifteen, they'd fought over everything from her funky wardrobe, to curfews and drinking. Then, at two o'clock one rainy morning, Andrea had screamed that she hated everything about her life—even her first name, which she said she wasn't going to answer to anymore. Benita's own nerves had been at the breaking point. Angrily, she'd lashed out at her ungrateful daughter, blurting out the truth about Andrea's birth.

The next morning, Andrea had taken two suitcases of clothes and moved to a friend's apartment.

At first, Benita's pride had kept her from calling. Then when she'd wanted to mend the breach, she found that Andrea had withdrawn the ten thousand dollars from her college savings account and left town without leaving a forwarding address. She'd never given up hope that she'd see her daughter again, but now...well, it might never happen. Benita might be dead in another month—or week.

Tears were streaming down her face as she closed the album. "Dear Lord," she whispered. "Please, let me see my baby again. Please, before I die."

WEARINESS DOGGED Mike as he stepped into the twilight of the parking garage. With his thoughts focused inward, the cars on either side of him were reduced to shadowy blurs. He knew his exhaustion had as much to do with being stuck in the middle of the Justine Hollingsworth case as it did with his early-morning stakeout. He knew that he was too tired to make a snap decision about turning down five thousand dollars. Keeping it would mean he wouldn't have to worry about his share of the office rent or the rent on his apartment for several months.

It would be smart to get some sleep. But as he headed toward his car, he decided to drive to Mount Olive Hospital—not home. Maybe if he looked into Justine's blue eyes again, he'd know the truth.

The noise of stealthy footfalls snapped his attention back to his surroundings. Someone was keeping pace behind him. With a sudden movement, he pivoted and found himself facing the guy with the weather-beaten skin and the fatigues who'd been following Justine two days earlier. The one who'd run away when Mike had confronted him.

They stared at each other, both tense, both ready to take appropriate action. Whatever that was. The scent of unwashed skin and cheap wine drifted toward Mike, and with a sudden, unbidden stab of anger mingled with pain, he wondered if this was how his father had ended up—a drunk on the street with no family and no friends.

The derelict moved from one foot to the other, his rheumy eyes regarding Mike with a wildly changing mixture of emotions—fear, determination and anger warring for dominance, with no clear victor.

The safest thing would have been to walk away. Mike stood his ground.

"We met the other day. Something I can do for you, buddy?" he asked, subtly shifting the initiative from the other man to himself.

The stranger licked cracked lips, took a step back.

"What's your name?" Mike hoped the abrupt question would elicit an unguarded answer.

"Gary." The man looked surprised that he'd answered.

Mike gave him an encouraging smile. "Well, Gary, what can I do for you?" he repeated.

"What happened to—"

Before he got any further, a car backfired somewhere out on the street. Gary dropped to a crouch on the oil-stained floor, his head bent, his hands and arms a protective shield. A high, keening wail came from his lips. "Noooooooo."

"Take it easy," Mike said, moving closer. "It's just a car."

"Make it stop."

"It has."

But Gary was in a world of his own. His eyes were wide, darting from side to side as if he expected enemies to emerge from the shadows. Scrambling up, he backed toward the wall, and from somewhere in his dirty clothing, he pulled a wicked-looking knife.

Mike wasn't a fool. He didn't move any closer. "It's okay," he tried in a reassuring voice. "Put the knife down, and we'll talk."

"Noooooo." With surprising agility, the frightened man turned and fled.

"Wait!" Mike shouted.

He could have saved his breath. The vagrant vaulted over a wall that separated the ramp from the parking deck and dropped to the next level of the garage. Mike heard footsteps pounding on the metal steps but when he reached the door to the stairwell and threw it open, the area was deserted. He debated going down, but he knew Gary had a tremendous head start.

Slowly, Mike walked back to his car, his brow furrowed. Gary was mentally unbalanced. That much was certain. And he'd been following Justine the other day. Did *this* encounter have something to do with her?

Mike unlocked the door of his Mustang and slid into the driver's seat, his mind replaying the bizarre encounter as he started the engine. Gary's terror when the vehicle had backfired had been tangible. He'd been reacting as if he'd been under fire.

Just what he needed. More questions.

Putting the car in gear, Mike left the garage and headed toward Mount Olive Hospital, determined to get some answers.

SEVERAL BLOCKS from the garage, Gary sucked in great drafts of air as he staggered along the sidewalk. His lungs burned, and his side ached, but he kept moving. Had to get away.

He risked a quick look over his shoulder. Stupid jerk! He'd made a bad mistake. He balled his hands into fists. Every time he tried to... tried to... He shook his head in frustration. One moment a thought would be there, the next it would skitter out of reach.

With an anguished sigh, he turned onto a narrow street lined with ancient row houses. Some had been demolished, leaving gaps in the ranks like teeth plucked from a decaying mouth.

"Can't let 'em find me," he muttered under his breath. "Gary made a mistake. Sure as hell made a mistake."

One of the houses ahead had boarded-up windows. With a stolen pair of wire cutters, he'd made a hole in the chain-link fence guarding the backyard. Then he'd put the edges back together nice and neat, so nobody could tell. He was good with his hands. He could do stuff. Like in the old days when he'd lived in a house. With...her....

A wave of anguish rolled over him, and a longing so palpable that it made his chest ache. He stopped and leaned against the wall, gasping, his eyes squeezed shut. When he could go on, he darted across a trash-filled gap in the row and made for the fence.

Almost there. Almost safe. He stopped to look over his shoulder to make sure nobody was watching. Then he squirmed through the fence, put the pieces back together and crossed the tiny yard. He didn't rest until he was in the basement stairwell.

Safe. In his snug little foxhole. He'd fixed it up nice and comfortable. And safe. Sinking down on the bed of newspapers and old blankets, he hooked his arms around his knees and rocked back and forth.

He'd given Mr. Private Detective the slip, all right. And the rest of 'em. The police, too. They didn't even know he had a beat-up car stashed a couple of blocks away with license plates he'd lifted across town. His transportation might look as though it belonged in a junkyard, but it ran good. And it was full of gas. He could go where he pleased anytime he wanted.

But he'd made a mistake today. He should've known better than to trust that detective. Should've known the guy would be on the other side.

"Stupid jerk. Gary made a mistake," he muttered, "Gonna get himself killed if he don't watch out." With shaky fingers, he felt inside his shirt. The knife was there. Just where he'd put it. Pulling it out, he cradled it in his lap. He was good with a knife. An expert. "That guy gets in my way again, I'll cut him good. Cut him good, for sure."

SHE WAS GETTING USED to it. The sensation of waking—the feeling of hope blooming like a small, bright flower unfurling in a protected garden. This time would be different. This time she would remember everything. Her life. Her job. The people she loved. Were they looking for her, worried about her? And what about the father of her child?

Oh, God, the father of her child.

She tried to wrap her trembling fingers around the flower, being careful not to crush the tender petals. But it was too late. The frigid wind had already blown into the garden, snatching the blossom from her grasp.

Her memory was no more than a pitifully short stretch of hours. The time since she'd first awakened in this hospital room and been told that a stranger had pulled her from a rain-swollen creek. The history of her life prior to that moment was a great yawning void.

Fear rose in her throat again. By an effort of will, she stopped herself from screaming. From deep in the recesses of her soul, she called forth the moral fortitude she instinctively knew she possessed. Until now, she'd been like a boat in a storm, helpless to fight the elements tossing her about. The only way she was going to survive was to stay calm and roll with the swells. From now on, she vowed, she was not going to lose control. *She would not.*

The resolve brought a measure of serenity. Lying very still, she opened her eyes a slit and examined her surroundings. To her vast relief, she was in the same room. Same walls, same furniture, same picture of the Mona Lisa. At least they hadn't moved her to the violent ward.

On the other hand, a trim-looking nurse was sitting in the corner of the room reading a magazine.

She longed to postpone the moment of reckoning, yet she'd learned there was nowhere to hide, either from the nurse or herself. So she stirred slightly in the bed.

The woman was instantly alert. "Mrs. Hollingsworth."

She grimaced, saw the nurse's gaze zero in on the movement. Under the covers, she pressed her palms against the mattress. This time she wouldn't make a big deal about the name. This time she'd go along with the program. Because they wouldn't let her out of here if they thought she was loony.

The woman watched her closely. "They told me you'd rather be called Lisa. Would you like that better?"

"Lisa would be fine, thanks," she said politely, surprised at the vast relief she felt.

"Why do you like the name?"

She pushed herself to a sitting position, making time to answer while the woman raised the head of the bed.

"It sounds real," she responded lamely. "I can't explain why.... Uh, are you a private duty nurse?"

"Yes. Dr. Habib thought it would be a good idea to have someone here when you woke up. Are you feeling any better?" she asked brightly.

Lisa considered the answer carefully. "Well, I still can't remember anything about my past. I'm sure you can understand how frustrating that is. And I find that I'm overreacting to things," she added for good measure.

"That's typical with a head injury."

"It is?"

The woman looked a bit puzzled. "Didn't the doctor talk to you about that?"

"We haven't talked much." Lord, had she forgotten something important? Vaguely, she recalled him telling her she might have trouble remembering things.

"Yes, well, why don't I let Dr. Habib know you're awake? Will you be all right by yourself?"

"Of course."

The woman left. That was a small victory. They trusted her to be alone for a few minutes. Actually, it was less than a minute before she caught a flash of motion in the doorway. Looking up, she expected to see the short, brown-skinned doctor, but it was someone else entirely.

A man in a worn leather jacket, faded jeans and a dark T-shirt. He stood in the doorway, filling the space, his left shoulder braced against the frame. His deep-set brown eyes regarded her as if he wasn't sure he'd be welcome.

The universe seemed to tilt. It was *him*. He'd been impressive in her memory, but memory didn't compare to the physical reality of the man.

The quizzical expression on his face said they must have some kind of relationship. It shifted to a look that told her he was trying to gauge her mood. She found she was going through the same exercise.

The first thing she decided was that he was making an effort to appear casual, with one hand thrust into the pocket of his jeans. Yet she sensed his underlying wariness, and a current of man-woman awareness that zinged from him to her and back again. Dr. Habib had called him a passing motorist. Had he deliberately misstated the situation to see how she'd react?

She wished to heaven she weren't sitting in a bed, wearing a nightgown. It took an effort to stop herself from looking down to see if her nipples showed through the thin fabric. Feeling them tighten, she plucked at the covers, dragging them higher to cover her bodice.

His lips twitched as he caught the movement. They were well-shaped, sensual. She didn't want to concentrate on his lips. Yet she found no safe focus. Everywhere her gaze rested, she liked what she saw. His features were craggy and honest, in a basic sort of way, as if he came from sturdy working-class stock. His dark brown hair was in need of a trim. His shoulders were broad, his hips narrow and his legs long. She guessed he didn't make a living sitting behind a desk.

But she didn't want guesses. She wanted to know all about him. For the first time since she'd awakened in this room, she was more interested in someone else than in herself.

She sensed she was teetering on the edge of some important truth. The frightening part was that she didn't know whether it was good or bad. Even worse, she knew she couldn't discover it by herself. She needed him. The way she'd needed him last night, whispering gentle words in her ear, keeping her safe in his strong arms. The memory of her fantasy made her face hot.

"I know you," she said in a husky voice.

Something blazed in his eyes.

"Are you my husband?" she blurted out.

His grim laughter filled the room, and she felt her skin go from hot to flaming.

... straighten her up in the safety cannula. The memory of Kendall inside her had...

... coming out the other end...

... Anyway you cut it, one hundred and...

... He was hoping he'd have his money before all was said and done...

... from her traumatic...

Chapter Five

"I'm...sorry," she stammered, momentarily bewildered and stunned. Too late she remembered the doctor had told her the man who'd rescued her was not her husband. But things had a way of getting muddled in her brain. Lord, what a mistake. "You have me at a disadvantage."

"That wasn't my intention," he demurred.

She tilted her chin up. "I take it you're not Kendall Hollingsworth."

"Hardly. I'm Mike Lancer."

"Mike Lancer," she repeated. It seemed to fit. She had the sudden image of a crusader trapped in the wrong century. Partly it was the name, of course. It was easy to picture someone named Mike Lancer wearing armor and charging full tilt on a warhorse with a lance at the ready. But it was more than that. It was the solid, steady aura that surrounded him. And the knowledge that he'd saved her life. "You're the man who pulled me out of the river."

"Yes, I'm also a private detective. You sent me a retainer in the mail. I got it this morning."

"I hired you? To do what?" Silently, she fought off disappointment. She'd been clinging to the hope that he was someone important in her life. Instead, they had a business relationship. Still, she knew she hadn't mistaken the sensual pull between them. It went both ways.

"You came to my office last week and said you were considering hiring me," he continued. "We never got around to discussing the particulars."

"So you didn't just happen to be driving by when my car went into the water."

"I was following . . . you."

She had the feeling he'd changed his mind about something in midsentence. "Why?" she probed.

"I saw you on the street outside my office. When I called to you, you ignored me."

"I wouldn't do that," she said with conviction. He was damn hard to ignore. More than that, she couldn't imagine being so rude. "I must not have heard you."

"On the way out of the parking garage, you stared right at me, Mrs. Hollingsworth, but you didn't slow down." His dark eyes bored into her.

"Don't call me that name." She wasn't sure why, but it was achingly important that he, above everyone else, believe she'd somehow gotten swept up in another woman's bad dream.

"Why not?"

She started to reach toward him, as if touching him might convey the bewilderment and upset she felt at being identified as this Hollingsworth woman. Then, embarrassed, she let her hand fall back. Midnight fantasies notwithstanding, she couldn't expect him to understand. All she could do was repeat what she'd said to the doctor and nurses. "It doesn't sound familiar. It doesn't feel right. What they've told me about her life seems totally alien. I can't be her."

He crossed his arms and continued his unnerving scrutiny, and she sensed he was struggling to maintain his cool demeanor.

"I asked Dr. Habib and the nurses to call me Lisa," she said, her voice suddenly defiant.

"How'd you come up with that?"

Feeling foolish, she pointed toward the picture.

He looked from her to the portrait. She knew she was blushing again and wondered if he caught even a little of the desperation behind her choice of name.

"I called your house," he said patiently. "Mrs. Justine Hollingsworth hasn't been home since your accident. Her staff thinks she's in the hospital. Her housekeeper brought down that nightgown you're wearing. It fits, doesn't it?"

She nodded tightly.

"You're a dead ringer for the missing Mrs. Hollingsworth."

She let out a long, frustrated sigh. "I can't explain why I look so much like her. But... but... why would I feel that people are trying to push me into someone else's life? Dr. Habib. The nurses. You."

He spread his hands. "Because there's something in your life that you don't want to face."

She studied the tight line of his lips, the disapproval in his eyes. What had she done to rattle this supremely confident man? Made a pass at him? Or was it the other way around?

"What did Justine Hollingsworth do to offend you, besides not saying hello when you saw her on the street?"

"Nothing," he shot back so quickly that she was sure he was lying.

She sat very still in the bed, fighting a silent war with herself. When he'd first appeared in the doorway, she'd hoped he'd come to rescue her from the prison of her mind. No, more than that, she added with bitter honesty. Last night when she'd been so alone and afraid, she'd made up a little fantasy that he was someone who cared about her. That if he took her in his arms, soothed his hands across her back, he'd ward off the terrible forces that threatened to annihilate her. Clearly, it wasn't going to happen.

Yet he'd said he was a detective. If he wasn't here to comfort her, maybe he could help her. She didn't want to be Justine Hollingsworth. But it could turn out to be true—whether she liked it or not. With a tight feeling in her chest, she acknowledged that she might be fighting the association because she didn't like the person she'd become. What if she'd once been the nice, innocent woman whose reactions seemed so genuine to her? What if, over the years, she'd changed into someone she was trying desperately to deny?

"I'm in trouble," she whispered. "Even if I can't remember what it is."

His features softened for a moment, giving her a little spark of hope.

"You must have some thoughts about why I came to your office in the first place. I mean, why does a married woman usually hire a detective?"

He shrugged. "The standard motives. Money. Sex. Revenge. Fear."

She cringed. So much for imagined hope. "Could you be more specific?"

"Well, you could be pretty sure that your husband is having an affair. Maybe you want to know whether he's getting ready to divorce you. Or you may want to make the first move—get the goods on him so you can get the best possible settlement."

She wished she hadn't asked. "You're not painting a very pretty picture of my domestic life."

His tone gentled a little. "There are other possibilities. Something from your past could have come back to haunt you. Someone could be blackmailing you, or harassing you, and you want ammunition to get them off your back."

A frightening scenario leaped into her mind. Oh, Lord, what if this had something to do with the baby? Was Kendall Hollingsworth the father—or was it someone else?

She pointed toward the chair the private duty nurse had vacated. "Why don't you sit down and tell me some things I don't know about Justine."

His expression was unreadable, his eyes hooded as he turned the chair to face her and made himself comfortable. "Okay, you're thirty years old—an age where women make reassessments of their lives, by the way."

She nodded.

"You come from Philadelphia." When she didn't comment, he continued. "You went to college at the University of Maryland—before you dropped out to get married. I assume you don't get along with your parents. They didn't come to your wedding."

"Maybe they're deceased."

He shrugged. "You got kind of wild in your teens. Beer. Pot. Sex. You might even have tried coke."

She cringed, then told herself that he was talking about someone else.

"In college, you met a guy who was different from your crowd. He was earnest. Hardworking. Putting himself through school. You were attracted to him. People who knew you then said you were crazy in love. He wanted to marry you when he finished school and had enough money to support you. Then you met Hollingsworth while you were working as a waitress at his country club and realized you liked life in the fast lane. For the past eight years, you've been one of Baltimore's wealthiest socialites."

"How do you know all that?"

He gave her a little shrug. "You'd be surprised at how easy it is to pick up information."

He couldn't be describing her. "Isn't there anything good you learned about me?"

"You and your husband give a lot of money to charity. You serve on a number of honorary boards. Your radar detector keeps you from getting traffic tickets."

She seized on that. "The day of the accident, I was driving a rental car. Why?"

"Maybe you were trying to give somebody the slip." He cleared his throat. "I didn't exactly follow you out of the garage. I was following the two guys in a Pontiac who were already tailing you."

She tried to absorb this new revelation. "You're sure they were following *me?*"

Methodically, he explained. "You took a circuitous route through the city. They stayed right behind you all the way. I dropped back a couple of hundred yards on Falls Road.

When I came around a curve, you were on the shoulder heading toward the Jones Falls, and the Pontiac was speeding away."

She felt goose bumps rise on her skin. She couldn't remember the accident, yet she could imagine her terror as the car slid toward the water. Not only for herself, but for the baby. She'd been shocked to learn she was pregnant, but now the power of her concern for her baby stunned her. There was no reason the baby should be any more real to her than the rest of this nightmare she seemed to be living; she didn't look pregnant, feel pregnant or even know how she'd gotten pregnant. Still, the prospect that her child might be in danger brought feelings of outrage and an instinctive protective need welling from some unknown place deep inside her.

Disturbing thoughts spun through her mind. What if her life with her husband was so empty that she'd sought refuge with another man? What if her husband had found out and wanted to get rid of her and the baby? She squeezed her eyes shut, unable to imagine herself engaged in that kind of betrayal.

"Who do you think those men were?" she asked.

"I don't know. Maybe I can find out."

"You think they caused the accident?"

"It's possible they were trying to frighten you."

"What did I do to them?"

His voice turned husky, as if he'd heard the bleakness in her tone and was offering comfort, but it was comfort given grudgingly. "It may not be anything you did. They could be trying to get at your husband through you."

Somehow, his speculation brought a measure of relief. Perhaps her troubles weren't something she'd brought on herself. "Why did they wait until he was in Alaska on a hunting trip?"

"He's away? Interesting. That gives him an ironclad alibi."

Once more she sensed a spark of sympathy. Lord, what she wouldn't give to have this man in her corner, not because she was paying him, but because he cared about her.

"I'd appreciate any help you can give me," she whispered.

He looked directly into her eyes. "It would make it easier if you could dredge up some pertinent memories—you know, give me something concrete to go on."

"Every time I wake up, I pray my mind won't be a blank—that I'll know my name. That I'll remember the important things. You've told me facts, but they're as sterile...as a gauze bandage fresh out of the wrapper. What you've said doesn't make me *feel* anything. Nothing's changed. I'm still struggling with the unknown."

"Well, then, it seems I have my work cut out for me." He looked as if he was already starting to formulate plans. At least she could hang on to that.

"Thank you."

When he rose, she stretched out her right hand as if to seal their agreement. For a moment he hesitated, then his palm clasped hers. His hand was large and warm and steady, the way she remembered. Hers shook slightly. The contact between them—not only his flesh against hers, but the locking of their eyes—stretched beyond the limits of social custom. She wanted him to feel something positive in the touch. She couldn't guess what *he* wanted, why he kept his palm pressed to hers.

For a second, she forgot why they were holding tightly to each other. Then he broke the connection and jolted her back to reality. She watched him closely, noting that the color in his cheeks had deepened. At least she had the satisfaction of knowing she wasn't the only one affected. What would he do, she wondered, if she asked him to spirit her out of the hospital, whisk her away from this horrible mess, in the same way he had pulled her from the river? That was asking too much. But maybe she could persuade him to do something that could prove even more valuable.

"Change your assumptions," she whispered.

"What?"

"Work from the premise that I'm someone who stumbled into another person's life."

He looked startled. And there was something else in his eyes, as well, a flare of warmth that made her insides turn liquid.

"Please don't discount it as a possibility. Don't write me off as an empty-headed socialite who screwed up."

He hesitated a moment, his jaw tight, but finally he agreed.

"Do you have a card, if I need to get in touch with you?"

Silently, he withdrew a case from an inside pocket and set a small white rectangle on the night table. Then he was gone. And she was alone again.

The hand that had clasped his slipped under the covers and pressed against her middle. Somehow, through some terrible cosmic twist of fate, she'd gotten trapped in Justine Hollingsworth's life. Regardless of the reason Justine had hired him, it was she herself who Mike Lancer was going to help. He was going to get her—and her baby—out of this predicament.

The notion comforted her for less than a minute before she ruthlessly told herself to put things into perspective. Mike Lancer had saved her life. He was the only thing she remembered from before the hospital. She was more than a little desperate, and she'd let herself get fixated on him. On his masculine strength. His tempting sexuality. Surely her reaction to him was natural in her fragile state. But it was also dangerous. Because in the end, as she'd known all along, the only one she could depend upon was herself.

Chapter Six

As he stepped into the hall, Mike flexed his fingers, remembering the touch of the woman who called herself Lisa. Her hand had been small and warm in his. The pleading look in her eyes as they'd held on to each other had almost melted his heart. Almost.

He knew more about Justine than he'd told her. Enough to know it would be suicidal to get involved beyond a superficial business level.

Despite that, as he strode toward the elevator, he couldn't get her image or her final heartfelt plea out of his head. She'd looked vulnerable and sexy in that simple nightgown, with the covers pulled up around her so he couldn't see her breasts. Either she was an excellent actress or she was so frightened and upset, she didn't remember how to be arrogant.

It was hard to deny that she believed what she was telling him, and he felt a stab of guilt that he was walking away. Slowing to a halt, he considered going back.

"Mr. Lancer?"

He became aware that someone was calling his name. When he looked up, he spotted a small, rounded man motioning him toward the nurses' station.

"Yes?" he said, approaching the man.

"I'm Dr. Habib."

Mike recognized the name from his answering machine.

"I'm glad to meet you." The physician held out his hand, and they shook briefly. "It was very heroic of you, plunging into that flooding creek to rescue Mrs. Hollingsworth," he said.

Mike shrugged. "Anybody would have done it."

"I think not. Thank you for coming down to the hospital. I understand you're a private detective?"

"Yes. I'm working for Mrs. Hollingsworth."

The physician looked surprised. "Did she hire you before or after the accident?"

Mike went through a quick mental debate and decided to fall back on the standard explanation. "I'm afraid our business is confidential."

"I was hoping you could help us come to some conclusions about her memory problem."

"You're convinced it's genuine?"

"Oh, yes. She's finding her condition very distressing. She's particularly disturbed by—" he hesitated, as if he, too, was dealing with questions of confidentiality "—her name. She asked us to call her Lisa."

Mike cleared his throat. "Can amnesia radically change a person's personality?"

Habib looked thoughtful. "Under certain circumstances. For example, if Mrs. Hollingsworth were playing a role in her everyday life, she could have lost the memory of that behavior."

"You'd be seeing her real self now?" Mike clarified.

"Yes. However, the trauma of her present predicament could bring out tendencies toward, uh . . . radical modes of coping."

"Like?" Mike pressed.

The doctor looked a bit uncomfortable with the direction of the conversation. "Earlier, she became quite agitated and we had to sedate her."

"Oh." A wealth of implications simmered in Habib's comments. Mike found himself wondering if there was some way to sneak a look at her chart.

"I was hoping you could give me some insights, but I seem to be doing most of the talking," Habib observed.

Mike didn't bother to explain his talent for getting people to open up. Part of his technique was simply to assume their cooperation. "I'm sorry I couldn't be of more help to you," he murmured. "But feel free to call if I can be of assistance."

The doctor said goodbye, and as Mike turned toward the elevator, his mind was playing with the tantalizing premise that Justine—Lisa—had proposed. What if the frightened, sensitive-looking woman in the hospital bed really wasn't Justine Hollingsworth? She looked the same—except for the shorter hair. If she wasn't Justine, who the hell was she? Even more pertinent, how and why had the real Mrs. Hollingsworth conveniently disappeared?

Were the two women part of some weird conspiracy? What if Justine had decided to disappear and had hired this other woman—this double—to take her place? Then the double had gotten into an accident and ended up with amnesia. What a mess for Justine. And for the double.

The whole scenario was pretty farfetched, but he'd heard of stranger things. And he wasn't in a position to exclude any angle. Even as he considered the outlandish scenario, he felt a curious spark of hope ignite inside him. If she wasn't Justine, if she wasn't Kendall Hollingsworth's wife, then he might be free to— His body reacted, and his blood began to simmer. He knew he was treading on very dangerous ground.

TAPPING HER low-heel pump on the portico of the Hollingsworths' palatial Mount Washington home, Estelle Bensinger waited for someone to answer the doorbell. She'd been here before to retrieve files from Kendall's private office and on other occasions to attend cocktail parties given for clients and associates. Then there was that day last year when she'd slaved eight hours to install software on Kendall's home computer, for all he'd appreciated it. And the weekend she'd had to reinstall almost all the programs because Justine had fooled with the machine and managed to screw up everything.

But no matter why she came, Estelle always felt the pull of the stately two-story mansion with its eight-acre partially wooded grounds. She'd imagined herself mistress of the house. Wiggling her toes in the plush carpet of the enormous master suites. Having mocha almond coffee and chocolate croissants in the formal dining room. Working out with her hunky personal trainer in a fully equipped gym, or taking a skinny-dip in the indoor pool that Kendall would build for her. She was normally a practical person, but the daydreams of enjoying all the decadent pleasures that money could buy had made Estelle shiver with secret longing.

The door wedged open to reveal the lined face of Maggie Dempsey. When Estelle had first entertained the fantasy of living here, she'd taken the time to cultivate the woman's friendship. After all, they had a lot in common. They were both overworked and underappreciated—and they shared a dislike for the present Mrs. Hollingsworth.

"Ms. Bensinger, this is a surprise. Are you needing something?"

"Yes. For Mrs. Hollingsworth in the hospital."

"Didn't the things I took over last night suit her?"

By an effort of will, Estelle kept her face neutral. She should have checked on that. "Who knows?" she temporized.

"All right. You see if you can please Her Highness. If you don't need me for anything else, I'll be getting back to my work."

Work, Estelle thought. She could hear a TV tuned to an afternoon soap opera. Maybe it was in the kitchen.

She breathed a little sigh as she climbed the stairs to Justine's room. Her past investment with Maggie had paid off. The housekeeper had practically invited her to search the upstairs suite. Of course, if she took too long, the woman might get suspicious. But efficiency was her forte. And with any luck, she'd find the ticking time bomb Justine had hidden and be out of the house before Maggie's favorite soap-opera heroine delivered her sobbing last line.

IN THE DARKNESS, Lisa shifted her position yet again. The green numbers on the clock told her it was ten fifty-eight. She'd been trying to get to sleep for an hour and a half and wasn't making any progress. The four walls of the hospital room seemed to press in upon her. Once again, her eyes flicked to the drawer of the bedside table. With a sigh, she gave in to the compulsion she'd been fighting all evening and pulled out Mike Lancer's unadorned business card. Turning it in her hand, she pressed the crisp edges against the pads of her fingers. She didn't look at the card. Instead, she pictured Mike's face—the assessing brown eyes, the square jaw, the sensual lips. He'd sent her a whole packing case full of mixed messages. Yet she wanted to believe that by the end of their conversation she'd convinced him to be on her side.

The door to her room opened and a man in a white hospital coat stepped inside. His footsteps were almost silent as he came toward her bed. She cringed, although she didn't know exactly why she was frightened. He looked well-groomed, and he smelled of expensive after-shave. Wordlessly, she closed her hand around Mike's card.

"I'm sorry if I've alarmed you," he said in a voice that had a distinct Latin accent.

"What are you doing in my room?"

"I'm Dr. Ray." He paused, watching her expectantly.

"Do I know you?"

"We've met at some of the hospital charity events, *señora*. I was hoping I might be a familiar face." He moved into the shaft of light from the street lamp outside, and she gazed into his deep-set eyes. Like his hair, they were dark. But his most distinctive feature was his pockmarked skin.

"I'm sorry. I don't recall you."

"A pity. I heard about your accident. I was making rounds, and I thought I'd stop by to see if there was anything I could do."

He continued to watch her intently, and she felt a little shiver.

"I should have come by earlier," he said. "But I'm so busy during the day."

"It's kind of you to visit." She knew she sounded insincere.

"Perhaps I can help jog your memory. Let's see, do you remember the cocktail party at your husband's office when he was celebrating the San Marcos contract?"

"Celebrating what?"

"A big business deal. You served champagne. And wonderful focaccia."

She shook her head She didn't know this man, but she was sure she didn't like him.

"Well, I'll see you again if I have the chance."

"Yes," she managed to say.

"Buenas noches, señora."

He exited as quietly as he'd come, and she was left breathing unevenly and wondering if the encounter had been a weird kind of dream.

She sat very still watching the numbers change on the clock, trying to come up with some sort of association. Hollingsworth's office. The San Marcos contract. But her memory of the man and the occasion was as blank as everything else.

Her fingers closed convulsively, and she realized she was still holding Mike's card. She thrust it into the shaft of light where the doctor had stood. After Mike's office number, his home number was listed.

It was after eleven. Was he awake? she wondered. Even if he was, it was clearly too late to call. Yet, as she stirred restlessly on the hard mattress, she knew that she was going to do it, anyway. He was the only individual in her limited memory to whom she'd related on any kind of personal level, and she needed to hold on to that human link. At least that was an edited version of what she felt. She wasn't going to think in terms of compulsion or the way their eyes had locked and held as he'd clasped her hand this afternoon.

After dialing, she leaned back against the pillows, closed her eyes and pressed the receiver to her ear.

He picked up on the fourth ring. "Hello?"

Her throat clogged, and she couldn't speak.

"Hello, is anybody there?" He sounded annoyed.

Before she lost her nerve, she cleared her throat. "It's Lisa," she answered in a shaky voice, glad he couldn't see her face. When he didn't respond, she continued, "You know. The woman in the hospital. The one accused of being Justine Hollingsworth. Guilty until proven innocent."

"You make it sound like a life sentence."

She wasn't sure what to answer. Maybe calling him had been a mistake. Silence stretched across the phone lines.

"I know it's late. I'm sorry to bother you," she finally said.

"No. I keep pretty irregular hours. What can I do for you?"

What indeed.

"I need to talk to someone familiar."

"You've remembered me from before the accident?" he asked sharply.

"No. I mean . . ." She paused again, knowing it would be folly to bare her soul to this man, deciding to risk it, anyway. "I told you, I feel lost—alone—isolated from everything that's normal. Trapped in a space where there isn't any past—or—or any future." She swallowed. "When I saw you standing in the doorway this afternoon, I had a feeling of connection to you. Or maybe it's just that I'm hoping you can help me," she added quickly as she wondered why she'd given so much away.

"How do you mean, 'connected'?" he asked warily.

"When I woke up in the hospital, you were the only memory I had." As soon as she'd said that, she knew he'd take it the wrong way, so she rushed to explain, "I mean, your mouth on mine. Your hands."

Oh, Lord. She was glad he couldn't see the hot flush spreading across her cheeks. She heard him suck in what sounded like a strangled breath.

"After... after you pulled me out of the car. When you saved my life. I didn't thank you for any of that."

"No need."

Oh, yes, there was need.

"Could we pretend we're friends?" she asked softly, surprised again at her boldness.

"That implies we've known each other long enough to get acquainted—beyond one afternoon swim, that is."

"Well, you seem to know a great deal about me. More than I know about myself," she murmured.

"After I left your room, I was trying to imagine what it would be like if my past were a blank."

"It's... frustrating."

"It could have its advantages."

"Why?"

"People carry around a lot of baggage. It would be nice to be free of some of it."

She wanted to ask what he'd like to forget. His childhood? A woman? Instead, she pleated the sheet under her left hand. "Is there anything you're willing to share?" she asked softly.

"There's not much to tell."

"Are you married?" Now why had *that* popped into her head?

He cleared his throat. "No."

"Why not?"

"Is this a survey for a dating service?"

Once again, she was glad he couldn't see her blush. Somehow, the conversation kept getting off on the wrong track. Floundering for something safe, she tried, "Uh, where are you—what room of your house? Apartment?"

"Apartment. I've got the top floor of an old row house. I'm in my bedroom. Propped against the pillows."

"Oh."

"I'm working late on my laptop to fill out a report for an insurance investigation."

Immediately, an image of his long, jean-clad legs leaped into her mind. His shoes were off but not his socks; his feet were crossed comfortably at the ankles, the way he'd sat in the hospital chair. His face was relaxed. His dark hair slightly mussed. She went back and edited a bit, putting a little smile on his face, pleased with the picture.

Was he still wearing his dark T-shirt? Or had he changed into pajamas? Almost at once, she canceled that notion. He didn't seem like the type for pajamas. It was easier to envision him sleeping naked or in a pair of briefs. She found herself wondering whether his broad chest was smooth or covered with hair. Hair, definitely, she decided. It would be dark, like on his head. Was there a lot, or only a sprinkling? In her imagination, she let her gaze drop lower. Shocked by her recklessness, she made an effort to pull her mind back to more acceptable images.

"I'd like to picture the room," she said in a husky voice.

"It's big," he answered. "With high ceilings and the kind of fancy woodwork that would cost a fortune today. The best feature of the room is the turret. It's got a window seat. But most of it's piled with stacks of magazines and videotapes."

"What kind of tapes?" She wanted to know more, and to keep listening to the sound of his voice. There was something heady about the secret warmth of talking to him like this in the dark. It was liberating. For a few minutes, they could be a man and a woman exploring possibilities. Was he feeling it, too? Did she hear it in the slight rasp of his voice, or did she only imagine what she wanted to hear?

"I collect old movies."

"I'm picturing plants in the window."

"Nope. Occasionally, a client gives me one, I forget to water it and it dies. I'm not very domestic," he added.

"You need—" She stopped short. She'd been about to tell him he needed a wife. To change the subject, she grabbed at his earlier comment. "How come you're working so late?"

"I've been busy, and I hate paperwork. But this report is due in the morning."

"So I guess you haven't had time to investigate Justine Hollingsworth's case."

He paused, and she was immediately sorry she'd asked the question. She should have known it would shatter the intimacy. "Actually, I checked out the license plate on the rental car you were driving. The vehicle was assigned to the Atlas office on Lombard Street."

"And I rented it in the name of Justine Hollingsworth?" She held her breath, waiting for the proof of the identity she didn't want to claim.

"I don't know." He sounded like a man who'd been cheated out of a poker jackpot.

Her brows wrinkled. "Atlas wouldn't show you the records?"

"The manager claims the paperwork's been mislaid."

"What do you mean, mislaid?"

"There's supposed to be a folder for each transaction. The one for that particular car is missing."

It was hard for her to get out the next question. "Are other folders for that day lost?"

"He wouldn't tell me. But I got the feeling yours is the only one. It's just a hunch, but I'm good at picking up nuances."

She stared into the darkness with unseeing eyes, wondering if the turn of events could possibly be a coincidence. "Why didn't you tell me about this?" she accused.

"I don't stop and report every little piece of information to a client. It's better to wait until some sort of pattern emerges."

"Better for whom?"

"In this case, for you. You haven't learned anything conclusive. All this has done is upset you."

"Yes," she admitted, her voice quavery.

He sighed. "It's late. You should get some sleep, but I don't want to leave you like this."

She gripped the phone more tightly, wishing he were beside her in the dark, wishing his arms were around her, warm and protective. The fantasy was even more potent now that she'd met him. And she couldn't help wondering how things would be if they'd met under different circumstances.

"You know what I feel like?" she asked suddenly. "Like I'm trying to claw my way out of an Alfred Hitchcock movie."

"Which one?" he asked, his voice taking on a note of tension.

"*The Man Who Knew too Much.* No, *Marnie,*" she answered. "She had amnesia, didn't she? And Sean Connery was determined to find out who she was."

"You remember Hitchcock plots?"

"My memory's selective. It's kind of like an old patchwork quilt, with a lot of the squares in the middle missing. The pattern's best around the edges."

"We . . . I used to watch a lot of Hitchcock movies."

"Who is 'we'?"

"Me and my college roommate. The way I remember it, Marnie didn't have amnesia. She was hiding her background from Connery," he added, speaking brusquely.

"Are you sure?"

"It's a tricky plot. He catches her stealing from him, and the only way he won't turn her in is if she'll marry him, but she's afraid to have sex. Finally, he gets really frustrated and, uh . . . forces himself on her."

Lisa felt a cold shiver sweep across her skin. In the darkened room, she curled to the side and burrowed lower under the covers so that only the top of her head and her face were visible.

"Of course, since the film was made in the sixties, we don't get to see the gory details."

"She tries to drown herself," Lisa whispered. The scene was starkly etched in her mind. Marnie floating facedown in a swimming pool. Only it wasn't simply a movie. It was her own near death in the creek, and she could feel the cold water lapping over her.

"He saves her life," Mike added.

"Like you saved mine."

He didn't answer. She was vividly aware of the other reason she identified with the movie. She felt shaky and scared, and the need to confide in him built inside her until finally, the pressure was too great. "I'm afraid of sex," she admitted with a ragged little gulp.

"You?"

Explicit pictures flashed in her mind. Pictures she didn't want to see. "I—I keep trying to...to imagine what will happen when Kendall Hollingsworth comes back and wants to—to make love to his wife. And I won't be able to respond because—" There were a number of things she could have said. She could have told him about the baby she was carrying. Or she could have described her fear of being vulnerable to a man she didn't know and didn't want to know. But even over the phone, she couldn't cross that line.

Several seconds of silence passed during which she sat in the dark listening to her heart pound.

"Maybe it will be okay," he finally said, his voice surprisingly husky.

She might have screamed that this wasn't what she wanted to hear. Not from him. But she'd promised herself not to give in to hysteria again. Instead, she forced her voice to sound normal. "Yes, well, as soon as you find out anything about the car, please let me know. And, uh, something else. A Dr. Ray came to my room a little while ago. He acted like he knew me and Hollingsworth."

"And?"

"It was a strange encounter. Could you check to see who he is?"

"Sure."

"Mike—"

"What?"

"Thank you for keeping me company for a little while." Before she said anything else embarrassing, she set the receiver gently onto its cradle.

FOR ALMOST A MINUTE after hanging up the phone, Mike sat staring across the room, wishing the conversation hadn't gotten quite so personal, especially that it hadn't taken its last, disturbing turn. He didn't want to talk to her about sex. Or making love to her husband. Or her most private fears.

Hell, he wished he could stop picturing her the way she'd looked that afternoon...in that revealing nightgown...before she'd pulled up the covers to hide her breasts. But he'd seen their rounded curves through the gauzy fabric, and the hardened tips of her nipples.

Gritting his teeth, he brought his attention back to the computer, and finished his insurance report. Then he printed a copy and switched off the laptop, setting it aside to get up and stretch. It had been a very long day.

With a deep sigh, he stripped off his clothes and pushed the computer and his case folders to the unoccupied side of his wide mattress. Piling work on the bed was a habit he'd formed since he'd started keeping the irregular hours of a PI. It was also a sure sign that he wasn't entertaining any overnight company.

He really should do something about that. Then he wouldn't be so fixated on tender, tempting Lisa.

No, he admonished himself. He'd better keep in mind that she was probably hard-bitten, savvy Justine Hollingsworth. But the image of Justine kept fading into the far more appealing vision of Lisa.

Annoyed with the turn his thoughts were taking, he pulled aside the covers with a snap of his wrist and slipped between the sheets. Then he shut off the light, determined not to lose any sleep over the woman, whatever the hell her name was.

Within five minutes, he was breathing deeply and evenly. While he knew how to govern his waking mind, he had no control over his subconscious or over his reaction to his late-night exchange with Lisa.

One moment, his body was relaxed, his mind drifting in the first stages of sleep. The next, he was caught in the snare of a dream. He was standing beside a river flowing high above its normal banks. The Jones Falls.

His head thrashed against the pillow, both his body and mind balking at the direction his subconscious was carrying him. With a feeling of inevitability, he stared down at the water. It looked different somehow. It should be muddier, more turbulent. But it was a clear, transparent turquoise like water in a swimming pool, so that he could see every nicely rounded rock on the bottom. And the current was lazy, not swift. He looked up, expecting to see a car plunging down the embankment. But there was no car. Instead, the woman he'd come to meet was floating facedown along the surface of the water, her arms spread out to her sides, her wild red hair drifting like the fronds of an exotic plant.

Fear rose in his throat. Fear that he'd arrived too late. Kicking off his shoes, he dived in after her, flipped her onto her back and pulled her toward the bank.

Then she lay on a bed of soft green moss, parts of which were covered with a quilt in a wedding ring design, only many of the squares were missing. She wore a thin gown. It was wet and plastered to her body, so that nothing was hidden. Not the tight, hard buttons of her nipples. Not the triangle of red hair at the junction of her thighs.

He forced his gaze to her face. The color was washed from her skin. Her lids were closed. She wasn't breathing. And he understood on some deep, primitive level that if he lost her, he'd lose part of himself.

Frantically, he went to work, clearing her throat and tilting back her head. But when he lowered his mouth to hers he felt her lips warm instantly. Her body came to life, and so did his. Desire, hot and unchecked, flooded through him.

"You're playing games. You don't need rescuing," he grated.

"Yes, I do. We both do."

He nodded. He'd known all along that he wanted her, known he was playing with fire if he got involved. He drew back, but her hand came up to grip his shoulder. Her eyes were open, and this time he was the one drowning—drowning in their crystal blue depths.

"Who are you?" he demanded, angry at her. Angry at himself for wanting to hear the answer.

"Lisa," she whispered, her voice pleading for understanding.

He gave a low laugh. "Wishing won't make it so."

"I'm not Justine. She has nothing to do with me."

"Prove it." He challenged her.

"You'll give me that chance?"

He nodded tightly. Instantly, he knew he'd made a mistake. But it was too late. She cupped her fingers around the back of his head and brought his mouth down to hers once more. It was a gentle persuasion, yet he couldn't break free from her hold, not when she'd kindled a fire in his belly.

As his mouth came down hard, her neck arched, silently pleading for him to increase the contact. He angled his head, ravaging her mouth, pressing his body to hers. And she responded with feverish movements of her hips and torso. Still, he might have pulled back from the brink. It was her wild, pleading little sobs that sent the inferno inside him raging out of control.

His hands tore at her gown, and, in the blink of an eye, they were both naked—heated flesh to heated flesh.

"I want you to need me as much as I need you," he ground out.

"I do."

He didn't believe her. Didn't believe that anything good could come of surrendering to this wild, hot passion. Yet he'd gone too far to pull back.

She was ready for him. More than ready. Urgently, she guided him to her, and the pleasure was so intense he was helpless to do anything but drive for release.

It was over very quickly. His body jerked. His breath came in a great gasp. Then he was awake, his flesh sticky, the bed covers in a tangled mess around him. He squeezed his eyes shut, but he couldn't shut out the woman in the dream. Who had he been making love to? Justine...or Lisa?

IT WAS FIVE in the morning when Estelle Bensinger pulled into the parking lot at Mount Olive Hospital. With the overnight bag gripped tightly in one hand, she strode through the lobby, as though she had an engraved invitation. A little digging had revealed that after a recent downsizing, the hospital was running understaffed on both the evening and swing shifts, and the security department had suffered the biggest hit. Her plan was to sneak into room 321 and get some answers from Justine, without anyone knowing she'd been there.

After taking an empty elevator to the third floor, she checked the wall map and started down the hall toward the nurses station. The ward was quiet but for the sound of a television coming from behind a partially closed door. Behind the counter, a nurse didn't even look up as she walked by.

Estelle figured she deserved a break. She'd nearly had a heart attack when Maggie had barged into Justine's room to complain that a special news report had interrupted her soap opera. What a time for some plane to crash in L.A. She'd barely escaped getting caught with her hand in a bureau drawer and had been forced to abandon her search with only a carry case full of silk nightgowns, French-cut underwear and a frumpy blue dress Justine wouldn't be caught dead in. But at least she'd come away with one startling piece of information. Maggie had told her that Justine claimed to be suffering from amnesia.

Damn the Hollingsworth bitch. What game was she playing now? Where had she hidden those documents she never should have gotten her hands on in the first place? What if they'd been in the car when she'd driven into the Jones Falls?

Estelle clutched the overnight bag as she stared at the closed door of Justine's hospital room. The lights were off, and she couldn't hear any conversation or TV. She reached for the knob, but a tap on the shoulder sent her spinning around.

"I'm sorry. Do you have a pass?"

"Do I need one?" Estelle asked innocently.

"I'm afraid so. You're not allowed here after visiting hours without one," the battle-ax of a nurse warned.

"But I've brought some more personal items for Mrs. Hollingsworth. And I'm sure she'd love to visit with me for a while."

"You can come back tomorrow. I'll see that she gets the things."

"How is she doing? Has she regained her memory?"

"You'll have to talk to her doctor about that."

Estelle weighed the odds of getting any useful information out of the woman, then decided that the probabilities weren't good enough to take the risk. With a little shrug, she handed the bag over and retreated down the hall.

Chapter Seven

As Dr. Habib entered the room, Lisa searched his face, trying to read the verdict before he spoke. After three days of exhaustive and sometimes painful tests, he certainly should be able to tell her something.

"All our tests confirm that you're in good physical health," he said.

"The baby, too?"

"As far as we can tell."

"Well, I can't wait to leave the hospital."

His expression changed from encouraging to grave. "I think under the circumstances it would be better if you stayed with us for a while."

"What circumstances?" she shot back. "You've done every medical test known to man."

He shrugged. "Not quite. But we have tried to be very thorough."

She plowed ahead. "And you've found out that I'm fine. How can you keep me here?"

"It's the logical course of action," he answered reasonably. "Your husband's away. You'd be alone except for your domestic help. My recommendation is that you check yourself into the psychiatric ward where our staff can help."

"No."

"I can't insist, of course. But if you leave the hospital, it will be against my advice, and I'll note that on your chart."

She had to hold tight to the edge of the sheet to keep from jumping from the bed. "I'll, uh, think about it."

He smiled encouragingly. "We have your welfare at heart."

Her answer was a slight nod as she struggled to keep her expression blank. But behind her staring eyes, her mind was racing. What if she did sign herself into the psychiatric ward? What if Kendall Hollingsworth came home and decided she was an impostor?

"You're *sure* of my identity?" she asked.

"Well, you have B positive blood, which is a fairly rare type. And you match Mrs. Hollingsworth on other important blood factors, as well."

"But that's not conclusive," she insisted.

"What would convince you?" the doctor asked, his tone maddeningly reasonable.

"DNA testing."

"I can initiate that process. An analysis will take over a month."

"Then get started, please. Do you need to take more blood or can you use some from the half gallon you've already drawn?"

"We have what we need."

He sounded agreeable enough, but then the uncertainty wasn't driving *him* crazy. Nobody was pressing to lock *him* in a psychiatric ward.

Feeling sick and shaky, she waited for Habib to leave. As soon as she heard his footsteps receding down the hall, she opened the drawer beside the bed and pulled out Mike's card.

When he hadn't called, she'd decided their phone conversation the night before had made him uncomfortable. And she'd vowed not to let things get so intimate again. But now Habib was trying to railroad her into a padded cell, and she had nowhere else to turn.

Mike picked up on the third ring. "O'Malley and Lancer."

She swallowed hard. "Mike, I—I'm glad I caught you in. It's Lisa."

"I told you I'd get back to you if I found out anything on the rental car. Or Dr. Ray," he added brusquely.

"Who is he?"

"There is no Dr. Ray."

"What?" She was already feeling shaky. The news made her head start to throb.

"There's no listing for him. Are you sure you have the name right?" he clipped out.

"I—that's what I thought I heard." She pressed fingertips to her pounding temple. Lord, *now* what kind of tricks was her mind playing? She wished she could picture the expression on Mike's face, the expression that went with his curt voice. Was he defensive because he hadn't learned anything? Or was he more uncomfortable about their late-night chat than she'd thought? In either case, he was cold and distant, and she might have hung up if she'd had any other alternative.

Instead, she hurried on. "I—I have a kind of urgent problem. Dr. Habib doesn't want to send me home. He says there's nothing physically wrong with me. But he's pressuring me to check into the psychiatric ward." Her voice faltered. "I . . . don't want to do that. I'm afraid if they get me in there, they'll never let me out." She clutched the phone, wondering why she felt compelled to share her deepest fears with this man.

"Yeah, that's scary," he said after several seconds.

Moisture clouded her vision, and she tried to blink it away. "He says if I check myself out of the hospital, it will be against his advice."

"Oh, yeah? Well, you need another opinion. Someone who's qualified to make that kind of judgment."

"A psychiatrist? I don't know one. I can't simply pick somebody out of the phone book."

"I've got a friend named Abby Franklin. She's a psychologist with a private practice here in my building. Jo O'Malley, my associate, and I have used her a number of times. She's good. Do you want me to see if I can arrange a consultation?"

"Yes. I'd really appreciate that."

"Sure. And listen—I'll let you know as soon as I hear anything on the car. I've been busy with some other cases."

She supposed it was a good sign that he was bothering to explain why he hadn't called. But he didn't prolong the conversation. Two minutes after she'd first picked up the phone, she was alone once more with her brooding thoughts.

"Lisa? I knocked, but I guess you didn't hear."

"Yes?" She paused in the bathroom doorway. She had exchanged her gown for bra, panties and a soft blue knit dress that Kendall Hollingsworth's secretary had brought to the hospital—bless her heart. What a relief to get out of her sleepwear—even if the bra was a bit too tight.

The dark-haired woman standing in the doorway looked to be in her early thirties. "I'm Abby Franklin," she said, holding out her hand.

"Dr. Franklin. I didn't expect you so soon." They shook hands briefly.

"I had a cancellation this afternoon, and Mike said you were anxious to see me."

"Yes. Thank you."

"It's a beautiful day. There's a little garden where we could sit and talk, if you like."

Lisa contemplated her all-too-familiar surroundings. "I feel like I haven't been out of this room since Columbus discovered America. But are you sure they'll let me go down in the elevator? I might run off," she added with a slightly bitter note in her voice.

"I stopped at the nurses' station and told them I'd be interviewing you. You've been here five days?"

"Yes."

"So how's it going?"

"Frustrating." Lisa slipped on the sandals Hollingsworth's secretary had left.

The doctor nodded sympathetically.

They didn't speak again until they reached a small, walled garden at one side of the sprawling hospital complex. Lisa took a deep breath of the warm, flower-scented air. It was like breathing freedom. She stooped to pluck a sprig of grass from between the paving stones, then followed Dr. Franklin to one of the comfortable patio groupings tucked under the shade of a spreading dogwood tree. She smoothed her fingers along the blade of grass as she studied the other woman. Dr. Franklin looked compassionate. Yet it was frightening to think that her future could be resting in this woman's hands. What if she agreed with Dr. Habib?

"Mike thinks highly of you," Lisa said.

Dr. Franklin smiled. "At 43 Light Street we're a very close-knit group. We've come to rely upon each other. Professionally, and personally."

"That must be wonderful."

"Yes. But we should be talking about you. How do you feel?"

Caution was the safest policy, but so much was bottled up inside her that Lisa found it almost impossible to hide her real feelings. "Physically, I feel okay. Mentally, I feel like I've lost control of my life. Only I don't know what my life is supposed to be. Dr. Habib told me there's no way to know when I might get my memory back. Can you tell me anything more definite?"

Dr. Franklin grimaced. "I wish I could."

Lisa flapped her arms in exasperation. "This is all so unreal. Particularly since everyone keeps insisting that I'm Justine Hollingsworth."

"Mike told me you disagree."

"What else did Mike tell you?"

"Not much. I know about the amnesia. I know he rescued you. I don't understand why you're so opposed to the identity. At least it's a place to start."

"It never sounded right. And the more I know about Mrs. Hollingsworth, the less the identity fits. I can't picture myself jilting someone I loved to marry a wealthy man. Or spending my time at a bunch of social events. Maybe the truth is, I robbed a bank or murdered someone."

"Are you worried about that?" the doctor asked gently.

Lisa laughed self-consciously. "Well, I've had a lot of time to speculate about why I was running away. Do you think I can't remember because I don't want to?"

"That could be a factor, although you did have a head injury. But let's go back to something else you said. Why do you think you're a fugitive?"

She crumpled the blade of grass in her hand. "Why hasn't anyone inquired about me?"

"Let's assume for a minute that you're not Justine," the doctor postulated. "Perhaps you're from out of town. You could have flown to Baltimore and rented the car you were driving. Your family could have left a message for you at the motel where you were staying."

"So now they'd be worried sick."

Dr. Franklin shook her head. "Perhaps nobody's tried to contact you. You could be on vacation and nobody's expecting you back for a while."

"Or I could be running away from the father of my child." She stopped abruptly, looked down at her middle and then back at Dr. Franklin. "If you read my chart, you know I'm pregnant. Unfortunately, I don't have any idea who the father is. Suppose we're married. Suppose we're not. I wasn't wearing a wedding ring," she concluded helplessly.

"How do you feel about the pregnancy?"

"At first, I was stunned. Now...well, the baby's become the only thing that I know for sure is real." It was true. At first, she'd found it hard to believe in the pregnancy. But it had become important to her—maybe the thing from her past that was most important. For a moment, she pictured herself cradling a child—her child—in her arms. But the terrible uncertainty of her situation intruded, and the half-formed image evaporated. "If I'm in a fix, the baby's in worse trouble, because she, or he, has to depend on me. I mean, what do I do for a living, if I'm not Mrs. Hollingsworth?''

"What are you good at?" the psychologist asked.

"I think I know something about computers. There was a program on the Learning Channel about surfing the Internet. I had a feeling I'd done that."

"Well, that's unusual. From what I understand, only a small percentage of Internet users are women."

Encouraged, she added another fact. "I'm getting good at reading faces, too. When I look at Dr. Habib, I know he wants to cover his ass—as Mike would probably put it."

Dr. Franklin chuckled. "Yes, Mike's very direct."

They shared a little grin.

Then the psychologist asked, "What do you see in my face?"

Lisa answered with the first words that came to mind. "Compassion. Open-mindedness. I think you want to help me."

"I do."

"So, do you think I belong in a psychiatric ward?" she asked in a rush.

"No."

The relief was so huge it made her giddy. "Thank God," she breathed. "But how do you know I'm not putting on some kind of act?"

The other woman laughed. "I can't be absolutely sure. But I certainly don't think you would have asked that question after I'd given you the go-ahead to leave, if you *were* putting on an act."

She flushed. "Right. That was somewhat rash of me."

"I'd recommend a change of scene for two reasons. The hospital isn't helping your mood. And if you *are* Justine, familiar surroundings might jog your memory. Do you remember anything from before the accident?"

Her brow wrinkled as she tried to give an answer that would make sense. "No. But when I wake up, I always have a strong sense of loss, like something important has slipped through my fingers. It's hard to describe . . . I feel like if I could only remember my dreams, I could connect them to my life. But they vanish the minute I try to hold on to them."

Dr. Franklin waited for her to continue.

"It gets worse. I—I'm left feeling relieved and...and at the same time frustrated. I know that must sound terribly muddled. Does it make any sense?" she asked anxiously.

The other woman nodded. "Your dreams may turn out to be important, a way to get in touch with your past."

Lisa gulped. "I'm pretty sure that part of the reason I'm not remembering is that I'm afraid to find out who I am. Or what happened to me."

"Don't push yourself too hard. Memories will come when you're ready. Maybe when you leave the hospital."

"I don't want to go to the Hollingsworth house. I realize I'm making assumptions from pitifully little information, but I don't think I'm going to like the people who live there."

"Perhaps Mike has painted a picture of Justine that isn't entirely accurate. We know he doesn't have the whole story. You have to keep an open mind."

Lisa nodded, wishing she could believe the therapist's optimistic assessment.

"What if you could make things turn out any way you wanted?" Dr. Franklin asked.

"I wish I could go home with Mike." She sucked in a breath, aghast at what had popped out of her mouth.

The doctor covered her hand. "He's a very appealing man. It would be easy to think of him as more than a friend. Especially when you're vulnerable and want someone to lean on."

Lisa shook her head. "It was a stupid thing for me to say. Even though I have a pretty good idea where it came from."

"Where?"

"When I woke up in the hospital, he was the only person I remembered. It was a very...strong recollection. Very...physical."

"He saved your life."

"I guess I want to think it, uh, created a kind of bond between us. But it wouldn't be smart to get involved with him. I'm a married woman, until proven otherwise. Then there's the baby." She gave Dr. Franklin a quick glance. "I don't want you to tell him about my being pregnant," she murmured.

"Why?"

"I want him to hear it from me." She kept her eyes lowered, unable to meet Dr. Franklin's gaze.

"But not right away?" the therapist guessed.

Lisa nodded tightly.

"Well, I respect your desire for confidentiality, of course."

"If he knows I'm pregnant, that will give him more reasons to dislike me," she whispered.

"He has no reason to dislike you."

"Maybe not me. But he doesn't have a very high opinion of Justine Hollingsworth."

"How do you know?"

"It slips out from time to time. He's made me sure I don't want to be like her." Lisa gripped the edge of her chair. "Does my keeping the baby confidential change your opinion of me?"

"Remember that honesty is always the best policy."

She lifted one brow, smiling, "You have a charming way of not answering questions when you don't want to."

Dr. Franklin spread her hands wide. "My professional training."

"Well, I'm glad you had time to see me so quickly. I feel a little better, now that I know I'm getting out of here."

"Only a little?"

"The idea of stepping into Justine Hollingsworth's life terrifies me. I wish I had some kind of proof that I'm not her."

"I think you have the strength to deal with either outcome."

Lisa let that sink in. She didn't feel strong, but she would try.

"Do you have any questions?"

She nodded gratefully. "Yes. Why are my emotions so...out of whack? It's like everything is...magnified."

"That can happen with a head injury. Also, with pregnancy. It's hard, but try to step back when you feel you're getting close to the edge."

She nodded, then asked one more question. "Do you know someone named Dr. Ray?"

Dr. Franklin frowned in thought for a moment before shaking her head. "Why?"

"He came to my room one night and acted like he knew me."

"Late at night? Could it have been a dream?"

"I guess I could have made him up." She sighed. "If I did, I wish I knew why."

The psychologist waited expectantly.

"No more wishing," Lisa said firmly.

"Don't be too hard on yourself. Give yourself time to heal."

"Time may be a luxury I can't afford."

TOO EXCITED TO RELAX, Benita Fenton lay on the narrow bed in Ed's den thinking about the article in the paper. She almost never read the sports section. Who cared whether the Phillies won three in a row or if the Flyers fired their coach? So it must have been fate that Ed had left the newspaper open to section D, page 3, on the dining-room table. The headline had jumped out at her as she started to clean up the dinner dishes. It read: Travis Stone Receives National Courage Award. Stone, the feature explained, was a former baseball player who'd fought a heroic battle with leukemia and won.

But it was more than his years of Major League accomplishments or his recent medical triumph that brought tears to Benita's eyes. His unwed mother had been tricked into giving him up for adoption when he was only a few hours old. And a Baltimore agency called Birth Data, Inc., had helped him track down his blood relations in order to save his life with a bone marrow transplant. A grateful Stone had taken over the funding of the charitable foundation, and many of the services were free to those who couldn't afford to pay. Birth Data, Inc., had become one of the most well-respected agencies in the region for reuniting adoptees with their birth parents.

Benita had recalled how Andrea had gone ballistic when she'd learned she was adopted, accusing her parents of lying to her for seventeen years. Benita had dug in and defended her position, saying she'd done what she thought was best. However, she'd come to regret having hidden her daughter's illegitimate birth from her. Andrea had stomped out of the house vowing to find her real mother.

What if she'd contacted Birth Data, Inc., as part of her search?

With shaking hands, Benita had picked up a pair of scissors, clipped the article and put it with the birth certificate she kept hidden in her jewelry box—the one with the names of Andrea's birth parents, Hallie Albright and Garrett Folsom. For years she'd pretended those people didn't exist. Now they could be the key to finding her long lost daughter.

First thing tomorrow, she'd call that agency. Then she'd tell Ed.

MIKE PUT DOWN the phone and sat staring out the office window. When he hadn't uncovered anything more on Lisa's rental car or the mysterious Dr. Ray, he'd approached the problem from a different angle. He'd contacted security at BWI, National and Dulles Airports and paid for a sweep of the parking facilities. The man at BWI had struck pay dirt. Justine's Mercedes was in the garage. According to the parking ticket on the dashboard, it had been there since May eleventh, the day the rental car had gone into the Jones Falls.

Mike scrawled a circle around the license number he'd written on the notepad. If Justine had wanted someone to think she'd skipped town, leaving her Mercedes at the airport would be the perfect ploy. Lisa could have been hired by Justine as a body double, then had her luck run out when the two thugs who were after Justine forced her car into the river.

On the other hand, suppose the real Mrs. Hollingsworth had taken a flight to parts unknown. And Lisa—or whoever she was—had come to Baltimore on the same day and rented a car. She'd been upset about something, driven around aimlessly and ended up in deep water, her purse swept away by the current, leaving her with no identification. But she looked enough like Justine Hollingsworth to be her twin sister.

Mike's stomach muscles clenched as he tried to picture Lisa and Justine, tried to figure out if they were really the same person. What if this very appealing woman with amnesia who kept insisting she wasn't Justine Hollingsworth was telling the truth? What if she'd had the bad luck to get caught in the middle of someone else's problems? Suppose she really was the sweet, vulnerable, frightened woman she appeared to be. Suppose she was in trouble and needed him . . . And suppose she was as attracted to him as he was to her. Against his better judgment, he allowed himself to contemplate the tantalizing possibility.

The cynical side of his nature wanted to dismiss the whole line of reasoning as hopelessly farfetched. The other more incriminating scenario he'd cooked up was equally plausible. But his softer side urged him to keep an open mind. Until he had proof of Lisa's identity one way or the other, it wasn't fair to condemn her, or to insert her into the middle of some criminal plot. And after all, he'd promised her he wouldn't make assumptions.

He considered calling Abby Franklin to find out how the interview had gone. Instead, he dialed Lisa's room at Mount Olive Hospital. "It's Mike," he said in an upbeat voice.

"Oh, hello!"

She sounded pleased to hear his voice, with no hint of recrimination that he'd been curt with her earlier.

"I want to thank you for recommending Dr. Franklin," she said.

"What did she say?"

There was a slight pause on the other end of the line. "A lot of things. The bottom line is, she thinks I don't belong in the hospital. I'm planning to sign myself out."

"That's good." He hesitated about two seconds, then asked, "Do you want me to drive you home, to smooth out the introductions to the Hollingsworth staff?" At least he'd have a chance to do some snooping around the house.

"Would you? I've been dreading going there alone."

"What time should I pick you up?"

"The sooner the better."

"I could get there by five."

"I'll be ready."

Mike hung up, fighting a mixture of anticipation and anger at his own rash behavior. Was he making use of an opportunity to poke around Justine's mansion? Or was he getting sucked in by sweet little Lisa?

Chapter Eight

Mike struggled to keep his expression neutral. This woman couldn't be Justine Hollingsworth. She looked too young, too subdued, too modest in an unassuming blue knit dress that brushed softly against her knees. And too pretty, which seemed to him a strange observation, since Justine was known among the wealthy crowd for her sleek good looks. But this woman had a different kind of beauty. Even with the ugly yellow of healing bruises on her forehead, there was a dewy quality about her that Justine had probably outgrown in grade school.

"All set?" he asked, his voice a little husky.

"No. But there's no point in putting it off."

Her voice had that soft lilt he remembered from their late-night phone conversation. It had turned him on then. It was having the same effect today. Pivoting on his heels, he led the way to the parking lot so that he wouldn't have to watch the feminine way her hips swayed when she walked.

A few minutes later, sitting in the car with her beside him, he caught the scent of lemon. Probably from her shampoo. It was less distracting than the feeling of nervousness emanating from her.

"You'll be all right," he said.

She swallowed, glanced at him and turned toward the window. He got the feeling her attack of the jitters had as much to do with being alone with him as anything else.

When had Justine ever been shy around men? he wondered.

He had the sudden impulse to reach out and cover her small hand with his. But in the close confines of the car, that was much too intimate a gesture, so he kept his hands wrapped around the steering wheel.

"Where do I live?" she asked.

As he pulled out of the parking space, he told her, "In Mount Washington near Western Run Park. You've got an estate off Old Court Road."

They turned left out of the lot. From the corner of his eye, he watched her stare at the substantial houses with their wide lawns. There was plenty of opportunity for sight-seeing with the traffic moving in fits and starts.

Lisa gestured apologetically at the double line of cars. "I guess I should have left after rush hour, but I couldn't wait to get out of there."

"I understand."

He took his eyes from the road for a moment, then had to slam on the brake as the pickup truck ahead of them screeched to a halt. The end of the pickup's skid was followed by an audible clunk.

Lisa gasped. "A dog. I think I saw a dog run into the street in front of that truck."

The pickup pulled over the white line and tore off down the nearest cross street, giving them a clear view of a black and brown German shepherd lying limply in the middle of the road.

Lisa made a strangled noise. Unbuckling her seat belt, she hopped from the car. Oblivious of the honking horns from the line of traffic behind them, she knelt in the street beside the injured animal, stroking his head and talking softly. The only thing Mike could do was join her.

More horns honked.

"We have to get him out of the street," Lisa said.

"Yeah."

Carefully, she worked her hands under the animal's shoulders. Mike took the dog's back quarters. A teenage boy who had been watching from the sidewalk came forward to support the middle. As gently as possible, they lifted the animal and moved him to the grass strip along the curb. He lay limply under the shade of a maple tree, panting.

Several other neighbors had seen the accident, and a stout woman came forward to announce, "That's Bruno. He belongs to the Caseys. Must have jumped the fence again."

"Tell them what happened," Mike ordered.

The woman hustled off.

"Hey, buddy, get your damn car out of the middle of the road," someone shouted angrily from the line of vehicles stacked up behind his Mustang.

Glancing toward the street, Mike bit back a sharp retort. "I'll be right back," he told Lisa.

She nodded without taking her attention from the injured shepherd. "It's all right, Bruno," she murmured as she smoothed her fingers over the black ruff. "You're going to be all right."

Incredibly, the animal gave a feeble wag of its tail.

Transfixed, Mike stood and watched, until another frustrated commuter gave him a sharp reminder of the traffic piling up. Striding to his car, he started the engine and pulled into the nearest empty driveway. Then he hurried back to the strip of grass. Lisa was still totally focused on the injured dog. When her hand slid along one back leg, the animal yelped, and she winced, as if she were the one in pain.

"Good boy," she said, her tone soft and soothing. "I know that hurts. Your leg is broken. But the vet can fix it."

Watching her, Mike sensed that her desire to help the animal was purely instinctive, as instinctive as her knowledge of how to give comfort. Her actions were spontaneous, her words genuinely spoken. Certainly, the dog seemed to understand that he was in good hands, Mike thought, seeing the animal's tongue lick Lisa's fingers as she scratched his head.

A gray-haired man in slacks and a plaid sport shirt lumbered up the sidewalk toward them. "Bruno. Oh, no.

Bruno," he gasped. When he reached the group, he dropped to his knees beside the shepherd.

At the sound of his master's voice, the animal lifted his head and wagged his tail again.

"Mr. Casey? Did your wife call the vet?" Mike asked.

"Yeah. He's expecting us." Casey stroked his pet. "Rita says the guy who hit him took off like a bat out of hell. Thanks for stopping."

"Anybody would," Lisa protested. "I think the truck just clipped his leg. I hope so, anyway."

Casey went on as if she hadn't spoken. "Damn. This is my fault. There's a low place in the fence, where a tree limb fell. Bruno got out before."

Mike watched Lisa pat the man's shoulder, ministering to him the way she had to his injured pet. The whole scene was so foreign to his image of Justine Hollingsworth that he felt disoriented.

Mrs. Casey pulled up in a station wagon, and Mike helped Lisa and Mr. Casey lift the dog onto a blanket in the back. As the vehicle maneuvered into the line of cars and drove away, Mike slipped his arm protectively around Lisa. Her body trembling, she leaned heavily against him.

"Come on." He led her toward his car, and she shuffled stiffly down the sidewalk to where he'd parked between a high wooden fence and a bank of forsythia.

She climbed in and sat with her eyes closed and her head thrown back, looking small and fragile and very sad. "That poor dog," she whispered.

Then, to Mike's great dismay, she burst into tears.

She started to cover her face with her palms, but he reached across the space between the seats and pulled her into his arms. Her fingers gripped his shoulders as her anguish poured out in great sobs that racked her body. There was nothing he could do but hold her and offer gentle words. After a little while, he sensed she was struggling to regain control.

"It's okay," he murmured. "He's going to be okay."

With a final gulp, she fumbled in her pocket. Pulling out a tissue, she blew her nose. "I hope so. I'm sorry I got so emotional."

"Don't worry about it."

She looked down at her hands. "I kept thinking how helpless he was. All he could do was lie there in pain and wait for someone to rescue him."

"We did."

"He made me think about ... about what happened to me. ... Mike," she said, her voice cracking, "what would I have done if you hadn't come along to pull me out of the river?"

"Someone else—"

She cut him off with a quick shake of her head. "I'd be dead."

"Don't think about that."

"I can't turn off my thoughts. Or my emotions. You saved me. But ... I'm not *me* anymore. I don't know who I am. And it's so awful."

She raised her eyes to him. They were large, and pleading for his understanding.

"You're going to be fine."

"You can't know for sure. I think I was acting like me when I was helping the dog. How I felt when I saw him lying there came from somewhere deep inside. But how can I be sure?"

He couldn't cope with either the hopeless look on her face or the aching feeling in his chest. He needed to make her whole. He needed to ease his own pain, as well. Somehow, the logical way to accomplish both was to gather her close once more.

This time she gave a little sigh of contentment as she came into his arms, her body molding itself to his. She pressed her face to his shoulder, swaying her forehead against his shirt. He felt her inhale deeply and reacted with a shiver that swept across his skin. He knew she felt it, because she raised her head and looked into his eyes, her gaze seeming to search his very soul. Her lips were only inches from his. They trembled slightly, parted, spoke his name so faintly he barely heard. Yet he caught the intensity of feeling.

He answered her in the same breathy whisper. "Lisa."

Neither of them moved. Then the most natural thing in the world was to lower his mouth to hers. For a startled moment, he realized what he was doing, and he intended to pull back. But she made a muffled sound that shattered his resolve, a sound of suppressed longing that zinged along every nerve in his body. It was too late for second thoughts. For any thoughts. Since he'd seen her sitting in her hospital bed, he'd wanted to kiss her. And so he did. Greedily, he angled his head, slanting his lips over hers for the most intimate contact, and she opened to him as she had in his dream. Her name was a groan deep in his throat.

If the kiss started with finesse, it rapidly progressed with a frightening lack of control. Her greed matched his. As did her restless drive to explore—to know. He felt like a skydiver without a parachute. Only the contact of his mouth with hers would keep him from crashing.

He couldn't catch his breath, even when his lips left hers to trail a hot, wet line across her jaw and down the beautiful curve of her throat to the wildly beating pulse point at its base. Her pulse kept time with the pounding of his heart. And the way she gasped his name over and over was a rich erotic counterpoint.

With some part of his brain, he knew they were parked in a stranger's driveway. But the fence beside his window and the tall bushes on the other side of the car gave the illusion of privacy. Yet the setting was almost irrelevant. Right now, he wasn't sure he would have been capable of acting differently, even if they had been sitting in the middle of the traffic lane.

Desperate for contact, his fingers glided up and down her ribs. When she sighed out her pleasure, his hands stole inward to cup her breasts. They were rounded and full in his hands. And when he stroked his thumbs across the nipples, he found them hard and tight with arousal. Like his body.

"Oh, Mike, that feels good. Oh, so good," she gasped, arching forward into his hands, driving him to a new level of excitement. "I've wanted..." The exclamation ended on a tiny sob. She turned her head and captured his mouth with hers again. He tasted carnal desire. He tasted need that matched his own.

Her dress had become an intolerable barrier. If it had opened down the front, he would have attacked the buttons. Instead, he skimmed his hand up the smooth curve of her leg, profoundly grateful that she was wearing only sandals and no panty hose. Pushing her skirt upward, he stopped to admire her delicate knees before homing in on the silky skin of her inner thigh.

Her legs parted, and she moved restlessly, invitingly. There was no doubt that she wanted his touch as much as he wanted to stroke her. He reached higher toward the heat radiating from her core....

And he froze as he heard a thump against the side of the car. They both jerked their heads toward the window.

A man in a business suit stood holding a briefcase in his hand. He was glaring at them.

"I'm afraid this is private property," he growled. "You'll have to find somewhere else for your little party—before my kids come out to play basketball and see something they shouldn't."

Mike felt his face redden. It had been a long time since he'd been caught making out in a parked car. From the corner of his eye, he saw Lisa frantically tugging at her skirt.

The homeowner marched past them and up his back steps. They were alone again, but Lisa didn't meet Mike's gaze as he started the engine and gunned it toward the street, tires squealing.

The traffic had abated somewhat. They drove for several blocks before she finally spoke in a strangled voice.

"I'm sorry. I didn't intend for that to happen. It appears my mother didn't raise me to be a lady."

"It was my fault as much as yours," he muttered, feeling like a jerk for letting things get out of hand.

After that, they rode in silence. From the corner of his eye, he saw her sitting stiffly in the seat, her arms folded protectively across her chest. She was motionless and looked as though she was struggling not to cry. He had to tighten his hands on the wheel to prevent himself from reaching over to touch her yet again.

IT TOOK an enormous amount of willpower to keep the tears in her eyes from spilling over and sliding down her cheeks, and giving away more than she wanted to reveal. Lord, it was hard to imagine a more mortifying scene—unless the homeowner had come by a few minutes later. When she felt in greater control, she stole a quick glance in Mike's direction. He was watching her. For a split second it looked as if he was going to say something. Then he firmly returned his attention to the road, leaving her glad that he was giving her some privacy, yet frustrated that he hadn't said anything. She'd been longing for some sign that he cared, but she hadn't been prepared for a white-hot flare of passion. She ached to know what he was feeling, but she knew he wouldn't welcome any questions. Even if she was brave enough to ask.

Maybe later, when she was alone, she could think about the pleasure of their lovemaking. While it had ended before either one of them was satisfied, it was by far the best thing that had happened to her in the short span of her recollection. But at the moment, it didn't make her feel better—or safer. She'd been trying so hard to keep Mike from knowing how vulnerable she was to him. Now her chest squeezed as she thought about how easily she'd given away her feelings. Yet what she wanted with all her heart was impossible. In fact, she didn't dare put it into words. At least while Mike was convinced she was married to another man.

Would it make a difference if she could prove she was free? The way he'd kissed and caressed her said there was hope.

A half smile began to form on her lips, but it was replaced almost at once with a rueful grimace. She was carrying another man's child. She wasn't free in any sense of the word. Not now, and almost certainly not when she remembered who had given her this baby.

But what if she never remembered?

Tears formed in her eyes. She mustered all her willpower to hold them back. Lord, she should have exercised more control. Only, she'd been hurting, and she'd reached for Mike. She hadn't realized what would happen, how quickly pain could be transformed into passion. It was a little like an alchemist turning lead to gold. Yet neither she nor Mike knew what to do with the riches. One thing was certain, though. She no longer could pretend that his saving her life was the only thing that drew her to him.

Lisa was unaware of the passing scenery. The daffodils and tulips in people's gardens sped by in a blur before her unseeing gaze. Then, all at once she realized Mike had turned the car between two stone columns, marking the beginning of a winding driveway flanked by graceful pink dogwoods. When they rounded a curve, Lisa stared in astonishment at an enormous two-story white house with a broad portico that looked as though it could have been transplanted straight from a southern plantation. Attached to the side was a four-car garage.

"Justine lives here?" she gasped, looking from the mansion to the wide lawn and carefully tended flower beds filled with perfectly coordinated white tulips and purple hyacinths.

"Not too hard to take, is it?" Mike retorted.

Before she could frame a reply, he pulled around the cobblestone circle to the front entrance, stopped the car and climbed out.

She was left staring at his back as he rang the bell. Then he stepped aside, and she saw a middle-aged woman in the doorway. Her salt-and-pepper hair was cropped short, her face was round and her plump body was clad in a black uniform with white trim. She looked about as friendly as a pit bull.

Taking a deep breath, Lisa climbed from the Mustang.

Mike made the introductions. "This is Maggie Dempsey."

"Mrs. Hollingsworth," she said in a voice that sounded artificially formal.

"I've been asking everyone to call me Lisa."

"Aye. They said." Mrs. Dempsey was perfectly polite while managing to convey disapproval.

Lisa stood uncertainly in the driveway. More than ever, she sensed that coming here was a mistake. She pictured herself leaping back into the car, throwing it into gear and driving away.

"How are you feeling, ma'am?" the housekeeper asked, as if she'd remembered it was her duty to sound concerned.

"Fine," Lisa answered automatically. "Do I call you Maggie or Mrs. Dempsey?"

"Whatever takes your fancy."

"All right then, Maggie, why don't you show me around."

The woman looked surprised by the choice of names. Wrong again, Lisa thought. She could see Mike watching the exchange, but she wasn't going to ask for his help.

"Thank you for bringing my things to the hospital, Maggie," she murmured.

"You're welcome."

Maggie looked away suddenly, and Lisa wanted to ask if the housekeeper had resented the extra duty.

Mike followed behind at a little distance, carrying Lisa's overnight bag. She knew he was interested in finding out how she interacted with her employee. She wanted to tell him she was as uncomfortable as Mrs. Dempsey apparently was.

The housekeeper led them into a wide hall with marble floors and flowered wallpaper. Then she stopped short, as though suddenly unsure of how to proceed.

Lisa realized the burden of smoothing the way was entirely on her shoulders. "Pretend I've come for a visit," she suggested. "Show me what I need to know to be comfortable here." She didn't add that the task was probably impossible; she could never be comfortable in such a pretentious place.

"Uh, this is the living room." Maggie gestured toward a large room done in pale white upholstery with a celery-colored rug.

Lisa wrinkled her nose, unable to imagine having selected such a color scheme or such stiff furnishings. It was the same in the relentlessly Chippendale dining room and the enormous ranch kitchen, where the counters appeared to be made of granite and the refrigerator was faced with maple panels so that it blended with the cabinets.

"Is everything all right?" Maggie murmured.

Lisa tried to take it all in. "Of course."

The woman seemed to relax a notch as Lisa went past the well-equipped home office, peering in quickly to see the personal computer and a row of filing cabinets integrated into a wall of bookshelves. Next, she peeked into the powder room off the side hall; it was large enough to hold a committee meeting. Only the sun porch across the back of the house, with its casual wicker furniture and enormous ferns and hibiscus, appealed to her.

A muscular man dressed in green overalls, who looked to be in his sixties, was watering plants and removing their dead leaves, which he stuffed into a small plastic bag. He stopped pruning and looked at her, as if he expected her to say something.

"You also work here?" she inquired.

He laughed as if she had told a particularly funny joke. "You know I do. Been taking care of the house and grounds ever since the place was built. Before you moved in," he added, as if he'd never considered the lady of the house a permanent fixture.

Lisa silently agreed with him—at least, as far as *this* lady was concerned. "I'm sorry. I'm sure you've heard about my memory loss."

"None of my business. I just do my work."

"May I know your name?"

"Frank."

"Well, Frank, for the time being, you'll have to pardon my little oddities."

He grunted and went back to work. Since she was all out of sparkling conversational gambits, she hurried out of the room.

They reached the front hall again, where Lisa gestured toward the huge vase of flowers on the sideboard. "Those are beautiful," she tried. "Did Frank pick them?"

"No, they're from Mr. Hollingsworth's business partner, Mr. Realto."

"Oh."

"He called several times to find out how you were."

Lisa nodded, wondering if she should send him a thank-you note. Her gaze fell on the overnight bag sitting in the hall, and she realized that sometime during the guided tour, Mike had disappeared. When she glanced out the window, she saw his car was still in the driveway.

"You go back to work," she told Maggie. "I'll be with you in a while."

The housekeeper hesitated, then started toward the kitchen. Lisa stood in the hallway, considering. Mike could be anywhere in the house. He could even be outside admiring the grounds. But she didn't think so. She was beginning to get a pretty good idea of how his mind worked. Quietly, she headed for the office. When she pulled open the door, she wasn't surprised to find him standing in front of a filing cabinet, riffling through the folders packed into one of the drawers.

Chapter Nine

It was a moment before he turned to look at her. When he did, his face was a study in composure.

"What are you doing?" Lisa demanded. Maybe it was irrational, but she felt betrayed. If he'd told her what he was going to do, it would have been different. But there'd been no discussion. She'd let him bring her here, and he'd lost no time in taking advantage of the situation.

"I'm doing the job you hired me for," Mike said casually. She couldn't match his nonchalance and heard her voice rise as she asked, "That includes going through the Hollingsworths' personal papers?"

"That includes finding out whatever I can about your problems." His eyes held an unspoken challenge.

She wanted to look away, but she held her gaze steady. "Did you offer to take me home so you could snoop around the house?"

"Partly. If you don't like it, I can return the part of your retainer I haven't spent on the investigation. That's most of it, actually."

Feeling trapped, she drew in a sharp breath. If he left, she'd be on her own in this house that was virtually enemy territory. But that wasn't the only reason she swallowed her pride. She needed to know someone was on her side—him, specifically. And she wanted him to understand that intuitively. But he was going to make her say it. "No. I don't want you to quit."

"You want me to keep working for you?" he clarified.

She longed to have him put it in personal terms. Didn't the kiss change anything? "Yes," she managed to say.

"Then let me do my job."

"Mike, please..."

"What?"

They stood tensely on either side of the room.

She swallowed. "We're both on edge about what happened...when we were alone. And...well, coming here to this house isn't making it any easier. I shouldn't have—"

"No." He cut her off, but as he continued, he wouldn't meet her gaze. "You didn't do anything wrong—or that I didn't encourage. So stop blaming yourself, and let's just forget about it."

Forget about it? Impossible.

What she wanted to say was, Mike, don't shut me out. But she didn't say it for two very good reasons. It wasn't fair either to make herself dependent on him, or to make him feel responsible for her problems.

Instead, she said nothing, simply stood with her hands clenched at her sides, and stared at him.

He gestured toward the files. "I need to know what was happening in your life before the accident. And you can't tell me."

"Not *my* life. *Her* life."

"Whatever."

"Are those Justine's files? Or her husband's?"

"His."

"Then why are you looking through them?"

"I told you, he could be the source of *her* problems."

She couldn't muster an argument. Swinging away, she found herself facing the computer. It was a top-of-the-line model, she noted, with a tower processor and a seventeen-inch screen. Sitting down, she booted the machine and scanned the Windows menu. There were several software packages—including a check-balancing program, a word processor and a selection of games.

"You know how to use the computer?" Mike asked.

"It would seem so."

"You're familiar with Windows?"

"Yes."

He looked surprised. "So which program do you want to access?"

"Finance."

"Smart girl."

A warm flush spread through her at his casual praise, and she chided herself for being so easily affected. Ridiculous that his opinion should matter so much. "I mean, it sounds the most familiar," she murmured.

Before she could test her theory, she heard someone in the hall.

"Where is Mrs. Hollingsworth?" an authoritative female voice demanded.

Maggie's muffled answer was followed by high heels clacking across the marble floor of the foyer. The door to the office flew open, and Lisa turned to find herself confronting a woman whose face was as homely as her tailored suit was businesslike. She seemed to assume that her very presence would elicit a response.

When the presumed Mrs. Hollingsworth didn't comply, the woman switched tactics and inclined her head toward Mike. "Who are you? What are you doing here?"

"Mike Lancer." He didn't answer the second part of the question. And he didn't offer his hand.

"Lancer." Her voice held an unmistakable note of derision. "You're the private detective Mrs. Hollingsworth hired before her bout with amnesia." As she spoke, the woman's gaze shot from Mike to Lisa and back again.

Neither of them offered what appeared to be the expected clarification.

"You seem to know a lot about what's going on," Mike countered. "Who are you?"

"It's my job to know what's going on," she clipped out. "I'm Mr. Hollingsworth's executive assistant, Estelle Bensinger."

"So why aren't you at the office taking care of business?" Mike asked with what sounded to Lisa like more than casual interest.

"I came to offer my assistance in helping Mrs. Hollingsworth get settled after her hospital stay," Estelle answered, her tone of voice matching the stilted cadence of her words.

Mike gave her a half smile. "Then I'll get out of your way."

Lisa felt her throat close. Until he'd said the words, she hadn't let herself contemplate coping with this house of strangers on her own. She sensed Estelle was watching her with keen interest, so she made an effort to address Mike as if he were simply working for her.

"Well, thanks for giving me a ride," she said.

He didn't seem to have any problem manufacturing an easy tone. "Sure thing."

"You'll be in touch if you dig up any more information?" she got out, an edge of panic in her voice.

He nodded.

Their eyes met. A moment of silence passed during which he looked as if he was sorry he'd brought up the subject of leaving. Or was she making that up? Lisa wondered as she watched him exit the room and cross the hall.

She had no time to consider what to do next. The moment Mike was out of the house, Estelle firmly shut the office door and pivoted, looking ready for a confrontation. Lisa took an involuntary step backward.

"I don't know why you came up with this new ploy, but you can stop the playacting now," Estelle said. With her nononsense business suit and grim face, she could have played a warden in a woman's prison movie.

"I'm not acting."

Estelle snorted. "You expect me to believe you don't remember *anything?*"

"I don't have to explain myself to you," Lisa countered with what she hoped sounded like conviction.

"That's not true. You can't change the rules in the middle of the game."

"What game? I don't know what you're talking about."

The woman ignored her comment. "Why did you go to the trouble of renting a car and changing your hairstyle if you were only coming back here?"

Why indeed? Lisa wanted to scream out her frustration with the whole absurd mess. Instead, she murmured, "I can't help what happened to me."

"What about our deal? What have you done with the damn folder from Kendall's files?"

Lisa stood very still, fighting a sense of vertigo. Every time she thought her situation couldn't get any worse, a new crisis arose like a monster from the swamp. Now what? Should she insist she didn't know what file Estelle was talking about? Or should she play along in hopes of gleaning information? The latter course was tempting but dangerous.

Temporizing, she shrugged. "My circumstances have changed."

The woman's mouth tightened into a dangerous-looking slash. "For all I know, you have that tape recorder in the stereo unit activated."

"I don't." Lisa felt her heart pounding as she tried to make sense of this weird encounter. Suppose Estelle had come here to size up the situation and report to her boss? Suppose she was laying a trap? That might explain what was going on.

"I guess you think you hold all the cards," Estelle said.

"No."

Abruptly, the secretary's manner changed, perhaps, Lisa thought, because she realized she was getting nowhere by being a bully. "Let me shut off the computer for you. You don't want to make Kendall angry by messing up his files." Deftly, she leaned over the desk and exited the Windows program.

"Thank you," Lisa managed to say, not bothering to explain that she could have done it herself.

"You don't have much time left before the manure hits the fan," Estelle said in a conversational tone as she straightened. "So think about getting over your amnesia and calling me before it's too late."

"What—what do you mean?"

The woman smiled without warmth. "I won't take up any more of your time. If you want to tell me where you hid those papers, you know where to reach me." Then, as Mike had, she turned and left Lisa standing in the middle of what she'd come to think of as enemy territory.

Shaken, Lisa reached out to steady herself against the edge of the desk. What precisely was going to happen when, as Estelle put it, the manure hit the fan? And exactly how long did she have before it happened?

The housekeeper's voice coming from the hall made her jump. "Do you want me to show you the upper floors?"

Lisa closed her eyes. It would be wonderful if she could simply ask Maggie what in the world was going on. Like, for instance, who was plotting with whom? And who was spying on whom? But she couldn't ask, couldn't afford to arouse any more suspicion. Not when she had no idea who was friend or foe. The only person she could rely on in this house was herself.

Lisa composed her face before stepping into the hall. "Thanks, but I'd rather look around upstairs on my own," she told the housekeeper.

"You know your way around?"

"I'll figure it out."

Climbing the stairs, she stifled the impulse to glance back and see whether Maggie was following her progress. When she reached the second floor, she saw that the housekeeper had carried the overnight bag into one of the bedrooms.

Steeling herself, she stepped into the room and was pleasantly surprised. Downstairs, Justine had clearly felt compelled to decorate in a style that befitted the grandeur of the house, either to suit her or her husband's taste. Here, however, she had chosen a country French motif, with rich, light-colored wood, simple rugs and matching curtains, and a bedspread with a tiny yellow and blue pattern. It was a place where Lisa could feel content. More than that, it was a place in which she *wanted* to feel safe, to crawl under the covers and pull them over her head.

The image brought goose bumps to her skin. She'd been so convinced she wasn't Justine Hollingsworth, but perhaps she had been fooling herself all along only because she wanted so desperately to be someone else.

Like a madwoman, Lisa rushed across the room and threw open the first door she encountered. It led to an enormous walk-in closet stuffed with enough clothes to fill a small department store.

"Princess Di, move over," she muttered. She could picture herself in a number of the more conservative outfits. Others seemed much too dressy, or too revealing.

After closing the bedroom door, she grabbed a narrow skirt and coordinating blouse. When she tried to put them on, she found it was impossible to zip the skirt all the way up, and the blouse was too tight across her breasts. She wanted to shout that these were not her clothes, yet the snugness proved nothing. Although she hardly looked as if she was carrying a child, she couldn't be certain that pregnancy hadn't already changed her body.

But the size of her feet wouldn't change, would they? Kneeling, she began to inspect the lines of shoes on two narrow shelves. Most had three-inch heels. When she slipped on a pair of white pumps, she felt as if she were tottering around on stilts. Did she really go in for these ridiculous things?

She tossed them onto the shelf, and slipped back into the thong sandals that felt much more comfortable. Then, since she'd already discarded her dress, she indulged herself and selected a jade green knit shirt and a pair of loose-fitting tan shorts with an elastic waistband.

Struggling for a sense of calm, she drifted across the bedroom and stood at the window to look out. The estate grounds were so extensive and so heavily wooded around the perimeter she couldn't see any of the neighboring homes, which only increased her feeling of isolation. Her gaze swept the wide lawns and neatly clipped shrubbery. Not her taste, she decided. If she could have any kind of garden she wanted, she'd go in for more flowers. Annuals like snapdragons and petunias in bright colors, clumps of perennials to provide a changing panorama throughout the growing season.

Hmm. Did that mean she knew something about landscaping? Maybe she had a flower garden at home. Wherever home was. The mere thought of home and family and a pretty little garden where she might spend the weekends puttering or chasing butterflies with her little girl—or boy— brought tears to her eyes.

"Oh, baby," she whispered, pressing a hand to her middle, "I don't think we belong here. I really don't."

A moment later, she clenched her teeth, struggling against giving in to self-pity. Dr. Franklin had said being pregnant—or the bump on her head—could be making her emotions so volatile. Regardless of the cause, she hated being at the mercy of her feelings.

Swiping away the moisture from her eyes, she brought her mind back to the scene below. Seconds later, she thought she saw a flash of movement at the edge of the garden. Going very still, she stared at an evergreen that appeared to have swayed. Was there a glimmer of contrasting color in the green foliage?

Lisa's heart started to pound as she imagined someone creeping through the shrubbery to spy on the house. Never taking her eyes from the evergreen, she waited several minutes. But nothing further happened, and she breathed out a little sigh. Maybe she'd seen a bird or a squirrel. Or that man Frank could have been in the garden pruning the bushes. Or maybe...

Before she could stop herself, her mind conjured a comforting fantasy, the one she kept reaching for whenever she was afraid. It was Mike. He'd changed his mind about leaving, and he was sneaking back to the house. He was going to take her away. Her chest squeezed painfully. She clung to the fancy for almost a minute, even though she knew it would get her nowhere.

With a grimace, she turned from the window. She might be jumpy as a cat on a trip to the vet's, but she had more important things to do than imagine either intruders or a knight in shining armor in the Hollingsworth garden. She had to look for clues to her identity—before it was too late, as Estelle had kindly told her.

THE MAN who had been staring at the house stood with the back of his fatigue jacket pressed against the wide trunk of an oak tree.

"Stupid jerk," Gary muttered, his voice low and full of self-accusation. "She was standin' at the window. She could have seen you. Now what are you going to do? Run back to your hidey-hole?"

He waited, every muscle in his body tense, expecting to feel a heavy hand clamp down on his shoulder and haul him into the open. He wanted to sink down until as much of his body as possible was in contact with the ground. But he knew that if he moved, they might see him. So he stood glued to the tree while agonizing seconds ticked by.

Nothing happened. Still, he remained in the shadows. The only part of him that moved was his hand. It inched toward the knife thrust into the waistband of his trousers. When his fingers closed around the handle, he breathed a little sigh. In that moment of peace, he tried to collect his scattered thoughts.

His junk car was stashed in the woods a quarter mile down the road where nobody would find it. He remembered that part. But the rest of it? He had come here to...

Sweat beaded his upper lip as he strained to make his mind function. He'd made plans. But they'd skittered out of reach like a crab scurrying across an empty beach.

A tear slipped down his cheek. He wanted to scream. But he gritted his teeth and stood with his hand clenching and unclenching on the knife handle until a measure of calm returned. He had made it this far. They hadn't found him. That was the important part. He could wait for the rest of his plan to come back to him.

Chapter Ten

Everything was so neat. Lisa continued to search through Justine's suite, thinking it looked as if someone had purposefully straightened up before her arrival.

She wondered if the mysterious folder Estelle had demanded was hidden somewhere up here. Whatever was in it must be damning in some way to Kendall Hollingsworth.

Stepping into the sitting room, she began opening drawers in the chest under the television set. The most interesting thing she discovered was a leather photo album decorated with gold scrollwork. Meticulously mounted in paper sleeves, complete with captioned dates, were pictures of a woman who looked so much like herself it made her gasp.

"Oh!" Now she understood why nobody believed her protestations. She and Justine looked like twins. Were they sisters . . . or was she herself really Justine Hollingsworth?

Mouth dry, she sank onto the love seat and stared at the face that looked so like her own. The woman in the pictures had the same blue eyes, the same red hair, the same cheekbones, the same chin. The creamy skin. And yet . . . there were subtle differences. Justine had the thinness of a woman who controlled her weight with an iron will. Her hair was long, and it was carefully arranged with a casual wildness that looked affected. Her nails, where they were visible in the photos, were long and dark—the hands of a pampered woman, someone who shunned labor, not someone who fantasized about puttering in a garden.

The earliest pictures dated back more than eight years. Justine was always with the same man. Lisa could only assume that he was Kendall Hollingsworth. Her hands shaking, she studied his face, trying to imagine kissing him. No spark of recognition flared within her as she stared at his sharp eyes and contemplated his narrow lips. All she felt was a kind of revulsion.

Her skin grew clammy, and she made herself stop focusing on him. Instead, she tried to evaluate the two people in the picture as a couple. In the early pictures, Kendall and Justine were smiling and relaxed, at ease in each other's company. But the last few pages of the photo album conveyed a different impression, as if simmering tension existed below the smiling facade. Or was she imagining things—looking for a reason for Justine's disappearance?

She shivered as the implications of the word *disappearance* sank in. She couldn't account for what had happened any other way. If she wasn't Justine, then the woman who lived in this house had vanished into thin air. Estelle had made it sound as though Justine had run away. But she could just as easily have been kidnapped—or she could be dead.

Lisa grew cold as an image formed in her mind. An image of a woman who looked very much like herself lying pale and still in the woods—or trapped behind the wheel of a sunken car. Shoulders hunched, she rubbed her arms, willing away the chill. For all she knew, Justine was on a Caribbean island soaking up the sun.

She went back to flipping the pages with morbid fascination.

Knowing she must face the enemy, she shifted her attention away from the woman, to the man whose image made her so nervous. She tried to be objective as she compared the way he looked in the earlier pictures to those labeled with more recent dates. He was older than Justine by maybe ten or fifteen years. In the first photographs, he'd been fit and tanned, with a full head of wavy dark hair tinged with gray. Moreover, he'd radiated the maturity and confidence of a man who was sure of his place in the world.

That impression remained intact over the next seven years of photos. But in the pictures at the back of the album, Hollingsworth seemed to have aged overnight. His hair was much grayer and receded from his broad forehead. Also, his body wasn't quite so trim; in fact, a slight paunch marred the waistline of his expensive slacks. More lines fanned out around his eyes, and his mouth appeared tense and drawn with suppressed worry—or anger.

Lisa didn't like that mouth. Again, she couldn't stop herself from shuddering as she imagined it coming down hard on hers. She tried to reason that she was manufacturing an irrational fear of the man. That she didn't know enough about him to be so frightened. But the pep talk didn't help. Quickly, she slammed the book of photos closed. Still, the daunting image of Kendall Hollingsworth lingered in her mind.

Her hand slid down to cover her abdomen. "The man in those pictures isn't your father," she whispered with conviction. "He just can't be."

Even as she uttered the heartfelt assurance, she admitted that she had no way of determining whether or not it was true. Feeling ill, she closed her eyes and sat very still. In fact, she had no way of knowing whether any assumption she'd made since waking up in the hospital was valid. As she'd told Dr. Franklin, the only thing about her that was irrefutable and verifiable was the existence of the baby inside her. Her child.

"We're in this together," she said softly. "I know it's scary. But no matter what, I'll make sure everything works out for both of us. If Mike can't...or won't help us, I'll get us out of this myself. I promise."

She took a deep breath and let it out slowly. It was foolish to keep holding out hope that Mike would rescue her. Again. He had no obligations to her—beyond the simple fact that Justine had hired his investigative services. Yet he must feel something for her, otherwise he wouldn't have lost his head and kissed her as if they'd been alone in a bedroom instead of sitting in a car ten feet from a public street.

The image brought a tiny smile to her lips. And without warning, she was lost, swept away by the memory of the passion—and the pleasure—that had surged between them. Lord, the taste of him. The feel of his hands. Her breath quickened, and her body felt hot and tingly and suffused with yearning. She longed to lose herself in the sweetness of being with him once more. In her mind, she transported them to a different setting. A walled garden with beds of scented flowers and a gently bubbling fountain....

But she soon found it impossible to remember the fleeting moment of happiness without recalling the mortifying interruption. The memory of the man banging on the car window made her cheeks heat, and not from pleasure. Getting caught had been bad enough, but the worst part had come when Mike had slammed the car into gear and driven off, tires squealing, and she'd sat there beside him almost able to see the wall he was erecting between them.

The wall meant rejection, and it had hurt. It *still* hurt. Her hands opened and closed helplessly as she experienced the pain all over again. It was worse that the rebuff had come on the heels of an intensely erotic encounter, but it would have hurt regardless of the circumstances. With no memory of any family or friend, Mike was, quite frankly, the most important person in her life, the person with whom she felt the strongest ties, the person who had known her longer than any other—known her from the moment he'd saved her life. The idea of being cut off from him—worse, that he had deliberately shut her out—was nearly unbearable.

And yet, clearly, she had no right to make any demands on Mike. It wasn't his fault that she felt so attached to him, that his face was imprinted on her mind forever as her first and most powerful memory. Yes, he was obviously attracted to her, but that didn't mean he had any desire to be emotionally involved with her. And, after all, how could a man be emotionally involved or committed to a woman who didn't know who she was? Even if she and Kendall Hollingsworth had never laid eyes on each other, she certainly carried the evidence of some intimate relationship.

"I'm sorry," she whispered to the baby. "I'm so confused. I know none of this is your fault, and I swear I'm going to love you the very best way that I know how. But, baby, I do wish everything weren't so complicated."

Sitting very still, she tried to let the connection to her child bring her comfort. She didn't know her past, but she could at least imagine her future with this child. A dreamy smile flickered on her lips as she pictured herself in a comfortable rocking chair, nursing an infant at her breast while a tiny hand curled around her finger. The soothing image held until she tried to imagine where the chair was exactly. What did the room look like? If she tried hard, she could put herself and the baby in a sunny room with a crib and a white dresser and blue-and-white-striped curtains at the window. But she knew that she'd made up the whole thing. Because there was no way she could already have started decorating a nursery.

The conviction made her heart squeeze. She longed to think about nice normal things a mother could enjoy with her child. Yet even that was denied her. At least until she had her memory back. But what if it never returned? A wave of fear swept over her as the possibility of never knowing her past took hold in her mind. The idea was so terrifying that she'd tried not to think about it. Yet it might be the reality she'd have to live with for the rest of her life.

Her hands clenched the fabric of the sofa cushions as horror threatened to swamp her. She was saved by Maggie's voice coming from the hallway.

"Mrs. Hollingsworth, are you hungry?"

With a grateful glance toward the door, she called, "I'll be right down."

In the bathroom, she washed her face and brushed her hair. When she stepped out of her room into the hall, she almost smacked into Maggie, who was standing directly beside the door.

"You didn't have to come up." Brushing past the woman, she headed for the stairs.

The housekeeper trailed after her. "It's late, and I'll be off duty in an hour. I came to ask what you'll be wanting to eat."

It was a perfectly plausible explanation, yet it didn't sound like the whole truth. She felt as if Maggie was spying on her—for Hollingsworth, perhaps, or even Estelle—and it only upset her further not to know if the notion was true or pure paranoia.

"Really, you don't have to bother with dinner. I can fix something for myself."

"I'd rather you didn't—" The woman broke off abruptly, looking as if she wished she'd kept her mouth shut.

"Why?"

"It's not my place to say."

In the front hall, Lisa turned and faced the housekeeper. "Since I'm having memory problems, it would help if you didn't find it necessary to hide basic facts from me."

Several hushed moments ticked by. Lisa hoped they made the housekeeper more uncomfortable than they made her feel.

Finally, Maggie spoke. "Last time you were in the kitchen, you were making cheesecake, and you didn't, uh, screw on...I mean, the top came off the blender. Cream cheese and sugar sprayed all over the place. You threw, uh, you stamped out of the kitchen, and left the mess for me to clean up."

"Well, I guarantee I won't blame my failings on you." *Even if I am Justine,* she added silently, heading down the hall in the direction of the kitchen. When she reached her destination, she stopped short, staring at the closed wood cabinets. She had no idea what was beyond any of the doors.

Maggie watched her surveying the room, a wary expression on her face. Why was the woman so tense? Lisa wondered.

"Pretend I've been hired to help out with a party, and you're showing me where to find everything," she said as Maggie came up behind her.

She knew the woman probably thought she was crazy.

After a slight hesitation, Maggie began to open cabinets and drawers and gesture toward the neatly arranged contents. "Well, here are the baking pans...the saucepans...the big pots. Knives, cutting boards, colanders, casseroles."

It certainly was a complete collection, Lisa thought. And expensive. Even the spices were in alphabetical order.

"Everything is so neat," she said.

"Decide on anything you'd like to cook?" Maggie inquired, her voice faintly edged with sarcasm.

"Pasta sauce." Lisa pulled down cans of Italian plum tomatoes.

"What seasonings do you want to use?"

"Basil. Thyme. Bay leaf."

"What about oregano?"

"I don't like oregano." She went very still as she realized what she'd said. It was true, she wasn't partial to oregano, but she hadn't known it until the words had popped out of her mouth. Just as she hadn't had a clue about what to cook until she'd spotted a can of tomatoes in the pantry.

"Should I fix a salad?" the housekeeper asked.

"Yes. Thank you."

"Is watermelon okay for dessert? I got some from Graul's."

"Fine."

Lisa hummed as she sautéed onions, then stirred the tomatoes into the pot and began to add seasonings. With a teaspoon, she tasted the mixture. It wasn't quite right, so she put in more thyme, along with salt, pepper and a little sugar.

Maggie interrupted her salad preparations to try the sauce. Her skeptical expression turned to one of surprise. "It's good. Have you been taking cooking lessons?"

"I don't know. I don't think so. Cooking feels natural."
Lisa glanced up to find the woman looking at her intently.

"You're different."

"How?"

"You're . . . nicer."

"Thank you," Lisa murmured. She would have liked to
believe that she'd taken a step toward winning the housekeeper's loyalty, but she was pretty sure it wouldn't be that
easy.

Maggie turned abruptly and bustled away to the pantry.

In forty minutes, the simple dinner was ready, and Lisa
felt a tremendous sense of accomplishment. She had discovered another ability in addition to her apparent knowledge of the computer. If worse came to worst, perhaps she
could support herself as a cook.

Lisa looked toward the formal dining room, with its long
table and dozen chairs. "Where do I like to eat when I'm
here by myself?" she asked.

"Sometimes I bring a tray to your room."

"And other times?"

"You like the patio."

"That sounds pleasant."

Maggie produced a tray, while Lisa fixed plates of pasta
and salad.

"I made a pitcher of iced tea," the housekeeper said.

"Maybe I'll have milk."

Maggie looked incredulous. "You hate milk."

"My tastes have changed," Lisa murmured. Actually,
milk wasn't what she would have chosen, but she was
thinking about the baby. In fact, probably she should make
an appointment with Justine's gynecologist for a prenatal
checkup. Then a new thought struck her, and she went very
still.

"Do you know the name of my dentist?" she asked
Maggie.

"Dr. Bishop. His phone number is in your phone book.
Do you have a dental problem?"

"No. I just wanted to check on something." Lisa felt a surge of disappointment as she glanced at the clock. Eight-thirty. Dr. Bishop's office was undoubtedly closed. But she was going to call first thing in the morning, because she'd thought of a way to settle the question of her identity one way or the other—by comparing her teeth to Justine's dental records.

ENOUGH TORTURE for one night.

Mike lifted his gaze from the computer screen and rubbed his eyes. He'd spent all evening trying to transcribe a week's worth of chicken-scratched notes—which ought to teach him not to let his work pile up—and he'd reached his limit. After saving the file, he leaned back in his chair and stretched.

No use pretending he was concentrating on work. He knew damned well where his head was. He kept picturing the defenseless look on Lisa's face that afternoon when he'd announced he was leaving.

Hell. He'd known how stupid it was to get any more involved with her. So why the devil had he kissed her?

The answer was instant: because of the way she'd fussed over the injured dog and cried in his arms. Comforting her had seemed the most natural thing in the world. Then, comfort hadn't been enough for either one of them. Unbidden, the passion of the kiss came back to him in a blast of heat.

Surging off the bed, he began to pace the length of the room. A short while later, he tried working at the computer again. But even that reminded him of Lisa—her sitting at the computer in Kendall Hollingsworth's den—and he went back to pacing. He cursed himself for missing an opportunity. The moment he'd stepped out of the house he'd realized his mistake. He should have stayed while Lisa accessed the financial program—if only to see if she was bluffing when she'd said that she knew how to use the system. If she did know how, then he could have collected some very useful information. Obviously, his judgment was warped.

Maybe he'd go back tomorrow and ask her to try.

The instant the thought occurred to him, Mike stopped pacing, squeezed his eyes shut and clenched his jaw. Wrong decision. What was he doing, thinking up excuses to get closer to her? Every time he drew a line and said he wouldn't cross it, he somehow ended up on the other side.

Scowling, he strode down the hall to the kitchen and yanked open the freezer. Shuffling through the assortment of TV dinners, he settled on spaghetti and meatballs, and stripped off the cardboard carton.

Inside was the familiar metal pan covered with foil. He'd been fixing these things for himself since he was seven. Back then, he'd been lucky to find anything in the apartment to eat since his old man habitually drank away most of the grocery money. Mostly he and Mom ate off of the tips from her waitressing job—and the uneaten food she scarfed from customers' plates when the manager wasn't looking. What kind of person would he be now if he'd had a normal family life? he wondered, not for the first time.

He sighed, annoyed that he was letting his mind wander over old pain. All that was way behind him. The scholarship he'd won to the University of Maryland had been his ticket to salvation. And he'd never gone back to the old neighborhood except as a police patrolman. Still, he sat surrounded by old memories and more recent reveries until the timer signaled him that dinner was ready.

At the dining-room table he peeled back the foil and burned himself from the steam. But his angry curse wasn't evoked simply by physical pain. He was cursing the foolish yearnings of his soul. He'd been disgusted enough with himself in the car, but walking into the Hollingsworth mansion had brought home a basic truth: Justine was married to Kendall. She belonged to someone else, and it didn't matter what Mike Lancer wanted. He'd never been the kind of person who stole anything, even if he was starving. And he wasn't going to start by stealing another man's wife. So if Lisa and Justine were the same person—and he had no proof that they weren't—he had no right to her. And that was all there was to it.

LISA STEPPED onto the flagstone terrace covered with a green-and-white-striped awning. A light breeze ruffled her hair, and she caught the scent of lilacs. Maggie, who had followed her outside, switched on a set of soft outdoor lights, and Lisa took in her surroundings—a wrought-iron table and chairs were at one end, a conversation group at the other. Probably, Lisa thought as she eased into a cushioned chair, these outdoor furnishings cost more than most people spent on their indoor furniture.

She couldn't picture herself actually living in this opulent setting, yet, as long as she was here, she could think of no reason that she shouldn't enjoy the tranquillity of the garden. It seemed to be having a positive effect on her appetite already. For the first time in days, she actually felt hungry.

She'd polished off most of the spaghetti, when her hand froze on her fork, as something flittered delicately at the edge of her vision. The evergreen branch she'd watched from the window swayed slightly. Again.

Trying to look nonchalant, she turned her head as if surveying the whole quiet twilight setting. She looked at the evergreen, but saw nothing special about that particular tree. In fact, as she watched, the wind picked up and began playing with shrubbery all over the yard.

The breeze sent a sprinkle of goose bumps over her skin. "Stop being paranoid," she ordered herself as she sipped her milk. But she suddenly found it hard to swallow.

Something wasn't right.

She started to push back her chair, when a furtive sound reached her ears. Straining to identify the source, she was sure she heard the crunch of stealthy footsteps on gravel deep in the shadows.

"Frank? Maggie?" she called, her gaze sweeping the garden that, only minutes ago, had seemed an oasis of peace and stillness.

No one answered. The hair on the back of her neck stirred, and in the next instant, she jumped to her feet, taking a stumbling step backward.

But it was already too late for escape. A man stepped out of the bushes and came toward her. Circling the table, he put himself between her and the house.

It was then that she saw the glint of metal and realized with a burst of terror that he was holding a knife.

Chapter Eleven

If she could remember her past life, Lisa thought, it would be flashing before her eyes. Instead, in a few terrifying seconds, she took in every detail of the knife-wielding intruder before her.

He was old and breathing hard, sucking in air as if he'd been running—or as if he was as nervous as she. She caught a scent of wine about him, saw that his skin was leathery and that he was wearing a dirty fatigue jacket and torn baggy pants.

His rheumy eyes sought hers, and she was transfixed by the odd assortment of emotions she saw cross his features, mostly fear and perhaps apology. He held her motionless with his gaze. She knew that only seconds had passed since he'd stepped from the shadows into her line of sight, but it felt like aeons.

By a tremendous effort of will, she managed to squeeze a few words past the painful constriction of her throat. "Please. Don't . . . hurt . . . me."

He shook his head. She didn't know whether he was agreeing with or dismissing the plea.

He licked his cracked lips, glanced furtively toward the house and then back to her. When he spoke, his voice was harsh, grating. "You're one of them."

One of *whom?* What part had this maniac given her in his paranoid delusion? She'd already had enough roles to play, none of them of her own choosing. "Please, leave me alone..."

He took another one of those heavy breaths, his gaze probing hers. "I can't. Got to tell you—" He stopped abruptly.

"Tell me what?"

His expression turned fierce and desperate. Without warning, he lunged forward.

Lisa's reaction was reflexive. Her hand shot out and snatched the paring knife off the watermelon plate. As she brandished it in front of her, the intruder went from bold to cowering in the space of a heartbeat.

"No...not you..." His body shrank into a protective crouch, arms curving above his head. From one second to the next, the balance of power had shifted. Now *he* was the terrified one.

"You frightened me, but I don't want to hurt you," Lisa whispered. "Who are you? What are you doing here?" Then, as a sudden thought occurred to her, she asked, "Do you know me?"

He looked up, his gaze darting around, scanning the area for the enemy, no doubt.

"Please," she said. "If you know something that can help me, tell me. Please."

"Too dangerous. They'll find out."

"Who?"

"The bastards who want to hurt me. Hurt you."

Her throat was so tight she could barely speak. "For Lord's sake. Tell me what you know!"

"I shouldn't have come here." His gaze shifted to the house. "Is he here?"

"Who? Hollingsworth?"

Instead of answering, he jerked around and ran, zigzagging across the lawn, his body low to the ground.

"Please! Wait! Who are you?" Lisa shouted at the receding figure. He didn't turn, didn't answer, he just fled.

She was left standing on the patio alone, wondering if her fevered mind had conjured an apparition. Yet no apparition could leave the smell of cheap wine and unwashed flesh hanging in the air.

"Lord, help me." She didn't realize how loudly she'd spoken until Maggie appeared on the patio, her features contorted with alarm.

"What's wrong, Mrs. Hollingsworth?"

Lisa's hand opened, and the knife clattered to the table-top. She grabbed the edge of her chair to keep from falling over. "A man—"

"Where?"

"He came from the bushes. He went back there." Lisa made a gesture toward the conifers where the intruder had disappeared.

Maggie took several steps forward and peered into the shadows. "I don't see anyone," she said in a doubtful voice.

"He was here. Don't you smell him?"

The housekeeper sucked in a draft of the evening air. "I can't tell."

"He was standing right in front of me! He had a knife."

"You were holding the knife," Maggie muttered.

"For self-defense. He had one, too. It was a lot bigger." Frustration churned inside her. She wanted to press her hands over her ears to block out Maggie's objections. Instead, she took several shaky steps toward the lawn.

"I believe you, Mrs. Hollingsworth."

But Lisa knew the woman was only trying to placate her.

Sinking to her knees, she began to crawl across the two-inch grass where she thought he'd stepped off the patio.

"What in the world are you doing, ma'am?"

Ignoring the disdainful voice behind her, she searched along the ground. For endless moments she found nothing. Then, changing direction, she found a place where the neatly cut grass was mashed flat.

"Over here!" she called.

Maggie hunkered down beside her as she pointed at a double row of indentations in the lawn. They led to the clump of evergreens where the intruder had disappeared.

"There. See?" she breathed triumphantly. "His footprints. He's got big feet. Bigger than mine."

Maggie looked pointedly from the large footprints to Lisa's size-six shoes. "Maybe Frank—"

"It wasn't Frank! He wasn't anywhere around when I came out. And the grass wouldn't stay flattened like that for very long."

Maggie gave a little nod, conceding the point.

"He was an old man—or maybe he only looked old. He was wearing a fatigue jacket and smelled like he hadn't had a bath in months..." Something in Maggie's expression made Lisa trail off, then ask, "Have you seen him around here before?"

The housekeeper's look became guarded. "No."

Lisa was almost certain Maggie was lying. "Call the police," she said.

"I wouldn't do that if I were you."

Lisa's head came up. "Why not? I want to know who was trespassing here and why."

"Mr. Hollingsworth doesn't like the law messing in his business."

Lisa felt a wave of cold sweep across her skin. "Why not?"

Maggie ignored the question. "Frank will have a look around." She'd spoken as if it were the end of the discussion, but Lisa wasn't about to let it go.

"Does Mr. Hollingsworth have something to hide?"

Maggie shrugged. "That isn't any of my business."

Lisa bit back a sharp retort.

Maggie continued, "All I know is that he got mad as a hornet when Frank called the police after some tools disappeared from the shed."

Lisa studied her pinched face. "This could be a little more serious than stolen tools."

"I'll do what you say, but I'm not going to take responsibility." The housekeeper pursed her lips. "Did *you* recognize him?"

Lisa shook her head. She sensed that Maggie could tell her more, but no additional information was forthcoming. Finally, she turned away. She could defy Maggie and call the police, but she knew the action would be reported to the master of the house. She didn't know Kendall Hollingsworth, didn't understand his rules, and she was already dreading meeting him. She didn't want another strike against her when he returned.

Feeling like an animal boxed into a corner, she walked stiffly toward the house. As she passed the tray on the table, she glanced at the discarded plates. A little while ago, she'd been hungry. Now the pasta and salad felt like rocks in her stomach.

Without a word, she stepped inside. Maggie was only a few paces behind her.

"Do you want me to bring the tray up?"

"No."

The curt syllable hung in the air. All she wanted was to close herself in Justine's bedroom and pretend she was in a nice, normal environment—like a plush hotel.

Halfway up the steps, she thought of telling Mike about the intruder. By the time she reached the landing, she'd already changed her mind. What could he do—come running over with a flashlight and shine it on the footprints? They'd be gone before he arrived. She sighed. If she couldn't call the police, there was no point in calling anyone. Time enough to tell Mike when he phoned her—if he phoned her—with the information about her rental car.

She closed and locked the bedroom door, then stared at it. It would never keep the man out if he broke into the house. With her insides shaking, wishing she'd brought the knife upstairs, she dragged the desk chair across the rug and tipped it so that the backrest was under the doorknob. For long moments she stared at the barrier, feeling a mixture of fear and chagrin. Probably the chair wouldn't help keep anyone out, either. But it made her feel a little better. A very little.

Clammy and cold with raw nerves, Lisa headed for the bathroom, thinking that a hot shower might warm her up and soothe her. She sat on the edge of the tub and began to remove her sandals, but, as she looked down, a flash of metal under the edge of the French provincial vanity caught her eye. Kneeling on the tile, she fished out a lipstick, then, bending to look beneath the vanity, she found a small hairbrush, a motel shower cap, a quarter and a nail file—all concealed to anyone who wasn't on hands and knees. They weren't dusty, so they couldn't have been on the floor for long. Still, they seemed totally out of place in this excessively neat house, which was run by an obviously meticulous housekeeper.

"Odd," she mused aloud. Then, addressing the owner of the room, added, "Did you drop your cosmetics case in your rush to disappear off the face of the earth?"

The absent Justine didn't reply.

Lisa stowed the articles in the lower vanity drawer. Then, stripping off her clothes and stuffing them into the hamper, she turned on the shower. Ten minutes under warm water with spicy-smelling soap and peach-scented shampoo made her feel better. Her improved state lasted long enough for her to blow-dry her hair, pull on an oversize T-shirt and underpants and climb into bed. Then her mind drifted back to the events in the garden, and her fragile contentment vanished.

The scruffy man in the fatigue jacket had acted as though he knew her—or at least the Hollingsworths. But *what* did he know?

"Has he been snooping around here before?" she asked the absent Justine. "Is that why Maggie was acting so weird?"

Her mouth twisted in a wry grimace. At the moment, she was the one acting weird. Talking to the woman who lived in this room—which was maybe the same as talking to herself. Either way, she didn't care. It helped to hear the sound of her own voice. She couldn't bear the silence.

Knowing she wasn't going to get to sleep anytime soon, Lisa decided to do some more investigating. Quietly, she got out of bed and went into the sitting room where she began to go through the end table beside the sofa.

Apparently, Justine liked to take home menus from expensive restaurants. A dozen of them were stuffed into one of the drawers. Underneath the pile, Lisa's fingers encountered a leather-bound book. The gold letters on the cover said Addresses. Eagerly, she began to thumb through the pages. Most of the entries were old, many of then crossed out entirely.

When she came to the L's, her breath caught in her throat. Mike Lancer's name was at the top of the second page. And it wasn't a new listing. He'd been in the book long enough for his address and phone number to have changed four times. The first two entries placed him in College Park, Maryland. After that, he'd moved to Fells Point, then St. Paul Street, where, she assumed, he must still live.

Lisa ran her finger down the list of addresses. "So, Justine . . . you've known him for a long time," she said aloud. "Funny, Mike didn't mention it. Does that mean he thinks that I'm you and he's waiting to see if I—I mean, *you*—remember him? Or is he hiding his relationship with you from *me?*" In either case, how big a fool had she been to let herself be so vulnerable to him?

She snapped the pages closed and tapped the book against her palm, contemplating this new piece in the puzzle of Justine's life. She thought about calling Mike to demand an explanation but if and when she brought up the subject, it would be face-to-face.

As she slipped the address book into her purse, she suddenly felt bone-weary, drained of both physical and emotional energy. A quick glance at the clock told her it was one-thirty in the morning. She'd been running on adrenaline for hours. Maybe, just maybe, she was tired enough to forget about the alien surroundings and the man in the garden and go to sleep.

On unsteady legs, she wobbled to the bed. When she turned off the light, she felt a surge of panic at letting herself relax in a stranger's room. But moments after pulling the covers to her chin, she slipped into blessed slumber.

STRANGELY ENOUGH, she knew she was dreaming. She was lying in Justine's bed, but she wasn't alone in the room. Maggie, Estelle, Mike, Kendall Hollingsworth and the intruder from the garden were all gathered there. Only, the disreputable derelict had metamorphosed into someone who looked like Charlie Chaplin playing the "little tramp." She watched them all warily, waiting to find out what would happen. On balance, she was more frightened of Kendall than of the tramp, which seemed awfully strange. After all, Kendall was supposed to be her husband.

Estelle leaned over the bed. "Where are the papers?" she demanded.

She stared at Estelle. "I don't know about any papers."

The secretary snorted. "You're lying."

"Give us the papers," the others chorused as they formed a circle around the bed.

She shook her head helplessly. "I can't."

Estelle regarded her with narrowed eyes, then turned to address the others. "We can't let her get away with this."

She tried to sit up, but Mike moved closer and put a restraining hand on her shoulder. His touch was gentle, yet it held her in place while Maggie, Estelle and the tramp began to search the room. Hollingsworth strode to her side and looked at her appraisingly. When she cringed against the pillows, he grinned. Then he silently turned and joined the searchers. At first, the process was orderly: the foursome opened drawers, sorted through their contents, carefully closed them again. But when they found nothing, the pace quickened. In a frenzy, they began to rush around the room, roughly sweeping everything from shelves and emptying bureaus. She watched as a lipstick, a quarter and an address book rolled under the vanity cabinet in the bathroom and vanished from sight.

"Look what you've done," she shouted.

But nobody paid any attention.

"Help them," Mike whispered. "Help yourself. Give them the papers."

"I can't," she protested, watching in dismay as the crew tore madly through her—or were they someone else's?—belongings. Somewhere in the house, a clock struck, and everyone in the room went still.

"Saints preserve us," Maggie croaked as a towel slithered through her fingers and pooled on the floor.

"You're a fine one to talk!" Kendall shouted, tossing a pair of shoes onto the rug.

The housekeeper glared at him. "Get out of here. All of you get out so I can put this place to rights before the master comes home."

The order didn't make much sense, since the master was one of the people who had made the mess. But like everyone else, he obeyed the command, fading through the wall like a piece of trick photography. For a long time, Maggie stood there, looking disinterested. Then she began to pick up the clothing scattered across the floor.

"Do you want me to help?" Lisa asked.

"No. You go back to sleep," the housekeeper replied.

Obediently, she closed her eyes.

Lisa's eyes snapped open. With an unsteady hand, she fumbled for the light, blinking against the glare as she surveyed the room that had been torn apart. Incredibly, it was as neat as it had been when she'd climbed into bed. The mess was gone, along with the early-morning visitors. She was alone, drawing in shaky breaths as she huddled under the covers.

Chapter Twelve

Lisa struggled to bring the dream into focus, hoping that somewhere amidst the disjointed rantings of her subconscious a clue to her real self might lie hidden. Eyes closed, she tried to fix each detail in her mind. The tramp. Mike. Kendall Hollingsworth. Maggie. Estelle. A hash of fantasy and reality.

Sitting up, she craned her head toward the bathroom. In the dream, she'd been able to see the vanity, but actually, it was hidden from view around the corner, which could be why the things that had rolled underneath had escaped Maggie's housekeeping efforts.

Of course, it was ridiculous to think the items had gotten there during a search. She had no reason to believe that the room had been ransacked as it had been in her dream, no reason at all even to entertain that notion—except Estelle *had* come asking about a folder of missing documents and she had brought clothes for Justine to the hospital—clothes undoubtedly taken from this room....

Once the thought entered Lisa's head, it was impossible for her not to wonder if, indeed, someone had carelessly destroyed the room looking for the same papers Estelle so badly wanted. She could easily see Maggie putting everything back in order—everything she could find—so that "the master" wouldn't know she'd allowed an intruder to get into the house. Or perhaps it had been Maggie herself who had done the searching.

Frighteningly, incredibly, it was starting to make sense. Unable to stop what her mind had begun, Lisa took the speculation a step further. Having to clean up an unexpected mess could explain why Maggie had been so nervous about showing her around that afternoon. She could have been waiting for her—*expecting* her—to notice that some things were out of order. Unfortunately, Maggie's behavior was only conjecture. For that matter, so was any speculation about someone's going through the house. But the papers were real. At least Estelle thought so. And both Estelle and Kendall Hollingsworth wanted them.

Lisa's pulse pounded as she considered the possibilities. If Justine had stolen valuable documents and stashed them in her bedroom, they might well have been found already, not by Estelle, but by one of the other players. But what if Justine had been smart enough to pick a better hiding place?

After a quick glance at the clock, Lisa climbed quietly out of bed. It was four in the morning. She could probably do a lot of snooping before Maggie or Frank got up. If they caught her walking around, she'd say she couldn't sleep and was using the time to get reacquainted with her surroundings.

Pulling on a robe from the closet, she tiptoed over to the closed door that connected her room to the other master suite. It seemed to her that Justine's most secure hiding places would be in Kendall's room. Or his office.

With a shudder, she turned the knob. She'd deliberately stayed out of his bedroom on her tour of the house because she didn't want to get that close to him—even in spirit. The very idea of being vulnerable to Kendall Hollingsworth made her queasy. But he wasn't here, she reminded herself as she opened the door.

For a minute, she stood quietly, breathing in the faint smell of cigar smoke. Then she turned on the small lamp on the bureau. In the warm glow everything was solidly masculine, with heavy walnut furniture and a plaid pattern repeated on the rug and wallpaper. In the center of the wall facing her was a king-size bed. She'd wanted to believe that

Hollingsworth and his wife kept separate rooms because they didn't have a sexual relationship, but the covetous look in his eyes in the photographs she remembered told her otherwise. More likely, he enjoyed the luxury of maintaining two ostentatious master suites.

Lisa stood looking at the wide bed, feeling her stomach tie itself into knots. Presumably, Hollingsworth had been celibate on his hunting trip. When he came back, would he be eager to exercise his marital rights? Would he want his wife even if she didn't remember who he was?

Her reaction to the sight of his bed was the same as it had been to his pictures. Her skin grew icy, and she rubbed her hands over her arms, moving the sleeves of the robe up and down. If he were a gentleman, he'd leave her alone. But nothing she'd learned about Hollingsworth made her think she could count on that. He'd stolen another man's sweetheart. He didn't want the police on his property, probably because he was engaged in something illegal. And he didn't trust his wife.

Would he be surprised to find her at home instead of in a car at the bottom of the Jones Falls?

She pictured him grabbing her, slamming her down on the bed, taking out the latent anger and frustration she'd detected in the pictures on the closest available target. The images were so vivid that a sick tide rose in her throat. For a moment, she imagined it already had happened. She tried to catch her breath, feeling as if she were being swept through a long, swirling, terror-filled tunnel.

Light-headed and unprepared for the strength of her reactions, she grabbed the door frame. She had to get out of here. Had to get away.

Backing out of the room, she closed the door, leaning against the wall as she struggled to bring her breathing back to normal. It was several minutes before she felt well enough to remove the chair propped against her door and step into the hall. For long moments she stood listening. Finally, on silent feet, she tiptoed down the stairs.

By the time she reached Hollingsworth's office, the inexplicable terror had receded, though her heart was still beating much faster than normal and her hands shook slightly as she turned the doorknob. After closing the door behind her, she flipped on the desk light. Beside it was the computer.

Maybe she could save herself some time, she thought, by poking through the files.

Sitting down in the desk chair, she booted the machine. Then, as she'd wanted to do earlier, she accessed the financial program. But the results were disappointing. The data had been erased from every file. At least it appeared to have been erased.

"Or maybe you don't know as much about computers as you think you do," she muttered to herself.

Frustrated, she glanced around the room. Back to plan one—searching for papers.

Experimentally, she pried at the edges of the carpet, but they were firmly attached. Turning over the chairs, she checked to see if anything was taped to the bottoms. No luck. Nor was anything fixed to the bottoms of the desk drawers. She even checked some of the file drawers, although she was sure Justine wouldn't be *that* bold. After a half hour's careful search, she was still empty-handed—and she was running out of both time and places to look.

The office was designed for practicality, with touches of elegance like the expensive pen and pencil set on the desk, the Casablanca ceiling fan and the wood panels on the front of the filing cabinets. Matching wood shelving marched up the walls on either side of the windows. On the lower levels were books on engineering and business management. Above them were leather-bound sets like the complete works of William Shakespeare, Charles Dickens and Theodore Dreiser, of all people. They looked out of place among the well-used engineering volumes.

Was Kendall's taste in literature really so elevated? Suddenly it occurred to her that, if he never read the books, they'd make the perfect hiding place. Pushing a chair toward the wall, she climbed onto the seat and pulled down *David Copperfield*. When she opened it at random, the spine of the book was stiff, and she suspected it had never been read. Encouraged, she began removing each of the volumes in turn. Ten minutes into the search, she began to wonder if this was another dead end. Then she extracted *The Merchant of Venice* and saw a manila envelope sticking out from behind the next volume.

With a giddy feeling of triumph, Lisa replaced the books and brought the envelope to the desk. She was about to read the contents, when a sound in the hall made her go rigid.

The doorknob turned.

"Who's in there?" a raspy voice called.

She almost shoved the envelope into the first hiding place that came to hand—the desk drawer—but then realized she might never get it back. For a frightening moment, she didn't know what to do. Then, quickly, she tucked the evidence under her robe and held it in place with an arm pressed against her chest.

Before she had time to look up, the door swung inward, and she was staring down the muzzle of a shotgun.

"On your feet!"

"Don't shoot," she quavered, scrambling up.

"You," Frank, the handyman, growled. Then he called over his shoulder. "It's her."

His face angry, he addressed her again. "What the hell are *you* doin' sneakin' around like this?" At least he lowered the gun barrel.

"I'm not sneaking. Put that thing away. You could hurt somebody," Lisa countered.

"You gave me and Maggie a start. We thought—"

"—someone had broken in," Maggie chimed in as she stepped through the doorway.

"Like they did before?" Lisa questioned.

"How do you know—" Maggie stopped abruptly.

Lisa tried to mask her look of victory, but it was gratifying to have her theory confirmed. "Suppose you tell me who was snooping around before I came home from the hospital.''

Maggie looked frightened. ''I don't know. They didn't touch Mr. Hollingsworth's office. Mostly it was your room and the kitchen.''

''The guy in the fatigues who came at me with a knife?''

Maggie shrugged. ''It could have been him.''

''What does he have against the Hollingsworths?''

''I wish I knew.''

''Then you've seen him around here before?''

Maggie blanched. ''I'm not sure.''

''Yes or no.''

''I may have seen him.''

Lisa pressed her advantage. ''What happened the night the house was broken into?''

''We didn't see. Somebody called and said they were from the hospital, that you wanted some things brought down right away. When Frank and I got home, we found a blooming mess.''

''Who called? A man or a woman?''

''A man,'' Maggie muttered.

''Thank you for informing me,'' Lisa said.

''Are you going to tell Mr. Hollingsworth?''

''I don't know.'' She was pretty sure she wouldn't. But it wouldn't hurt to hold the threat over the housekeeper. ''Does Mr. Hollingsworth have any enemies?''

''I—I wouldn't know.''

The faltering answer made Lisa press harder. ''If you don't want him to hear about the break-in, tell me what you know!''

Maggie paled.

''Did he talk to you about someone?'' Lisa tried.

''No. But one night he had an argument with Mr. Realto.'' The housekeeper looked as if she wished she'd kept her mouth shut.

''The man who sent the flowers, Mr. Hollingworth's business partner?''

''Yes.''

"What were they arguing about?"

"I don't know."

"Business?"

Maggie shrugged.

Lisa stared at the woman's downcast eyes, suspecting she had gotten all she was going to get. Pulling her robe tighter, she pressed the envelope more firmly to her body, and exited the room. She heard Maggie and Frank turn but didn't spare a backward look. Walking with studied care, she made quickly for the stairs, but her heart was pounding so hard that she felt dizzy.

Once inside her room, she stood with her back braced against the door, picturing Frank and Maggie coming after her with the gun. She had to remind herself that they hadn't really been after *her.* They'd thought someone had broken in. Again. Maggie said it was a man who'd called to draw her and Frank out of the house, so the culprit couldn't have been Estelle. What about one of the men who had forced her off the road, or the business partner—Realto—with whom Hollingsworth had argued? She'd pressed Maggie pretty hard. Probably she'd made an enemy.

With a decisive click, she locked her bedroom door, then carried the envelope to the bed, where she fluffed up the pillows and made herself comfortable. Yet her hands still weren't quite steady as she began to inspect her booty, which turned out to be photocopies of engineering specifications and construction plans for a project from the K. H. Group. That must be Hollingsworth's company.

"You understand these?" Lisa asked Justine as she began to examine order forms for steel beams and other materials. Why had Justine taken this stuff, anyway?

She was flipping back and forth between the spec sheet and the schematic, when her hand went very still. She didn't know about Justine, but she was having no problem reading the highly technical information. Wasn't that a bit unusual?

Unfortunately, an answer popped into her head. If Justine had worked in her husband's business, she could have acquired considerable technical knowledge. Suppose she'd found the proof she hadn't wanted to find—that she really was the woman who lived in this house.

With a grimace, she tried to convince herself that she'd drawn the wrong conclusion. From the remarks Mike had made, she gathered Justine hadn't worked after her marriage. Yet she could no longer rely on the truth of anything Mike had said. Not until she found out what his name was doing in that address book, with four changes of addresses.

Her lips pressed into a firm line, she went back to examining the papers. After a few minutes, her vision blurred, and she realized her brain wasn't in any shape to cope with so much detail.

Well, now she had a legitimate reason to contact Mike, she decided, not bothering to square the conclusion with her previous assessment of his honesty. She would show him the papers and ask what he thought. Then, perhaps, she could introduce the topic of the address book.

How long had he known Justine, and what exactly was their relationship? Silently, she admitted that she wanted answers to those questions as much as to any of the others tormenting her. She knew her feelings were confused, that reason and emotion were playing a tug-of-war inside her. She didn't have the right to quiz Mike about his past—if it had no bearing on her present problems.

How could she expect honesty from Mike when she wasn't being honest with him? she asked herself abruptly. She was hiding something from him, all right. She was keeping her pregnancy a secret, and she didn't like being the kind of person who lied even by omission.

Oh, she could come up with excuses. She was frightened and alone and attracted to the man who had saved her life. Perhaps her amnesia or her head injury was affecting her judgment. But really, she could think of no reason that pardoned her behavior. The next time she saw him, she was going to share her secret.

LISA AWOKE with a start to find herself sitting in bed with the light on. Her arms were folded tightly across her chest, and she remembered she'd been clutching the envelope of construction specifications.

But the envelope was gone.

With a gasp, she sat up straighter. A shaft of sunlight knifed though a crack in the curtains, and a glance at the clock told her that it was almost one in the afternoon.

Frantically, she searched the top of the bed, hoping to find that the papers were under the covers. When she couldn't locate them, she climbed out of bed and hunted across the rug. But the envelope had vanished.

Maybe it had never existed. Had she dreamed she'd found it, as she'd dreamed about the people rummaging through her room?

No, she vividly remembered Frank stepping into Kendall's office with the shotgun leveled at her.

She glanced toward the door. She'd locked it last night. But Maggie certainly would have a key.

Damn. She should have hidden the envelope. Now it was too late.

Still angry with herself, she began to get dressed. Brushing her teeth, she remembered there was something else she had planned to do that day. She pulled out the address book, and called the dentist's office. In a voice that quavered, she said she was Justine Hollingsworth and asked to come in and see her records.

The receptionist's answer was a crushing anticlimax. "I'm sorry, Mrs. Hollingsworth," the woman apologized. "Dr. Bishop is out of the office this morning, and you'll need his authorization. Can you call back after three?"

"Yes," Lisa replied before hanging up. She'd been so sure she'd have the answer to her identity this morning. The hours before three o'clock stretched ahead like an eternity.

With a sigh, she descended the stairs, relieved when she stepped into the kitchen to find it empty. Yet as she fixed herself breakfast, she kept thinking how quiet the house was. If Frank and Maggie weren't here, anyone could have come in while she was sleeping. And surely bedroom locks were easy to pick.

Insecurity made her find a tray and carry her juice and cereal upstairs to the bedroom. As she ate, she thumbed through the address book, wondering what kind of response she'd get if she phoned some of the women listed. Nobody had called to chat since she'd gotten home. Perhaps these were women who worked with Justine on volunteer committees, not close friends.

When Lisa was finished eating, she eyed the phone again. Despite her decision of the night before, she was nervous about calling Mike. And when she finally mustered the courage to dial his number, her bad luck held; she got the answering machine. Not wanting to say too much over the phone, she left a brief message. Then she carried her breakfast tray down to the kitchen.

Grocery bags that hadn't been there a half hour ago sat on the kitchen counters and on the floor in front of the refrigerator. A noise in the back hall made her glance up quickly to see Frank striding through the doorway with two more bags in his arms. Maggie followed a few seconds later with two satchels labeled Graul's, which she carefully set beside the sink.

Lisa gave them both a long look. Maggie brushed past her to open the freezer.

"Are we having a dinner party?" Lisa asked as she looked at the mountain of supplies. *Did you take some papers from my room?* The question screamed in her mind, but she didn't ask.

"Not likely. Mr. Hollingsworth is coming home today," Maggie tossed over her shoulder.

Lisa felt the bottom drop out of her stomach. "Today?"

"That's right. I keep forgetting, you don't remember," the woman answered sarcastically. Apparently, the nighttime encounter in the office had been a declaration of war.

"What time?"

"Before dinner."

Lisa nodded and backed out of the room. Lord, she'd been hoping she had a few more days before she had to face her so-called husband.

A cold sweat beaded on her skin as she stepped into the hall and heard the sound of a car in the driveway. She expected to see Hollingsworth emerge from a Jaguar or some other equally luxurious car. To her vast relief, the vehicle was Mike's old Mustang. Climbing out, he trotted toward the house.

Before Maggie had a chance to interrupt them, Lisa sped across the marble floor and pulled open the door. Mike's hand was hovering at the bell. When he saw her, he went very still.

She was so glad to see him, it took a great deal of effort to keep from throwing herself into his arms. The look in his eyes made her think he might be fighting the same impulse. Or perhaps she was reading too much into the tension etched on his face.

"Come in." She took a step back.

He followed her into the hall at the same moment that Maggie appeared around the corner. She looked inquiringly in Lisa's direction.

"You can finish unpacking the groceries," she said stiffly.

"Very good, ma'am," the housekeeper replied like a bit player in a drawing-room comedy.

When she'd disappeared, Lisa whispered, "She's been keeping tabs on me."

Mike nodded and ushered Lisa into Hollingsworth's office. She would have preferred some other room, but this was probably the most private place. Unless she took him upstairs, and she could just picture Maggie gleefully reporting to Hollingsworth that "your wife entertained a male friend in her bedroom." If she was last night's thief, she could cap her success by handing him the papers his wife had stolen.

"You don't trust her?" Mike asked in a low voice after he'd shut the door.

"I don't trust anybody."

"Good, because...I'm sorry, there's no other way around this...I have a piece of information you're going to find disturbing."

Lisa tensed, waiting for the bad news. Mike took her gently by the shoulders, pitching his voice low as he spoke. "Yesterday I asked a friend of mine who's a mechanic to check out the car you were driving. There was a hole in the power-steering line. It could have gotten punctured by accident—maybe even when you plowed into the river. Or it could have been put there deliberately."

Chapter Thirteen

Lisa shivered. "You're saying somebody tampered with my car? They wanted me to have an accident?"

"I can't be sure."

"But you think so."

"I'd rather err on the side of caution. If somebody went after your car, and you escaped, they might want to get a little more personal now that you're back home."

All at once, her encounter last night in the garden leaped into her mind. "Somebody was here," she said quietly. "Yesterday evening, while I was eating dinner."

His eyes were instantly alert. "Are you okay?"

"Yes. It was an old man with a knife."

Mike's hands swept up and down her arms as if to assure himself that she was unharmed.

"He didn't hurt me. He ran away when I picked up a paring knife from the table."

"Good."

"Maybe not. He said, 'You're one of them,'—or something like that. I think he believes he knows me. Or Justine. He could be somebody with information about her. Or he could know who I really am," Lisa added.

Mike frowned. "Was he wearing a fatigue jacket?"

Her eyes widened. "You know him?"

"I saw him in the parking garage the day of your accident. He could have been in the garage waiting for you."

"Or for Justine," Lisa reminded him.

Mike made an impatient gesture. "Whatever. The point is, he could be the one who tampered with your car."

"Or the person who broke into the house while I was in the hospital."

Mike looked startled. "How do you know somebody broke in?"

"I tricked Maggie into admitting it last night. I got another lead out of her, too. Hollingsworth had a fight with his business partner. Someone named Realto."

Mike pulled out a notebook and wrote down the name.

"Can you find him?" she asked. "Or the vagrant? I'm almost sure Maggie's seen him around here before."

"I'll try to find the old guy, but he could be anywhere in the city. If he doesn't want to be found, it might be pretty difficult. Did you call the police?"

"Maggie discouraged me."

Mike snapped the notebook closed. "Oh, yeah?"

"She said, 'Mr. Hollingsworth doesn't like the law messing in his business.'"

"Great."

"Something else. Last night I found some papers Justine apparently stole and hid from her husband. Now they're missing."

"Where did you find them?"

"In an envelope behind those books." She pointed to a line of Shakespeare's plays near the top shelves.

He raised an eyebrow. "Kind of a lucky guess on your part."

"Yesterday after you left, Estelle—Hollingsworth's secretary—demanded the papers."

Mike's eyes narrowed. "How did she know about them?"

Lisa shrugged. "I haven't figured that out yet. But I, uh, realized it would be stupid for Justine to hide them in her room—or anywhere obvious. So I started thinking about where Hollingsworth wouldn't look. That's how I happened to search behind the books he probably never reads."

"Now the evidence is missing?"

"Yes. I took the envelope to my room. But I was exhausted and fell asleep. When I woke up, it was gone."

Mike swore and looked toward the closed door. "You think the housekeeper took them?"

"When I finally woke up, it was almost one o'clock, and she and Frank were out getting groceries. I guess anyone, from the men who were following me the other day, to the guy in the fatigue jacket, could have come into the house."

He snorted. "You must sleep pretty soundly."

Defensively, she replied, "I've hardly slept at all since I woke up in the hospital—except when Habib drugged me."

He conceded the point with a sigh. "What was in the envelope?"

"Engineering specifications for a construction project."

"You're sure?"

"Yes. I could tell that much at least. They must be important, or why would Justine have hidden them?" She looked down at her hands. "I feel like a fool for letting them slip through my fingers. Or maybe you think I'm making them up."

He didn't say anything for several moments, and she suddenly wanted to get out of the room.

She took a step toward the door, but he blocked her path. "Don't leave."

"Why?"

"I don't think you're making them up."

"That's something, anyway."

She saw his throat move as he swallowed hard. It was only a small gesture, but it broke loose more words locked inside her.

"Mike, I don't want to stay in this house!"

"You live here."

"Do you really believe that?" she demanded.

He looked perplexed, a man being forced to challenge basic assumptions. Several heartbeats later, he answered. "I don't know. If you're not Justine, that makes things a hell of a lot easier for me. I haven't felt like I was on very strong moral footing lately."

She kept her gaze steady. "What do you mean?"

"I'm not in the habit of making love to other men's wives."

MIKE WATCHED Lisa's reaction to his words closely—saw her surprise, saw her blush.

"Lisa," he began, then saw her expression change again at his use of her chosen name. Her relief was almost tangible.

When he'd driven her "home" yesterday, he'd wondered if he really was doing the right thing, but he'd tried to ignore the nagging doubts. Now the defenseless look in her eyes melted through another layer of his resolve. Honesty forced him to admit that nothing about Lisa reminded him of Justine—except her physical appearance. Everything under the surface was different, so different that it made complete sense to him that she was someone else who had gotten snared somehow in the middle of Justine's problems.

"I've been doing a lot of thinking," he admitted. "There are things we ought to get into the open. Things I haven't exactly handled...honestly."

"Like your name in Justine's address book?" she questioned softly.

Mike felt his cheeks grow hot. "You found that, too?"

"Since you left yesterday, I haven't had much to do besides search this place—or sit around asking myself questions."

They stared at each other across three feet of space, and he saw his own feelings of relief, as well as his wariness, reflected in her gaze. He waited, barely breathing, wondering if the gap between them would widen or close. When he couldn't stand the separation for another heartbeat, he took a step closer. She moved toward him at the same time. Then his arms were around her, and she let out a deep, shuddering sigh.

"Mike."

His embrace tightened. It felt completely natural to hold her in his arms, and he wished things could be this simple, this uncomplicated. A man and a woman who needed each other, who belonged together, despite all the evidence to the contrary. She moved her cheek against his jaw, and he worried fleetingly that his beard would scratch her tender skin. Like putting his brand on her, he thought, conceding that there were other ways in which he wanted to claim her as his own, wanted it more than he'd like to admit.

"I'm so confused," she breathed.

"So am I."

"You? You're not the one in trouble."

"Trouble is relative."

"I don't have a past. I'm frightened of the future. I shouldn't be dragging you into my problems."

"You're not dragging me."

She relaxed against him, and he knew she'd needed his reassurance.

"I can't help myself. This feels right. It feels good," she added as she ran her hands over the strong muscles of his shoulders.

"Oh, God. I want you to understand what I've been going through," he grated. "I don't have any rights in this situation. You're supposed to belong to someone else. And I've been fighting that. And fighting my basic instincts. Do you understand?"

"Yes." She clasped him tighter. "Too well. You don't know how much I wish I could give you some kind of proof that I'm not Mrs. Anybody."

He knew she felt the ripples of reaction he couldn't hide. She tipped her face upward and their eyes locked. Then his lips brushed hers. A very light touch, yet the contact set a shiver across her skin.

"I might not remember my past," she murmured, "but I'm sure no man ever...ever affected me this way. When I'm with you like this, I can't think about anything but getting closer." The last part came out on a little sob.

His hands moved up and down her back, pressing her closer, molding her body to his. "When I found out about the car, I had to come over and make sure you were all right," he told her. "No. That's not exactly true. I was looking for an excuse to come back."

"Oh, Mike."

His mouth came down on hers, taking what he'd been wanting for an eternity. She kissed him with the same intensity and he knew that any confessions he might make were less important than the need simmering between them. Carnal need. And something more—the need to mate, to bond. They'd aroused each other to fever pitch the day before. In seconds, they were back at the same level of hunger. She made little noises deep in her throat as she moved against him.

His hands slid to her hips, pressing her tightly to his erection.

"Not here," she whispered.

"Where?"

She drew in a shaky breath and looked wildly around, like a sleepwalker who suddenly wakes and realizes where she is and what she's been doing.

"Mike, we can't. I mean, I promised myself I'd tell you…things. But not here. Take me away from this house. Please. Before it's too late."

But it was already too late. Outside, tires screeched as a Mercedes pulled up behind Mike's car in the driveway. They both turned guiltily toward the window as the car door shot open and a man bolted out.

"Oh, Lord, it's Kendall Hollingsworth," Lisa gasped.

"You know him?" Mike asked sharply.

"I recognized him from the pictures in Justine's photo album."

Hollingsworth was wearing a knit shirt and jeans. His graying hair was a beat too long. And his lined face was tanned. For a moment, he peered at the Mustang that was probably occupying his favorite parking place. Then he looked toward the house. Through the windowpanes, Mike

saw the other man's gaze scanning Lisa and himself standing with their arms around each other, and he saw Hollingsworth's face cloud with anger. The irate man strode
toward the front door, and a couple of seconds later, it
slammed open. Hollingsworth blew into the office with
hurricane force.

He gave Lisa a scathing look before rounding on Mike.

"What the hell are you doing here with my wife?" he demanded.

"I'm working for her," Mike answered coolly.

"Working? Is that what they call screwing these days?"

Mike's hands balled into fists, but he kept himself from
slugging the offended husband. "You've got the wrong
idea," he growled. "Mrs. Hollingsworth—"

"—has had the hots for you since you tutored her for that
college biology lab," Kendall interrupted. "I knew you'd
eventually show up in her life again. She has a nasty habit
of getting what she wants."

Mike saw Lisa's mouth drop open, then her eyes riveted
to his face, which he was certain had guilt plastered all over
it.

"Y-you said," she stammered. "That . . . that story you
told me in the hospital . . . about Justine being engaged to a
guy in college." Her eyes were very round. "That was you."

"Unfortunately, yes," he admitted.

"You should have told me. I would have—"

"You would have what? Put me through the wringer all
over again?"

"No," she denied. "I would have understood why you've
been sending me such mixed signals. I can't remember the
past, but *you* can. You weren't playing fair."

"Are *you?*" he shot back. "Wasn't there something important you wanted to get off your chest?"

Hollingsworth was listening, too, but Mike focused on
Lisa. Her face drained of color, and he took that as evidence of guilt. What had she wanted to tell him? That this
whole amnesia thing was a performance she'd made up to
protect herself? He should have kept Justine's penchant for

deception in mind before he'd gotten swept away by wide-eyed, innocent Lisa.

He didn't want to be confused. Or uncertain. If anybody knew who this woman was, it should be Kendall Hollingsworth.

Her gaze was fixed on Mike. He wasn't sure what would have happened if he'd been alone with her at that moment. He was prepared to tell her anything she wanted to know in exchange for her confession, whatever it was. Then he'd get the hell out of this mess—for good. But the initiative was no longer in his hands. Hollingsworth had apparently heard enough.

"Were you with her last night?" he grated.

"Of course not," Mike retorted, angry that he was being accused of something he hadn't done. Lucky the husband hadn't arrived fifteen minutes later.

"Get out of here," Hollingsworth ordered. "And stay away from my wife."

"I'm not—" Lisa began.

Hollingsworth's deadly glare made her close her mouth. "You and I have unfinished business. But I'm not going to talk to you in front of an audience."

Her gaze shot from Hollingsworth to him, clearly pleading with him not to leave her here. The terror in her eyes nearly made Mike forget the excellent advice he'd given himself moments before. For a blinding instant he almost grabbed her by the hand and pulled her out of the room, out of the house, away from the angry man who looked as if he wished he were holding a shotgun. But the impulse died as quickly as it had been born. He himself was the one who had no rights in this situation.

"I'm sorry," he said. Sorry that they'd gotten caught. Sorry that he'd let himself get emotionally involved up to his eyeballs.

She didn't answer, but he could feel her gaze on him as he left the room. His anger with himself didn't allow him to look back. Nor did he glance through the window as he climbed into his car and jerked it into gear.

Yet nothing could erase the terrible look in her eyes that was part fear, part accusation. Ruthlessly, he tried to push the image aside. Justine Hollingsworth could take care of herself. She would always come out on top. But he couldn't quite make himself believe it.

STARING AT Mike's retreating back, Lisa struggled to make her brain absorb what she'd just learned. But the information was still too new. Too raw. Too overwhelming. All along, she'd sensed that there was some hidden undercurrent in her relationship with Mike. Something he didn't want her to find out about Justine. Well, he'd just dropped it on her like a case of explosives and left her to cope with the aftermath.

She had no time to cope with anything, though, before Hollingsworth's voice knifed through the thickened atmosphere of the room.

"So," he said tightly.

The syllable hung between them like an indictment. Staring at the closed door, feelings of abandonment and desolation washing over her, Lisa couldn't reply.

When the silence stretched on, he barked, "Turn around and look at me!"

For a split second, she pictured herself dashing toward the door. The notion was immediately followed by the image of Hollingsworth's grabbing her shoulders and hauling her back. She could almost feel his hands on her, and it made her cringe. She'd gotten the shakes simply from contemplating a confrontation with this man. And here he was, large and intimidating. Worse, in his mind he had good reason to be angry.

"Dammit! Answer me!" he shouted.

Forcing composure into her features, she turned to face him, though she wasn't able to meet his gaze for more than a couple of seconds at a time.

He snorted in disgust. "I leave for a little vacation and come home to find my wife in the arms of her old lover. Now, you tell me—what have you got to say for yourself?"

Fighting to control the shaking of her voice, she replied, "A lot of things have happened this week."

"Oh, yes. An accident. And amnesia. And your ridiculous insistence on being called by another name. I don't know what your game is, Justine, but it won't work on me. Your doctor might have been willing to play along. I'm not."

No, she thought, he definitely wasn't the kind of man who'd play games of someone else's choosing. Nor could she envision him indulging his wife, no matter now injured she may have been.

"You talked to the hospital before you came here?" she asked.

He nodded. "And Estelle."

Lisa drew a ragged breath. "And you're convinced they're right and I'm lying."

His eyes raked her face, her body. "I don't need anybody else to convince me. I've lived with you for eight years, and I damn well know who you are." With a sneer, he added, "Butchering your hair and letting yourself get fat is hardly what I'd call a creative disguise. But then, you never did have much of an imagination, did you?"

Neither did he. At least, not enough of one to see her as anyone but the woman he'd expected to find. And it was eminently clear that he didn't like that woman. The edge of violence in his voice made Lisa's insides quake and her legs feel like water. Still, she tried with increasing futility to keep the fear out of her voice.

"It was a mistake to come here," she said. "I'm sorry your wife is missing. But I'm not her."

He uttered a harsh laugh. "Is that supposed to be an excuse for you to climb into bed with Mike Lancer?"

She lifted one shoulder in a tiny shrug. "What's the point in denying anything? You won't believe me."

"You've got that right. Not after the hot little scene I caught through the window. The two of you looked like you were about to rip each other's clothes off."

She blushed. He was too close to the truth for comfort.

"I told you, if I ever found you with him again, you'd be sorry."

She couldn't disavow the embrace, but she wasn't going to admit to the marriage. "Justine hired Mike before she disappeared."

"To do what—give her a jolt in the afternoons?"

Was that part of it? Lisa couldn't help wondering. She now knew with certainty—and with a vague, undoubtedly irrational feeling of betrayal—that Justine and Mike had been lovers in the past. More than that, Mike had loved her. He had made plans to marry her when he graduated from college. Justine had hurt Mike badly by dumping him for Kendall Hollingsworth, which went a long way toward explaining Mike's wariness. He was afraid to let himself trust Justine again. And Lisa could hardly blame him.

"She hired him to do some investigating," she said.

Hollingsworth scowled a warning. "Stop talking about yourself in the third person. It's getting on my nerves."

"But I'm not—" The protest died under his angry glare. Biting her lower lip to keep it from trembling, she looked away.

"So," he continued, "when did you get together with him again?"

Anger warred with fear as she replied, "He fished me out of a river. Or didn't the doctor tell you how I ended up in the hospital?"

"I heard the story."

"It's no story. Two men forced my car off the road. My *rental.*"

"Why were you driving a rented car?"

"I don't know.... Do you?"

"What's that supposed to mean?"

"What do you know about the accident?"

The dangerous glint in his eyes told Lisa that she may have gone too far. His voice, when he spoke, was frighteningly quiet.

"My dear, I think you may possibly have lost your mind."

Lisa wasn't sure what he would have said or done next if the phone hadn't rung. Her gaze shot to the desk before she realized that the sound was coming from a cellular phone that Hollingsworth pulled out of his pocket.

He flicked it open and pulled up the antenna. "Yes?"

Someone on the other end of the line started to speak, and Hollingsworth turned his back. As the conversation continued, he stepped into the hall and shut the door. A few moments later, she saw him through the window, standing in the driveway, rocking back and forth slightly on his heels. The person on the other end seemed to be doing most of the talking. Then he rang off and strode rapidly back into the house.

"I have to go out," he announced.

"Don't let me keep you."

"I won't. But don't get any stupid ideas about splitting. You'd better be here when I come back," he added, making his meaning perfectly clear, "because I want some answers."

"You haven't been listening. I've given you all the answers I can."

"I don't think so."

"I don't have any reason to stay in your house."

"And *I* don't have time for an argument. I have to leave, but I'm not going to let you take advantage of me again. If you run away, I'll find you."

She swallowed, somehow knowing he would.

His expression changed, and he gave her a malicious grin. "And if by some remote chance I can't find *you*, I'll go after Lancer. I'll make sure your boyfriend is very sorry he tried to pick up where the two of you left off."

Chapter Fourteen

The implied threat hung in the air.

"Do you understand?" Hollingsworth asked, his voice stabbing at her.

Woodenly, Lisa nodded. She'd come here to find out if she was Justine, believing she could leave anytime she wanted. In her wildest dreams, she hadn't imagined that her actions could put Mike in danger.

What in God's name was she going to do? Could she risk calling Mike to ask his advice? Would he even take her call?

"And don't you dare call your lover!" Hollingsworth added, chilling her with what seemed an uncanny ability to read her mind. It chilled her further when he added, in that steely tone, "Because, I promise you, I'll know."

She didn't doubt him. Didn't dare. Nor did she doubt that he had both the power and will to carry out his threats. His face was a twisted mask of venomous fury, and she knew she'd been right to fear this man. She couldn't begin to envision what living with him would be like.

"Got that?"

"Yes," she managed to say.

He stared at her for a full thirty seconds, his expression now reflecting obvious pleasure at his victory. Then he walked out of the room.

"Ms. Dempsey," he bellowed from the front hall.

"Yes, sir," Maggie replied almost instantly.

"I expect Mrs. Hollingsworth to be here when I get back. I'll hold you and Frank responsible if she isn't."

"Yes, sir."

The front door slammed behind him, and Lisa felt the sound reverberate through her. She was cold to the bone, shaking like a leaf and giddy. If she didn't sit down soon, she was going to fall down.

The moment she saw Hollingsworth's car pull from the house, she left the office. She kept her eyes straight ahead as she made for the stairs and willed her legs to carry her up the carpeted flight. She walked directly to her room, but as soon as she closed the door behind her, she felt her knees buckle and had to grab the back of a chair.

Her gaze flew to the phone. She could disobey orders and leave a message at Mike's office. But what if all calls from the house were being monitored? Her actions could get Mike killed.

Sinking onto the couch in the sitting room, she cradled her head in her hands. A hysterical little laugh bubbled out of her when she realized she wasn't going to get over to the dentist's office, after all. Hollingsworth had said he thought she was losing her mind. He was too close to the truth. How could anyone hope to stay sane with shock piling upon shock? The revelation about Mike and Justine would have been the final straw. Except that there was so much more.

She concentrated on breathing deeply until the hysteria passed. The only thing she knew for sure was that she couldn't stay in this house. She'd felt trapped from the moment she'd stepped across the threshold. She should have left while she could. Now she'd have to wait and try to sneak out in the middle of the night.

But where could she go with no money and no identity?

Well, at least she could solve one of those problems.

Rising from the couch, Lisa crossed to the bureau and began to rummage in one of the drawers. She'd discovered that Justine kept stashes of cash on hand, which had remained despite the break-in. When she'd found the money, she had decided she wasn't going to touch it, but present circumstances forced her to rethink that decision.

In a box of designer panty hose, Lisa located one hundred forty dollars, all in twenties. She stuffed the cash into the pocket of her slacks. Then, from the bottom drawer of a jewelry box, she withdrew ten one-hundred dollar bills and tucked them into a purse taken from the walk-in closet. Eleven hundred and forty dollars ought to take her somewhere—anywhere—out of Kendail Hollingsworth's reach.

How long would he be gone? she wondered. And would he be in any better mood when he came back? Either way, Lisa figured it wouldn't be good news for the woman he thought was his wife.

THE LUXURY CABIN CRUISER was moored at one of the docks on the far side of Baltimore's harbor. Estelle had always thought of it as a nice little retreat, a place to which she and Kendall could slip away for a few hours together. It was off the beaten path, yet close enough to downtown that they could pop over for a long lunch.

Today, when he'd called and asked her to meet him, she'd suspected it wasn't for a lovers' tryst. After hanging up, she'd thought about going home, packing a bag and taking a very long vacation. But she'd never been good at saving for a rainy day. Without the cash she'd been promised, she wouldn't get very far. So she'd simply have to tough things out for the next few hours, and hope plan B clicked into action.

With hands that trembled, she set two glasses on the galley counter, a whiskey glass for Kendall and a tumbler for herself. He always drank scotch. She never touched anything stronger than a wine cooler. But if she had been a drinking woman, this would be a good day for it, she thought as she poured white wine over ice cubes, added soda and took a swallow.

Estelle was fumbling for the makings of Kendall's drink, when the boat swayed. Panic seized her, and she almost dropped the bottle of scotch. Quickly, she finished her preparations as heavy footsteps crossed the deck.

"Kendall?" she called.

"Were you expecting someone else?"

Blood was pounding in her ears, but she forced herself to turn slowly, extending a hand with the glass of whiskey. "You need a drink."

"Later."

She saw the embittered look on his face and struggled to keep her own expression friendly. But she knew the smile she gave him was stiff. "Welcome back," she managed to say.

He set his briefcase on the table. "You've been busy while I was gone."

"Nothing I couldn't handle."

"Perhaps you'd like to tell me why you were making copies of the San Marcos confidential files."

She felt her heart skip a beat then begin to race. "That's ridiculous. You keep those records locked in your safe. I would never—"

"Cut the innocent act."

He moved purposefully toward her. She retreated until her hips pressed against the sink.

"Who are you spying for?" he growled.

"I don't know what you're talking about. You've got to believe me."

Kendall's large fingers dug into her shoulder, and she winced. She'd seen him manhandle Justine, but he'd never touched her like that.

"No mistake, Estelle. I had a surveillance system installed when you were in Atlanta last month. The guy reviewing the footage called a little while ago. I've got you on videotape with your hand in the cookie jar."

"Jesus, no," she gasped, struggling to get free.

"Do the ethics of stealing confidential information from your employer bother you?" he asked sarcastically.

Her lips moved, but no words came out.

As quickly as he'd pounced, he released her, and she stumbled against the counter, rubbing her shoulder.

An instant later, he faced her, a videocassette in one hand, a gun in the other. He was angry, and she could almost feel him drawing energy from her fear.

Putting down the tape, he reached for the glass of scotch and drained it in a couple of swallows.

Light-headed, she struggled to keep her expression blank.

"You'd better start talking, and I mean now. Who hired you? Realto? Or someone else?"

"I..."

"Talk."

God, if only Justine had played fair. But the bitch had left her twisting in the wind.

"Your wife," she whispered.

LISA SAT on the love seat in her room, trying to choke down the dinner Maggie had brought, her ears peeled toward the front door. When it opened, every muscle in her body tensed. The sound of voices in the hall was followed by heavy footfalls coming up the stairs. Automatically, she looked at the clock. Six-thirty. He'd been gone for hours.

Hollingsworth stepped into the room, and Lisa was shocked by the change in his appearance. He looked weary, his shoulders slumped, and his hair was mussed. He gave her no more than a quick glance as he crossed to his own bedroom, went inside and closed the door. She could hear him emptying change and keys. Then the toilet flushed. Water ran. When he opened the door again, he was drying his face on a blue towel. After pitching it in the general direction of her hamper, he lowered himself into the chair opposite her.

His presence made her heart hammer. At least he hadn't claimed the other end of the love seat, Lisa thought, wishing she'd been eating in the dining room when he appeared. Here in the bedroom, there was no place to take refuge if things went the wrong way.

Picking up her glass of orange juice, she took several tiny swallows to moisten her throat.

He cleared his. "I'm sorry."

She blinked, certain she couldn't have heard him correctly. "Sorry? About what?"

"Being on a hunting trip when you had that accident. You always hated my hunting trips."

Wary of his solicitous tone, Lisa frowned. She pictured him rehearsing the line all the way home. It sounded stilted enough. And she didn't believe it. Yet, under the circumstances, it would be worse than stupid to provoke a return of his anger.

"It wasn't your fault," she said carefully.

He seemed to relax a notch and started to speak again, but at that moment, Maggie appeared at the door.

"Come in," Hollingsworth called in response to her deferential knock.

The housekeeper swished into the room carrying a tray with another dinner plate. However, instead of orange juice, he'd apparently requested a bottle of scotch and an ice bucket along with his fried chicken, green beans, mashed potatoes and gravy.

"Thank you," he murmured. "I won't be needing you for the rest of the evening."

"Yes, sir."

Maggie left rapidly. She probably knew enough to get out of the way when her employer was drinking, Lisa thought as she watched Hollingsworth drop ice into a short glass and slosh in amber liquor. He belted back the first glass, then poured himself another. From the looks of him, she'd be willing to bet that he'd had a few on the way home.

With any luck, at this rate, he'd pass out before he finished eating.

He polished off the mashed potatoes on his plate and poured more liquor into his glass. Stretching out his legs, he drank the scotch, studying her across the coffee table between swallows.

The silence lengthened between them. Lisa consciously kept her palms pressed to the sofa on either side of her, fearing that if she moved at all, he'd see her shaking.

At last, he said, "If you've really lost your memory, you've got to be wondering about the two of us. As lovers, I mean."

She swallowed painfully. "I was hoping we could worry about that later."

"I'm not worried. I've been thinking about you the whole time I was gone. Absence makes the heart grow fonder."

His meaning was very clear.

In a small, breathy voice, she said, "I—I hope you're not planning to do something we'll both regret."

"It was too late for regrets when I came home and found you with Lancer."

So his apology had all been a facade. He was still blazing angry.

Feeling her throat clog, Lisa started to rise. But before she could escape, Hollingsworth was out of his chair, fairly leaping across the coffee table, shocking her with his speed and agility. As big as he was—and half-drunk, at that—he shouldn't have been able to move so quickly.

He came down on her hard, knocking the air from her lungs. As she struggled for breath, he pressed her into the sofa cushions. His face was very close. She smelled the liquor on his breath and turned her head to the side, but he put his hand under her chin and brought her face back to his. Then his lips covered hers in a hard kiss that was more punishment than passion.

"No—" She tried to twist from his brutal hold, but his free hand held her fast, clamping around her arm.

"Please! You're hurting me."

"Relax, honey. You always did like me to be a little rough. Don't you remember?"

"No! Don't do this!"

The protest was lost on him. His touch was devoid of all tenderness as his hand moved to her breast, squeezing painfully. Her gasp made his chest rumble with laughter.

"That's right. Let me know how much you like it."

"No! I don't like it. Let me up!" She was caught in a nightmare. A nightmare that was doomed to repeat itself over and over. For a confused moment, she imagined it was another man on top of her, another man she was trying to push away. The image blurred, lost in a haze of light-headed terror and bewilderment.

Then Hollingsworth spoke and she knew who he was.

"Close your eyes and pretend I'm Lancer."

"Don't—"

She might have saved her breath, for all it affected him. If she screamed at the top of her lungs, would Maggie come? She doubted it.

Hollingsworth grabbed Lisa's leg, straightening her body so that she was sprawled along the length of the short couch.

When she lashed out with her foot, he growled a warning. "Do any damage, and you'll really get hurt."

Then his body shifted, and he groped for the placket at the top of her knit shirt. The buttons popped, and the fabric tore.

From the moment she'd seen his picture, she had imagined his touch with deep, abiding distaste. But she hadn't imagined rape. Against her leg, she felt the hard length of his erection and knew he meant to use it as a weapon.

In total panic, she reached behind her, frantically searching the surface of the end table for something she could use in her own defense. She almost sobbed in relief when her fingers closed around the neck of the candlestick lamp. But when she pulled it upward, it only moved a few inches, then seemed to stick.

Oblivious to her struggle, Hollingsworth tugged at the waistband of her slacks, and she felt them moving relentlessly lower. She yanked at the lamp, and it came free with a jerk. Her arm completed the arc, and she brought the shaft down on Kendall's head.

He grunted, then abruptly went still, his weight pressing her down.

She wriggled out from under him, pulling up her slacks as soon as she was free from his grasp. For several moments, she sat huddled on the coffee table shaking uncontrollably and sucking in great drafts of air. Realizing she was still holding the lamp, she let it slip through her fingers. It hit the rug with a dull thunk.

She knew she had to get away before the madman on the sofa grabbed her again, but she wasn't sure she could stand. And she could see he wasn't moving.

Lord, what had she done? Reluctantly, Lisa forced her gaze to the top of Hollingsworth's head, where the lamp had connected with his skull. A red stain was spreading through his graying hair.

"Kendall?" she whispered.

He didn't move.

Heart in her throat, she knelt beside him and felt for the pulse in his neck. To her relief, it was strong and regular.

Pushing herself to her feet, wobbling slightly, she made her way to the dresser and grabbed the purse in which she'd put the money she'd found. Turning, she started to flee, then stopped dead. She had no keys. No car. No means of escape.

A picture flashed in her mind of Frank and Hollingsworth tracking her across the lawn, shotguns in hand, and the image was followed swiftly by the taste of bile rising in her throat. She glanced toward the couch. Hollingsworth was stirring. She had to leave now or it would be too late. And the solution to her problem was really quite simple: she would take Hollingsworth's car.

She crept into his room, looking to see where he'd emptied his pockets. In a little hall that led to his closet, she spotted an antique dresser, his change, keys and wallet strewn across the top of it. She was reaching for the prize, when the door between the rooms flew open. Hollingsworth swayed in the doorway, his face red with effort, his eyes glinting with emotion that went far beyond anger.

With a sob, Lisa snatched the keys.

"What happened?" he asked in a woozy voice, wincing as he fingered the top of his head. He winced. Then his gaze traveled the room and zoomed back to her.

"You hurt yourself," she answered. And as far as she was concerned, it was true. She'd only hit him because he was going to rape her.

His eyes closed, then snapped open again. "Christ. You whacked me, and I saw stars." Again he touched the bump on his head, this time more carefully. "You bitch." He moved to block her escape route, raising his hands with fingers spread to grab her.

She took a step back and then another, her knees coming up against the edge of the bed.

"Gotcha!" Lurching forward, he lunged for her.

She dodged out of the way, and he swayed on his feet. She thought he would fall, but he made a quick recovery, and moving faster than she anticipated, grabbed for her again. His fingers grazed the hem of her shirt, and for a terrible moment she thought she was done for. Then he overbalanced and pitched forward, catching himself on the edge of the bed. Apparently, the effort was too much, and he sank to his knees, clutching at the spread, pulling it askew.

Darting around him, Lisa pounded down the stairs, thanking God that no one was standing in the front hall, waiting to block her exit.

It was dark outside, but she didn't stop until she was away from the glow of the porch light. Her lungs burned as she dragged in several deep breaths. The keys were in her hand, but she'd left the purse with the money in the house. Yet there was no way she was going back inside.

The car was a little farther along the driveway. She ran to it, yanked open the door and slid into the driver's seat. It was too far back for her to reach the gas pedal. She fumbled frantically, trying to locate a lever that would move her forward. Every few seconds, she glanced toward the house, expecting to see the enraged man she'd left upstairs barreling through the door with a gun in his hand.

Finally, she found the release mechanism, and the seat shot forward. She bumped against the wheel. More precious seconds ticked by as she eased herself to the right position.

The sound of the engine coming to life as she turned the key in the ignition was the sweetest music she had ever heard. But she wasn't home free yet. Footsteps thudded to her right. With a moan, she glanced toward the window expecting to see Frank. Her mouth fell open when, instead, she beheld the tramp who had come at her with the knife. The man must have been lurking again—waiting for her.

Careening across the lawn, he made for the car, waving his arms for her to stop.

Not on your life, she thought as she tromped on the accelerator. The car shot forward just as the man stepped into the driveway. Into her path.

Yanking madly on the wheel, she swerved into the bushes. Branches scraped her left fender, and the tire bounced onto a hidden curb, making the car tip at a crazy angle. She missed the man by inches, then fought to bring the vehicle back to an even course. But the tramp surged forward, trying to block her path again.

His eyes were wild, his face contorted, as he shouted something at her. With the windows closed, she couldn't hear the words and didn't want to.

"Get away," she screamed as she lurched down the driveway, hunching forward so she could make out the dark shapes of the trees. "Get away. Get away. Get away." The words became a chant. She strained to see in the darkness, barely avoiding a stately blue spruce as the driveway twisted and turned. Several hundred yards from the house, she realized that she hadn't turned on the lights. With a whimper, she searched for the right knob and found it.

The road leaped into focus, and the trees receded into the background, speeding past on either side, dark and indistinct shapes. She couldn't believe it was over. She kept expecting the tramp to loom out of the shadows.

Mercifully, no one stepped into the path of her headlights as she wove her way down the endless driveway. She considered it a stroke of luck when a glance at the console beside her seat told her that Kendall had left the portable phone in the car.

Her luck changed, though, when she reached the end of the private road. Illuminated by a set of floodlights, the gates were firmly shut across the blacktop. For a split second, she thought about trying to crash through. Then reason overruled panic, and she slammed on the brakes.

Chapter Fifteen

On a sob, Lisa jumped from the car and ran toward the gate. Floodlights perched atop the entrance posts blinded her, and she shaded her eyes to locate the metal latch that held the gates closed. Fumbling with the catch, unaware of the whimpering noises coming from her throat, she unlocked the gate and swung it open.

Behind her, footsteps thumped against the hard surface of the driveway. She didn't wait to see who was coming. She simply ran for the car.

With hysteria not far off, she jumped into the Mercedes as a figure appeared in the darkness, his arms waving.

"Wait! Justine! Wait!"

Teeth chattering, she choked back a scream, slammed the car door closed and pressed the gas pedal to the floor.

Left or right? She hadn't a clue where she was, anyway, so it didn't matter. She chose left and zoomed away from the open gates.

She'd gone three hundred yards, when headlights filled her rearview mirror. Glancing between the dark road ahead and the mirror, she couldn't tell if the vehicle behind her had followed her through the gate.

Lisa turned onto a side road. The other car followed, picked up speed. She increased the pace. Ahead, a traffic light turned yellow. Stepping on the gas, she shot through the intersection, watching the signal turn red as she passed.

Ioments later, a van on the cross street started up, and the
:hicle behind her was blocked.

Praying the light was a long one, she turned up another
de street, then another...and another. Wooded lots
owded close to the narrow road on either side. When she
ıw a winding driveway, she pulled in past the first bend,
ıut off the headlights and waited, her heart pounding.

Seconds ticked by. She saw, through the trees, the lights
: several cars pass, and each time, she reached for the door
ındle, ready to jump out and take her chances in the
oods. But no one stopped. After fifteen minutes, she al-
wed herself to believe she had, indeed, escaped. Relief
ickled in slowly, followed swiftly by utter exhaustion. She
umped in the seat and, without pause for thought, reached
r the phone and dialed Mike.

Her breath rushed out in a heartfelt "Thank God" when
ıe heard his voice, but then she realized she was talking to
ı answering machine, and disappointment swept over her.
ıe had nowhere else to turn. Still, if she was found dead in
.e car, she wanted someone to know what had happened.
) when the beep sounded, she began to speak.

"Mike, I-I'm in H-Hollingsworth's car," she began, fear
aking it hard to breathe—or speak. "I—I stole it. I had to
:t away. H-he tried to— He attacked me. I—I hit him, and
:hink he's—"

The phone clicked. "Lisa. Where are you?"

'RONG STREET. She wasn't up here. Lennie Ezrine
reeched to a halt, then whipped the Pontiac around in a
ght U-turn. Beside him, Jack Ordway sat with his meaty
ıgers wrapped around the butt of a revolver.

"You lost her," Jackal muttered.

"She's around here somewhere," Lennie insisted with
ore confidence than he felt. Damn, the bitch had sure
cked her moment—with him taking a piss in the woods.

"You shoulda stayed in the car," Jackal growled.

"Oh, come on!"

"Well, you shoulda run the red light back there."

"And smashed into that van? Then we'd both b
screwed." From the corner of his eye, he could see Jack:
squeezing his fingers around the gun butt. "Put the piec
away," he snapped, "and get on the scanner. She makes
call from the car phone, we've got her."

Jackal laid the gun on the console and turned on th
scanner bolted to the dashboard.

Lennie made a turn down another residential street an
crept past the long driveways. Mouth set in a grim line, h
bit back the curses seething behind his lips. Jesus, if they lo:
track of her now, what the hell were they going to do?

The green numbers on the display changed, and th
monitor crackled, bringing in various conversations. Som
jerk was talking to his broker. A woman threatened 1
ground her kids if they didn't clean up their rooms by th
time she got home. Talk about pissing away money. Sh
could tell them the same thing for free in five minutes.

The scan continued.

"Wait. Stop," Lennie ordered, recognizing her voice fro:
the phone calls she'd made that he'd monitored.

Jackal adjusted the volume, and the voice came in loude:
Lennie slapped his palms against the wheel. "It's her."

"Yeah, but where is she?"

"She'll give herself away," Lennie answered as he turne
down another street. Maybe they'd even hit it lucky and fin
her while she was still talking.

"MIKE! Oh, thank God," Lisa cried. "I thought yc
weren't home."

"I was screening my calls. Where are you?" he repeatec

"I'm in the car. I don't know where. Mike, I think som
body was following me."

"Hollingsworth?"

"I don't know."

"You lost him?"

"I hope so."

He was silent for several moments, then said, "It's ea
to monitor a call on a cellular phone."

She sucked in a breath. "Somebody could be listening?"

"Maybe. I don't want to take the chance. Do you remember where we rescued the dog? Don't say the name of the street!" he said quickly. "But do you know where we were?"

"Yes."

"Can you find the place again?"

She peered through the trees toward the road. She might as well be in the middle of the north woods. "I think I can find it if I can figure out where I am now. I'm all twisted around."

"I'll meet you where we saw the dog."

"What if I can't... can't get there?"

"Ask directions at a gas station. Or ask for a map." His voice was calm and practical, steadying her. "If you run into any trouble, call me. I'll be right there." He gave her the number of his car phone and made her repeat it.

"Thank you," she breathed.

"I'll be on the road in three minutes. Don't give your location unless I tell you to."

LENNIE'S EYES NARROWED when the line went dead. He'd been hoping for more, but they were still in the game.

"That son of a bitch Lancer is smart," Jackal said.

"Yeah, but his girlfriend can't be more than a few blocks from here."

Jackal hunched forward, peering into the darkness. "Last time we followed her, she got lost. Maybe she'll have to call him for directions."

"Yeah."

"Why'd she change her name to Lisa?"

"Guess we'll have to ask her about it when we find her." Jackal laughed, an evil sound.

"She's got to be heading for a main road," Lennie muttered. "Too bad she knows we spotted her."

"So what? That won't do her no good when we catch up."

"Unless Lancer gets to her first."

Jackal fingered the gun. "He won't expect company."

Lennie made a disgusted noise. "I hope you're not planning to plug him on a city street."

"Do you think I'm dense? After we deliver her to the boss, we'll take Lancer somewhere a little more private."

"Fine by me." Lennie headed for the nearest gas station, hoping his quarry wasn't too far off target.

THE SECOND she hung up the phone, Lisa began to shake. She'd told Mike she could find the place they'd agreed to meet, and, reassured by the sound of his voice, she'd believed she could do it. But sitting there in the dark, alone, hounded by fear of being followed, she wanted only to curl up and cry. She wanted Mike to come and get her. She wanted him to make her safe. She wanted...him.

For long moments, she stared into the darkness, trying to steady herself. If she didn't get a grip and start moving, whoever had been following her might find her before she could meet Mike. She could end up back where she'd started—or worse.

Starting the engine, she backed out of the driveway. Less than five minutes later, she was at a major intersection with a gas station. She parked close to the office door, went inside and bought a map. Concentrating on the task instead of her fear, she found her present location. Then she was able to plot a course.

She arrived at the spot where the dog had been hit before Mike. Pulling to a stop on the shoulder, she put the car in park, then, with the engine running, slouched in her seat and trained her eyes on the traffic passing by. Again and again she had to remind herself that nobody else knew this location. She was safe. Yet she couldn't stop picturing a big gray car with two tough-looking men—one grinning wickedly at her out the window—blocking her escape. The image was so powerful she thought it might actually be real, her occluded memory giving up a piece of reality to fan the flames of imagination. As if the flames needed fanning.

It seemed an eternity before she saw Mike's familiar Mustang pass her. She straightened in the seat, and, with tears of relief blurring her vision she watched as he made a U-turn and pulled up alongside her.

She was about to jump out, but he motioned through the closed car windows for her to stay put, then opened his door and stood up long enough to scan the block in all directions. Lisa looked, too, and saw no other cars. When she met Mike's gaze again over the roof of the Mustang, he gave her the high sign to hurry.

Scrambling out of the Mercedes, she yanked open the Mustang's door and climbed into the passenger seat. She barely had the door closed when Mike said, "Hold on," at the same time he hit the gas and took off down the road.

The next few minutes left her too breathless to speak, which was just as well, for she was sure anything she tried to say would be incoherent. When Mike made a sudden sharp turn up a side street, she braced herself with a hand on the dash. He made several more quick turns, zooming through narrow residential streets until, finally, he turned left onto a well-lit, multilane road. There, he slowed to a reasonable pace.

With heart still pounding, Lisa saw Mike glance several times at the rearview mirror. His features, illuminated in snatches by the streetlights, were taut. He looked haggard and worried... and furious.

After several blocks, he said, "No one's following us."

But they were. She could feel them. They were out there, looking for her, and they wouldn't give up until they found her.

"Are you all right?" Mike cut into her thoughts.

"Yes," she whispered. "Just...scared."

"What happened?"

Her lower lip trembled. "Hollingsworth got a phone call and went out. When he came back, he...he'd been drinking. He seemed better, though—better than when he left. Less angry. He kept drinking until...until he grabbed me."

Mike swore, the fury she'd seen in his face surfacing in a flash. But it wasn't directed at her; he was angry on her behalf, and that made all the difference in the world.

His touch was gentle when he lifted a hand from the steering wheel to finger the front of her shirt where the placket was torn. "Did he hurt you?" he asked.

She looked down at the damaged fabric, remembering Hollingsworth's hands on her flesh. Shuddering, she replied, "He was—he was going to rape me. But I—I got away."

"Christ, Lisa..."

"Take me somewhere safe," she pleaded.

His hand reached down to cover hers where it clutched the seat. "I will," he said. "Tell me how you got away."

The heat from his hand seeped into her cold flesh, warming her. "I knocked him out with a lamp. Then I stole his keys. He came to and almost grabbed me again. But he was still groggy, and...and I got past him."

Mike was silent for several long minutes, his knuckles white as he gripped the wheel. When he spoke, his tone was controlled. "Why didn't you leave when he went out?"

Lisa dragged in a deep breath. "He told Frank and Maggie to guard me. And...and he said if I ran away and he couldn't find me, he'd come after you."

"You believed him?"

"He meant it, Mike. I know he did."

Mike fell silent again. Lisa considered telling him about the tramp who'd tried to prevent her escape that evening. But she was suddenly unsure of herself. He was sitting rigidly in his seat, both hands now fused to the wheel. She cast several glances at his harsh profile. It might have been carved from granite.

He wasn't an easy man to read. And the task was made harder because she had to rely entirely upon intuition and what little she'd learned of him in a week's time. Intuitively, she felt as if she knew him very well indeed; she knew he was an honorable man who she could trust with her life. Practically speaking, she didn't know him well at all. At the moment, she had no idea what he was thinking or feeling. And that scared her. A lot.

It also made her frustrated and upset with herself. Clearly, he was a private man—in some ways, a hard man—who didn't share his thoughts or feelings easily. She knew she shouldn't take it personally or assume that his withdrawal meant he was rejecting her. Yet, when she looked at his shuttered features, she couldn't quite prevent the feelings of loss and abandonment from creeping in to haunt her.

Despair settled over her, and the feeling grew as she watched street signs flash by. They passed some enormous mansions, then a long section of old semidetached houses. The semidetacheds gave way to block after block of four-story row houses with marble steps leading to their front doors. Mike turned right, into an alley, then right again into another alley that ran between two sets of skinny back-yards. Halfway up the block, he parked.

He didn't touch her as she climbed from the car, or as they walked through the narrow, fenced yard to the back door. Silently, he turned the key in the lock and ushered her into a dimly lit hallway, then preceded her up two flights of worn stairs. Still without speaking, he unlocked one of two apartment doors on the landing, and pushed it open.

She hesitated, unconsciously hugging herself against a sudden chill as she looked from the open doorway to him.

"Come inside," he said, his tone low and strained by some emotion she couldn't guess.

Stepping across the threshold, she watched him throw the bolt behind them. The living room was in shadows. Only a dim bulb glowed from a table lamp near a window on the far side of the room. In the shadowy light, his tension was almost palpable. Down on the street, an occasional car passed, a distant reminder that the world had not shrunk to the two of them standing in this unfamiliar, dark room.

When she couldn't take another second of his silence, she asked, "Do you think it was my fault—what happened tonight? That I provoked him?"

"Jesus! Of course not," he exclaimed.

"Then...what's wrong?"

He cleared his throat, yet when he spoke, his voice was gritty. "I should never have left you with that bastard. If I hadn't, none of this would have happened. You wouldn't have been in danger. You wouldn't have had to...to fight off a rape." His voice cracked. "Lisa, I'm sorry."

She couldn't tell him it was all right that he'd left. It hadn't been all right. It had been awful. Still...

"It's true, I was scared," she whispered. "But even I couldn't have imagined that he'd be as...wicked as he is."

Mike continued as if she hadn't spoken. "When I left, I told myself you were Hollingsworth's wife. That you'd made your bed, and you could lie in it."

Her breath caught. "You want to think the worst of me?"

"No. Maybe. Or maybe the worst of myself." He shook his dark head. "I don't like wanting something I can't have. I never did. My only excuse is that I was trying to protect myself." He ran a hand over his face, then back through his hair. "I haven't let a woman get under my skin since Justine left me. You scared me. You were my most compelling fantasy come true. Justine coming back to me. The old Justine, before she changed." With an angry gesture, he added, "But I couldn't trust it! And I couldn't defend it morally. I didn't *want* to be attracted to you. I didn't *want* to like you.... But I couldn't help myself."

Lisa stared at him, wide-eyed. "Oh," she whispered, and a wealth of feeling accompanied the syllable.

He took her by the shoulders, turning her so they were face-to-face. "Since I've been old enough to make decisions, I've lived by certain rules, and they almost always worked. But you make me want to forget all the rules. All I can think about is wanting to make love with you."

Those words and the horrible, haunted look on his face made her heart turn over. Suddenly, the basic equation between them changed. She wanted to heal him. She wanted to love him. Nothing was as important as giving him everything she could. Nothing except...

Lisa hesitated, knowing she had to tell him about the baby, knowing she had to tell him *now*. In another minute, it would be too late. But if she told him, would he still want to make love with her? Or would his code of honor insist that he couldn't make love with a woman who was not only pregnant with another man's child, but who didn't even know who the man was?

She knew the answer. And she couldn't bear it, couldn't bear even the thought of him turning away from her yet again. She needed him as much as she suspected he needed her, and neither dishonor nor disloyalty entered into it. She had no history, no memory of any man she had loved, and she might never remember. Unless she was to go on for the rest of her life alone, she had to begin again somewhere.

Fate had given her a place to start—here, with this man standing before her, watching her with such intense longing in his deep brown gaze. She couldn't deny either of them this chance to heal, to love, to begin life anew.

WHEN LISA TOOK a step toward him, Mike went very still. With effort, he managed to remain still as she laid a hand against his cheek. But a tremor raced through him when her fingers trailed down his neck, down his arm, then back up again, her hand coming to rest on his shoulder.

Pressing her face against his shirtfront, nuzzling his chest in a way that made him stifle a groan, she whispered, "All right. I look like Justine. Everybody seems to agree and, having seen her picture, I can't deny it. But you know me well enough to tell the difference."

With his arms plastered to his sides, he muttered, "What do you mean, I know you well enough?"

"You know *me*. The woman you followed on a rainy afternoon. The woman you fished out of the river. Think about it. Do I talk like Justine Hollingsworth? Do I move like her?" Lifting her face to look at him, she let her body rest lightly against his. "More important, what do you feel when you're with me?"

He swore softly. "I've never felt anything like this."

She gazed at him with her lovely blue eyes full of hope and longing. "Mike, be honest with yourself—and with me. In your heart, do you really believe I'm Justine?"

It was as if he was being tested—faced with salvation packaged to look like his worst nightmare. He could turn away, let his head overrule his heart, let his fear overcome his instincts, and go on living behind the brittle wall of pain and loneliness he'd built over the past eight years. Or he could trust his instincts, and believe what his senses told him was true. Suddenly it occurred to him that he'd be out of his mind to let this chance pass him by. Because, God knows, he'd never have another one like it again.

"No," he said softly. Then, louder, "No, I don't think you're her." With a low sound of suppressed need released, he wrapped his arms around her and crushed her to him. "Lisa," he whispered as his mouth covered hers.

He kissed her hard, a desperate kiss filled with hunger, and with every second that passed, his conviction grew stronger. It had nothing to do with reason or common sense, nothing at all to do with evidence or mental guesswork. It had everything in the world to do with instinct. He simply knew. The woman in his arms, all soft and warm, couldn't possibly be the same woman who'd teased and baited and ultimately betrayed him all those years ago.

His senses only confirmed what his heart already knew. He'd never tasted a mouth so sweet, or one that melded with his so perfectly. He'd never smelled this woman's scent, or run his hands over these same lush curves. She was no one he'd ever touched before. She was new to him.

She was Lisa. And loving her was like waking up from a bad dream to discover that the world was bright and shining and full of promise. Some inexplicable twist of fate—a good twist, for a change—had given her to him. And nothing between heaven and earth was going to persuade him to let her go. Ever.

He tried in every way he knew to tell her that. Feasting on her, angling his head one way and then the other, deepening the kiss as if she were the source of all life. His hands moved feverishly, across her back, down her spine, to her hips, molding their bodies, sealing them with heat. She met his hunger and his need, her mouth surrendering to his, her hands clutching at him, pulling him closer. The tiny, whimpering sounds she made fueled his passion, urged him to take it all, everything she had to give.

And he did. During that one endless kiss, he touched her everywhere—breasts, hips, the warm, secret place between her thighs, claiming her body through the barrier of her clothing until she was liquid in his arms. Her knees buckled, and he took her weight against him, slowly easing her down to the rug. They swayed together, clinging, hands and lips moving urgently—touching and kissing everywhere they could reach.

He let her go long enough to struggle out of his shirt, then to strip hers away along with her bra. Then he gathered her close again, feeling the hardened tips of her breasts graze his chest, moving from side to side to increase the pleasure for both of them.

"Oh...oh, Mike," she whispered, her warm breath brushing his neck below his ear.

"I want you naked in my arms," he growled. "Naked under me. So hot you can't think about anything but what we're doing."

She moaned softly. "I'm already so hot I can't think about anything else."

"Good. I plan to keep it that way."

He was as efficient in removing the rest of her clothing as his trembling fingers would allow. She helped him, her own hands shaking as much as his. When they were both naked, lying side by side on the carpet, he let his gaze rake her body from head to toe, let himself revel in the sight of her lush breasts, and her white, nearly translucent skin that felt like silk to touch. The narrow waist, the sensuous curve of her hips, and the smaller curve of her belly came together to frame the nest of red curls at the juncture of her thighs. His gaze lingered there for a long moment, his blood pounding hotter at the thought of what was to come.

When he finally lifted his gaze to meet hers, he saw in the muted light that she was blushing. She started to roll toward him, but something in her eyes—a trace of nervousness or fear—made him hold her back with a hand on her shoulder.

Softly, he asked, "Are you frightened of me?"

"No," she replied, her blush deepening. "Only afraid that you won't like what you see."

"Oh, sweetheart," he murmured, "you couldn't be more wrong." Stroking her from breast to thigh, he added, "You're beautiful—soft and lush and so damn sexy.... I wouldn't change a thing."

Her gaze made a slow trip down his body, then traveled the same path back up to meet his once more. "Neither would I," she whispered. "Only..."

"Only what?"

"Being with you...like this...it's new to me."

He thought about that for a moment or two, then asked, "Do you have any memory of ever making love?"

She shook her head a little. "Not really. Only a sort of vague sense that I have, but nothing specific." Then, with a flicker of dismay crossing her brow, she said, "Oh, Mike, I don't know if I'm any good at this. But I want to be. Tell me what you like."

If he hadn't already been convinced that she wasn't Justine—and seeing her luscious and totally unfamiliar body had given him all the physical evidence he could have wanted—he would have been then. Justine had never shown so much as a scrap of self-doubt and, indeed, had always acted just a little bit like anyone she took to her bed was damned lucky. Certainly she'd never put anyone's pleasure above her own.

A slow smile formed on his lips. "I like this," he said, pulling her to him. "And this..."

Taking her mouth in another hot, deep joining, he moved his hair-roughened leg between her smooth ones. At the same time, his hand found her warm center, fingers parting the folds.

Her hand splayed across his hips, fingers digging into his flesh as he stroked her, her mouth tearing away from his as she drew in ragged gulps of air.

But it was his own breathing that went ragged when her hand found his sex, her fingers exploring gently, curling around him.

"Oh, Lisa," he groaned, hips straining toward her.

"And this," she said. "You like this."

"Oh, yeah. And these," he murmured as his lips and teeth nuzzled at her breasts.

"Please. Now. Please," she begged, her hand guiding him to her.

He covered her body with his, whispering her name, spreading her thighs wide, his mouth finding hers as he probed for entrance. Then she seemed to blossom open, and he was sliding inside her, and she was taking him in, hot and full and deep.

She gasped his name, fingers clutching his back, hips tilting to take him deeper.

"That's it, sweetheart," he murmured close to her ear. "That's right. Let me know how you want it. Show me..."

His hips began a slow rhythm, his hands beneath her hips angling her body until her response told him that he'd found the right spot. He let her set the pace, let her responses guide him, moving faster now...and faster...until she was nearly frantic beneath him. Until he'd lost all sense of deliberation or control and was aware only of the unbridled desire driving him. It was a purely intuitive move when his hand slid upward to find her breast, his fingers capturing the nipple and squeezing it gently.

She surged against him, and the high, keening noises she'd been making suddenly dropped a couple of registers. He felt the first quaking spasm hit her. He let it take him. Let it carry him over the edge until he felt the hot convulsion begin deep in his belly. Then they were both lost. The climax washed over them in one long, voluptuous wave, locking them together to ride it out, rippling back and forth between them, until, at last, it left them spent and breathless on a newly discovered shore.

LISA WAS STILL QUIVERING with aftershocks when Mike rolled to his side and folded her into his arms. She burrowed closer, not at all ready to be separated from him even by a few inches. She felt shattered—and not merely from the storm of physical pleasure but from the gift he'd given her: he believed, *truly* believed, that she wasn't Justine. Finally, she'd convinced someone—the most important someone. And, in convincing Mike, she realized, she'd also convinced herself. She hadn't been fully aware of how terrified she'd been that she might be Justine. Seeing—*feeling*—Mike's utter certainty that she wasn't . . . well, the relief was nearly overwhelming.

Yet, so was the confusion. If she wasn't Justine Hollingsworth, who was she?

At the moment, in all honesty, she didn't have the energy to care. She knew enough about herself to feel satisfied with the sort of person she was. And lying safe and warm in Mike's arms in the afterglow of passion, she found it impossible to be worried about much of anything. Surely she could put aside worry for one night. Surely she could begin again tomorrow—this time with Mike's full support—to unlock the door to her past.

For an instant, a tendril of fear curled through her at the thought of her pregnancy. Would unlocking her past destroy the present? Would some previous commitment make it impossible for her to fulfill the commitment she felt she'd made to Mike?

She refused to think about it. Tomorrow would be soon enough.

Wiggling onto her side, Lisa pressed a kiss to Mike's shoulder, loving the salty taste of his skin. In response, he kissed the damp skin along her hairline.

"I should have taken you to bed," he said quietly.

She smiled. "I couldn't have walked that far."

His chest rumbled with the sound of soft laughter. "I'm not sure I could have, either."

"I'm still too limp to move," she sighed. "Can we camp out here?"

She heard the smile in his reply. "Maybe you were a Girl Scout when you were a kid."

"I think the Scouts discourage this kind of behavior."

He laughed outright at that. "Well, at least let me make us more comfortable." He reached to the couch and pulled down a pile of pillows and cushions and an afghan, fashioning a makeshift bed on the rug.

Snuggling at his side beneath the afghan, she murmured, "You don't look like the crocheted granny-square type."

"My seventy-year-old landlady made it," he replied. "She'd be mortally offended if I stuffed it in the closet."

Lisa contemplated the notion of Mike Lancer worrying about a little old lady's happiness. "You want people to think you're tough. But you're not—where it counts."

"Don't tell anybody, okay?"

"Why not?"

"Tough is safer," he muttered.

She moved so that she was cradling his head against her breasts, realizing quite well that he'd tried to play it safe with her—and failed. She also realized that, at this moment, she held his complete trust in her hands. It was both a gift and a burden. She wanted to protect him, to be the one who made him happy—forever. She could only hope that whatever fate had plucked her out of her old life and plunked her down in this new one would allow her the time she needed to show him that his trust was not misplaced.

Quietly, she repeated his words, "Tough is safer. How did you come up with that philosophy?"

His hand trailed lazily down her arm as he replied. "My dad was a mean drunk. He was meaner if you let him know you were scared."

"Oh, Mike."

He murmured something against her breast that she didn't catch, then said, "I survived."

"Didn't your mother stand up for you?"

"In the beginning. By the time I was six or seven, she'd given up." He grunted softly. "I think she ran out of lies to tell in the emergency room for how she got the broken ribs—or arm or nose."

"Good Lord," Lisa breathed. "Why didn't she leave him?"

"I spent a lot of years asking myself that same thing—until I became a cop. By the time I'd been on the job six months, I'd lost count of how many domestic disputes I'd covered. And I'd stopped blaming my mother for what she did or didn't do."

It didn't surprise her to hear he'd been a policeman; it seemed to fit his personality exactly. Afraid to hear the answer, Lisa asked anyway, "Wasn't there anyone else you could turn to?"

Mike let out a heavy sigh, his breath warm against her skin. "I had some friends at school. But nobody I trusted enough to bring home."

Lisa's fingers toyed with the silky dark hair at the back of his neck.

"And I did have one teacher," he continued. "A gym teacher in junior high who took an interest in me. I thought it was because I was good at sports. But years later, when I thought back on it, I wondered if he knew something was going on at home. Anyway, he seemed to understand that I needed some kind of outlet. He got me started walking, which turned out to be not just an outlet but a means of escape.

"Where did you go?"

"Everywhere," he said. Shifting her so that she was tucked against his side, her head on his shoulder, he held her close as he continued. "Starting from home, I'd walk to Dundalk Marine Terminal and watch them unload cars from ships. Or to Greenmount Cemetery and try to find the headstone with the oldest date. And Herring Run Park—that was one of my favorite places. When I got sick of looking at East Baltimore, I started taking buses across or up town. I'd go someplace like the zoo in Druid Hill Park, then walk home."

"But you were only... what? Eleven or twelve? Wasn't it dangerous for you to be out in the city, all alone?"

He gave a short laugh. "Not as dangerous as being home with my father. Besides, I was always pretty much on my own."

Lisa bit her tongue so as not to speak the words that came to mind—that she found the notion of a little boy being on his own worse than appalling.

Perhaps in response to her horrified expression, he hurried on. "By the time I was sixteen, I knew Baltimore like the back of my hand." He snorted softly. "Of course, by then, I wasn't walking because I was afraid of my father. I was bigger and stronger than he was, and if he'd hit me, I'd've hit him back. But I kept walking, anyway. Still do it, almost every day."

He took a breath as if to speak, then hesitated. Finally, he said, "Walking is how I met Justine."

A sudden chill ran through her. Justine wasn't at the top of her list of favorite topics. But Mike was.

"Oh?" she prompted.

"Hmm." He drew back a little and looked at her—checking her out, she thought, to see if she minded hearing about his past lover—the lover who'd jilted him and who was the cause of her own current woes.

She gave him an encouraging smile. "Go on."

He snuggled her against him again. "We were both at the University of Maryland, living on campus. She walked every day, too, and we kept seeing each other, until one day we started walking together."

It sounded harmless enough, she thought. A perfectly normal way for young people to meet.

"Walking led to talking," he said. "Pretty soon, I was helping her with her science classes, and she was helping me with French. If it had been up to me, it probably would have stayed at that. Hell, she was beautiful and had a great sense of humor, and she was popular as hell—and I figured I didn't stand a chance. But one day, she said she was tired of waiting for me to ask her out, so she'd decided not to wait anymore. She asked me to take her to a showing of *North By Northwest* at the student union." He paused, casting her a downward glance. "I'm kind of a classics buff."

"I figured that," Lisa said softly. She'd noticed the framed posters of *Citizen Kane* and *Psycho* on the living-room walls. Oddly, they struck a chord inside her. Somehow, she felt that she could have remembered plots, even minute details, of dozens of old movies—if she'd tried. At the moment, she was too tired to bother.

Stifling a yawn, she said, "Go on."

His hand came up to her chin, and he tilted her face to his. "You're falling asleep," he said, planting a kiss on her forehead.

"No," she protested. "Tell me more."

"Not tonight." He smiled. "If you're determined to get the rest of the story—and God knows why you'd want to, 'cause none of it's what I'd call riveting—you'll have to wait for the next installment."

"It's riveting to me," she whispered. "Mike, how long were you and Justine together?" she asked softly.

"We had two great years before things fell apart. But we're not going to talk about her anymore tonight."

He lowered his head and kissed her, then his lips moved against hers in a whisper. "You need to sleep."

Unfortunately, she had to agree. Her eyelids were leaden, and even the thought of sleep brought her close to the edge of it. Close enough for a quick flash of memory to slip through her guard—a piece of the waking nightmare from earlier that evening. She gave a little shiver.

"It's all right," he said. "I'll keep you safe."

She sighed. "I know."

He kissed her again, then trailed a line of kisses down her neck to her breasts, kissing each one in turn before working his way back up to her lips. There, his mouth settled for a brief but tender moment. Their lips parted with a soft, moist sound, then he pulled her tightly beside him. Eyes closed, she listened to the reassuring beat of his heart, strong and steady. Her last conscious thought was that his living-room rug was the most comfortable place she'd slept in her short but eventful life.

FAINT GRAY LIGHT came through the window when her eyes fluttered open. For several disoriented moments, she wondered why the mattress felt so hard. Then she realized where she was, and that Mike was beside her.

His body was levered up on one elbow and his hand was on her shoulder, lightly shaking her. Suddenly, she became aware of the tension radiating through him.

The smile faded from her face. "What's—" He cut her off with a finger pressed against her lips. For a moment, she was confused. Then she heard it.

Outside in the hall, a floorboard squeaked—the sound of someone moving stealthily. It was followed by a gentle twist of the doorknob, then the indistinct jingle of keys.

Chapter Sixteen

Lisa lay rigidly, trying to imagine who was on the other side of the door.

Mike whispered urgently in her ear, pointing toward an overstuffed chair by the window. "Get behind there. Now!"

Pulling the afghan around her, she scrambled across the room. From her hiding place, she saw Mike moving in a blur. He appeared simultaneously to douse the lamp, grab a hiker's walking stick that stood by the coatrack in the corner, and position himself by the door. Naked, he looked like an ancient Greek athlete about to compete in some arcane sport.

She held her breath as a key slipped into the lock. Nothing happened, but she heard a muffled curse on the other side of the door. Then the intruder tried another key. This time it turned, and the door opened a crack.

Peering around the corner of the chair, Lisa watched the crack widen. To her horror, the first thing through was the long barrel of a gun. It was followed by a hand and the rest of the gun, then an arm, and finally a man who moved on silent feet.

Mike yanked him across the threshold with one hand while using the other to bring the walking stick down on the back of his neck. With a muffled groan, the intruder crumpled to the rug. Before Lisa had time to sigh in relief, another figure leaped into the room, weapon drawn.

Lisa screamed. Mike sprang aside as a low thunk sounded, followed by the splatter of plaster falling from the opposite wall. Lisa realized immediately that the long barrel on the gun was a silencer, and that the assailant was aiming again for Mike.

Mike used the stick in an upward sweep to knock the gun from the second man's hand. The weapon sailed across the room. Recovering his balance, the man sprang at Mike. They went down in the pile of discarded clothes, thrashing about as each tried to get the upper hand.

Still clutching the afghan, Lisa made for the corner where the gun had landed. It took several frantic seconds of searching before her fingers closed around the cold metal. When she turned, the men were rolling across the floor, trading blows like sailors in a saloon brawl. Except that one of the combatants was naked.

Mike landed on top. He slammed the other man's head against the floor. The man only grunted, then reversed their positions.

Lisa saw blunt fingers press into Mike's windpipe. He tried to pry them loose but couldn't. As she watched in horror, his face began to turn red. Nearly wild with panic, she tried to get a clear shot at the intruder but was afraid she'd hit Mike.

Then, suddenly, she realized that she didn't have to shoot anybody. Heedless of the afghan that had slipped to her waist, she raised the gun in the air and fired. It didn't make much noise, but it was enough to attract the assailant's attention. His head swung toward her, his eyes bugging out.

She smiled grimly. "That's right. Next time I'll blow your head off," she snarled, advancing with the gun leveled at him, hoping it was too dark for him to see how badly she was shaking.

Her commando act worked. As the man's attention focused on her, Mike broke free. He landed a blow on the other man's chin. Then another. And another. The intruder let out a strangled sigh and went slack.

Mike was out from under him in an instant. "Keep them covered," he growled.

Lisa sagged against the chair, dropping her hold on the afghan to wrap both hands around the gun. But her effort to keep it steady was futile; she was shaking all over.

Mike darted to the closet and emerged with a roll of heavy tape. He closed the front door, then used the tape to bind the two unconscious men's wrists and ankles. For good measure, he sealed their mouths and left them trussed up and lying strewn about like logs washed up on a beach.

Lisa, who had never felt closer to collapse, marveled at Mike's cool common sense when he stooped beside each captive in turn and rummaged through their pockets until he found their wallets and located identification.

"Lennie Ezrine," Mike muttered with a nod toward the larger of the two intruders, the one he'd knocked out first. "And this one's Jack Ordway."

"Hollingsworth said he'd send someone after me," Lisa whispered, her voice shaking as badly as the rest of her.

Mike snorted with disgust. "Lucky, it's so hard to get good help these days." Dumping the wallets on top of the two unconscious bodies, he stood up, rubbing the knuckles of his right hand against his left palm. Then he crossed to her and pried the gun loose from her frozen fingers.

He led her around the corner into a dining alcove. A square pine table and two chairs filled most of the space. Mike put the gun on the table and turned to her.

"You hurt yourself," she said, taking his hand and running a gentle finger over the reddened knuckles.

"I'll be all right." He gathered her into his arms.

She clung to him, still trembling. He felt so good, his body so strong and lean and healthy. "I put you in danger. If they'd . . . hurt you or—"

"Stop it," he admonished gently. "It's not your fault you've stumbled into Justine's mess."

"It may have been hers to begin with, but it sure seems like my mess now."

Beneath her cheek, his muscled, hair-dusted chest rose and fell in a heavy sigh. "Until we figure out who you are—or where Justine is—yeah, I'm afraid you're right. And I should have realized it. I should have taken you somewhere else." He gave a self-deprecating grunt. "So much for keeping you safe."

"But you did keep me safe," she whispered. "If I'd been alone, still driving around in the car, when they found me—"

His hands tightened on her back. "Don't think about it."

"I knew they were coming. In the car, on our way here, I could *feel* someone out there, looking for me. And I knew they wouldn't give up."

"Did you recognize them?" he asked.

"No." She looked up at him, frowning. "Should I?"

"They're the creeps who followed you out of the garage next to my office. The same ones who drove you into the Jones Falls."

She shuddered violently, burying her face against his neck. "I don't remember anything from before the accident."

The barest trace of humor crept into his tone as he said, "So, Annie Oakley, you don't know if you've ever fired a gun."

She shook her head. "No, but it felt ... odd. Foreign. I don't think I have."

"Well, whether you have or not, you did exactly the right thing with it. You were very brave."

"I didn't feel brave. I felt terrified."

"I've never seen it written that you can't be scared and brave at the same time. But I tell you what—" he leaned to glance around the corner into the living room "—unless you want to face them awake again, we'd better split."

Another violent shudder ran through her. "I don't ever want to see them again—awake or otherwise."

He grunted softly. "Right. So let's get—"

"Mike, tell me the truth," she interrupted. "They meant to kill me, didn't they?"

He studied her for a moment, and she could see that he didn't want to answer.

"I can't be sure," he said finally. "But my guess would be, yes, they were sent to kill you. Sweetheart, I'm sorry, but nobody uses a silencer unless he means business."

"Where can I go?" she whispered. "Until I know who wants me dead—or who wants Justine dead—it doesn't seem like anyplace is safe."

"I'm working on that," he said. "But first things first. I'd like to wake these bastards up and see what kind of information I could get out of them. But they might have backup outside, waiting. I want to get you away from here—fast."

She nodded. "Okay."

He gave her shoulder a reassuring squeeze, then left her while he went into the living room. Lisa took a small step forward to peek around the corner, her gaze following Mike as he began picking up couch pillows.

"Are you going to call the police?" she asked.

"Not from here," he replied.

She watched as he carefully retrieved her bra and shirt from under one of the combatant's feet. Shuddering as he held out the garments to her, she said, "I can't wear them."

"Then you'll have to borrow something of mine." He dropped her unwanted clothing, grabbed her sandals off the floor and led her to his bedroom. There he found sweatpants and a dark T-shirt for her and jeans and a shirt for himself. The clothes were far too big, but she didn't mind. They smelled like him, which gave her a sense of feeling safe and cared for.

"Afraid I can't lend you shoes, unless you want to play Bozo the clown."

Nodding, she slipped into her sandals. As her thoughts started to clear, she began to wonder who, indeed, had sent the two men tied up in the living room, and who exactly they'd come seeking. It was reasonable to assume they were after Justine, who apparently knew she was being followed and had escaped.

But it was also possible that the attackers had been looking for *her*. She knew next to nothing about herself. Before her accident, had she been involved in something that would make her a target for murder? Recent events led her to believe that anything was possible. Even that she could be running away from the father of her baby.

That thought led to speculation about a messy divorce and a wildly possessive husband. Or maybe a man married to someone else, who was driven to the point of madness because she'd refused to have an abortion. She couldn't envision herself having an affair with a married man, but at this point, it would be foolish to discount any possibility.

Sitting on the edge of the bed, she pressed her fingers to her suddenly pounding temple. "Mike, how did I look when you saw me on the street that first time? I mean, did you have any clue about my state of mind?"

He stopped in the act of loading a clip of bullets into a gun he'd taken from a bureau drawer. "You looked upset. Why?"

"I'm trying to figure out what I was doing in Baltimore with a rental car—or why I was in your office building. I mean, since I wasn't there to see you."

"Good question, but save it for later," he ordered gently. "We've got more pressing problems right now. Let's go."

The gun was in his hand as he preceded her down the hall and past their still-unconscious visitors. As they approached the front door, Lisa heard a thump. Both she and Mike froze. His gun came up into firing position. Another thump sounded—closer this time.

Mike grimaced. "Newspaper. Christ, if he throws it against the door, one of our visitors could wake up." Tucking his gun inside his jeans at the small of his back, he opened the door and stepped quickly into the hall. "We're going out, so I'll take it," he said to the delivery boy. Before the sleepy-eyed kid got a step closer, he drew Lisa by the hand into the hallway with him, and closed the door behind them with a quiet click.

After handing over the paper, the boy trudged back down the stairs, and Mike gave the paper to Lisa. "Here. Carry this."

She hugged the paper to her in an unconsciously protective gesture as Mike pulled out the gun. He motioned her to be quiet, and they stood listening to the delivery boy's steps as he descended the stairs. After the back door banged shut behind the boy, Mike led the way downstairs and into the yard. In the early-morning light, Mike's gaze darted up and down the alley, his attention on full alert. He held the passenger door of the Mustang open for her, then closed it after she climbed inside.

As he swung into the driver's seat beside her, she turned to toss the paper onto the back seat, but a headline on the front page caught her eye, and she stopped cold.

"Oh, my God," she breathed.

"What's wrong?" Mike asked.

"He's...dead," she managed to say, nearly strangling on the words. "But he...he can't be!"

"*Who's* dead?" Mike pulled the paper toward him. "Holy mother of...Millionaire Developer Kendall Hollingsworth Found Dead," he said, reading the headline aloud. As she listened in shock, he quickly summarized the story. "It says his housekeeper found him unconscious with a lump on the back of his head. His wife is missing and...*shit*. She's wanted for questioning."

"But, Mike, he was alive!" Lisa exclaimed. "I swear he was! He was alive enough to walk across a room and try to grab me."

Mike's dark brows were drawn together in a ferocious scowl. "Sweetheart, I believe you. But I think we'd better find someplace less public than this alley to figure out what happened."

As he drove slowly between the backyards, Lisa fought off the feeling of unreality that threatened to swamp her. None of this could be happening. But every few seconds, when the surreal sensation numbing her brain let up a little and reality seeped in, she knew that it was, indeed, happening.

It didn't seem matters could get any worse. She didn't know who she was. Didn't know where she lived or even her real name. About the only facts she did know were her height, weight, hair and eye color, blood type... and that she was pregnant. She'd been mistaken for some woman who had disappeared into thin air and who was married to a monster. A man who had tried to rape her and who was now dead. And the police thought she might have killed him.

"Are you taking me to the police station?" she asked in a small voice.

Mike gave her a startled glance. "No."

"Maybe you should."

He made a right onto a one-way street. "Why? You're not Justine."

"What if I was the last person to see him alive?" Feeling sick, Lisa picked up the paper and began to read. "It talks about his wife being treated for amnesia, and—" She sucked in a sharp breath.

"Read it to me," Mike insisted, his gaze flickering between the empty, predawn street and the rearview mirror.

"Are we being followed?" she asked.

"I don't think so. It would be hard to follow anyone this early in the morning and not get caught. Keep reading."

Lisa went back to the article. "They got a quote from Maggie Dempsey. "'I was working in the kitchen when I saw Mrs. Hollingsworth through the window,'" the housekeeper told reporters. "I thought it was strange that she was outside after nine o'clock in the evening. So I called to her, but she didn't answer.''''"

"You were with me at nine o'clock," Mike said. "I looked at the clock on the dashboard right before we went inside my apartment. It was eight-thirty."

"But Maggie says—"

"She saw *someone,*" Mike finished the sentence. "What if it was Justine?"

Lisa stared at him, her mouth slightly open.

He explained. "Justine's been hiding out all week. Her car was at the airport, remember? Suppose she came back last night. Suppose she wanted to get back at Hollingsworth for all the times he raped *her*. Suppose she killed him."

Lisa let out a long breath. "Only, I'm the one who's going to take the blame."

Mike's face was grim. "We've got to find out who you are. And prove that you're not involved in any of this."

"But, Mike, I *am* involved," she insisted. "For heaven's sake, I hit the man over the head!"

"In self-defense," he muttered. "And if you *had* killed him, it still would have been self-defense."

His calm assurance didn't stop shivers from racing over her skin. "If Hollingsworth was dead last night, he can't be the one who sent the men this morning," she said.

Mike shook his head. "He could have set something in motion before he died—like yesterday before he came home from his trip. Hell, he could have set it up weeks ago."

Lisa gave a little nod. Wrapped in the shock of Kendall Hollingsworth's demise, she hadn't been paying attention to where they were going. When Mike made a right into an alley, she sat up and took notice. He pulled to a stop behind an aging brick row house and parked.

She gave the alley a nervous once-over. "Where are we?"

"A friend's house." Hesitating, he explained, "Pat's a bit strange, so be prepared."

"How do you mean, 'strange'?" she asked.

Lifting one shoulder in a shrug, he said, "Rough. Keeps to himself. I arrested him a long time ago for petty larceny. When he got out of jail, he was nailed for an armed robbery he didn't commit. I caught the guy who did." Again, Mike shrugged as if to say what he'd done was no big deal. "He does me favors from time to time."

"And what favor are you asking today?" she asked.

"I want to make some phone calls."

"To the police?"

"I think we'll wait on that one until I've got you out of town. But I'm interested in the question you asked a while ago—about what you were doing in my office building. You didn't come to see me, but you must have been there for *some* reason. Somebody in one of the offices must have seen you. And they might know who you are."

Lisa's eyes widened, a spark of hope flaring inside her.

Mike nodded. "Exactly. We've got a couple of lawyers, an architect, Dr. Franklin, a herbalist . . ."

He went on to name several dozen others. None of the names were familiar, but, she thought grimly, that didn't mean a thing.

Suddenly, a crash from somewhere nearby made her jump.

"Probably a rat in a trash can," he muttered. Still, he waited awhile before getting out to reconnoiter the alley.

When he was satisfied that no one was watching, he ushered her toward a door covered with peeling black paint. He knocked and, after a short time, the door was opened by a middle-aged man with broad shoulders, wearing a green plaid shirt and jeans.

"Mike!" The man's lined face creased in a smile.

"Sorry to bother you so early, Pat, but I need your phone."

"Sure, come on in." The man led them down a hall. "I just got off work, so you didn't wake me up."

"Still working at High's?"

"Yeah, it's good. Too bad more ex-cons don't have a Mike Lancer to find 'em jobs when they get out of the joint."

Lisa's gaze flashed to Mike as they entered a dark sitting room with faded overstuffed furniture. So, he'd done a little more for Pat than keep him out of prison. Is that how he thought of her—as simply another Red Cross case?

Dismissing the notion as implausible, given the night before, Lisa turned her attention to her shabby surroundings. From the sofa, a gray tabby looked at them curiously.

"Lisa, this is Pat Lemon," Mike said.

Lisa murmured something polite and shook the man's hand. He seemed nice enough, and he certainly seemed to like Mike. But the seedy, worn-out surroundings only added to the surreal, almost grotesque feeling of the morning.

"Can I get you anything?" Lemon asked her. When she shook her head, he ambled toward a flight of stairs, telling Mike, "I'll be working on my crossword puzzle if you need me."

After watching her taciturn host depart, Lisa perched on the sofa. When the cat moved two feet to curl next to her, she began almost unconsciously to pet it. And as Mike plunked down in a decrepit armchair beside the phone, picked up the receiver and began dialing, she went on stroking the purring animal, the soothing action helping to control her mounting tension as she listened to Mike's conversations.

A few people he tried didn't answer, but when he got someone on the line, he always started by mentioning the article in the paper about Hollingsworth, then asking if anyone had seen the woman in the picture. Lisa knew from his expression that the answers were negative.

After a dozen calls, he replaced the receiver with a sigh. "Sorry, I thought it was a good idea."

She spoke past the tightness in her throat. "It made sense to try."

"I want you out of the city," he said emphatically, picking up the phone again and punching in another number. Almost immediately, someone answered. "Jenny, it's Mike," he said. "I've got a problem."

Lisa listened, her anxiety growing, as he launched into a more detailed explanation about her amnesia, the murder and her being wanted for questioning. As she took in the earnest, worried expression on his face, she realized he fully intended to solve her problem. He really meant to find out who she was, and she had no doubt that he would move heaven and earth to do it.

Which made her aware in a way she hadn't been before that she absolutely had to tell him about the baby. It couldn't be put off any longer. And not only because he had a right to know. How could she expect him to do his job without all the information? Her pregnancy might be a major clue in leading him to her identity.

She'd intended to tell him that morning—perhaps over breakfast together. But events had precluded breakfast and had certainly left no time for intimate chats about her condition. Now, the more she thought about it, the more difficult telling him seemed.

Last night it had all been very clear. As far as she was concerned, there was no man but Mike in her life. She loved him, and she longed to tell him she would love him forever. Yet, in the light of day, she faced the truth that she had no right to make such a promise, not without knowing what her previous commitments might be.

Moreover, she had no idea how her revelation would affect Mike's feelings about her. It didn't seem possible that he could have made love to her as he had and not love her. Even so, what if he *did* love her? How would she feel when he learned she was pregnant with another man's child?

Betrayed. Angry. Hurt. The words flashed into her mind, and she reluctantly had to accept that they could be accurate. Given his emotionally impoverished background, falling in love with Justine must have been an enormous step for him. Probably for the first time in his life, he'd dared to be happy. And it had lasted for two years. Justine's betrayal had made it almost impossible for him to trust a woman— particularly one who looked so much like Justine. It wouldn't take much—no, not much at all—to destroy his trust once again.

Lisa huddled on the couch, petting the cat, steeling herself to tell Mike about her pregnancy. Her attention snapped to the present, though, when she heard him ending his conversation with the woman to whom he was speaking.

"I really appreciate this, Jenny," he said. "We'll be there in about thirty minutes." He hung up the receiver and gave her a thumbs-up sign. "We're all set. You can stay at Jenny's while I canvass my office building with your picture."

Lisa nodded. "But, Mike, I have to—"

"The only thing you have to do is stay out of harm's way." He gave her a warm smile. "Now, let me handle this, okay?" Standing up, he walked toward the door, calling over his shoulder, "Come on."

Filled with all sorts of new trepidations, Lisa followed.

When they were back on the street once more, she started again to tell Mike that she was pregnant.

Before she could speak, he gave her a quick smile, saying, "Let me tell you about Jenny. She's a computer programmer." He paused for an instant, then added, "She's blind. But she insists on being self-sufficient. She lives by herself in an old farmhouse outside the city, in a little town called Elkridge. It's pretty isolated. Perfect for us. There isn't a chance anybody will think about looking for you there."

He shot her an expectant look, as if he was waiting for approval, and Lisa obliged him with a nod. She wasn't worried about the location; she trusted his judgment. There were other things about the arrangement, however, that bothered her.

They were on a major highway now, heading out of the city, and Lisa kept her gaze directed straight ahead as she said, "You didn't tell Jenny that I'm suspected of murder, did you?"

"The article doesn't say that," he replied.

"Why else would I be wanted for questioning?"

"First, they want Justine—not you. Second, they want to talk to the dead man's wife because she's missing. Hell, they could be thinking she's dead, too." He reached over to squeeze her hand where it lay clenched on her lap. "So try not to jump to conclusions. When I get you settled, I'm going to call a contact I've got in the department."

Lisa stared out the side window at the flat, marshy stretches of land flashing past. "Jenny could get in trouble for letting me stay with her, couldn't she? She and you both could be... what's it called? Accessories?"

"Lisa, stop it. Nobody's going to get in trouble for helping you, because you didn't kill anyone."

"Suppose I did," she insisted. "Suppose he had a brain hemorrhage or something."

Mike let out a sigh filled with exasperation. "Then, like I said before, it was self-defense. Sweetheart, you've got enough other things to worry about. Don't make yourself sick worrying about something that isn't going to happen. You're not going to get charged with a murder you didn't commit."

Lisa wasn't at all sure he was right that she wouldn't be charged with murder, but he was certainly right that she had enough other things to worry about and that worry was making her sick. At least, *something* was making her sick. She felt awful, dizzy and exhausted and decidedly queasy. Was it only shock and worry? Or was morning sickness finally rearing its ugly head?

Wouldn't that just be the perfect way to break the news that she was pregnant—to throw up all over his car.

It soon became impossible to think about telling him anything. She couldn't talk without wanting to vomit. She considered it a blessing when Mike switched on the radio to a light rock station, making conversation unnecessary. For the remainder of the trip, Lisa concentrated on taking slow even breaths and studying the unremarkable horizon.

It wasn't long before Mike slowed the Mustang at a gravel driveway leading to a Victorian farmhouse perched atop a hill. The house was surrounded by a stand of huge spreading maples, covered in new, pale green leaves, and stately old hemlocks. A couple hundred feet away was a big red barn.

As Mike pulled the car to a stop by the front porch, the door opened. A slender young woman came out and made her way to the railing, tapping in front of her with a long white cane. Her brown hair was pulled back into a single braid. Her gaze, Lisa noticed, was directed toward the car as if she could see it.

Mike rolled down the window. "Okay if I park in the barn?"

"Sure," the woman called back.

Mike drove through the double doors and cut the engine. As they started walking toward the house, Lisa felt shyness and anxiety wash over her at the impending meeting with Jenny, and it occurred to her that, since waking up from the accident, she'd felt the same way each time she'd met a new person. It wasn't only a matter of nerves made raw from recent events. It was the notion of facing a stranger when she was a stranger to herself. Halfway to the house, Lisa's steps faltered. She didn't know if she could face this woman who Mike thought of as a friend and who was clearly important to him.

It was as if he knew what she was going through when he put his arm around her waist and tugged her close in a brief hug. "It's okay, Lisa," he said. "Jenny's the last person on earth who'd give you grief."

His lips curved upward in an encouraging smile, and she offered him a tentative smile in return.

"That's my brave lady," he said, then leaned down to give her a quick kiss. And just before they reached the porch, he murmured close to her ear, "Promise me you won't tell Jenny I was fighting burglars at dawn bare-ass naked. She might think it was...you know...undignified."

Despite herself, Lisa giggled.

He missed her grateful look as he mounted the porch steps, saying, "Jenny Larkin, I'd like you to meet Lisa. Lisa, this is Jenny."

"It's nice to meet you," Jenny said, her blue gaze appearing to follow the progress of their footsteps up onto the porch.

"Thank you for letting me come here," Lisa returned, stopping beside Mike. "But I'm worried you could get in trouble if the police find out."

Jenny didn't answer. She was frowning slightly, her head tipped to one side. "I've heard your voice before," she said.

For an instant, Lisa simply stared at her, confused.

"Say something else," Jenny said as she made small circles with the tip of her cane on the porch floor.

Lisa cleared her throat, feeling extremely self-conscious. "Um...what should I say?"

"Anything."

"Uh..." Nervously, she scrambled for something reasonably coherent. "I've had some upsetting things happen lately. I guess it started with my car going into a river."

Jenny's features, which were small and regular and pretty, softened in a sympathetic look. "I know this is awkward, but I identify people from their voices. Try telling me that you have an appointment with Mrs. Stone."

"I have an appointment with Mrs. Stone," she managed to say, feeling her throat constrict. Had she spoken those exact words before?

"I'm almost certain you were in my office," Jenny said. "We talked to each other."

With her heart suddenly racing, Lisa whispered, "What office?"

"Birth Data, Inc."

She blinked, at once bewildered and unbearably excited. "I—I came there? What is it?"

Before Jenny could speak, Mike answered the question, and his voice was strung with tension. "It's a family-search organization for adopted children run by Erin Stone. She was one of the people I called this morning, but she didn't answer."

"You wanted to locate your birth parents," Jenny added.

Dumbfounded, Lisa glanced from Jenny to Mike, then back to Jenny. "I'm adopted?"

"I presume so," Jenny replied.

Her knees buckled. Suddenly, as if the ground had opened under her feet, Lisa felt herself falling. Mike moved quickly to catch her, his arms coming around her waist from behind.

She could hardly breathe, but as she leaned against Mike for support, she managed to get out a few words. "Do you know my name? Do you know who I am?"

Chapter Seventeen

"The name you gave was Leigh Barnes."

"Leigh Barnes," Lisa repeated, squeezing her eyes closed. She waited for the magic door to open. Any second now, it would all come back to her—family, job, home, the father of her baby. But the place in her mind reserved for such memories was still only empty space. Nothing. Not even a hint of anything familiar.

The disappointment was so acute, tears filled her eyes, and she had to fight hard not to cry. She let Mike guide her with an arm around her waist into the house. Jenny followed. Lisa crumpled into a corner of the sofa, sinking deep into the fluffy cushions.

"Did you remember something?" he asked.

She shook her head.

To Jenny, he said, "Are you sure Lisa is the same woman you spoke to?"

Jenny's brow wrinkled. "I thought so. It was last week. Ellen, our receptionist, was on lunch break, so I talked directly to Leigh Barnes." Closing the front door and propping her cane against the wall, she crossed to the sofa and sat beside Lisa. "I'm sorry. I shouldn't have been so quick to speak."

Swallowing the tears clogging her throat, Lisa replied, "It's not your fault. I could be the person you met, but I simply don't remember."

Outside, a horn honked. "That's my ride," Jenny said. "I can tell them I'm not going in to work today."

"No," Mike countered. "Better follow your normal routine, in case anybody's nosing around Light Street."

She looked torn. "I hate to leave you like this."

"Go on," he said gently. "We appreciate what you're doing for us."

"Yes," Lisa added.

With what Lisa thought was remarkable confidence, Jenny rose and crossed to a small table by the door. She picked up her purse and the white cane—one of the only clues that she was blind—then said, "Make yourselves at home. There's an extra house key in the drawer beside the fridge. If you want to get some sleep, the guest bedroom is on your left at the top of the stairs. But please don't move any furniture, or leave anything lying around where I might trip over it."

"We'll put everything back where we found it," Mike assured her.

After Jenny left, Lisa sat with her head cradled in her hands. Grimly, she tried to push her thoughts through the blank wall in her mind. "Leigh Barnes," she repeated over and over. All she got for her efforts was a headache.

The sofa beside her sagged, and she let her hands fall from her face as Mike sat and pulled her into his arms.

"Don't make demands on yourself that you can't fulfill."

"How did you know what I was doing?"

He laughed. "If I were you, I'd be giving myself a migraine trying to crash through the memory barrier."

"I hated being called Justine—I mean *hated* it—enough that you'd think it might force me to remember who I am. If amnesia is part physical and part emotional trauma, it makes me wonder what on earth happened to me. I guess it was so awful that I've blocked out everything."

He stroked his knuckle against her cheek. "At least you know why you picked the name Lisa."

She managed a smile. "Yes. Leigh. Lisa. It must have sounded familiar."

"And you know why you were in Baltimore at 43 Light Street." With one arm still around her shoulders, he stretched for the phone sitting on the table next to the sofa. "Let's see what Erin Stone has to say. I'll try her again at home. Maybe she was in the shower earlier." Mike punched in the numbers, then gave her a quick nod at the same time she heard the faint "Hello" come through the receiver.

"Erin, it's Mike," he said. "Sorry to bother you so early, but I have an urgent request...."

It was quickly obvious that things weren't going the way he had anticipated. "But this is a matter of life and death," he argued. "I want to prove Lisa had no motive for assaulting Kendall Hollingsworth, except that he was trying to rape her." After a pause, he sighed. "Okay. I appreciate your position." He put his hand over the mouthpiece and spoke to Lisa, his expression exasperated. "Erin's sorry, but information on clients is confidential."

"Let me talk to her," Lisa said. Mike handed her the receiver, and she took a deep breath. "Mrs. Stone?"

"Yes," a pleasant voice answered.

"I'm sorry to bother you at home. I'm at Jenny Larkin's house because two men came into Mike's apartment this morning and tried to kill us."

The woman on the other end of the line sucked in a startled breath. "Mike left out that little detail."

"Yes, well, a lot of frightening things have happened recently, starting when the same two men ran my car into the Jones Falls. I would have drowned if Mike hadn't been there to pull me out. The problem is, I woke up from the accident with amnesia. I don't remember a thing—not even my name, much less where I live, where I work...nothing. My purse was lost in the accident, so I don't have any identification. When we got here this morning and Jenny said she'd met me in your office, that was the first clue I've had to my identity." Lisa heard the desperation in her own voice as she finished. "So you see, Mike wasn't exaggerating. It truly seems to be a matter of life and death."

A short pause ensued. When the other woman finally answered, her tone made Lisa want to cry again.

"I don't know what to say. God, what you've been through sounds dreadful! But, well, I can only hope you'll understand why our files are closed. Information about adopted children and their birth parents is very sensitive."

"But you may be the only one who can help me!" Lisa said, impatience getting the better of her. "What if I came to your office? If you recognize me as Leigh Barnes, would you release the file?"

This time the pause was longer.

"Yes. All right," the woman said finally.

"Oh..." Lisa bit back a sob. "Thank you. You don't know..." Her hand sought Mike's, which was resting on her shoulder, and gave his fingers a squeeze. Then, she asked, "Did I fill out some kind of form?"

"Yes."

At the positive response, Lisa asked the question burning in the back of her throat. "Could you give me one piece of information? Did I say I was married?"

"I believe you said you were single."

"Thank you," she breathed.

"Let me have the phone." Mike took the receiver from her trembling fingers. "Erin, I don't want to bring Lisa to Light Street. Whoever sent the thugs to my apartment might have the office staked out, too. Could you meet us, say, at that little coffee shop near the Walters Art Gallery? ...All right. Noon. Yeah, that's fine."

Replacing the receiver in its cradle, he was silent for a moment. The lines of tension in his face mirrored the strain in his voice as he spoke. "Well, what's the answer to the question? Are you married?"

She shook her head. "No."

"Thank God." He grabbed her hand, clutching it tightly.

This was it, she thought. There would never be a better time to tell him. "Mike..." She drew a slow breath, trying to calm her churning stomach. "I wish it were as simple as my not being married. But it isn't."

He uttered a humorless laugh. "I'm just glad to hear my worst fear isn't going to come true—that I don't have to turn you over to some other guy."

"No, but . . . there are other complications."

Leaning away from her a little, he gave her a sharp look. "You remember something you're not telling me?"

She shook her head. "Not on a conscious level."

"Then are you trying to say that last night didn't—" he broke off, his gaze falling from hers "—that it didn't mean something to you?"

Her eyes misted. "Oh, Mike, of course it did. It meant the world to me. I love you. Or I wouldn't have made love with you."

He gathered her close. "Lisa—"

"Oh, Lord, I shouldn't have told you that."

"Did you mean it?"

"Yes, but I'm not free to say it."

"You're afraid there's some other man in your life."

"No. I mean, that's not the point. The point is that I'm . . . I'm pregnant."

He suddenly went rigid and very still. "You're what?"

She didn't repeat it. She knew he had heard.

Several dreadful moments went by in utter silence.

Rising, he took a couple of steps away from the couch and turned to look down at her. "You knew that last night?"

Heart pounding, Lisa nodded. "Dr. Habib told me."

"So why didn't you tell *me*?" he demanded.

Sighing raggedly, she said, "At first it was too personal. Then I tried to tell you a couple of times. I was going to do it right before Hollingsworth came home from his hunting trip and found us in his den."

An injured look crossed his features, but he quickly regained control. "But it slipped your mind last night."

"I wanted you so much," she whispered. "Mike, last night we needed each other—you know it as well as I do. And I was afraid if I told you, you wouldn't want to make love with me—that you would think it was wrong or...I don't know...dishonorable.''

"Well, you got that right.''

"But don't you see,'' she pleaded. "It *wasn't* wrong or dishonorable! I have no idea who the father of my baby is, and I might *never* know. Should I have to go on for the rest of my life without anyone? Or condemn my baby to having no father just because I'm waiting for my memory to come back?''

"So, what if you don't remember?'' he countered. "It's only been a week. It's not at all unlikely that either you'll find out who you are or that somebody is looking for you— and that he'll find you.''

She gave her head a quick shake. "It wouldn't matter. Mike, I love *you*. I could never go off with some man I didn't even know, much less love, no matter who he is or what he's been to me! It would be like promising eternal fidelity to a total stranger! No. Worse than that. It would be like keeping a promise that some other woman made!''

In the silence that followed, Lisa saw Mike waver, saw the longing in his eyes war with the anger and pain of what she knew he perceived as her betrayal. But the battle was over quickly. Anger and pain won. He turned away, walking over to stand at the window, his back toward her.

She stared at the rigid set of his shoulders. "Mike, please,'' she begged. But he didn't turn around, and she knew it was hopeless to try again. The wall was in place between them, more impenetrable than ever.

Had she lost him forever? The possibility brought a strangled sob to her throat, and tears soon followed, hot and heavy. Scrambling off the sofa, she dashed toward the stairs, but with tears blurring her vision, she was clumsy. She slipped, banging her knee against a stair tread.

Ignoring the pain, she pushed herself up and kept going. In the guest room, she shut the door and threw herself on the bed, where she curled into a ball and cried. She needed Mike there, on the bed with her, holding her, telling her everything would be all right. But she knew he wouldn't come, not now. And maybe never.

LENNIE SQUINTED as he emerged into the watery sunshine outside police headquarters.

Beside him, Jackal breathed a long draft of warm spring air and let it out slowly. "I need a drink," he muttered.

"Later," the high-priced lawyer snapped as he led them rapidly down the block.

Lennie had never met the guy before, but he'd been impressed at how fast he'd gotten them sprung. As they turned the corner, Lennie saw a black Lincoln that looked as out of place in the neighborhood as a champagne bottle in a cooler of beer.

"He wants to talk to you." The mouthpiece gestured toward the sedan, then walked away.

Lennie peered at the car but couldn't see through the privacy glass. Wiping his sweaty palm on his pants, he reached for the handle and opened the door. The man in the back seat looked as though he was on his way to a board meeting. A uniformed driver sat behind the wheel, eyes straight ahead.

Lennie eased into the back seat. Jackal took the space by the window and closed the door. The air inside the luxury sedan was heavy with the aroma of expensive after-shave. Probably fifty dollars a bottle.

"I hear you had considerable difficulty this morning," Señor Realto observed in his slightly accented English.

Lennie hesitated, afraid to trust the man's mild tone.

"Yeah, but it wasn't our fault," Jackal jumped in. "We woulda put Lancer away and grabbed the broad—if the son of a bitch had taken her to bed instead of screwing her on the living-room floor."

"He heard us at the door," Lennie added.

"Heard *you*," Jackal pointed out, to Lennie's disgust. "You were the one with the lock pick."

The car pulled away from the curb and nosed into traffic as Realto said, "There's no point in assigning blame."

Relaxing a little, Lennie said, "Thanks. And thanks a million for springin' us so fast."

Señor Realto nodded, his expression completely neutral. The man was always hard to figure. He was from some banana republic, and he only came to Baltimore a few months a year. When he was around, he paid real good—if you did your job and kept your mouth shut.

"Tell me what happened, *por favor*," Realto asked.

"Lancer was ready for us when we came in the door," Jackal whined. "It was just bad luck."

"*Sí*. But I'd like to hear about it."

As they drove up Fayette, Lennie answered questions. No, they hadn't squealed to the cops. Yes, as far as they knew, the woman was still with Lancer. No, they didn't know where he might have taken her.

"I think it's time for me to handle things personally," Realto murmured.

Lennie breathed a sigh of relief. He and Jackal were off the hook. This job had been bad news from the start. He wished they'd never picked up Miss Rich-Bitch's trail at that parking garage the week before. They'd known she had an appointment with Lancer, but they hadn't expected her to be driving a rental. Or to go into that Birth Data office. They'd been playing catch-up ever since.

The Lincoln stopped in back of an abandoned warehouse.

"Where are we, anyway?" Jackal asked.

"You'll be safe here," Realto said in a tone that sent a warning shiver up Lennie's spine.

The chauffeur pressed a remote control. The door opened and closed again as the car rolled into a dimly lit space.

Realto stepped out, then turned to look at them. His voice still bland, he said, "I'm sorry I overestimated your abilities, but I've learned when to cut my losses."

Jackal's "Hey, wait—" turned into a gurgle as a slug from the chauffeur's gun tore into his chest.

Lennie knew he didn't have a chance. Heart pounding, he leaped for the open door. He was half out when the bullet caught him, making a neat hole in the side of his head.

LISA HAD NO NOTION how long she'd been crying when she heard Mike's footsteps in the hall. Quickly, she wiped her hand across her eyes.

"You have an appointment with Erin Stone," Mike said through the closed door. "She's breaking her rules for you, so let's not keep her waiting."

Lisa struggled to pull herself together. A box of tissues sat on the bedside table, and she took one and blew her nose.

"Lisa, did you hear me?"

"Yes."

Her knee throbbed as she stood up and limped to the door. She hesitated before opening it, her hand on the doorknob, not wanting to face him. But it couldn't be avoided.

She found him looming in the hall, arms folded across his chest like protective armor. Ducking her head, she scooted past him into the bathroom. She stared at herself in the mirror. The woman who stared back looked awful, eyes puffy, skin splotchy, and splashing cold water on her face didn't help.

Trying not to limp, she met Mike at the front door. His expression was stony. He left her standing on the porch to go retrieve his car, and he didn't speak as she climbed in beside him. The silence continued during the ride into the city. She wanted to say something, to make him understand why she'd done what she'd done, but it was clear that he was in no mood to listen. So she simply stared straight ahead, wishing she had some makeup or, at least, a pair of dark glasses to hide her blotchy face.

They drove back through the city the way they'd left, and at some point Lisa realized Mike was looking for a parking place. She noticed a coffee shop on the next corner and assumed it was their destination. Her stomach, which had been none too stable all morning, began to churn once more with nerves over the impending meeting. A meeting that quite literally could determine the rest of her life.

Straightening in her seat, she cleared her throat. "Thank you for bringing me back to town. You can let me off at the corner. I guess you'd better return the balance of the retainer to Justine. I-I'll pay you back the rest as soon as I can. How much did she send you?"

"Five thousand dollars."

Lisa gasped.

"I'm working for her until further notice," Mike said, skidding to a halt behind a car pulling into traffic from a parking spot at the curb. He slipped his Mustang into the vacated spot, saying, "I think my expenses on her account were legitimate."

Lisa frowned, confused. His tone and expression told her that he was angry, but if that was so, why wasn't he doing as she'd asked, dumping her out at the corner?

"Do you have any money?" he muttered. "Anywhere to go?"

"I found some cash in Justine's bedroom," she replied. "But some of it's in the pocket of the slacks I was wearing last night and the rest is in the purse I left at Hollingsworth's. But, Mike, that doesn't matter. Mrs. Stone is going to tell me about Leigh Barnes, and it certainly looks like that's who I am. I presume I have a job—a home. Somewhere."

When he didn't respond, she cleared her throat again and said, "Maybe the best thing for me to do is contact the police."

That got a reaction.

"Like hell," he stated flatly. "You're not in any shape to answer a barrage of questions from a hostile interrogation team. Kendall Hollingsworth was an upstanding citizen, and they'll be under pressure to name his murderer. Right now, all they've got is you."

Lisa winced at hearing the truth put so bluntly.

His expression was still dark and brooding, but his tone less angry as he said, "Listen to what Erin has to say before you make any decisions."

"Won't it look bad that I'm hiding out?"

"Not if we can figure out who killed Hollingsworth—or, failing that, where Justine is. Or who you are."

Lisa noted his use of the word *we* but didn't dare speculate about its implications. Before she could ask how exactly they were going to solve a murder, Mike got of the car, fed a couple of coins into the meter and started toward the coffee shop. Lisa followed as fast as her injured knee would allow her to hobble.

Mike waited for her at the entrance of the small shop and held the door for her to enter. As they stepped inside the almost empty restaurant, she saw an attractive, dark-haired woman sitting in a booth near the back. She had seen them, too, and was looking toward them expectantly. With Mike following her, Lisa started down the narrow aisle, toward the woman who was presumably Erin Stone. As she approached, she was relieved to see a spark of recognition in her eyes.

"How did you hurt your leg?" she asked as they drew near her table.

"Oh . . . I tripped on the stairs." Lisa slid onto the opposite bench, casting a quick glance at Mike, who seemed to hesitate before sliding in next to her.

"I guess it's badly bruised."

Her hand fluttered in a dismissive gesture. If Mrs. Stone wanted to assume that was why she'd been crying, so much the better. She was acutely aware of Mike's shoulder and arm brushing hers. Tension was radiating from his body. It took more energy than she was capable of mustering at the moment to put the distraction entirely aside as she asked, "Mrs. Stone, are you reasonably confident that I'm Leigh Barnes?"

"Please, call me Erin. If you're a friend of Mike's, there's no need for us to be so formal." She smiled. "And, yes, I'm sure you must be Leigh Barnes. You look like her, and Jenny's right, you sound like her."

Lisa squeezed her eyes closed and uttered a sincere "Thank God." Then, looking once more at Erin, she said, "Since I woke up in the hospital, people have been trying to convince me that I'm Justine Hollingsworth."

Erin opened a briefcase and pulled out a slim folder. She was about to hand it to Lisa, when a waitress appeared.

An eternity seemed to pass while Mike ordered coffee. Lisa shook her head. She couldn't have swallowed a thing; her stomach was roiling.

When the waitress left, Erin passed the folder across the table. Pulse pounding in her ears, Lisa scanned the information. She was thirty years old. She lived in Philadelphia.

The waitress came with Mike's order and left again. Lisa kept reading, vaguely aware that Mike didn't touch the coffee.

"I'm an architect?" she asked, incredulous. From the corner of her eye, she saw Mike's startled look.

"That's what you said. Do you have reason to doubt it?"

"No, it just seems...unusual. But I guess it explains why I know how to operate a computer—and how to read construction specs."

As her eyes scanned down the page, more facts leaped out at her. High school. College. Childhood illnesses. Her adoptive parents, Sheila and William Barnes. They were both deceased, according to the information she'd written. But the words might as well have been about someone else.

"None of this means much to me," she admitted to Erin. "Did I tell you anything about myself? About why I came in?"

Erin threw Mike a quick glance. "I have notes from our conversation. But it's all extremely personal information."

Mike stood up instantly. "I'll make myself scarce." Before Lisa could stop him, he strode away.

She wanted to call him back, didn't want to keep any more secrets from him. But she wasn't sure he wanted to know more about her than he already did, which appeared to have been too much. She watched him exit the restaurant and head in the direction of his car. Then, with a sigh, she turned back to Erin.

Erin pulled several typed sheets from her briefcase and ran her eyes over the contents. "Some of this will be disturbing."

"Please, just tell me."

"You came to us because you were pregnant."

"Yes, the doctor at the hospital told me that."

"You said you wanted to know your heritage and your medical background so you could do the best for your child."

Lisa leaned forward. "Did I mention the baby's father?"

"Leigh—"

"Call me Lisa. I'm comfortable with that. Leigh still sounds foreign. Maybe I'll stick with Lisa permanently."

Erin nodded. "You said the father of your child is a man you met professionally. When you told him about the baby, he insisted that you get an abortion."

Lisa blanched. "I could never have an abortion."

"That's what you told him, and he threatened to get you fired. Apparently, he has some pull with your boss."

"Oh."

"You said that if you had to, you'd find a job in another state. That was another reason you came to Baltimore. You sent résumés to several architectural firms here, and you had interviews scheduled."

Feeling giddy and extremely unwell, Lisa pressed her fingers to her forehead. "Too bad I don't remember a thing about designing buildings," she muttered. "Did I happen to say if I had any money saved?"

Erin looked unhappy. "You mentioned some medical bills you're paying off."

"Oh, Lord." Under the table, her fingers clenched together as she wondered how she was going to support herself, let alone a baby. She didn't know. She didn't know how she was going to manage anything.

It was the final straw. Her stomach lurched in complete revolt. Suddenly, the smell of coffee and food wafting through the restaurant became nauseating, and she knew no amount of steady breathing was going to help.

"I'm going to be sick," she managed to say hoarsely, struggling to slide out of her seat.

As she bolted from the booth, she saw Mike coming through the door. Mortified, she darted to the back of the shop and shoved open the door marked Ladies. She just made it into one of the stalls, where she heaved into the toilet.

Several minutes later, she was sponging her face at the washbasin when the door opened and Erin came in.

"Are you all right?" she asked kindly.

"Embarrassed," Lisa murmured. Cupping her hands, she took a sip of water.

Erin looked at her sympathetically. "Morning sickness is part of the package."

"This is the first time for me. At least, it is as far as I know." A sudden, unbidden thought chilled her to the bone. Her head came up sharply. "Oh, Lord, what if it isn't? What if I've got other children who don't know where I am? What if—"

"Lisa, stop," Erin ordered firmly. "You'll make yourself crazy. If you do have children, the chances are excellent that they're being cared for and will be perfectly fine until you can get back to them."

Staring at Erin's reflection in the mirror above the sink, Lisa caught her breath, then let it out slowly. Erin was right, and as she became aware of how extreme her reaction had been, a little of the anxiety seeped out of her.

Erin continued on a sensible note. "If it will make you less worried, have a doctor examine you. She can tell whether you've ever delivered a baby. Maybe they even did an examination at the hospital while you were unconscious, to see if your pregnancy was threatened by the accident, in which case, all you have to do is call and ask." She concluded with a little shrug and a reassuring smile.

Lisa sighed. "Actually, I'm not sure I even want to know right now. I've already got more to worry about than I can handle—like, for instance, how I'm going to take care of *this* baby. It seems, with what you've told me, that I may be unemployed."

"Well, I have some ideas about that, too." Studying her, Erin said, "You look better. Are you ready to go sit down again?"

"I think so."

They left the ladies' room and began walking slowly back toward the table.

Halfway there, Erin said, "Birth Data, Inc., is part of a larger organization called the Stone Foundation. It was started by my husband, Travis Stone. We have many different programs, and I think we could help you."

Lisa shook her head. "I don't want to take anybody's charity."

"Would you take a job with us?"

She gave Erin a surprised look. "I—I suppose so, but... well, what sort of job? I don't remember any of my technical background."

Erin stopped beside their table. "I can arrange for aptitude tests. Then we'll have a better idea of what you've studied and where your interests lie."

Lisa's spirits rose a little. She might never be an architect again, but then, she had no memory of being one before. The important thing was that she'd have a job. Erin was offering her the chance to solve one of the many, seemingly unsolvable problems facing her. It felt good to be able to take positive action.

"Yes," she said. "That sounds fine. Thank you."

Erin slid into her seat. "It must be awful losing your entire memory—and on top of everything else! I can hardly imagine what you've been going through."

Looking down at the tabletop, Lisa fingered the spoon lying beside Mike's abandoned coffee as she muttered, "I have the feeling I don't want to remember the shambles I made of my life. If only I could—"

"Lisa."

She jumped at the sound of Mike's voice beside her.

"I'm sorry," he said. "I didn't mean to startle you."

Her hands fluttered at her waist. "It's okay. I just didn't [se] you."

"Are you all right?" he asked, glancing briefly at Erin, [th]en back at her.

"As well as can be expected, I guess." She searched his [g]aze, wary of the urgency she saw reflected there. "Why? [W]hat's happened?"

"I have some news." His voice was grim.

The knot in her stomach tightened in anticipation.

"I checked in with my office from the car phone," he [sa]id. "There's been another murder."

Chapter Eighteen

Lisa could hardly bring herself to ask. "Who?"

"Estelle Bensinger."

She pressed her hand over her mouth. "Oh, Lord."

Holding her gaze, Mike went on. "She was found floaing in the Inner Harbor—with a bullet in her back."

Lisa stared at him in numb silence, trying to grasp tl implications of this latest catastrophe. The jingling of tl bell above the shop door failed to break through her daz but the sight of a uniformed policeman coming through tl doorway yanked her back to the present with a snap.

"Oh, no," she gasped. "Mike..."

At her stricken look, he glanced over his shoulder. The without hesitation, he took her hand and pushed her into tl booth, sliding in after her until she was tucked between hi and the wall, their backs to the door.

"Sit tight. He's probably just getting a cup of coffee," I hissed as he cupped his arm around her shoulder.

She huddled next to him, heart pounding, her gaze rieted on Erin, whose eyes followed the policeman's proress. Lisa expected that any second the officer would strie over, grab her by the shoulder and whip out a pair of hancuffs. Several horrible minutes passed before she saw Erintense features relax.

"He's gone," she said. "Mike was right. He only wante a cup of coffee."

Lisa let out the breath she'd been holding. Without thinking, she turned her palm up to clasp Mike's hand and lowered her head to his shoulder. "Thank you," she whispered.

His acknowledgment was little more than a grunt, and it made her remember that she didn't have any right to lean on him. Straightening, she detached her hand from his, her cheeks growing warm under Erin's curious gaze.

"I hate feeling like a fugitive," she said, her voice strained and ragged. "What if I just go home? To the address I listed on my application." As soon as she'd said it, she thought, wait a minute, bad idea. Given the new knowledge of Hollingsworth's and Estelle Bensinger's murders, it seemed almost certain that the two men who'd broken in that morning had been looking for Justine, not her. But suppose they'd been sent by her baby's father—the man who'd threatened to get her fired. Philadelphia would be the first place anyone wanting to harm Leigh Barnes would look.

"No, forget it," she said.

"Right," Mike agreed. "You're in danger. And the only thing we know for sure is that whoever's after you isn't Kendall Hollingsworth. He's dead. So is his secretary. It seems pretty clear to me that Justine is high on the hit list. And even if they realize you aren't Justine, they might *still* follow you home because they think, by now, you know too much." Mike shook his head slowly. "The way I see it, you have one choice. You've got to lie low for a few days until we figure out who's behind the murders."

He was right. Lord help her, she knew he was right. But she wasn't only terrified for herself and the baby. She raised reddened eyes to Mike. "They know you're helping me. Maybe they wanted to kill you this morning, too."

"I can take care of myself," he repeated his earlier assurance.

She dragged in a shaky breath, knowing there was no use arguing with him. But he wasn't the only one she was endangering.

"I can't go back to Jenny's. I can't put her in jeopard
too."

"There isn't a snowball's chance in hell that anybody
going to know you're there," Mike assured her. "The on
way they'd know is if they followed us, and you can damne
well bet I'm not going to let that happen. I'll drop you of
Then I'll show up at the office, so anyone keeping tabs c
me will see I'm alone."

She didn't bother arguing. She knew it wouldn't do a
good.

"I hate to leave you like this," Erin said.

Gathering what wits she had left, Lisa asked, "May I ta
my folder? Maybe looking at it will trigger a memory."

"You can take the copy. I need the original."

Lisa folded the papers and put them into her purs
"Erin, you've been a tremendous help. I can't tell you ho
it feels to know that I *am* somebody. I may not rememb
my past or my current life, but having facts about the
makes a big difference."

"I'm glad." Erin handed Lisa a business card and starte
toward the door. "Call me if there's anything else I can do.

Lisa watched Erin's departing figure, then, as Mike ro:
to leave, dragged herself after him to his car.

Dropping into the passenger seat, she leaned back, e:
hausted. From the corner of her eye, she watched him driv
His eyes seemed fixed on the road ahead, yet every few m
ments his gaze flickered toward her.

"Well, are you going to tell me about your lover?" he f
nally asked as he wove though the traffic.

She stared at his hands. They were clamped around th
wheel so tightly that the knuckles were white. "I still don
remember anything," she said. "According to Erin Ston
I don't have a lover."

"So it was an immaculate conception?"

She folded her hands in her lap. "It seems I was involve
with someone who didn't like the idea of fatherhood. H
wanted me to have an abortion."

She saw his jaw tense, and a second or two later, he said,
You can force him to cough up child support.''

Lisa shivered as she recalled Erin saying the man had
threatened to get her fired. "I don't think so."

A few minutes of silence passed before Mike spoke again,
is tone reluctant and a little bitter. "Did you love him?"

She wanted to say, no, she hadn't. The best she could
o—with honesty—was, "Erin didn't say. I guess I didn't
ll her."

Silently, Lisa wondered if she could have slept with a man
he didn't love. She hoped not. Yet she also couldn't imag-
e falling for the kind of person who would have tried to
rce her to have an abortion.

"I only know one thing for sure," she whispered. "I love
is baby."

She waited tensely for Mike to say something. When he
dn't respond, she gradually felt herself giving in to
mbing fatigue. Letting her eyes drift closed, she allowed
ep temporarily to bury some of her anxiety.

IKE DROVE toward Jenny's house, trying to ignore the
oman sleeping next to him. But his eyes kept wandering
om the road to her. She was slumped at an angle, so he
uldn't see much of her face, only the gentle curve of her
eek and the small slope of her nose. He wished he didn't
nd them so appealing.

What a sucker he was. Twice in his life he'd let himself
re about a woman, and both times, he'd been screwed.
sed. Taken in. Whatever he called it, it amounted to the
me thing: it hurt. Bad. Bad enough that he couldn't shrug
off or push it away or pretend it didn't exist. But this time,
admitted, was worse than the last. This time, he cared
ore about the woman.

Which was maybe why he was so angry. Where the hell
d Lisa get off, thinking it was okay to make love with him
ithout mentioning that she was pregnant? Despite her ra-
onalization, somewhere, someplace, she did have a past,
d it did matter. She couldn't simply ignore it.

He couldn't ignore it, even if he did understand her ar gument that she might never remember her old life.

Unfortunately, he also couldn't ignore the overwhelmin tenderness and protectiveness that he felt toward her. It ha been bad enough, knowing she was lost, without a mem ory, while people were running her off roads and trying t rape and kill her. It hadn't helped to get to know her, to fin out she was as warm and loving as she was bright and en gaging. But, ironically, knowing she was pregnant was th final straw. It made everything he felt about her a thousan times worse.

He wanted her, wanted to be with her, wanted to protec her. And nothing he told himself about how she'd betraye his trust made a bit of difference. Yeah, he was angry an hurt. But he was old enough and mature enough to realiz that his anger and hurt were mostly leftovers from Jus tine's betrayal; they had little, if anything, to do with Lisa And if the man who'd fathered her baby was really the bas tard it sounded like…well, she was probably right, he didn' matter, and she was better off not remembering him.

Mike clenched his teeth. He couldn't walk away from her Not now. Not, at least, until he knew she was safe Then…hell. Face it. He didn't know what he was going t do.

IN THE SMALL WAITING ROOM at Birth Data, Inc., Benita sa nervously next to Ed, twisting the strap of her oversiz purse. Ed hadn't wanted her to make the two-hour car tri from Philly to Baltimore, but she'd insisted with as much o her old energy as she could muster. Finally, when he'd re alized that taking her where she wanted to go was the onl way to give either one of them any peace, he'd agreed.

When the office door opened, she looked up eagerly.

"I'm Erin Stone," a slim young woman said. "Can I hel you?"

Benita started to push herself to her feet. Ed levered a arm under her elbow to help her. "I'm Benita Fenton. An

his is my husband, Edward. I called you about my daugh-
er."

"Oh, yes."

"We drove down from Philadelphia to give you a special
picture of her that I had made. I thought it might help you
ind her."

Mrs. Stone nodded, although she looked a little puzzled.
Benita figured she was wondering why anyone would come
o far to deliver a photo in person. Benita didn't want to
xplain herself. She'd been seized by a terrible urgency that
f she didn't get the ball rolling right away, she wouldn't live
ong enough to see her daughter. She hadn't even been able
o tell Ed. She sure couldn't tell this stranger, no matter how
:ind she looked.

"Why don't you come into my office?" Mrs. Stone sug-
;ested.

Benita shuffled after her, with Ed silently bringing up the
ear. When they were all seated, Benita unsnapped her purse
ind brought out a large envelope.

"After I wrote to you, I sent Ed to the library to do some
esearch." She gave her husband a little smile. "He found
ut about a new technique, where they take a picture of a
nissing child and somehow they put it into a computer.
They use the computer to add years to the person's face.
Make them look the way they would now."

Mrs. Stone nodded. "Yes, I've seen it done."

"Well, I found a place that would do that for me. And I
vanted to bring you the picture of Andrea as soon as pos-
ible." Opening the envelope, she looked at her daughter's
ace, amazed once more at the transformation. It was her
precious Andrea, but she looked so grown-up. Passing the
ltered photo across the desk to Mrs. Stone, she said, "Isn't
he pretty?"

"Oh!" Mrs. Stone gasped, her eyes widening.

"What's wrong?" Benita asked worriedly.

"This is your daughter—Andrea?"

Benita gripped the arms of her chair. "Tell me! Has
omething terrible happened to her?"

"I—I don't know," Mrs. Stone began, then quickly continued. "I talked to a woman this morning who contacted us to help find her birth parents. She looks like this enhanced photo of your daughter." She picked up a folder from her desk and hastily scanned the contents. "But according to the information she gave us, she was adopted by Sheila and William Barnes."

Benita suddenly felt hot all over. Leaning forward in her chair, she said, "If she looks like my Andrea, I've got to see her. Right now. I'll know if I see her." Her voice rose in panic. "You are going to give me her address and phone number, aren't you?"

Ed slung an arm around his wife's shoulders. "Honey, take it easy. You know what the doctor said about getting overexcited."

Her heart was pounding against her chest like a kettle drum, but she shook him off. "Ed, don't fuss."

"Mrs. Fenton, does Andrea have any distinguishing marks?" Mrs. Stone asked.

Benita frowned. "Marks? I'm not sure.... I... Oh, yes. There's a scar—about three inches long, I'd say, on her right thigh. You remember, Ed, the time when she was nine. She fell on a soda bottle and broke it. I'd never seen so much blood. Even when it healed, you could still see that scar." Benita began to sweat, the beads of moisture rolling down her face. "Mrs. Stone, you've got to help me find her."

"I'll do my best."

Benita gave her a weak smile that turned into a grimace as a sudden crushing pain spread through her chest, up her neck and down her left arm. With a low moan, she slumped in the chair.

"Oh, my God!" Ed gasped. "It's her heart. Mrs. Stone. Please, call 911. We need an ambulance."

LISA WOKE to an odd combination of sensations—warmth and contentment mingled with small physical discomforts. Grimacing a little at the crook in her neck, she realized vaguely that she was curled against Mike with her head on his chest, one hand hooked over his shoulder and the other gripping a fistful of his sweatshirt. His arm was curved around her hip.

Enveloped by his warmth and his familiar scent, she thought hazily about the taste of him . . . and the feel of his hands on her body. She snuggled closer, then lifted her mouth for a kiss, sighing in anticipation of feeling his lips cover hers.

Instead, she felt every muscle in his body go rigid. Her eyes blinked open in time to catch a yearning look on his face, but his features quickly became an expressionless mask. And suddenly she remembered. She wasn't supposed to be in his arms. He was furious with her over her lie of omission.

Her face turned hot with embarrassment, and she quickly looked away. Sitting up slowly, she said, "I'm sorry. Why didn't you wake me?"

"You needed some sleep."

"I need . . ."

"What?"

She wanted to say "you." Instead she said, "Courage." Tears hovered behind her eyes. Lord, she was turning into an automatic watering system. Press an emotional button, and she cried.

Opening the car door, she made for the house. But her knee had stiffened since she'd whacked it, and she stumbled. Mike caught her.

"I'm okay." She waved off his help.

"You should have put ice on that knee."

"I wasn't thinking about it."

She took another step and winced, and he swung her into his arms.

"Mike, you don't have to carry me. I can walk."

"Shh." He ignored her weak protest, carrying her across the gravel driveway toward the porch.

Closing her eyes, she anchored her arms around his neck and pressed her face against his shoulder. He shifted her weight as he searched for Jenny's key in his pocket. Pushing open the door, he crossed the living room and stood in front of the sofa for several seconds without setting her down, as if he was reluctant to let her go. Finally, he lowered her to the sofa. She stared up at the wet patch where her face had been pressed against his shirt. He followed her gaze, looked momentarily embarrassed, then seemed to snap into another gear.

"Ice," he said.

"What?"

He cleared his throat. "Ice. For your knee."

"Oh." She looked at her leg, feeling helpless and hating it. "I guess."

He turned and strode into the kitchen, where she heard him yanking drawers open, rummaging through them and slamming them closed.

Slipping off her shoes, she stretched out on the couch and tried to focus on her surroundings. The room was sunny and welcoming. Jenny's home was very appealing, with lots of warm colors, handmade pottery and paintings on the wall.

As Lisa studied a pink and green Mexican bird on the mantelpiece, a fantasy began to play through her mind: she and Mike were a married couple and this was their house. She'd hurt her knee, and he was worried. He'd gotten very protective since she'd told him that she was pregnant....

The fantasy spun out pleasantly for a few minutes, then came to an abrupt halt when Mike returned with a towel-wrapped bundle of ice.

"Are you all right?"

She nodded.

"Your face is flushed."

"Hormones, I guess."

He sat beside her, and she thought for a minute that he was going to roll up the leg of her sweatpants—*his* sweatpants.

"Um . . ." He hesitated.

Rather than wait for him to ask her to perform the task, she simply reached down and did it. She tried not to wince as the fabric grazed her knee. Her skin was marked with a large purple bruise.

"You'd better put this on," he said, carefully handing her the towel without touching her hand.

She gingerly set the lumpy compress in place. "That should help. Thanks."

"Uh-huh."

"Why did you leave the police force and become a private detective?" she asked.

He looked startled. "What kind of question is that?"

"A personal question."

Standing up, he crossed the room. "Then why are you asking?"

She regarded him steadily. "What do I have to lose? Of course, you don't have to answer if you don't want to."

He hesitated briefly, then spoke in a flat tone. "I was set up to take the fall in a drug bust that went bad. I resigned rather than go through a bunch of garbage with Internal Affairs."

Lisa frowned. "Set up? By whom?"

"A faction I'd annoyed."

"A faction? You mean in the department? Policemen do that to each other?"

"I made some enemies in high places. Questioned authority. That kind of thing."

Lisa was indignant. In fact, it stunned her to realize how angry she was about the injustice done to him. She had to work hard to tamp down her anger in order to speak.

"Is that why you didn't want me to turn myself in?" she asked.

"Yeah. Most cops are okay. But they can get overzealous when they're being squeezed for results. "

"Then aren't you taking a chance by harboring a fugitive?"

"I'm used to taking chances."

On some things, she wanted to say.

Their gazes seemed to touch over the invisible wall that stood between them. The telephone made them both jump.

Mike answered it. "Yes. She's here." Handing her the receiver, he said, "It's Erin. Do you mind if I listen in?"

She shook her head, then spoke to Erin, her voice shaky. "I didn't expect to hear from you so soon. Have you found something?"

Mike moved rapidly out of her line of vision. In the background, she heard him pick up an extension.

Erin asked, "Does the name Andrea Fenton mean anything to you?"

Lisa closed her eyes and tried to think. "Andrea Fenton... No."

"A Mrs. Benita Fenton is trying to locate her adopted daughter who ran away from home ten years ago. This morning, she brought us a computer-altered picture showing how the girl probably looks now."

Confused, Lisa said, "I thought you did searches for birth parents."

"That's usually true. But in this case, Andrea hasn't contacted the family since she left home." Erin paused. "Lisa, the picture looks startlingly like you."

Lisa drew a sharp breath, then grabbed her purse off the floor where she'd dropped it and pulled out the papers Erin had given her that morning. With trembling fingers, she found the application she'd filled out the week before. Swallowing hard, she asked, "Can you tell me if Andrea's birthday is May 12, 1966?"

Chapter Nineteen

"Yes," Erin answered. "That's right. May 12, 1966."

Breathless, Lisa said, "That's the date I put on my application."

"It's Justine's birthday, too." Mike's voice carried a trace of excitement as he spoke from the extension.

Lisa felt the hairs on her neck stand up and gooseflesh race down her arms. When Erin told her she was adopted, she'd wondered if she and Justine were twins, but it hadn't seemed likely. Now it seemed not only likely but probable.

"Mrs. Fenton was quite upset," Erin continued. "She, um, had a heart attack in my office, which makes her search a matter of some urgency."

"Oh, no!" Lisa gasped. "Is she all right?"

"She's in the hospital, in stable condition."

"The poor woman!"

"Erin," Mike cut in, "do you think Lisa may be this woman's daughter?"

"Fenton isn't the name I gave for my mother," Lisa pointed out, looking at the application she was clutching. "I put that my mother was Sheila Barnes. And my father was William Barnes."

"You could have given false information," Mike said.

His words brought a stab of pain. She realized immediately that he was implying she might have deliberately lied—after all, she'd lied to him. But she couldn't allow his lack of faith in her to get in the way of her quest. With effort, she spoke in a reasonable tone. "What would have been the point of my doing that?" When he didn't reply, she suggested, "Maybe Mrs. Fenton is Justine's mother. Maybe Justine ran away from home and changed her name."

Mike uttered a harsh laugh. "Sure. Why not?"

"Well, there may be a way to find out," Erin said. "Mrs. Fenton told me her daughter has a three-inch scar on her right thigh."

Fumbling to tug her pants down below her hips, Lisa thought how absurd it was that she had to look—how bizarre it felt not to know her own body. Exposing her right thigh, she examined the skin. It looked and felt smooth as she ran her fingers from hip to knee.

"I—I don't see any scars," she said, readjusting her clothing. "I guess it could have faded since Mrs. Fenton last saw it. But I just don't see why I would have put Sheila Barnes on my application if my adoptive mother was Mrs. Fenton. It doesn't make sense. I mean, if I was really interested in locating my birth parents, it would have been plain stupid not to provide accurate information."

"That's certainly true," Erin agreed.

Reluctantly, Lisa asked, "Mike, did Justine have a scar?"

He was silent for a moment, and, when he did finally answer, his tone was gruff, as if he didn't want to admit he knew the answer any more than she had wanted to ask the question. "No. At least I don't remember one."

Lisa sighed. "Of course, that would have been too easy. Erin, what else did Mrs. Fenton tell you?"

"When she first contacted us," Erin replied, "she sent a copy of her daughter's original birth certificate."

Lisa's fingers tightened on the receiver. "With my birth parents' names?"

"Well...Hallie Albright and Garrett Folsom. They're your birth parents—if you're the Fentons' daughter, or if you and Justine are sisters and *she's* their daughter. Or if, somehow, you're their daughter's sister. But if you're Justine's sister, and Justine *isn't* their daughter, that would mean there are three of you, wouldn't it? God, Lisa, I'm getting as confused as you must be about all this.''

"Erin, I don't know what to say. Hallie Albright and Garrett Folsom aren't any more familiar to me than Sheila and William Barnes were. But I guess that doesn't mean anything.''

"I can tell you're upset," Erin said. "I'm sorry. I was hoping the information might help you remember something.''

"I was hoping so, too," Lisa murmured. "And I really do appreciate your help. I keep expecting one of these pieces of information—a name, a date—to trigger my memory, and for it all to come flooding back, but it doesn't happen." She gave a small, humorless laugh. "I guess a lightning bolt will have to strike me first.''

Erin had to ring off then, when her next appointment arrived. Dazed and slightly giddy, Lisa didn't move until she'd heard Mike hang up the extension, then, with a sigh, she carefully replaced the receiver.

She should be excited, hopeful, about the new information. She had names to work with now—lots of them. And a birth date. But the date was only a spot on the calendar. And the names meant no more to her than the label on one of Justine's designer dresses. Less. She'd heard of some of the designers. The thing that bothered her most, though, was the near certainty that she and Justine shared some familial connection. How could she feel excited or hopeful about being related to someone she found just short of loathsome, from the way she decorated her mansion to the way she had treated Mike?

She glanced up to see Mike standing in the doorway, watching her with an unreadable expression on his face. One more reason to dislike Justine, she thought. For she was certain that it was the memory of Justine's betrayal, more than anything she herself had done, that had turned him away from her. He was afraid of being hurt again, and so he was making himself as inaccessible to her as a stranger.

He shifted his weight slightly. "I'd better get down to the office."

She felt a hollow place open in the region of her heart. She had the terrible feeling that if he left now, she would never see him again.

"You look like you're suffering from information overload," he said.

"Yes." Sitting up a little straighter, she tried to dispel her dark thoughts. "Erin's given me some facts, but they don't touch me inside, where it counts. It's a weird feeling."

Mike took a few steps into the room. "Will you be all right by yourself?" he asked.

"Yes," she lied, figuring she'd better start remembering how to be independent. "It's probably better, anyway. I—I need to sleep."

Mike paused by the couch. Their eyes locked, and the moment stretched. She felt her heart pound as they regarded each other. She waited for him to say something, but he remained silent, his eyes and hers the only point of contact. Then he broke the connection. Giving her a brief nod and a mumbled "I'll see you later," he walked out the door. And she was left sitting on the couch, alone.

BY AN EFFORT OF WILL, Mike kept his mind on business as he drove into downtown Baltimore. As soon as the autopsy report on Hollingsworth was available, he was going to call in a favor and get the results. Meanwhile, he wanted to find out what was happening with the two guys he'd left on his living-room floor. And he intended to accomplish both tasks without giving away the information that he had the prime suspect stashed in an Elkridge farmhouse.

The prime suspect. He didn't call her by name. Not even in his thoughts. He was trying hard not to feel anything about her. But unwelcome emotions like longing and need and compassion kept sneaking past his defenses. When they did, he felt his heart twist.

As he parked and walked out of the garage across from 43 Light Street, he couldn't stop picturing her face as he'd ft Jenny's house. There were dark smudges under her eyes, er skin was pale and her mouth was pinched. He knew he'd wanted to ask him to stay, that she was afraid of what ight happen in the next twenty-four hours. Probably even ore afraid of the future. But she hadn't said a word. That ad taken a kind of courage most people didn't possess. He dmired her for it. He admired her for a lot of things.

IAND PRESSED against the knife under his shirt, Gary edged oward the side of the parking deck where he could watch he detective head for his office. Lancer was alone. So where as Justine? Or was it Leigh? He wasn't sure about her ame anymore. But it didn't matter so much, he reassured imself.

She'd come running out of the house last night and he'd ried to catch her, but she'd gotten away in the car. This norning he'd been hoping he'd find her with the detective. Leeping low, Gary crept toward the car and took a quick ok in the back seat. Empty. The girl wasn't hiding in the ar.

Sinking to the oil-stained floor, he cradled his head in his ands. Sometimes when he tried real hard, he could make is brain work almost as good as it had before he'd gotten ll messed up. He knew he could do it. He'd done it before. Like when he'd gone back to that no-good lawyer who'd elped screw up his life.

The guy was old and sick now. In a nursing home. Maybe, Gary figured, the lawyer had felt sorry about what he'd one all those years ago. He *should* be sorry. But it didn't atter anymore. The important thing was, for the first time, he old goat had given him some answers. Enough infor- ation for him to come to Baltimore and start nosing round.

A shiny sports coupe pulled in to park in the same lane of ars as Lancer's Mustang, and a man got out. Gary went ery still. It was another guy he'd seen at the Hollings- orths' estate a couple of times. *Señor* something or other. Iostly he didn't drive himself around. Usually he was sit-

ting in the back of a big black car with a chauffeur in th
front.

So what was he doing down here alone? Did he kno
where to find Leigh?

Maybe, Gary thought. And maybe he ought to follo
him. Yeah, that was what he should do, all right.

THE DOOR TO O'Malley and Lancer was unlocked. When h
entered the waiting room, Mike could see Jo sitting at h
desk, talking on the phone. She gestured toward his offic
indicating that someone was inside. Apparently, whoever
was wanted privacy, because the door was closed.

The cops?

Trying to keep cool, he planned what he would say
them. He also prepared for a fight, in the event that it wa
another pair of goons.

When he pulled open the door, the breath froze in h
lungs. She was sitting in the easy chair in the corner, look
ing very much the way she had when he'd left her a half hou
ago—dark circles under her eyes, pale skin, and tension line
around her mouth. What struck him hardest, though, wer
the ways in which she *didn't* look like the woman he had le
sitting on Jenny's couch. The differences were indefinable
yet, to him, couldn't have been more obvious. He wor
dered how he ever could have been fooled.

"Justine. Where the hell have you been?"

The slender redhead gave him a cool smile. "Minne
apolis. I got in last night." At his surprised look, sh
shrugged. "It seemed as good a place as any to lie low. B
I've been keeping tabs on the situation."

"How?"

She brushed a hand lightly across the front of her tigl
blue skirt. "Maggie told me about the woman's accident an
amnesia when I called, pretending to be one of my friend
from the country club. After that, I got some informatio
from the hospital. How does my double fit into the pic
ture? Did you bring her in to pinch-hit for me?"

Without answering, Mike crossed to his desk and sat down. He couldn't take his eyes off her. Couldn't stop his brain from cataloging the subtle differences between her and Lisa. Justine was polished in a way Lisa would neither care nor seek to be. Thank God. Justine was hard, even cruel, where Lisa was soft and warm and almost too sensitive for her own good. Justine looked like a woman with an agenda. She also looked too damned skinny. And he could think of a lot of other ways to describe her, too, none of them flattering.

"No," he replied to her question. "She got tangled up in your life by accident." Pausing, he added, "She's most likely your twin sister."

It was with considerable satisfaction that Mike saw Justine's face go even paler.

"That's impossible!" she snapped.

He shook his head slowly. "It isn't if you're adopted and your birth mother had twins."

She stared at him, her composure slipping another notch. "I am adopted. But I—I didn't know there were . . . two of us." Giving her head a quick shake, she spoke briskly, "But at the moment, I've got other things more pressing to worry about than some long-lost sister."

"Apparently." Mike picked up a pen from his desk and pulled a pad of paper in front on him. "You say you've been keeping tabs on the situation around here. So you know Kendall is dead?"

"Yes. That's why I'm in your office. As his widow, I'm going to inherit a sizable fortune. And I wouldn't want my stand-in to get the inside track."

Mike's voice turned steely. "But you were content to let her cope with the chaos you left behind."

She lifted one slender shoulder in a delicate shrug. "She gave me some breathing space."

How could he ever have been so entranced by her? It didn't help much to remind himself that he'd been young and immature. He felt he should have seen the seeds of callousness and avarice in her from the start. But then, those seeds had been buried beneath the shining surface, and he hadn't had enough experience with intimate relationships to know how to see beneath that surface. When Justine met Kendall Hollingsworth, the seeds had sprouted, taken root and grown like weeds to choke out anything that might have been worth having. God, how she'd changed.... God, how lucky he felt to be free of her.

Slowly laying his pen on top of the pad of paper, he spoke in a glacial tone. "What do you want from me, Justine?"

She shifted in her chair so that her skirt rode up a little farther, giving him what he guessed was supposed to be a tempting view of her legs. "You're the best, Mike," she said. "I know you can protect me—while I probate the will." At his complete lack of response, she added quickly, "When the will is settled, I'll be able to pay you a lot more than that measly five thousand."

"I thought the fee was fair."

She lowered her lashes and smiled. "There could be substantial fringe benefits."

He didn't want to hear about them much less accept them, but this wasn't the time to say so. He kept his expression carefully neutral.

"I've missed you," she said. "You and I had something good together. And now...well, with Kendall gone..."

"You and I could pick up where we left off," he finished for her.

"I knew you'd understand."

He understood, all right, and it made his stomach turn.

"I, uh..." She fidgeted a bit with the strap of her purse. "I know something you'll be interested to hear."

"Yeah?"

"It was Kendall who had you framed in that drug bust. He's the one who got you off the police force."

Caught off guard, Mike couldn't hide his surprise. "*You* knew?"

"Mike, I learned about it last year, but there was nothing I could do then. I'm telling you now."

And he was supposed to thank her? Clearly, she thought he should be grateful for the information.

His face hardened once more into a mask. "Tell me exactly why you came to me a couple of weeks ago," he said.

She squirmed a little in her chair. "It's complicated."

"Let's start with some basic information. Do you know who killed Kendall and Estelle?"

Her head jerked up, and she met his gaze directly, her eyes wide with astonishment. "Estelle's dead?"

She wasn't faking it, he decided. She really hadn't known.

"She was found floating in the Inner Harbor this morning," he told her. "With a bullet in her back."

Still holding his gaze, she whispered, "Kendall could have killed her—if he knew she was helping me."

Mike frowned. "Let me get this right. You and Estelle were working together on something?"

She nodded. "We had a deal. She took some papers from Kendall's office for me. Stuff about his San Marcos construction project with Johnny Realto that I could use as insurance."

Lisa had asked about Realto, Mike remembered, but when he'd checked, the man's name hadn't come up in connection with the K. H. Group. "Explain it to me—slowly," he ordered.

Justine brushed away an imaginary stray hair from her face, and he noted that her hand was trembling.

"Realto's a silent partner," she said. "I think he lives in Miami."

"Why would *you* need insurance?"

She flushed. "Okay. I was stupid enough to sign a prenuptial agreement. If Kendall wanted out of the marriage, I would only get a minimum settlement."

"He wanted a divorce?" Mike asked, understanding a little better why she hadn't been perfectly straight before. Kendall was her trophy husband, so to speak. If he didn't want her anymore, it meant that she was a failure.

"We weren't, uh, getting along all that well," she murmured. "I didn't know if I could hold it together."

"Why would Estelle want to help you? Wasn't she hi
devoted executive assistant?"

Justine gave a harsh laugh. "Sure. And his mistress. I've
known that for years, but I didn't care because it took some
of the sexual pressure off me. It turns out the two of us
weren't enough for him. He was cheating on her, too."

Mike digested the information quickly. "Let's go back to
the papers."

With a sigh, Justine explained, "They're construction
specifications for the housing projects Kendall is building in
San Marcos. Realto has government connections down
there. He arranged to have the inspectors pass on stuff that's
not up to code. The partnership was saving millions of dollars by cutting corners."

"So you could have put Kendall in jail by spilling the
beans," Mike concluded.

She nodded.

"And Realto."

"Yes."

"Well, that would certainly piss them off—if they found
out."

A look of genuine fright crossed her features. "Yes, that's
why I hid the specs before I left. I was afraid if Kendall
caught me with them, he'd kill me then and there."

"So why did you come back last night?"

She shot him a quick glance. "I got nervous wondering
what that woman who looks like me might be doing in my
house. I couldn't stand it anymore. I had to make sure the
specs were safe. And they aren't. They're gone, Mike, and
I'm scared."

He watched her try to control her features. She was right.
Hollingsworth would have killed her if he'd thought she was
going to expose his scam. But the danger hadn't ended with
Hollingsworth's death.

"Help me, Mike," she said in a small voice.

"I'll try," he answered, not for old times' sake or because he still wanted what she might deign to give him. He'd

o it because, at this point, helping Justine meant helping
Lisa.

"But this time I need the truth. Did you kill Hollingsworth?" he asked bluntly.

She drew back, indignant. "No."

"Where did you go last night after you left the estate?"

"I have a room at the Hyatt Regency."

That much he could verify. He wished her vow of inno-
ence could be proven as easily because she could be lying
hrough her teeth, and he wouldn't know it.

THE RINGING OF THE PHONE catapulted Lisa from a restless
leep, dogged by nightmares. Her eyes snapped open, and
he was overwhelmed by a crushing feeling of loss.

Mike. Where was Mike? For an instant, she didn't even
now where she was. Then the phone rang again, and sud-
enly the details of Jenny's living room swam into focus.

She sat up and reached for the receiver, scattering the
Birth Data, Inc., papers she'd been studying before ex-
austion had claimed her.

"Hello? Mike?"

No one answered.

"Hello?" she tried again.

There was no reply except the moaning of the wind out-
ide. It had begun to blow since she'd fallen asleep.

"Is anyone there?"

The line went dead, and she was left clutching the re-
eiver. Carefully, she replaced it in the cradle, her still-foggy
rain wondering vaguely who had been on the line. Wrong
umber or someone expecting Jenny?

Then all thoughts of the phone call evaporated as an im-
ge from the nightmare she'd been having flashed into her
mind: a man with a charming smile. Yet the smile sent a chill
p her spine.

She went very still, knowing with inexplicable yet terri-
ying certainty that she was teetering on the edge of some-
hing dangerous. Dangerous but significant. Lord, what was

it about the man in the dream? It seemed suddenly that she'd been dodging him every time she woke up.

Her breath came rapid and shallow as she started to banish his face from her conscious thoughts, back to the place where she'd been hiding it. But something stopped her—the question leaping into her mind: Where would the image of that man's face take her? If she dared to go.

For a moment or two, she hesitated, frightened, trembling, the image still swimming hazily in her head. She felt repulsed by him, and her entire being revolted at getting any closer. But she'd reached the point where not knowing her past was a suffocating burden, much worse than anything she imagined she might learn. She knew she had to look, had to know. And the sooner, the better.

She pressed her hand to her face, hiding behind the screen of her fingers. Then, heart pounding, she concentrated on pulling the dream into her mind, reeling in the details....

It had started at dinner in a restaurant with starched white napkins and gleaming cutlery. She was with a good-looking man. He was paying close attention to her, lavishing compliments on her. He had conservatively cut brown hair, laugh lines around his eyes...and strong, blunt fingers that she found appealing. He was older than she, more experienced, and she was flattered that he wanted to get to know her better. They talked about the contract her company had with his firm. And she nodded when he gave her advice, thinking how clever he was and how much she could learn from him. After dinner, they danced....

Sitting on Jenny's couch, Lisa began to tremble. The bad part was coming. She could feel it as every nerve in her body grew taut in anticipation. At the last minute, she tried to back out, tried to stop what she'd started. But then abruptly, the choice was taken from her. The dream—the memory—sprang into her mind all at once, and in all of its hideous detail....

"I'll walk you to your room," her companion offered.

"You don't have to."

"You shouldn't be alone in a big city hotel at this time of night."

She opened her door, and he slipped inside with her.

"Hank, I have to catch an early flight."

He didn't listen. Reaching for her, he pulled her into his arms and ground his hips against hers.

"Hank, no."

"Don't tell me no. You've been sending me signals all week that you want to go to bed as much as I do."

"But I don't know you well enough—"

"We're going to get to know each other a lot better, honey."

She tried to break free from his grasp, but his arms tightened around her, and his mouth came down hard on hers. Frantic now, she pushed at his chest but he grabbed both her wrists in one of his hands.

"I know you're a nice girl," he soothed. "I know you have to pretend to resist. But you're as hot as I am, aren't you?"

"Let me go. Please. If I gave you the wrong impression, I'm sorry."

"Stop playing games. Relax and enjoy it." The advice was punctuated by his free hand closing over her breast.

She gasped. He cut off the sound with his lips. Then her back was pressed against the bed, and he was on top of her, pushing up her dress and tugging at her panty hose. He tore the clothing from her lower body and thrust painfully inside her, his hips pounding against her until his body convulsed....

OUTSIDE THE FARMHOUSE, thunder rumbled in the distance as Lisa sat hugging her knees and rocking back and forth on the couch. Choking sobs rose in her throat and escaped. And as the scene that had taken place on that hotel-room bed gradually receded, the door to her past swung open. Unlocked by the shattering encounter she'd been struggling so hard to repress, her memory flooded back, full force.

She sucked in a breath, drowning beneath the deluge. Lightning seemed to crackle inside her head, and each flash was a new memory that made her slender frame shiver and her teeth chatter with reaction. *This* was what she had prayed for. Yet she felt that the onslaught might tear her apart.

Recollections shook her body: the important contract she'd won for Williamsburg Architects; the business trip to Chicago to work out the details with Fairland International; Hank Lombard, the contract manager who'd been so enthusiastic about her work. They'd gotten along very well—until he'd pushed his way into her room and forced himself on her. What had she told Erin—that the father of her child had threatened to get her fired if she didn't have an abortion? Lord, it was true. He could, and probably would, do it. He and her boss at Williamsburg were longtime friends. So she'd taken a month's vacation—to try to find another job.

How helpless she'd felt. How powerless. Leigh Barnes. The brainy architect who didn't have a clue about men.

A sick feeling rose in her throat, and she pushed it down. With shaking hands, she reached for the Birth Data, Inc., application. She'd been pouring over the form, memorizing her birth date, her street address, where she'd gone to elementary school. But the entries had only been words. Now like magic, they'd become real.

Tears welled in Lisa's eyes and ran down her cheeks. She wasn't Benita Fenton's daughter at all. She was the much-loved daughter of Sheila and Williams Barnes. Yes, she remembered her adoptive mom and dad and the wonderful, loving home they'd provided. They'd been too old to adopt through an agency, so they'd found a lawyer who knew about a pregnant woman whose boyfriend had been shipped off to Vietnam. She'd always known she was adopted—and very precious to her parents.

They'd been so proud of her. She smiled as she remembered things about them: Dad teaching her to ride a bike and, later, getting her one of the first home computers on the market. The whole family gathered around the Christmas tree, eating cookies and hanging decorations. So many good memories. And a few that were painful.

Dad had died five years ago. Mom had broken her hip and gone into a nursing home, and she'd passed away last year. That was why Leigh—she—was still paying off medical bills.

Wiping tears from her face, she laid the application carefully on the coffee table, then sat back to draw a slow, deep breath. Now she knew. The worst—and the best.

MIKE COCKED HIS HEAD as he heard someone rush into the outer office. Then a loud, urgent knock sounded at his door.

"Come in," he called.

Erin tore into the room and stopped dead, a look of relief spreading across her face when she spotted Justine. But the look rapidly gave way to confusion. "You aren't Lisa," she said.

Justine straightened in her chair. "I'm Justine Hollingsworth, if that's what you mean."

"When I saw you, I thought—I hoped you were Lisa." She turned to Mike and raked her hand through her hair. "God, I'm sorry. After the Fentons left, I was doing some research on Lisa's birth mother—trying to contact the hospital where she was born. I should have put her file away, but I didn't think anything would happen."

"Slow down. Tell me what you're talking about," he suggested.

Erin drew a steadying breath. "I usually grab a bite at my desk, but Travis was downtown and asked if I wanted to go out to lunch. When I came back, Lisa's folder was missing."

He frowned. "Did anybody else put it away?"

"No." She shook her head. "Jenny thinks someone may have been in the office. She isn't sure because she was in the bathroom for a few minutes."

Fear clutched at him, making his voice curt as he asked, "What was in the folder?"

"The application Lisa filled out. My notes." Erin hesitated. "And the phone number at Jenny's."

Mike swore. "Anybody with a computer directory could figure out where she is."

"Call her. Make sure she's all right."

He was already reaching for the phone. He dialed, waiting tensely for the numbers to go through. When they did, all he got was a weird-sounding busy signal. "She may be talking to someone," he muttered, although he had no idea who she might call. "Or the line has been disconnected."

Erin waved an arm in a helpless gesture. "Mike, I'm so sorry."

"Not your fault. How could you imagine that your own office wasn't a safe place to leave papers?" Unlocking his bottom-right desk drawer, he pulled out his gun. He stood up and strode toward the door, saying, "I'm going out there."

"What about me?" Justine called after him. "We're having a conference."

"Not anymore."

"But *I'm* the one who paid you!"

Over his shoulder, he tossed, "I'll send you a refund." Then he slammed the office door closed behind him.

SHE HAD FOUND a kind of peace. Lisa sat alone with her memories for another hour. But, gradually, the desire grew to share the news with someone. With Mike. A little smile played around her lips. She could finally come to him whole and complete. She could tell him who she was, that she'd had a safe and happy childhood, that she'd done some good things in her life, that she wasn't a money-hungry, manipulative female who would use a man, then leave him for greener pastures.

She could tell him all those things—if he ever forgave her.

Her smile slowly faded. Who was she kidding? Mike was probably never going to forgive her or trust her again.

Something scraped against the window to her left, and for an instant, she froze. When she looked to the window, she saw that it was a tree branch swaying in the wind. The sky was darkening fast—the storm was getting close. She'd hardly been aware of it.

With a little sigh, she rose from the couch and wandered into the kitchen, where she set the ice pack in the sink and picked up the mug of soup she'd made after Mike had left. Earlier, although she hadn't felt hungry, she'd forced down a few swallows by reminding herself that she needed to eat for the baby.

The baby. It didn't matter how her child had been conceived. She'd come to terms with that, she recalled, before the accident. She remembered her doctor giving her the results of the pregnancy test, remembered being upset at first—and scared. Most of all, she remembered wishing her parents had been alive, because she'd never needed them more. But in all her turmoil and upset, she'd never once thought of rejecting the baby. Really, it had been easy to accept the life growing inside of her. In her mind, the baby had nothing to do with Hank Lombard. It was *her* child.

Outside, the wind tore at the trees, and a clap of thunder shook the old house. Lisa stood holding the soup mug, staring blindly at the magnetic braille calendar on the front of the refrigerator. As the thunder receded, she heard a noise somewhere behind her.

She jerked around, and her eyes flew to the window over the sink. It was open. Lord, she'd been so lost in her own world, she hadn't even thought of closing up the house.

She set the mug down and reached for the window, then froze, her hand halfway there. This time she was sure she heard something that didn't sound like any noise a storm might make. Thinking Mike had come back, she started to call his name, but then realized he wouldn't steal into the house unannounced.

Sliding open a drawer, she began to look for a knife or something she could use as a weapon, but only came up with dish towels. Trying to stay calm, she opened another drawer.

But it was already too late. She knew someone was in the room before she turned. Someone who smelled of expensive after-shave.

"Close the drawer and turn toward me slowly," a voice grated. When she hesitated, a large male hand clamped down on her shoulder and spun her around.

Chapter Twenty

A scream rose in her throat and bubbled out.

"Quiet! Don't move, or I'll kill you."

Lisa looked at the gun in his hand, then back at his eyes. *He'd do it,* she thought wildly. *He'd kill me without a moment's hesitation.* His eyes looked malevolent, boring into her, and ... and she'd seen them before.

Staring at him in terrified confusion, she tried to remember: dark eyes and hair, temples flecked with gray and a complexion pitted with acne scars.

"Dr. Ray," she breathed. She'd come to think the late-night encounter in her hospital room had been a dream. But the man holding the gun to her ribs was all too real.

He smiled. "Yes. You remember our brief visit. But Ray is not my name. I'm Juan Realto. Johnny to my friends. But then, *señora,* I wonder if you do not know already who I am."

Lisa could hardly breathe, much less speak. Gasping, she managed to say, "Kendall Hollingsworth's partner?"

His eyes narrowed. "So you *do* remember me."

His tone was mild, even casual, but his look was fierce. Lisa realized dimly that her responses were critical, but she had no idea what he wanted to hear, what would satisfy him.

Trembling all over, she gave her head a tiny shake. "No. I—I only remember you ... from the hospital. But Maggie said Señor Realto sent me flowers, and ... and when I—I asked who ... who that was, she told me."

He seemed to consider her answer, then he smiled again. "I must say, *señora,* either you are telling the truth, or you missed your calling as an actress."

"What do you want?" she whispered.

The smile left his face. "I want the documents Estelle Bensinger took from Kendall's files."

"I don't have them," she whispered.

"You are lying," he said. "I see it in your eyes."

"N-no," she stammered, "I only know there are some papers that Estelle wanted back from Justine. She came asking for them the day I left the hospital. She wanted them badly, but I . . . I didn't know what she was talking about. Because I'm *not* Justine. My name is Leigh Barnes. I swear it!"

He gave her a long, hard stare. Her heart pounded so hard she thought she would collapse, and she gripped the counter behind her for support as she waited for his verdict.

Finally he said, "I believe you are not Señora Hollingsworth. But, unfortunately for you, I had a talk with Señorita Bensinger, and she told me everything—everything except where the stolen papers are now."

"But I don't have them!" Lisa insisted.

"Señors Ezrine and Ordway weren't so sure."

"Ezrine and . . ." Frantically, Lisa tried to think who he was talking about. "The two men who tried to kill me by running me off the road."

Realto scowled. "Their orders were only to frighten you. *Pero* you do not have to worry about them anymore. They are gone, and I am here. Now we are going to see if pain will force you to tell me what you know. And if you know nothing more . . ." He shrugged. "*Sí, es la vida.* That is life. I must make certain that you cannot tell anyone else about my business dealings with my late lamented partner."

He was going to kill her. He'd tortured and killed Estelle—Lisa was sure of it—and now he was going to do it to her. It didn't matter whether or not she was Justine. It didn't matter whether she told the truth or lied. Either way, she was going to die.

Realto gestured with the gun. "Into the living room where we can be more comfortable."

She couldn't fight him. Nobody else knew he was here and nobody was coming to save her. For a moment, despair overwhelmed her terror, and she nearly broke down in tears. Then she thought of the baby, thought about the injustice of her child's life being taken away before it had been given the chance to grow.

And she thought of Mike—of never seeing him again. Never loving him again. He was hurting so badly, thinking she'd selfishly made a fool of him. What if she never had the chance to convince him otherwise?

It could all end here. Unless somehow she found a way to stop this criminal lunatic.

In a flash, Lisa achieved a clarity of thought she hadn't possessed since the accident. With steely resolve, she let her shoulders sag, as if in defeat, and started walking toward the living room. But as she passed through the kitchen doorway, her hand shot out and gave the door a hard slam backward. The ploy took Realto by surprise, and the heavy wood hit him in the face. A split second later, the gun went off, several slugs tearing through the wood inches from her.

But she was already running full tilt for the front door. When she threw it open, the wind whipped her hair around her face and shoved her sideways. She pelted down the steps and across the yard, trying with every ounce of inner strength to ignore the shooting pain in her knee and simply run. At first, she had some dim idea of disappearing into the woods, but she quickly realized she wasn't going to make it. She could hear Realto behind her, breathing hard and cursing angrily, the wind carrying his words away on a high, keening note.

It was hopeless to think she could outrun him.

Veering left, she made for the barn, hobbling now in pursuit of a place to hide. As she yanked open the door and crossed the threshold, the gun cracked again. Two more shots. Did he have two left, she wondered, or was that only in the movies?

Near the door, a pitchfork stuck out of a bale of hay an she snatched it, then searched wildly for cover. With on seconds to spare, she made a dive for a dark corner.

TREES BENT and swayed along the roadside as Mike race toward Jenny's house. When he turned into the drivewa lightning streaked across the sky and raindrops began splatter his windshield. If he made it to the porch witho getting soaked, he'd be lucky.

Halfway up the winding driveway, he heard the bloo chilling sound of gunfire. Outside.

"Oh, God..."

Pressing the gas pedal to the floor, he reached for the ca phone. He'd stashed Lisa here to keep her away from t law—but saving her life was more important. Dialing 91 he quickly got the Howard County Police and requeste help; at the same time, he swerved to a halt at the top of t driveway. When he grabbed his gun and jumped out, th first thing he noticed was the barn door was open. He wa sure he'd left it closed. But what if he guessed wrong abou where to find Lisa? Quickly he glanced at the surroundir woods. There were empty. No sign of movement. Eyes na rowed, he headed for the barn.

OUTSIDE, the storm broke, sending a torrent of rain onto th barn's metal roof. Lisa heard water begin to drip onto th concrete floor somewhere to her right.

In the cool darkness, she crouched behind a stack of ha bales, curling to her side to make herself as small a target possible. Her knee throbbed abominably, and she rubbed with one hand, the fingers of her other hand clutching th pitchfork.

Footsteps pounded on the concrete floor, and she fe every muscle in her body tense.

Realto's voice sounded, harsh and grating. "There is n way out, *señora*. I have you trapped. The longer you mak me look for you, the angrier I will be when I find you."

Tough. Let him be angry. He couldn't be any angrier than she was.

"Come out, *ramera*. Whore."

Lisa gripped her makeshift weapon with both hands. It was hardly a match for Realto's gun, but it was all she had. And the long, pointed prongs could be lethal—if she had the opportunity to use them. It was either kill him or let him kill her baby, and, between those two extremes, there really was no choice.

Through the open door, a bolt of lightning split the sky. Hard on its heels, thunder shook the old building to its foundation.

Please, God, she prayed silently. *Let me save my baby. Give me the chance to be a good mother.* Paradoxically, alongside those prayerful thoughts, Lisa contemplated the best way to inflict damage with her dubious weapon.

Rain drummed on the roof. More drops found their way to the floor. Thunder clawed at the eaves, drawing her gaze upward. She scanned the rafters high overhead at the same instant a bright streak of lightning illuminated the shadowed space.

Her heart skipped a beat, then thudded painfully in her chest when she made out the profile of a man creeping across the loft. Realto had climbed a ladder to the second floor.

But no! Recognition sizzled through her like an electric charge. It wasn't Realto. It was Mike.

Gun drawn, he moved stealthily through the shadows. Could he see her from up there? She wanted to let him know where she was, but she didn't dare move.

Somewhere close, Realto was on the prowl again. She heard his footsteps crossing the floor and knew he wasn't bothering to hide his whereabouts. Why should he? He was confident of how this game of cat and mouse was going to end.

Waiting for him to pounce was agony. Worse, though, was watching Mike as he edged closer to the rim of the loft, closer to making himself a target. She wanted to scream at him to stay back, and she prayed as hard as she'd ever prayed in her life that he would be careful. That he wouldn't get killed trying to save her, because she'd never be able to live with it if he did.

Frantic for his safety, she scrambled furtively in the straw looking for something to throw to divert the gunman's attention. She found several loose clods of dry earth, and her hand closed around them, testing their weight. Then, cautiously, she lifted her arm, aiming at the boards of an open stall on the other side of the barn.

She was about to fling the clods, when metal clattered in the loft above, ringing clearly over the drumming rain. Realto whirled, lifted his gun and fired. Mike shot back, but the killer ducked into a stall and got off two more shots. Lisa watched in horror as Mike grunted and staggered backward.

Seeing him go down, something seemed to break loose inside her. She launched herself, half-crazed, pitchfork in front of her like a bayonet, at Realto's back. But before she reached her target, inexplicably, she was flung aside.

The pitchfork went flying, and she landed in a heap on the straw, gasping for breath and utterly confused. Then, as she struggled to a sitting position and looked to see what had hit her, a hysterical sound—half scream, half laughter—escaped her. It was the tramp. The man in the fatigue jacket who'd been dogging her steps everywhere she went. Like a ghost or some grotesque kind of guardian angel, he'd materialized again, out of nowhere.

With a savage howl, he spun Realto around, knife in hand. The knife flashed as the tramp's arm came down, and the blade plunged into the side of Realto's neck.

For a split second, Realto went rigid, his eyes wide with shock. With a clunk, the gun fell from his hand. Then, with an eerie gurgling sound, he crumpled to the barn floor and lay still.

"You miserable scum," the tramp snarled, yanking the knife from his victim's neck.

Lisa hadn't a clue if the tramp was truly her guardian angel come to save her from certain death, or if he would go for her next. She didn't wait to find out.

Springing to her feet, staggering a bit as her injured knee rebelled, she looked frantically for a ladder up to the loft. When she spotted it at the other end of the barn, she ran toward it, leaving the vagrant crouched over Realto.

Gritting her teeth against the pain in her knee, she climbed up the rungs and made for the place where she'd seen Mike fall. He was sitting against a stack of hay bales.

"Mike! Oh, Lord!" she cried as she came down beside him.

His skin was gray and his breathing ragged. "Lisa..." He tried to sit up straighter, gulping air to speak. "Lisa, are you all right?"

"I'm fine." Anxiety strained her voice. "Where? Where are you hurt?" she demanded, feverishly running her hands over his chest, horrified at the amount of blood soaking his shirt. When she touched his shoulder, he winced.

"Oh, God, I'm sorry," she said. "Please don't die. I love you." She pressed her palm against his chest, wishing she could enfold him in her arms but afraid she'd hurt him worse.

His hand came up to cover hers. "I'm not going to die," he said, his voice a little steadier. "It hurts like hell, but it's not fatal. Knocked me over, though. Musta' hit my head. Clumsy." He gave a low grunt of disgust. "Just give me a minute. I'll be okay."

She wanted to believe him, wanted to believe he wasn't simply trying to reassure her as he quietly bled to death. Even as she watched, the blood continued to spread steadily across his shirt.

In the background, Lisa heard the wail of a siren.

"Are you sure you're all right?" Mike asked urgently, his eyes searching hers.

"Yes," she replied. "He didn't touch me."

His head fell back against the hay bales, relief momentarily wiping pain from his features. He sat with his eyes closed, his fingers wrapped tightly around hers, while Lisa listened tensely to the sirens getting closer.

Shaking his head as if to clear his thoughts, Mike opened his eyes to look at her. "What the hell happened after Realto nailed me?"

"That vagrant . . . you know, that man who—"

"The smelly guy in the fatigue jacket?" Mike's eyes widened. "He's *here*?"

She nodded. "He came out of nowhere. Just . . . jumped out of the shadows with his knife. I had a pitchfork, and I was going to try to stab Realto with it, but before I could the tramp attacked him."

Mike started to say something, but suddenly the sirens screamed into the yard with a vengeance. Mere seconds later, the barn was filled with the sound of running feet.

Lisa cringed, huddling toward Mike.

"It's okay," he said. "I called the police when I drove in and heard gunshots."

Below them, she heard a man's voice snap, "What's going on here, buddy?"

Nobody answered.

Wincing, Mike pushed himself away from the hay bales and edged forward.

Lisa reached to stop him, but he shook his head urgently. "Got to tell them who's up here—before we get shot."

Numbly she listened while he shouted down, "This is Mike Lancer, private detective. I called the police. I'm up here with Lisa . . . Barnes."

He shot her a quick glance, and she guessed he was asking for approval of his choice of her name. She shrugged a little and nodded. It hardly seemed to matter.

Moments later, a face appeared over the edge of the loft. It belonged to a uniformed officer, who quickly took in the situation.

"You okay?" he asked Mike.

"I'll live."

The uniform nodded. "An ambulance is coming. It won't help the guy on the floor, though. He's dead."

"The tramp stabbed him," Lisa said. And because she felt she owed the man a considerable debt, whoever he was and whatever his intentions toward her, she added, "He saved my life. The man who's dead—Juan Realto—was going to shoot me."

The cop's expression remained noncommittal. "Well, the guy's not saying anything. We're taking him in."

Drawing a deep breath, Mike started to get up.

"Mike, wait." She tried to stop him. "Let somebody help you."

But he waved her away. As he struggled to his feet, she could see he was determined to leave the loft under his own power. Heart in her throat, she watched him make his way awkwardly down the ladder, using one hand to grasp the rungs. At the bottom, he moved aside so she could follow, and she scrambled down as quickly as her knee would allow.

When she reached the ground, she turned to see that Mike was even paler and his forehead was beaded with sweat. He leaned heavily against one of the support posts, cradling his left arm against his body.

"Mike, you need to lie down," she said.

"No," he insisted. "I need to talk with the police. *Now,*" he added sharply.

Another officer strode through the door and approached them. He stopped in front of Lisa. "Is your name Justine Hollingsworth?" he asked.

Shaking inside, knowing she had no choice but to face this moment and get it over with, she met the officer's gaze directly. "No, my name is Leigh Barnes. I live in Philadelphia, and I work for Williamsburg Architects. I only look like Justine Hollingsworth." She didn't add that the resemblance was most likely due to their being twins.

The officer raised one eyebrow in a skeptical look. "Do you have some identification?"

She hesitated, then admitted reluctantly, "No. But if you talk to Erin Stone at Birth Data, Inc., she will identify me. I can give you her phone number and address."

"What she said is true," Mike put in. "And if you go to the Hyatt Regency in Baltimore, you'll find Justine Hollingsworth herself." When he caught her shocked glance, he nodded. "She came into my office this morning and told me where she's staying."

The officer's skepticism cracked a little, took on a mildly perplexed cast. But his confusion soon passed. "Where were you last night between five and eight o'clock?" he asked her.

Before she could reply, Mike snapped, "You don't have to answer. You can demand that an attorney be present."

She pressed her lips together and kept silent, although it seemed like postponing the inevitable. She didn't look at Mike, was afraid she'd come apart if she did. She had to get through this. And, Lord, she'd just escaped death, surely the worst was over.

It wasn't.

"You're going to have to answer sooner or later," the policeman said. "You're under arrest for the murder of Kendall Hollingsworth. You have the right to remain silent. Anything you say can and will be used against you in a court of law. You have the right to an attorney..."

The rest of the words went by in a blur. This wasn't happening. It couldn't be. Not after everything else.

Mike shoved away from the post. "Wait just a damn minute. You can't—"

"An arrest warrant's been issued," the officer cut him off. At the same time, he pulled out a pair of handcuffs and reached for her hands.

She croaked out a few words. "No. Please. I didn't kill him."

"Yeah, well, you'll get your chance to prove it," the officer said.

Lisa's gaze sought Mike's, her eyes filled with desperation. But he looked pale and sick and as helpless as she.

Sinking back against the support column, he rasped, "Lisa, don't say anything without talking to a lawyer first."

"I don't know any lawyers," she said, her voice a thready whisper.

"I do." He heaved a breath, squeezed his eyes closed. "Don't worry. It's going to be all right."

But it wasn't. Somehow, she knew it wasn't. When she'd gone into the river and hit her head, something had changed in the universe, and since then, nothing had been right. And at the moment she was thoroughly convinced that nothing would ever be right again.

It was too much. Far too much. She was beyond upset, beyond anger, beyond feeling anything.

She stood quite still while the officer snapped the cuffs around her wrists. The metal was cold against her skin.

Dimly, she was aware of Mike arguing with the policeman, and soon other officers came to intervene. She didn't hear what they said. She was somewhere else, floating out of her body, away from this place, this time, her conscious mind in a state of total shutdown—her only defense against the unendurable.

As the officer led her out of the barn, her feet moving automatically one in front of the other, she vaguely registered the rain pouring down to soak her clothing. It was cold. Cold like the handcuffs.

Cold like the bleak, empty future that stretched endlessly before her.

Chapter Twenty-One

"It's going to be all right." Mike's last words to her rang in Lisa's head as she lay on the narrow bunk in her tiny cell. She was trying hard to believe it but without success.

She scarcely remembered the process that had brought her here. She did remember being shuffled through several police stations, somehow landing in the Baltimore City Jail. She also recalled a judge pronouncing her a flight risk and refusing bail. Mostly, the past twenty-four hours were a blur. She thought she might actually have slept through a lot of it.

Amazingly, it seemed she'd slept through the night, as well, although conditions weren't conducive to rest. The place was hot, airless and crawling with bugs, and the smell was enough to make her gag. Still, she'd awakened somewhat revived—physically, at least. The problem was, the emotional turmoil that exhaustion had staved off had come flooding back.

At the moment, despair threatened to sweep away her sanity. Squeezing her eyes closed, she shut out the grimy walls covered with hateful messages scribbled by previous prisoners. But the imprint of the lumpy bed against her back was a constant reminder of her circumstances.

Despair gave way to fear. Not only for herself. For Mike.

The thought that he might be in the hospital was driving her crazy. After all, the last she'd seen of him, he was dripping blood and close to collapse. She had to content herself with the knowledge that he'd been well enough to make a phone call, because he'd sent Laura Roswell to see her.

Laura had come early, announcing she was a colleague of Mike's and an attorney. Lisa had asked her immediately how he was, but all Laura could tell her was that his arm was in a sling. Then she'd forced Lisa to go back over the gory details of the past incredible week. Next, she'd demanded the police show her the autopsy report on Hollingsworth. Unfortunately, it named the cause of death as respiratory arrest brought on by a subdural hematoma resulting from a blow to the head. It hadn't helped Lisa's case at all.

At that point, Laura had advised her to tell the police everything—from the time of the car accident, to her escape from Hollingsworth's estate. The police were unimpressed. They had only her word that she'd been attacked. Given the autopsy report and her admission that she'd hit Hollingsworth, she was still the prime suspect. Moreover, they had checked the Hyatt Regency, and Justine wasn't registered, which reinforced their notion that *she* was Justine.

Laura Roswell had left saying she would make it a top priority to get Lisa some positive ID. Because, if she wasn't Justine, the only motive she would have had for hitting Hollingsworth was self-defense. Armed with every phone number and name Lisa could remember, starting with her colleagues at Williamsburg Architects, Laura had promised to make phone calls that afternoon. "Meanwhile," she'd told Lisa, "don't worry."

Easier said than done.

Lisa shifted a little, trying to get comfortable on the hard cot. The frustration of not being able to help herself was enough to make her scream. She wanted to be doing something. Anything! And the only thing she could do was lie here. And wait. And worry.

Down the hall, the heavy door to the lockup squeaked as it swung open. The sound was followed by purposeful footsteps drawing closer. They stopped in front of her cell, and she saw a prison guard and Ben Brisco, one of the detectives who'd interrogated her. Ben was tough-looking, but he wasn't as hard-nosed as Munson, the other officer who had questioned her.

"You've got a visitor," Brisco said.

Lisa sat up, her hopes surging. "Mike?"

"No." Brisco hesitated for a second, and she thought he was going to say something else. But all he said was, "Sorry."

Lisa's spirits plummeted. "So, who is it then?"

Brisco's reply was laconic. "You'd better see for yourself."

Sighing, Lisa sat up. She was hot. Mike's sweats that she'd put on yesterday morning were undoubtedly starting to smell, and she felt in dire need of a shower. Hardly a state in which to receive visitors. She didn't even have a brush for her hair. She winced as she stood up. Her knee was better, but it stiffened when she wasn't using it.

"You okay?" Brisco asked as the guard unlocked the cell.

"Mentally or physically?" she muttered, unable to keep the sarcasm out of her voice.

He muttered back, "Keeping you here isn't my idea."

She shot him a surprised look. Did she actually have an ally in this hellhole?

He gestured for her to precede him down the hall. They waited while the guard unlocked the gate, then he ushered her to one of the interrogation rooms. With the guard stationed outside, Brisco motioned her through the open door of the windowless, gray cubicle containing three metal chairs and a table that had seen better days.

But when she stepped into the room, it wasn't the decor that riveted her. It was the auburn-haired woman sitting with her hands clasped on the scarred tabletop. The woman was a copy of herself. Except that her hair was carefully coiffed, her makeup in place and she was wearing a blue silk blouse instead of ill-fitting, dirty sweats.

Lisa felt as if she'd had the breath knocked out of her, and she grabbed the back of a chair for support. For a full minute, she couldn't speak. Finally she managed to wheeze, "Justine?"

The woman raised her chin, and Lisa gazed into blue eyes that were mirrors of her own.

"That's right," the woman answered. Her voice was cool, but her wide eyes and pale, drawn expression told Lisa she was not unaffected at meeting her double.

With a scrape of metal against tile, Lisa pulled out the chair she was holding and dropped into the seat. Maybe, she thought, if she'd always known she was a twin, this experience wouldn't be so shattering. As it was, she'd had only the pictures in Justine's photo album as evidence of their similarities. And looking at a picture was nowhere near as unnerving as this.

"Wh—what are you doing here?" Lisa breathed.

Justine waved an impatient hand, looking as if she wished she was anywhere else on earth. "Mike made me come."

Before Lisa could comment, Brisco said, "Mike found her. After she left his office yesterday morning, she checked out of the Hyatt, where she was registered under another name, and checked into the Harbor Court."

Justine shot the detective an angry glare. "Do you really have to be here? I've already given you my statement, admitting I was at my house the night Kendall was murdered. That's all you're going to get."

"You were there?" Lisa gasped.

Tearing her heated gaze from Brisco, who remained steadfastly present, Justine looked at her. "I must have arrived after you'd gone. Kendall was already decked out on the bedroom floor."

Lisa frowned. "So, if you were there, why didn't you stay? Why did you wait for Maggie to find him dead?" And as a stunning thought hit her, she whispered, "Or did you kill him?"

"No, I didn't kill him," Justine muttered. "Although there've been times..." Recovering her composure, she shrugged. "I didn't stay for the same reason I went away in the first place. I needed some breathing space."

Lisa's jaw went slack. "And I gave it to you? How long have you known what was happening to me?" When Justine didn't reply, she guessed, "From the beginning?"

Still no reply.

Anger overriding shock, Lisa fixed her sister with a burning look. "I think you owe me some honesty, don' you?"

Justine tried to stare her down—and failed. Her gaze slid away. "Okay," she said, grudgingly. "I've known since the day after the accident. I called Maggie, pretending to be a friend of mine from the country club. She started babbling about your car going into the Jones Falls."

"And you let me go through hell, tangled up in your life without saying a single word."

The slender shoulders rose and fell in a shrug. Justine fidgeted in her chair. "I was scared, all right? Is that so hard to understand? You saw enough of Kendall to know what he's like. I'd done something I knew would make him angry, and I was scared he'd find out. So I let you cover for me. And . . . well . . . I'm sorry."

She wasn't sorry, Lisa thought—at least not for what she'd done. She was only sorry that she'd been caught.

Lisa stared, repulsed, yet unable to look away from the woman she was forced to believe was her own flesh and blood. It was beyond her comprehension that one human being could use another as callously as Justine had used her.

She didn't know what to say. Truly, she didn't have *any-thing* to say to Justine, which saddened her deeply. She'd found a sister only to discover they didn't have a single thing in common.

No, that wasn't true. Incredibly, by some bizarre cosmic twist, they'd both been attracted to the same man. The difference was, she loved Mike. Lord knows what Justine had felt for him—but surely it wasn't love.

Lisa was saved from having to speak when Justine continued, her voice low and a little shaky. "You can't imagine what living with Kendall has been like. What did you have with him? A couple of nasty hours?"

"About that," Lisa whispered. "He was awful."

"Yes, well, try multiplying those hours by eight years." Drawing herself up, Justine made a fuss of straightening her skirt and tucking in a stray hair, but her hand was shaking, and her trembling lips and little frowns kept ruining her cool demeanor. "He was wonderful to me," she continued, "when he wanted a pretty young wife. By the time I found out what he was really like, it was too late."

"You could have left," Lisa said.

Justine uttered a short, harsh laugh. "Oh, sure. And he would have stood back and let me, right?"

No, Lisa realized suddenly, he wouldn't have. Kendall Hollingsworth wouldn't have let anything he considered his possession get away from him. She'd heard him order her not to leave and set his housekeeper and handyman to guard her. No, he would never have allowed Justine to walk out on him.

"I thought I could handle him," Justine murmured. "But I was wrong." She shot Lisa a quick glance. "Maybe if you'd had to live with him for all those years, you'd have done the same thing I did."

Lisa doubted it. Yet, slowly, she was beginning to understand how desperate Justine had been. She knew about desperation. Was learning more about it every day. More than she'd ever wanted to know. But she didn't think it was possible that she'd ever be desperate enough to let another person suffer on her account, while she sat back and watched. At least she hoped she'd never sink that low.

A loud knock at the door cut off Lisa's thoughts, and Detective Munson burst in. He looked from Lisa to Justine, his gaze stony and unrevealing.

"Okay," he said to Brisco. "I'm ready for them."

"Ready for what?" Justine demanded.

He focused on Lisa as he replied, "There's a crazy man in custody. The one you say stabbed Realto."

"He did!" Lisa insisted for the dozenth time.

Munson gave her a long look that made her wish she'd hung on to her self-control. "Yeah, well, I'd like confirmation."

Lisa seethed. Brisco and Laura Roswell had explained that since Mike had been on his back behind a bale of hay, she and the tramp were the only witnesses. "Why don't you get confirmation from the man who had the knife? Ask *him* who stabbed Realto."

It was immediately obvious that Munson wasn't about to answer questions asked by prisoners. Before he could repeat his order for her and Justine to follow him, Brisco stepped in.

"The guy clammed up on us as soon as we got him to the station house. Wouldn't even say what he was doing at the farm. Just sat for hours with his mouth shut. Then he started saying he was willing to make a deal. Said he'd write out a confession—if we let him talk to you."

"But *I* don't have to talk to him." Justine stood up. "I'm free to leave whenever I want."

Brisco gave her a look that put her back in her seat. "By admitting that you were at the estate the night your husband died," he said, his voice ominous, "you cast doubt on the identity of the woman who struck him."

Justine's composure slipped a notch. "But it wasn't me."

"So you said. But if we put you and Lisa in a lineup, I bet your housekeeper won't be able to tell you apart."

Another notch down, Lisa thought. Yes, underneath all that polish and silk, Justine was really frightened. Only, for some reason that Lisa didn't know—and didn't particularly care to know—Justine was driven beyond reason to try to hide her fear.

"Mike didn't say this would happen," she snapped. "He told me it was perfectly safe for me to come down here."

Brisco shrugged. "If you cooperate with this investigation, you'll be less likely to end up behind bars. Leave now, and I won't guarantee that you won't be picked up again within the hour."

Justine's face went pale, and in another minute, Lisa was ertain the sophisticated facade would be in tatters.

Brisco seemed to sense it, too, because his tone was mild s he said, "The sooner we clear things up, the sooner you an go. Okay?"

Munson gestured impatiently. "Can we get on with this?"

Lisa was as uncertain as Justine about seeing the tramp, ut she'd go along with almost anything that got the guy to alk.

Munson led the way down the hall to a large room, where ehind a glass window two uniformed guards stood on either side of the vagrant.

He was dressed in a jailhouse-orange jumpsuit, which, lthough ugly, was a distinct improvement over his former ttire. Moreover, he'd showered. His previously matted hair vas clean, and standing out in clumps around his head. He vas sitting with his arms folded, a stubborn mien deepening the lines on his weather-beaten face.

His head jerked up expectantly as the door opened. When e spotted Lisa and Justine, his hard expression melted, aking on a dreamy softness.

Lisa shrank back, confused. This man had followed her, :ome at her with a knife and killed Realto. He was dangerusly unpredictable.

At a nod from Brisco, the two tough-looking guards left.

"Okay, Gary," Munson barked. "We've filled our end of he bargain. Now tell us about Realto."

The man called Gary ignored him. All his attention was ocused on her and Justine.

"Please," she whispered. "Tell them what happened."

He spoke as if he hadn't been listening. "You're here. Two of you are here. But where's Andrea?"

"I told you, we don't know," Brisco answered calmly. "This is the best we can do."

Gary sighed. "I guess I got to be grateful for that. Here I am with two of my baby girls. Leigh. No, you want to be called Lisa. And Justine."

What on earth was he talking about? As his gaze na
rowed on her, Lisa took an involuntary step back.

"How do you know who I am?" Justine croaked.

His face fell, his disappointment so acute Lisa felt s
should be able to touch it.

"Don't you understand?" he pleaded. "You're my gir
My baby girls. Mine and Hallie's."

Lisa's mouth fell open, and for an instant her hea
stopped. *This* was Garrett Folsom? A quick glance at Ju
tine confirmed that her sister was equally shocked. T
gether they listened, speechless, as the peculiar ma
continued.

Head hanging low, swaying back and forth, he mutter
"I should have married her before they shipped me off
Nam. Brains got scrambled over there. Posttraumatic stre
syndrome, they call it." His head snapped up, his ga
shooting from Lisa to Justine. "No shame in that, y
know. No shame."

Light-headed, Lisa wobbled on her feet. She barely n
ticed when Brisco eased her into a chair.

Justine's reaction leaned toward outrage. "You can't
serious!" She looked down at the disheveled man as if he
just crawled out from under a rock. "You're claiming to
my father? Why—do you want money?"

"Money?" He looked bewildered. "Don't need money.

Lisa pressed her hands together on the table and tried
remain very still, tried very hard not to become hysterica
How many shocks could one person absorb? Whatever tl
number, she'd passed it. Justine, her sister. Now, this ma
saying he was her father. Hers and Justine's and...ar
somebody named Andrea.

Andrea...*Fenton?*

Lisa gasped. "Wait! Do you mean there are *three of us?*

He gave her a beatific smile. "Yes. Three little girls. Thr
little babies Hallie gave me." His smile faded. "But by tl
time I got back from Nam, you were all adopted and n
body would tell me nothing. Social Services kept saying
was better that way—'cause of, you know, my stress sy

drome." And with a hint of the bulldog determination that she herself had witnessed, he added, "But I didn't give up. I kept trying. All these years. I finally got the lawyer fellow who arranged the adoption...he's in a nursing home now...I got the names of your families from him. That's how I knew Justine was in Baltimore. And Leigh was in Philadelphia." He shook his head sadly. "Can't find Andrea."

Not twins but triplets. Lisa drew a ragged breath—at the same time, Justine, sitting beside her a few feet away, also heaved an unsteady sigh. Lisa met her sister's gaze. They studied each other for a moment, and Lisa saw that Justine was no more able than she to cope with this.

Justine sighed again and looked away. "Well, this is all perfectly unbelievable. And, frankly, I've got more important things to worry about than long-lost relatives."

Fortunately, Brisco rescued them both from having to respond to Garrett Folsom's desire for a family reunion.

"You were following Lisa around because she was your daughter?" Brisco asked.

Gary nodded vigorously. "Leigh...I mean, Lisa and Justine. See, I was trying to help! Like when I got those papers...you know, those papers? I got them the night Lisa fell asleep, and I put them in a safe place."

"*You* took them?" Lisa and Justine cried in unison.

He grinned. "Sure. I've got 'em. Got the folder from the rental car company, too. Yes, indeed, I do. Nice and safe."

"You mean, from Lisa's rental car?" Brisco asked.

Gary bobbed his head. "Saw the company sticker on Lisa's car. Knew where to go. Waited 'til late—real late— then got in and went through the records. Matched up Leigh's name...Leigh Barnes...that's her right name, you know. I'm sure it is. Yes. Matched up Leigh's name with her car's tag number."

The detective frowned. "But why did you take the records?"

Gary drew back. "To keep Leigh safe, of course."

Brisco shook his head over Gary's muddled logic. Rather than seek further clarification, the detective steered the questioning back to the previous topic. "Tell me more about these papers you took from Leigh. Are you talking about the ones Justine got from Kendall Hollingsworth's files and hid?"

Gary frowned. "Don't know where they came from. Just know Leigh found them in Justine's house." He looked at Lisa. "You fell asleep, and I was afraid somebody would take 'em. You know that housekeeper is pretty nosy. Can't trust her. So I grabbed 'em for safekeeping. Been watching over you," he said smugly. "You and Justine. I can slip in and out of that house when old Maggie is asleep."

Justine made a strangled noise.

Lisa held her breath when Brisco finally asked what was to her the most important question.

"Did you kill Realto?"

Gary looked incredulous. "Of course. What did you think?"

"Just tell us why you did it," Brisco suggested.

Gary snorted in disgust. "Don't you understand anything? He was going to shoot my girl. Shoot Leigh. Couldn't let him do that." He gave Lisa a beseeching look. "I'm not bad. Really. Never got a chance to prove I could be a good father. If Hallie hadn't died—God, I wish she hadn't died— her and me would have kept the three of you, and things would have been different." His gaze shifted between Lisa and Justine. "Don't hate me. Please don't."

"I don't hate you," Lisa answered automatically, with no real idea what she did feel. At the moment, she didn't think she would ever be able to accept this man as her father. She'd had a father, a very good one, and William Barnes could never be replaced.

Still, the truth was unavoidable; Garrett Folsom was her flesh and blood—the man who had given her life. And despite the fear he'd engendered in her with his bizarre behavior, he had saved her life. More than once.

Again Brisco relieved her from having to commit to anything definite.

Clearing his throat, the detective told Gary, "It will help Leigh if you tell us what happened at the farm."

Gary sat up straighter. "I want to help her. I do."

"Come on then," Munson said, putting his hand on Gary's shoulder. "Let's go do it."

Hesitantly, Gary rose. "Where are we going?"

"Where you can write down what happened," Munson answered, guiding him toward the door.

"But I want to talk to my girls some more."

"Later."

Gary threw Lisa and Justine one last look as he left the room. "You understand?" he asked urgently.

Lisa nodded, even though she wasn't sure what he'd meant.

"What's going to happen to him?" she asked Brisco when the door had closed.

The detective said, "He'll probably go to a veteran's hospital."

Justine pushed back her chair and stood. "I can't take any more of this. I've got to get out of here."

"I don't think so." Brisco took a step to the right and blocked her path. "I think you're going to sit tight right here while I make a phone call to my lieutenant."

"And then what?" she snapped.

"We'll see."

Folding her arms tightly around her waist, Justine fell back into her chair and stared at the wall. Her light, rapid breathing was the only sound she made. Lisa was sure she was wishing she'd never come back to Baltimore, much less to the police station.

"And me?" Lisa asked. "What's going to happen to me?"

Brisco sighed. "Sorry. I don't know. It's not my call."

It was what she'd expected. Yet the thought of going back to her cell made her throat tighten and her eyes sting. The detective opened the door and stood holding it for her. She rose slowly and started to leave.

"Wait."

Justine's voice stopped her at the doorway.

Lisa gave her a questioning look.

Justine studied her intently, a slight frown flitting briefly across her brow, her expression filled with indecision. Finally, the frown disappeared and she spoke bluntly. "You do know, don't you, that Mike is in love with you?"

Lisa stared at her, her lips parted slightly in shock. "Did he tell you that?"

Justine gave a delicate snort. "He wouldn't tell me anything if I tried to torture it out of him. No, he didn't tell me. It was obvious."

Not knowing what to think—and more than a little wary of believing her—Lisa asked, "Why are you telling me this?"

Justine looked at her for another long moment, and slowly, a tiny crack appeared in her armor—a softening of her mouth, a trace of warmth creeping into her eyes. Quietly, she said, "I don't know. Maybe because I owe him. Maybe because I owe you both. Maybe because I know him well enough to guess he hasn't said a thing to you about how he feels." Drawing a deep breath, she straightened, and the armor was suddenly intact once more. "What you do with the information is your own business. But, honey, I'll tell you this—the pastures don't get any greener anywhere else. And men don't come any better than Mike Lancer."

Lisa's mouth curved into a small, sad smile. "I know."

Chapter Twenty-Two

The instant Lisa stepped into the hall, she heard angry male voices coming from the other end of the corridor. Her heart skipped a beat, and her head turned sharply to look—because one of those voices was gloriously familiar.

"All I'm asking is that you *listen* to me!" Mike shouted, shaking a manila folder under the nose of a uniformed guard. A white sling cradled his left arm, but otherwise he seemed—and definitely sounded—healthy.

"And all I'm asking is that you follow procedures!" the guard shouted back at him.

"Dammit! I want Lisa out of jail!"

"And I'm telling you—"

"What's going on here?" Brisco started toward the two arguing men, giving Lisa all the excuse she needed to follow.

Mike whirled at the sound of Brisco's voice. "Ben! Thank God! I'm trying to get this—" He broke off, and Lisa saw his gaze swerve past the detective and come to land on her.

With Justine's startling revelation still ringing in her head, her instinct was to keep walking until she was in his arms. But uncertainty brought her to a stop several feet short of him.

Her eyes searched his features but found nothing on which to pin her hopes. He had dark shadows beneath his eyes, stubble across his jaw and he looked worried, exhausted—and furious.

"Your shoulder . . . ?" she began. "Are you—"

He waved aside her concern. "It's fine. Nothing seri ous." His gaze raked over her once. "Are you all right?"

She nodded.

"What have you found out?" Brisco asked.

Mike's gaze flashed to the detective, but instead of an swering the question, he said, "Don't take her back to he cell. She didn't kill Hollingsworth."

Brisco hesitated. "Mike, you know it's not up to—"

"I can prove it."

The two men appraised each other in silence, and as th moment stretched on, Lisa could feel the tension rising.

Finally, Brisco relented. "Okay. Let's hear what you've got to say."

Hope surged inside her, and her gaze automaticall sought Mike's. She wanted so badly to go to him. But sh didn't. No matter what her untrustworthy sister had said she had to assume he was here because he'd agreed that firs day in the hospital to help her—and Mike Lancer kept hi promises. To read anything else into his presence was wish ful thinking. Lisa reminded herself of that as she followe Brisco into another ugly interrogation room and sat dow at the table.

Brisco closed the door behind Mike, then walked to th head of the table, where he straddled a chair. "All right," he said. "What've you got?"

Mike plunked the folder he was holding onto the table an took the chair across from hers. Giving her a quick, inscru table glance, he spoke directly to Brisco, "I got a secon opinion on Hollingsworth's autopsy report."

Brisco's look was wary. "Something wrong with the firs one?"

Mike's features twisted in derision. "Tappenhill signe it."

"Oh, Christ."

Lisa caught the look the men exchanged, and it brough her to the edge of panic. Was she going to be tried for mur der on the basis of a report done by an incompetent? Hand

enched together in her lap, she listened closely as Mike
ontinued in clipped phrases.

"So, we start with the assumption that Tappenhill's re-
ort is a piece of trash," he said.

"I'm listening," Brisco muttered.

"Last year I did some divorce work for a Dr. Paul Mey-
rs. He's in pathology at Johns Hopkins. He told me that if
ever needed his expert opinion, I had it. Between mid-
ight and two this morning, he gave me a crash course on
e interaction of certain drugs."

"And...?"

"Hollingsworth was already a dead man walking when he
as hit on the head. The blow isn't what killed him."

Lisa sucked in a sharp breath.

Brisco cocked an eyebrow. "So what did?"

"You're gonna love this. Just listen. Hollingsworth was
n Capoten for his high blood pressure. I've confirmed that
ith his physician." Mike pulled out a sheet of paper from
e folder and handed it to Brisco. "The police pathology
port states that Hollingsworth had lithium in his sys-
m—a drug regularly prescribed for bipolar disorder. But
ccording to his medical records—" another sheet ap-
eared and was passed across the table "—he's never been
iagnosed with or treated for any mental condition."

Brisco studied the sheets, then looked at Mike. "And?"

Mike handed him several more sheets. "These are copies
f pages from the *Physician's Desk Reference* and some
harmacology texts, documenting that lithium in combi-
ation with Capoten produces toxic effects. The time of
nset of symptoms varies from one to six hours, which
ould have given Hollingsworth plenty of time to get back
rom his meeting with Estelle Bensinger before he bought
."

"You're getting ahead of me," Brisco muttered. "Slow
own."

Lisa stifled a groan. In the past two minutes, the tiny
park of hope she'd felt hearing Mike tell Brisco he could

prove her innocence had grown to a blaze. She could hardl
contain her eagerness for him to get on with it.

"Estelle Bensinger," Brisco repeated. "The dea
woman."

Mike dragged in a deep breath and let it out. "Righ
Hollingsworth's secretary—and mistress. I'll get to the
meeting in a minute." Handing over more papers, he co
tinued, "These are copies of several articles found in Be
singer's apartment about the consequences of combinin
lithium and ACE-inhibitors like Capoten. And don't ask m
how I got them."

Brisco gave him a jaded look. "I don't want to know."

"Two weeks ago, she obtained a prescription for lithiu
from a physician in Washington. But only a small amoun
is missing from the bottle found in her medicine ches
Probably only the quantity that went into the drink sh
served Hollingsworth when he met her on his boat."

"Boat?"

"He owns... *owned* a cruiser that's docked at the Inne
Harbor. She didn't have time to clean up from their littl
rendezvous before she was killed, so the glasses were still o
the counter. I had the residue from both glasses analyzec
The lab confirms the presence of lithium in the one tha
contained scotch—which is what Maggie Dempsey, th
Hollingsworths' housekeeper, swears Kendall Hollings
worth drank exclusively."

"Wait a minute." Brisco held up a hand to stop the on
slaught of information. "How do you know they met on hi
boat the day he died? Our investigation didn't turn that up.'

*That's because your colleagues weren't trying to find ou
who really killed Hollingsworth*—Lisa almost said the word
aloud. If she hadn't been so ecstatic over the mountain o
evidence Mike had amassed to absolve her, she easily coul
have been furious at the police for their smug assumptio
that they already had the killer behind bars. Cautionin
herself not to get too ecstatic too soon, she couldn't quit
hold back a sound of excitement. It came out as a tin
whimper.

Mike's gaze snapped to her, and he frowned. "You okay?"

She nodded, her eyes shining. If ever a woman had wanted a hero, he was it. She knew he must see her love for him written plainly on her face—she couldn't help it—and when his frown deepened to a scowl, a shard of pain lanced her. That scowl took the joy and hopefulness right out of her and made the thought of freedom nowhere near as bright. She listened with leaden spirits as Mike turned back to Brisco to finish making his argument.

"You know Bensinger and Hollingsworth had been having an affair for years," he said.

Brisco nodded. "Yeah, we got that."

"I checked out all their regular hangouts. They were both seen boarding the cruiser Monday afternoon, before he died. She got there a half hour before he did. I've got witnesses who are willing to sign statements."

Brisco was clearly amazed. "How the hell did you manage all this—" he flapped the papers in his hands "—in twenty-four hours?"

Mike combed his fingers through his hair, heaving a deep, tired sigh. "I've had a lot of help." Shrugging his good shoulder, he added, "I also have a record of Hollingsworth's phone conversation with a detective agency he employed, in which he's told about a videotape of Estelle Bensinger removing a folder from his confidential files."

"Where did you get *that?*" Brisco asked.

"From the same company that was videotaping his office."

"Christ." Brisco studied him for a moment, then shook his head. "I told those bastards they didn't know what they were losing the day you left the job. I like being proved right."

Lisa watched Mike's neck and cheeks turn ruddy, and she was a little surprised when he didn't try to deny Brisco's praise.

"Thanks, Ben," Mike said. "Your confidence means a lot to me. But I'm not in this for myself. I'm only here to prove

that Lisa didn't murder Kendall Hollingsworth.'' His lip
thinned to a grim line. "The point is, Estelle Bensinger ha
a motive for killing Hollingsworth. She also had the weapo
that killed him, the knowledge to use it and the opportu
nity."

Brisco gave a low grunt. "Too bad Juan Realto drilled he
a couple of hours later."

"You've got confirmation on that?"

"Yeah, the ballistics report came back. The bullet the
took out of her was fired by his gun. No doubt about it."

"Ben, I want you to turn Lisa loose."

Brisco shook his head. "Mike, you know I don't have th
authority."

"Dammit!" Mike's fist hit the table with a bang, the an
ger and frustration Lisa had read on his features erupting.

"Take it easy," Brisco said. "You've made your case, an
it's damned convincing. Now let me put the cards on th
table, and we'll see how it plays."

Mike stared at Brisco in silence, his nerves visibl
stretched to the breaking point.

Lisa knew that she, too, was on the verge of exploding
and she was awed by Mike's self-control. Her own was rap
idly deteriorating. Finally, she couldn't prevent herself fron
reaching across the table to place a hand on his arm.

She felt the muscles in his forearm tense beneath he
touch.

"Thank you," she whispered. And she managed a grate
ful smile that he didn't return.

His eyes searched hers, his dark gaze smoldering witl
emotions she couldn't begin to read. Finally, he gave her
single nod, then looked away.

She withdrew her hand, fighting back tears, and turne
to Brisco, who was busy politely ignoring the private ex
change taking place. When he caught her gaze, he mo
tioned toward the door. She nodded, and, without furthe
speech, he ushered her out of the room and back to her cell

AN ETERNITY. That's how long it seemed to Lisa that she sat cross-legged on the bunk in her cell, literally biting her nails. In fact, it was five hours. She looked up at the sound of approaching footsteps. Brisco appeared with a guard in front of the bars—and he was smiling.

"You're free to go," he said as the guard unlocked the cell door and opened it.

She squeezed her eyes closed against sudden tears, relief pouring through her so strongly it made her giddy. "Thank God."

"And Mike Lancer."

"Yes, and Mike Lancer," she murmured, rising.

Brisco led her through the locked gates and dingy corridors to a large room where guards were supervising prisoners visiting with friends and relatives. A row of tables bisected the room, divided by bars separating the free from the incarcerated.

Lisa searched for Mike, but he wasn't here. A little desperately, she asked Brisco, "Have you seen Mike?"

The detective shook his head. "He stayed until we found out the charges were being dropped. That was around two. I don't know where he went then." His tone was apologetic. "I had to wait for the paperwork before I could release you."

She nodded. "I understand."

She also thought she understood why Mike wasn't here. He'd fulfilled his obligation, gotten her cleared of the charges and now she was on her own. He could hardly have made it plainer if he'd said it to her, face-to-face.

"Where are you going?" Brisco broke into her thoughts as he led her to the jail's front entrance.

"I was staying in a Sheraton in Towson," she replied, swallowing the lump in her throat as she tried to return her mind to practical matters. "My things are all there. But I don't know if they're holding my room—or, for that matter, how I'd get into it without the key or some ID." Her hand fluttered in a helpless gesture. "I guess I'll have to convince them that I am who I say I am." In Mike's bor-

rowed clothes and with the grime of the Baltimore City Jai
clinging to every pore in her body, it seemed unlikely to he
that she'd succeed.

"I'll call and talk to the manager," Brisco offered. "I'l
make sure you get your key."

She gave him a grateful look. "I'd really appreciate it."

"No problem. Do you have money?"

"No." Heat crept into her cheeks at the admission. Tha
she had come to this, that she could be standing in a jail i
a strange city, penniless and wearing borrowed clothes wa
beyond humiliating. Her voice was scarcely a whisper as sh
explained, "My wallet, credit cards, money...everythin
was washed away in the accident."

Before she could argue, Brisco took out his wallet an
handed her two twenties.

"Oh, I couldn't—"

"Sure, you can," he insisted. "I wouldn't be able to slee
tonight if I put you out on the street without a cent."

"Thank you," Lisa whispered, wadding the bills into he
clenched fist. "I'll pay you back."

He gave a brief laugh. "Well, you know where to find me
Look—I've got to get going, but I'll call you a cab before
leave. Just wait out front for it."

Thanking him again and saying goodbye, Lisa steppe
through the main door onto the sidewalk. She was shocke
to see that it was still daylight. The sun was just droppin
below the tops of the tall brick and gray stone buildings
bronzing their surfaces in amber tones.

She waited ten minutes, standing on the busy city street
disoriented and dirty and saddened beyond anything she'
ever experienced. Probably it wasn't really cold outside, bu
she stood shivering in the light wind. When the cab ar
rived, she slumped in a corner of the back seat and gave th
driver the name of her hotel. As the vehicle made its wa
through the bustling downtown traffic, she stared out th
window, oblivious to the passing scenery.

She was back to square one. The place she'd been last Tuesday morning when she'd left Erin Stone's office in tears.

No, that wasn't quite true. She'd acquired two identical sisters, one of whom she happily could have done without and one of whom she probably would never meet. She'd also acquired a biological father who was well-intentioned but who needed more than therapy. For her baby's sake, as well as her own, she thought it might be better to forget she'd ever learned of her blood relations.

Which left her and the baby with no family at all. Oh, she had friends. Some very good ones, she remembered. Melody and Esther would stick by her, but they weren't going to raise her baby with her. In all ways that counted, she'd be on her own.

She also had to find a new job, even if Hank Lombard didn't get her fired; her firm did too much business with his for her to be able to avoid him. Under ordinary circumstances, she wouldn't have doubted her ability to find a good position. But how would prospective employers respond when she told them, as she surely would, that she was pregnant?

Still, there was something worse than financial uncertainty, she thought sadly. Since her parents' deaths, she'd thought she felt as lonely as a person could feel. She'd been wrong. She still missed her parents dreadfully, yet she had memories of them, a lifetime of having known them and their love, to comfort her.

She had no memories of a lifetime with Mike to console her. She'd wanted a partner, a friend, a lover. She'd wanted a father for her baby. Somehow, she'd known intuitively, even in those first foggy moments she'd laid eyes on him, that he could fulfill her needs and desires as no other man could. It was agony to know she would never hold him again. Never feel the strength and vitality of his body pressed to hers. Never feel his tenderness—or his passion. Never hear his laughter. Having tasted what love between them would be like, she had to accept that there would be no more.

Tears threatened to spill down her cheeks. She would have to thank him, of course. He'd moved heaven and earth to get her out of jail, and he'd saved her life, several times over. She couldn't simply leave town without acknowledging her debt to him. If he didn't want to see or talk to her, she would have to find some other way to tell him how grateful she was.

And then she would have to tell him goodbye.

At that moment, riding silently in the back of the shabby yellow cab as it headed out of the city, Lisa knew what it felt like to have a broken heart. The pain stabbed at her and she fought to hold herself together for just a little longer.

The cab dropped her at the Sheraton and she went to the desk, where, to her relief, the manager met her with the key to her room. Blushing at the curious looks of the hotel staff and guests in the lobby, she hurried onto the elevator.

With a prayer of thanks that no one was in the hallway on her floor, she walked quickly to her room and opened the door. Stepping inside, she was struck for a moment by the eerie feeling that she'd been gone only since that morning. There was her suitcase on the bed, her blue linen suit hanging in the open closet, her bottle of Chanel No. 5 on the bureau . . . her sneakers, her briefcase . . . all of it exactly as she had left it. How odd that nothing had changed when she would never be the same again.

Closing the door behind her, she went immediately to the bathroom, where she stripped off her clothes, turned on the shower and stepped under the stream of nearly blistering hot water. When she'd lathered and scrubbed everything once, she started over and did it all a second time.

The steam still billowed around her when she belted a terry cloth robe around her waist. A knock at the hotel-room door brought her out of the warmth and security of the bathroom.

Unable to imagine who it could be, she peeped through
the security viewer. In the next instant, with her heart racing, she had the door unlocked and open.

"Mike!"

"Thank God," he said. "You made it out here all right."

Stunned by the sight of him, she could only manage a
nod.

"I went home to shower and shave," His tone was gruff,
businesslike. "I planned to be back at the jail when they released you. But I sat down on the couch to eat a sandwich,
and that's the last thing I remember. I fell asleep."

"You looked exhausted," she said, thinking that he still
did, despite the clean clothes and shaven face. Much as she'd
like to reach out to him, she had to hold back her hands.
Mike had come here as a detective closing a case, not as a
man claiming a lover.

His arm was still in a sling. Shrugging his good shoulder,
he said, "That's no excuse. I should have been there to get
you. I'm sorry."

She shook her head. "The last thing you need to be is
sorry. I owe you a lot more than a nap."

He scowled. "You don't owe me anything."

"Mike, I owe you my life," she said with quiet insistence. "What you've done for me went way beyond the call
of duty." Her gaze fell to the floor. "I'll never be able to
thank you enough."

He was silent for a moment, then spoke in an oddly
strained voice. "Lisa, we have to talk."

Her gaze flew to his. From the look and the sound of
him—all those harsh lines in his face and brusque, short
words—it wasn't anything she wanted to hear. Yet she
couldn't help hoping that it might be.

"Okay," she whispered.

"Can I come in?"

She nodded, then stood aside to let him pass. Bolting the
door behind him, she turned to find him standing stiffly a
few feet away. He was half turned away from her, his right
hand shoved into his back pocket.

"Lisa," he began, then hesitated, casting a quick, sideways glance at her. "Or I guess I should call you Leigh shouldn't I?"

She shook her head. "No, I'm going to keep the name Lisa."

"Oh? Why?"

She tightened the belt at her waist. "You'll think it silly."

"No, I won't. Tell me." His voice was quiet, more encouraging than it had been a minute ago.

"Well..." She lifted one shoulder in a tiny shrug. "I woke up in the hospital, and I wasn't Leigh Barnes anymore. I was Lisa. Now I remember who Leigh Barnes is, but I feel like a new person—I guess that's the best way to put it. Leigh and Lisa combined." Feeling horribly exposed, she gave him a fleeting glance. "It probably sounds totally schizophrenic."

"No," he said softly. "In fact, it makes a lot of sense." He paused for a moment or two, then said, "Tell me what brought your memory back."

"It was a dream," she replied in a scarcely audible tone. "After you left Jenny's yesterday afternoon, I fell asleep on the couch. I dreamed about something that—" She stopped abruptly, the words lodged in her throat. She wasn't ready to tell him about the dream, not when she had no idea why he was asking. "It was something that happened a couple months ago," she continued. "It was...very bad. I've dreamed about it ever since it happened, but yesterday, the phone woke me up in the middle of the dream, and I remembered enough of it that I was able to force myself to remember all of it. Once I had, the rest of my memory...well, it just sort of switched back on."

"I wish it hadn't happened like that—when you were alone," he murmured. "And I hope not everything you remember is bad."

With her gaze directed at her fingers, which were twisting the belt of her robe into knots, she replied, "No, most of it is very good. I had a wonderful childhood with terrific parents. They weren't rich, but they gave me love and security and good values.'' She wanted to tell him more but didn't know if he wanted to hear. He was standing there so rigidly. He kept asking questions, but she still didn't know why he was asking them. With each answer, she felt more defenseless, more raw. Why couldn't he say what he'd come here to say and then leave?

He heaved a sigh. "So, what will you do now?"

She frowned, still unable to summon the courage to look at him.

"What are your plans?" he prompted. "Are you going back home soon, or will you...still be looking for a job in Baltimore?"

This was it. This was where he would extricate himself from whatever claims of dependency he felt she had on him.

Swallowing against the tightness in her throat, she said, 'I suppose I'll go back. It seems like—'' she drew a jerky breath ''—like the logical thing to do.''

A quick glance caught him staring fixedly at the blank TV screen across the room.

"Do you..." He stopped midsentence. "I mean, is there anyone special waiting for you?"

"No, it's only me...and the baby," she said softly.

He sucked in a deep breath, held it for a second or two, then let it out. "What if...what if I asked the two of you to stay?"

Her head snapped up, her gaze flashing to his face. Slowly, his head turned toward her, and their eyes met. Gone was his harsh mask and the guarded look. His features were open, vulnerable. His eyes, as they searched hers, were soft and warm with some emotion she was afraid to name.

"You *want* me to stay?" she asked, hope swelling inside her.

He nodded once.

"Here? With you?"

Again, he nodded. "Here. With me."

"Mike—" Lisa's hands flew to cover her face as a so
escaped her. "Oh, Mike, I . . . I thought you were gettin
ready to say you wanted me to leave. At the jail . . . yo
looked so angry. I thought—"

"God, Lisa, didn't you realize . . . ? Sweetheart, I wasn'
angry at *you*."

Suddenly he was right in front of her, drawing her clos
against him. Even with only one arm, his embrace was soli
and secure. He spoke with his lips buried in her damp curls

"I was angry at the cops, at Justine . . . at the world i
general. When I saw you, all I wanted to do was grab yo
and run, get you out of there and take you someplace
could hold you. It was hard enough even speaking to yo
without— If I'd touched you or held you . . . Lisa, I'd hav
lost it. And I *couldn't* lose it. I had to keep it together to ge
you out of there. I'm so sorry, sweetheart. I didn't realiz
how you'd take it."

With her face buried against his neck, Lisa sobbed, "Oh
Mike, I'm sorry, too. I know I hurt you, and I know
should have told you about the baby in the first place. Bu
I was confused and worried and frightened, and I wasn'
thinking straight."

"It's okay, sweetheart," he told her. "It doesn't matte
anymore."

"But you were so angry." She gulped. "When you walke
out Jenny's door to go back to the office, I thought I'
never see you again."

His arm trembled as it tightened around her. "You looke
so sad. So . . . lost. But I felt used and manipulated in a wa
I hadn't since . . . since Justine. The only way I could dea
with it was to tell myself that I'd be better off without you
Except I knew I wouldn't be. Deep down, I knew yo
weren't really trying to deceive me. I was only lying to my
self, and the only excuse I've got is that I was mad . . . an
scared."

She lifted her head to look at him. "Scared?"

"Damned right," he muttered. "I was scared as hell o
how much I love you and how bad you could hurt me if yo

wanted to.'' Before she could speak the words on her lips, Mike raised his hand to her mouth. ''Let me finish. When I got to my office, Justine was there.'' He laughed harshly. ''Seeing her made me realize how different the two of you are. Not that I didn't already know it, but... well, let's say I gained a perspective I'll never lose.''

And Lisa saw clearly that it was true—he wouldn't ever confuse her with her sister again. ''She did something for me too.''

''Did she?''

She nodded. ''Justine told me that you were in love with me. I can't say that I like her very much, even if she is my sister. And I like her even less for what she did to you. But I think she's sorry for what she did—to both of us. I also think she's scared and I'm *certain* she had a very bad time of it with Kendall Hollingsworth.''

His puzzled expression deepened to confusion. ''Why are you defending her?''

Lisa shrugged. ''I guess I'm hoping that if you stop judging her so harshly, you'll judge yourself less harshly, too. You blame yourself for being taken in by her, but your only sin was to trust the woman you loved. And that's no sin at all. She may even have loved you, too, but she was immature and impulsive. I'd bet anything that's how she decided to marry Kendall Hollingsworth—on the spur of the moment. I'd also bet she regretted it like mad almost as soon as she'd done it.''

''And I bet you're right.'' He sighed. ''You're a smart lady, Lisa Barnes. Which is only one of the many reasons that I love you.'' His hand came up to lie against her cheek, his thumb tracing the line of her lips as he whispered, ''Marry me, Lisa.''

She sucked in a sharp breath, her heart racing.

''I want to hear you say yes.''

''Yes,'' she breathed. ''Oh, yes!'' She threw her arms round him, barely remembering to be careful of his shoulder. ''I love you so much.''

''Lisa...''

He lowered his mouth to hers for a searing kiss tha
promised much more. But when his hand slid up her ribs to
find her breast, she drew back, gasping for breath.

"Mike . . . wait. I have to tell you something first—abou
the night the baby was conceived."

She saw a shadow flicker in his eyes. "Lisa, you don'
have to—"

She smoothed a finger across his furrowed brow. "I do.'
Her voice dropped to a whisper as she told him of her job a:
the only female architect at Williamsburg, how she'd strug
gled to win a position on the liason team, and finally of tha
fateful night in Chicago.

She paused for breath, glanced at Mike to see that he wa:
watching her closely, then lowered her gaze once more. "
tried to fight him off, but I couldn't."

"Lisa . . ."

"Mike, it's okay. It's what I dreamed about at Jenny's
and when I woke up, instead of pushing it away like I'd beer
doing, I *made* myself remember it. Because somehow
knew I had to if I was ever going to remember anything else
That night was . . . it was the worst thing that's ever hap
pened to me. But I faced it and it's over. He hurt me, but
survived. And I've got this baby that I do want very, ver
much. That's why I was at Birth Data, Inc. I wanted to lear
my baby's heritage."

His hand stroked her back, caressing, soothing. "Yo
looked so upset that day."

"I guess I was feeling pretty down, wondering how I wa
going to cope with being a single mom and working."

He kissed her cheek, her hair, then her mouth, gentl
kisses, tender and healing. "I don't have much experienc
with happy family life. But when I said I wanted you,
meant the whole package." His voice broke a little. "I swea
to you, Lisa, I'll do my damnedest to be a good father t
your child."

She gave him a smile full of love. "I know you will."

"It'll be so good—the three of us together. Or the four o
us, if you want."

"I want," she whispered. "I want your babies, too. But mostly—" She gasped as his mouth found its way to the base of her neck and his teeth nibbled at her shoulder. "Oh, Lord, Mike, mostly, I want you."

"You've got me," he growled. "For keeps."

His lips joined hers in a passionate kiss, and as he slowly began to walk her backward toward the bed, she realized that they were alone, and safe, in a snug bedroom where they wouldn't be disturbed. Finally, she was free to show him exactly how much she loved him.

When the backs of her knees bumped against the mattress, she lifted her gaze to find him smiling at her, as if he had come to the same conclusion. While he fumbled one-handed with the knot of her robe, she lifted one finger and gently traced the arch of his cheek, the curve of his lips, the line where his dark hair met his brow. Then she traced the same path with her lips.

"Damn," he muttered, giving up on the knot. "This sling is a nuisance."

"Not to worry," she said. With a provocative smile, she untied the knot and let the robe slide off her shoulders to pool around her feet. His heated gaze raked over her, and he felt her nipples harden against the silk of her nightgown as if he'd touched them.

He sucked in a quick breath, lifting his hand to cup her breast. "So sexy. So beautiful," he murmured.

She leaned into his touch, yearning for more. Still, she was determined to continue what she'd started. The first time, he'd undressed her, and he'd made it a delicious, carnal experience. This time, she wanted to do the same for him.

Reaching for the top button of his shirt, she began the task, and she continued to make it an erotic journey punctuated by lingering kisses and tantalizing touches. By the time she had him naked—but for the sling and his shirt, which she left unbuttoned and spread open across his muscled chest—they were both at fever pitch.

When it looked like he was about to lose all restraint and take control, she pushed him gently down onto the bed to lie on his back and lowered her body onto his. He gasped as he slid inside of her. For a moment, her eyes closed and she gloried in the feel of him filling her completely. She opened her eyes to find him smiling, then his hand slid down to curve gently over her abdomen, and she went very still. The smile left his face, and his eyes held hers as he spoke on a husky, solemn note.

"Years from now," he said, "when we talk about the time you got pregnant, this is the night we'll remember. This is the night we made this baby—together."

For the space of several heartbeats, she couldn't speak, could only gaze down at him in wonder. How had she gotten so lucky? She didn't know, but she would be grateful for the rest of her life to whatever god or fate had brought her to him.

"Oh, Mike," she whispered, tears glistening in her eyes.

His fingers laced together with hers, clasping hers tightly. "Ah, sweetheart," he said, his hips moving beneath her. "Don't make me wait any longer. Do it now."

Her eyes locked with his as she began to move. He let her set the rhythm. As the pace quickened and her own pleasure surged, she found exquisite joy in watching the mounting tension in his face.

"This is the way it's supposed to be, isn't it?" she whispered, her eyes never leaving his.

"Yes, this is the way it's supposed to be," he repeated a little later, cradling her against his side.

Epilogue

More peppermint tea?"

Lisa smiled as Benita Fenton offered to pour her another cup. They were sitting in the older woman's Philadelphia home, Benita nestled in a wing chair, an afghan spread over her lap. Her health was still delicate, but lately, she'd made remarkable strides.

Lisa shook her head. "No, thank you, I'm fine. You sit still and let Andrea and me take care of the dishes."

Benita sighed. "I hate being waited on. Especially by two women with bellies out to here." She held her hand out in front of her, slightly exaggerated, to indicate the state of Lisa's pregnancy—and her daughter's, which was a little farther advanced.

Lisa joined her sister in clearing dishes, thinking that it had been five months since her fateful encounter at the Jones Falls. Over the course of those months, she'd been busy getting married and settling into happy domestic life with Mike and had all but forgotten her living nightmare.

The biggest surprise had been getting to know her sister, Andrea. Erin Stone had found her living with her husband and son in New Jersey. Lisa had welcomed Erin's offer to set up a meeting. Erin had also helped to facilitate a reconciliation between Benita and her daughter. In fact, when Andrea had learned about her mother's precarious health, she'd been determined to mend the breach that had kept them apart for so many years.

Lisa followed her sister to the kitchen and began loading dishes into the dishwasher. In the living room, she could hear Gordon, Andrea's husband, telling Mike about the relative merits of various mutual funds. She sighed. The guys were never going to be best buddies, but Mike had claimed he was learning something. With Gordon's advice they were starting a college fund for the baby.

"How was Gary when you saw him last week?" Andrea asked, her voice low to guard against her mother's overhearing. Any mention of Garrett Folsom sent Benita through the roof, and no amount of reassurance would convince her that the man posed no threat to her relationship with Andrea.

"Better, I think," Lisa replied. "The doctor says the new medication is helping."

Both she and Andrea had been visiting their father regularly at the veterans' hospital in Baltimore. At first it had been so strange, thinking of him as her father. But as time went on, she was getting comfortable with him.

"I like to listen to his stories about Hallie," Andrea murmured.

Lisa nodded, pouring detergent into the dishwasher and closing the door. "Me, too. I loved my parents dearly, but can't help wondering how things would have been if Hallie had lived and she and Gary had married."

"Different, that's for sure," Andrea said. "Maybe Justine would have turned out okay."

Lisa sighed at the mention of her other sister. The black sheep of the family, without doubt. When she'd left Justine sitting at the table in the Baltimore City Jail, she hadn't expected—or particularly wanted—to see or hear from her again. It had shocked both her and Mike when Justine sent them a wedding present, then months later a beautiful handmade quilt for the baby. So, who knew what might happen? Lisa had given up making predictions.

Andrea, who hadn't yet shown any interest in meeting Justine, glanced over her shoulder as she hung a dish towel on the rack to dry. "Mom was strict," she said. "And

ırned into the epitome of the rebellious teenager—impul-
ive, inconsiderate, willing to do anything for the sheer risk
ıvolved. After I ran away, I was sorry, but I didn't know
ow to come back."

Lisa made a sympathetic noise. "I had some impulsive
ᴇndencies, too, when I was that age. But I was lucky. My
ᴀrents knew just where to set the limits without making me
ᴇl trapped."

"I thought a couple of times that I'd wind up either in jail
ɪ dead," Andrea muttered. Then, laughing, she added,
Who would have thought I'd end up married to a stock-
roker."

"You never know," Lisa agreed.

The back door banged, and Tony, Andrea's four-year-old,
ame in from the backyard with his grandpa. Lisa watched
ᴇr sister kneel to hug the boy. Soon, she thought, she'd be
olding her own baby—and she could hardly wait.

"We've got to get going," Andrea told Tony. "Go give
ɪrandma a big goodbye kiss."

"I don't wanna leave!" Tony protested.

No, Lisa thought with a smile, not when he had two new
oting grandparents who had to be restrained from overin-
ulging him.

"If you're a good boy, we can come back and see
ɪrandma and Grandpa next Sunday," Andrea assured him,
ᴠhich seemed to satisfy the youngster.

A half hour later, having said their goodbyes, Lisa walked
ᴠith Mike to the car to begin the ride home to Baltimore. He
lid an arm around her expanded waist as they walked, and
he rested her head against his shoulder.

"I heard Gordon talking your head off," she murmured.

He chuckled. "Gordon's a little talkative, but he's part of
ᴇ package."

She stopped walking. "What package?"

"My ready-made family," he said, his voice thick. "I
ᴇver had one. Now I've got you, and this little one—" he
ᴀtted her swollen belly "—and I've got your sister and her

husband and the Fentons. Before it's over, God help me, might end up with Justine, too.''

"God help us both," Lisa sighed.

"If it happens, it happens. After all, she's part of th package, too.'' He gave her a tender look as he spoke in husky tone. ''Sweetheart, you've brought me so much.''

"Oh, Mike." Lisa put her hand on top of his where i rested on her abdomen. She didn't think he'd ever be en tirely comfortable revealing his deepest feelings. On th other hand, he hadn't seemed to feel the need to retreat be hind his wall of reserve since the night he'd asked her to marry him. So, again, who knew what might happen? With Mike, anything was possible.

The baby started to kick, and she knew Mike felt it, be cause he grinned at her.

"He's getting stronger every day," he said.

"*She's* getting stronger every day," Lisa corrected. It wa an ongoing mock battle between them, although neither o them really cared whether their baby was a girl or a boy.

Their baby. The child they'd made together that night i the hotel room. Mike had fixed the memory in her mind fo all time.

Rubbing his hand gently against the mound of their child he said, "Seems to me, early indications are that he's goin to keep us busy."

"I expect *she* will," Lisa said, a frown flicking across he brow. "Andrea warned me that the first few months with baby can be pretty rough. No sleep, no social life. No sex.'

"I promise you, we absolutely will *not* let that happen,' he muttered.

"Mmm. And it doesn't exactly get easier."

His eyes held hers. "We'll do it together, Lisa. And we' make it good."

"Yes, I know we will," she whispered. And it was true Because if she'd learned anything during her ordeal, it wa that she could get safely through the fires of hell—as lon as she had this man at her side.

And there's more 43 LIGHT STREET!

If you liked FACE TO FACE,
you won't want to miss any of the 43 Light Street stories
that are coming your way, as "master of suspense"
Rebecca York continues this award-winning series in
Harlequin Intrigue.

Turn the page for a bonus look at what's in store for you
in the next 43 Light Street book:

FOR YOUR EYES ONLY

*Jenny Larkin has spent her life trying to make up for a
mistake. But now that mistake is about to cost her, for this
sightless woman has been targeted by an on-line stalker
who "sees" all her guilty secrets.... And after he kills her
friend Marianne, he's going to come after Jenny.
The only man who can help her is one she'll never let into
her life—no matter what the risk.*

Don't miss FOR YOUR EYES ONLY!
Only from Rebecca York . . . and Harlequin Intrigue!

Available in February 1997, wherever
Harlequin Intrigue is sold.

Prologue

He felt the excitement in his blood. In his bones. In his fingertips where they lightly caressed the computer keyboard as he waited for the modem to make the connection.

Got ya!

Today was the day. He knew it with the instinct of an avid hunter who has finally run his quarry to ground.

With barely controlled excitement, he typed in the bogus membership number and password he'd acquired. Marianne was already on-line. Waiting for the man she thought of as Oliver.

He'd given the pseudonym a good deal of thought. It came from his broad reading background. This time the book was that piece of romantic claptrap, *Love Story,* about a young husband named Oliver. He was devoted, sensitive, sweet and understanding. Nobody named Oliver could be a murderer.

Marianne responded to his log-on with an immediate greeting.

"Hi," he typed. "I've been counting the hours until I could get back to you."

"It's been a long day."

He picked up on the hint immediately. Women liked when you commiserated. "Bad day at work?"

"Mmm-hmm."

He had to sit through a five-minute recitation of how her boss had given her a report to complete that shouldn't have

been her job. But he was ready with the right sympatheti
responses.

"Poor baby. Why don't you unwind with me over din
ner?" he typed.

There was a short pause before she responded. "I'm no
so sure that's a good idea."

"Why?"

"We've never met."

He came back with a reassuring answer. "We're not go
ing to meet until you break down and let me into your life.'

"I know."

"We've been friends for two months now." A long tim
to wait for gratification. "You've told me so much abou
yourself. And I think you know me pretty well."

"As well as you can know someone over a computer net
work," she hedged.

"I'd like to take the next step."

"What if—I mean—what if you're disappointed?"

So that was it. She wasn't worried about *him*. She wa
worried about what he'd think about *her* when they finall
met. Sweet anticipation swelled in his chest. He was glad h
was typing instead of speaking, because he knew he couldn'
keep his voice steady. "I know I'm not going to be disap
pointed," he soothed. "I already know you so well. You
sense of humor. Your intelligence." He stopped there be
cause he didn't want to lay it on too thick.

"Oliver, there's something I haven't told you. Some
thing that might make a difference."

"We've come so far. You can trust me with the rest," h
coaxed.

She answered quickly, getting it over with. "I have a vi
sion problem. I'm not blind. But I do need to wear ver
thick glasses. And I use a special computer that reads t
me."

A feeling of power gathered in his body like warm, swee
honey. This was it. The knowledge that made the relation
ship work for him. She had told him her secret. "Do you
seriously think that would make any difference to me?"

"I was afraid it would."

He pretended to be hurt. "Marianne, I thought you trusted me."

"I do. And I feel so relieved."

"Meet me tonight. At this little bar and restaurant in Fells Point that I bet you'll love. We'll start with drinks—then dinner. And the band is wonderful. It's a good place to unwind."

"All right."

He gave her the address, and they chatted for a few more minutes. When he disconnected, he sat rubbing his hands together, squeezing them harder and harder—anticipating the feel of his fingers digging into the smooth skin of her throat.

* * * * *

Don't miss this next 43 Light Street tale—
FOR YOUR EYES ONLY—
coming to you in February 1997. Only from
Rebecca York—and Harlequin Intrigue!

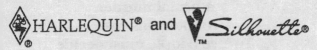

HARLEQUIN® and **Silhouette®**

are proud to present...

HERE COME THE GROOMS™

Four marriage-minded stories written by top
Harlequin and Silhouette authors!

Next month, you'll find:

The Bridal Price	by Barbara Boswell
Annie in the Morning	by Curtiss Ann Matlock
September Morning	by Diana Palmer
Outback Nights	by Emilie Richards

ADDED BONUS! In every edition of
Here Come the Grooms you'll find $5.00 worth
of coupons good for Harlequin and Silhouette
products.

On sale at your favorite Harlequin and Silhouette
retail outlet.

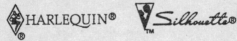

HARLEQUIN® **Silhouette®**

A brutal murder.
A notorious case.
Twelve people must decide
the fate of one man.

Jury Duty

an exciting courtroom drama by

Laura Van Wormer

Struggling novelist Libby Winslow has been chosen to sit on the jury of a notorious murder trial dubbed the "Poor Little Rich Boy" case. The man on trial, handsome, wealthy James Bennett Layton, Jr., has been accused of killing a beautiful young model. As Libby and the other jury members sift through the evidence trying to decide the fate of this man, their own lives become jeopardized because someone on the jury has his own agenda....

Find out what the verdict is this October at your favorite retail outlet.

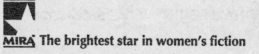

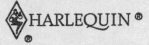

1997
Reader's Engagement Book
A calendar of important dates
and anniversaries for readers to use!

Informative and entertaining—with notable
dates and trivia highlighted throughout the year.

Handy, convenient, pocketbook size to help you
keep track of your own personal important dates.

Added bonus—contains $5.00 worth of coupons
for upcoming Harlequin and Silhouette books.
This calendar more than pays for itself!

 Available beginning in November at
your favorite retail outlet.

 HARLEQUIN ®  Silhouette®

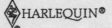